CRIMEBITS:

100 OPENING GAMBITS FOR GREAT THRILLERS & LINKED MYSTERY PUZZLES

CRIMEBITS:

100 OPENING GAMBITS FOR GREAT THRILLERS & LINKED MYSTERY PUZZLES

SELECTED BY

LEE CHILD

AND

LUCA VESTE

PUZZLES BY

ROBIN STEARS

This first paperback edition published in 2024
by Black Spring Press
An imprint of Eyewear Publishing Ltd
The Black Spring Press Group
London, United Kingdom

Cover design by Matt Broughton
Typeset and interior design by Evie Rowan
Illustrations by Annie Wicks

ISBN 978-1-915406-83-5

www.blackspringpressgroup.com
Printed in Canada

FSC www.fsc.org
MIX
Paper | Supporting responsible forestry
FSC® C103567

Lee Child is one of the world's leading thriller writers. He was born in Coventry, raised in Birmingham, and now lives in New York. It is said one of his novels featuring his hero Jack Reacher is sold somewhere in the world every nine seconds. His books consistently achieve the number-one slot on bestseller lists around the world and have sold over one hundred million copies. Two blockbusting Jack Reacher movies have been made so far, plus a TV show *Reacher* on Amazon Prime. A multi-award winning author, he was appointed CBE in the 2019 Queen's Birthday Honours.

Luca Veste is the internationally bestselling author of nine novels, including *Trust In Me*, *The Bone Keeper*, and *Dead Gone*. He is the host of the hit podcast *Two Crime Writers and a Microphone*, bass player in the Fun Lovin' Crime Writers, and the co-founder of the Locked Up Festival, which raised over £25,000 for the Trussell Trust charity. He is the crime editor for The Black Spring Crime Series. He studied psychology and criminology at the University of Liverpool, and lives on Merseyside with his wife and two daughters.

Robin Stears is a writer, editor, and puzzle setter from Ohio. Her puzzles have appeared in the *L. A. Times, Games, Women of Letters, The Crossword Club, Penny Dell Puzzles, The Inkubator*, and in *Daily POP* by PuzzleNation and *Crosswords Free* by Redstone Games mobile apps.

How To Use This Book

We hope you enjoy *CrimeBits* as much as we did putting it together.

In here you'll find the 100 top CrimeBits – opening gambits for the start of fictional crime thrillers that may or may not actually exist yet – with Lee Child's selection of the top 5.

You'll also find specially constructed puzzles each inspired by the CrimeBit. Please note, in honor of Lee Child's most famous character, Jack Reacher, many of the crosswords are in the American form, with some answers in American spelling.

To make this a really fun grab-bag of a book, we also added in some trivia, writing prompts and tips from Luca Veste, a best-selling crime author, to inspire the creative writer within you.

Let the CrimeBits begin!

CONTENTS

Introduction by Lee Child 1

CrimeBits & Puzzles 11

Afterword by Luca Veste 343

Solutions 357

INTRODUCTION by LEE CHILD

Like all lifelong readers my age, about twice as much of my reading happened before the internet as after. I can't really make up my mind which phase was better. In the old days, we lacked a reliable recommendation network – every book was essentially a random choice at the library, or the result of a random suggestion by an older sibling or a crusty old great-uncle, or simply the book's presence on the family shelves, or its discovery lost on a bus, or – for some titles, certainly – its furtive under-the-desk distribution by sniggering pals at school.

In a way I loved the randomness. I read all kinds of things I might not have, had I been following a curated A–Z path. But equally, looking back, I resented it, because I missed a lot, too. That's the problem with randomness. I was a fairly late adopter of the internet, but quickly came to appreciate the order it imposed – other people's also-bought or also-enjoyed data steered me in many excellent directions, and I learned to navigate the wild matrix of recommendations found down various rabbit holes, mostly to great effect. Overall, a solid win for new technology.

Except that the new technology wasn't limited to book stuff on the internet. There was a generalized explosion of new media that brought with it a radical fragmentation of attention spans. Suddenly there were video games, VHS and DVDs, on-line videos, bite-size journalism, emails, cell phones, cable, satellite, dozens of TV channels, then hundreds, then streaming. The old idea of settling down with a book for hours and hours on end started to fade away. Competition for leisure moments became frenetic, ever faster and faster.

The impact on how books were written was marked. For instance, I remember a workmate recommending *Captain Corelli's Mandolin*, by Louis de Bernieres, back in 1994. Those were still the old days. I had a rotary landline, no cell phone, no computer, and just four channels on my TV. My friend said, 'It's a great book, but you've got to give it fifty pages before you make up your mind.'

He was right. Great book. But fifty pages? How quaint that sounds these days! Now we find ourselves judging by the first fifty words. The first paragraph, basically. The first page, maximum. Ever faster and faster. Fragmented attention. Suddenly we had a hundred different things competing for our next hour, which suddenly made us tense and anxious about possibly wasting it.

Authors had to adapt. Fair enough. We play the hand we're

dealt. Those first fifty words quickly became seen as crucial. They either sold the book, or they didn't. But how? To adapt an old (and very adaptable) writer joke: 'A great opening needs two things. Unfortunately no one knows what they are.'

Actually a great opening needs way more than just two things. It must set the tone, the mood, and the voice. It must hint at – in fact promise – an experience of a certain kind, a story of a certain pace and nature, a narrative point of view we're comfortable with, the likely appearance of characters we'll enjoy – all the while simultaneously setting a hook we're intrigued by.

And all the while without trying too hard. A reader picking up a book is asking a basic subliminal question: 'Am I going to enjoy this? Is it going to be exciting?' The worst possible answer from the writer is: 'Yes! Yes! You're going to *love* it!! It's going to be *incredibly* exciting!!!' That's over-egging and over-selling. Readers generally don't appreciate being coerced to that degree. They feel manipulated. Much better is for the writer to say, with a kind of cool insouciant confidence: 'You might like it, or you might not . . . it is what it is, and the decision is entirely yours.' All the while making damn sure there's some subtle thing there to bait the hook. You pretend not to care, while simultaneously paddling like crazy under the surface. It's incredibly difficult to do. The stakes are high, but you have to ignore the make-or-break implications, relax, and trust your instincts.

My own first-ever opening went like this: *I was arrested in Eno's diner. At twelve o'clock. I was eating eggs and drinking coffee. A late breakfast, not lunch. I was wet and tired after a long walk in heavy rain. All the way from the highway to the edge of town.*

I had no real idea what I was doing back then, but I was happy with it, and in retrospect I can (almost) see how and why it works. I started in *media res* – in the middle of things – with no throat-clearing or scene setting. The arrest is the motivating incident that drives the subsequent story, and it's right there in the third word. The voice is established as a first-person narrative, by a person who has no fancy tastes – he's in a diner, chowing down after a disrupted start to the day – and who recounts events in a halting, slightly inarticulate manner involving verbless sentence fragments, as if he's unaccustomed to speaking out loud. Probably lonely, probably a drifter, operating in the margins of society.

Subliminally the reader asks, Who are you? Why are you being arrested? Are we going to like you? Are you a bad person? What's going on here exactly? And I didn't answer. Not right away. The whole art of creating momentum and suspense is to ask questions and then delay the answers. The first answers come on the second page – the as-yet unnamed about-to-be arrestee sees the cop cars coming and expertly deduces they're coming for him.

Clearly he's smart, a thinker, probably familiar with such situations, so he's characterized to an extent, although not completely – he could be a repeat offender, or even a master criminal (Are we going to like you? Are you a bad person?) But reassurance shows up immediately – ahead of the coming arrest, he puts a five dollar tip under his saucer, so that he doesn't stiff the waitress. No reason why she should suffer for his personal troubles. I wrote that line with no thought whatever – probably it's what I would do – but anecdotal reports from early readers found it vital and foundational. He's a decent and honorable man. That line really helped, and it was the product of pure instinct.

More answers come over the next few pages, establishing the still-unnamed narrator as calm, tough, some kind of high-stakes expert, half irritated and half amused by a local police department he judges as second rate. By the end of the chapter the reader sees the basic shape of the story to come. And simply by *getting* the reader to the end of the first chapter, the opening has done its job.

Suppose I had started like this: *I was arrested in Eno's diner. For a crime I didn't commit. It took a lot of time and trouble to get myself off the hook. Because something bad was happening in that small Georgia town.* Would that have worked? Absolutely not, in my opinion. Over-eager, over-explaining, tipping my hand, certainly over-selling – practically *begging* the reader. Truth is, I *was* begging the reader, like we all are, but I couldn't let it show. Like I said, it's about instinct, and it's very difficult.

This collection shows how the current generation of intending writers approach the problem. These samples were submitted for a competition, and I picked a winner and four runners-up. Now it's your turn. It's up to you to decide which work, and which don't. You might disagree with me. That's OK – you're a reader too, just as much as I am. Which of these would make you want to devote the next hour to reading on? And if you can figure out the exact reasons why, be sure to write in and let me know, because even after nearly thirty years of doing it, I'm not sure I've figured out the precise alchemy yet. Or better still, write your own novel. If the first fifty words genuinely pull me in, I'll read on for sure.

Lee Child

New York

2024

CRIMEBITS
&
PUZZLES

The Logic Puzzles

- Our CrimeBit logic puzzles are composed of a list of clues and a working out grid.
- Each item within the different categories (people, places, objects etc.) will match with an item in another category.
- No two items in one category will ever be matched to the same one item.
- Using the clues provided, determine which items match with each other, marking them true.
- If a row or column has one true answer, then each of the remaining answers should be marked false.
- As true and false answers are marked, the relationships between the items on the grid are revealed and the puzzle is solved.

CRIMEBIT No. 1

Runoff

YOUR RATING /100

John Adamcik

The six o'clock news drew our impromptu family reunion around my uncle's big-screen television. We were waiting to see history. Or, at least a replay. Sure enough, the news helicopter had aerial video of police chasing the robbery suspects down our grandparent's rural mid-Michigan road. We nodded when the reporter compared this to the Purple Gang's route decades earlier.

While my cousins commented on the getaway car shredding gravel, a lifetime of my father's fishing lessons kicked in and guided my eyes to a silver speck on the screen. It flashed like a bass hitting a spoon. Everyone else hollered when the car fishtailed into the massive field ditch about a mile past our family farm, but I was making mental notes about where the speck had disappeared in the cattail runoff near my grandparent's driveway.

The police obviously didn't see it. The reporter didn't mention it. I almost said something to the family. Instead, stopping off at the farm on my way home, it didn't take me long to find a silver key in the ditch. I recognized the hotel name, and I knew I could beat the police there.

PUZZLE No. 1

Family Reunion

Across

1. Malign in print
6. Some barn birds
10. TV tavern that sells Duff Beer
14. Prizefight site
15. Labor
16. Wild about
17. Will Ferrell film
19. Follow a script
20. Attached, in hotel lingo
21. Emanation from a New Jersey skip
23. Sound surly
25. Shirts named for a sport
29. Apple or quince
32. Whoopi Goldberg film
35. Ark landing site
38. Head of a college
39. ___ Bo
40. David who starred in "The Fugitive"
42. Place before, grammatically
44. Had a date, say
45. "Jellicle Ball" show
47. Church activity
48. Overprotective sort
51. Flat fish
52. Burning issue?
53. Radio part
56. Shape of some medals
59. Casablanca's country
63. Prefix for "both"
66. "1984" personage
68. Bank deal
69. Olympic weapon
70. 40-40, at Wimbledon
71. Have a yen (for)
72. Forest fauna
73. Trims the lawn

Down

1. Load cargo
2. Modern home of ancient Susa
3. Places for roses
4. Manual writer's audience
5. Put aside for later
6. Everyone else
7. Aim to win
8. Ride to the red carpet
9. Slope slider
10. Reflect
11. Single digit?
12. Zeta follower
13. Turf in a roll
18. Metro map abbr.
22. Barkeep's gadget
24. Tupperware topper
26. Forever or Jackson
27. "Juno and the Paycock" writer
28. Directs
29. ___ party
30. Soapbox user
31. "The Fife Player" and "The Balcony"
33. Month before Oct.
34. Dropcloth
36. Mountaineer's goal
37. Eye drop?
41. Degree in abstract mathematics
43. Repeated by rote
46. Play place
49. Doing a carwash task

50. Karaoke selection
54. "... ___ any drop to drink" (Coleridge)
55. Take the edge off?
57. Danny's role in "Community"
58. Fully grown
60. Guzzle
61. Grammy-winning Winans
62. Minecraft players dig them
63. The lot
64. Bovine remark
65. Make taboo
67. "Do tell!"

CRIMEBIT No. 2

Cache Call

John Adamcik

The metal detector and shovel were useful. Although his father put sod down before they moved, the toy cars Burton dug up now proved this had been his sandbox. Still, he was tired. A revelation the day before had prompted his spontaneous thirteen-hour drive and unannounced homecoming: new technology yielded a DNA match on a cold case. His cold case. His hometown. National news for the second time in thirty years. He was stunned to recognize the face of the man who had saved his life.

The shock brought clarity to Burton's memories: his grandmother had picked him up from school before she was killed when a stolen armored truck crashed into them. The thieves took Burton, dragging him and several briefcases through a nearby woods, unaware they were less than a mile from his house. The men argued about what to do with him when one of the three shot the other two and apologized to Burton before running away. Burton had grabbed a briefcase and ran, burying it in his sandbox before his mother found him in their garage.

He had never told anyone about his cache. It had to be here. Unless the man had returned.

PUZZLE No. 2

Buried Loot

BOOTY
BOUNTY
BREAD
BUCKS
CABBAGE
CAPITAL
CASH
COINS
CURRENCY
DINERO
DOUGH
FUNDS
GELT
GOODIES
GREENBACKS
HAUL
JACK
LETTUCE
LUCRE
MOOLAH
PELF
PLUNDER
PROCEEDS
SCRATCH
SHEKELS
SILVER
SPOILS
STASH
STERLING
STUFF
TAKE
WEALTH

D	L	G	M	D	F	Z	K	S	B	V	G	K	R	E	O	F	F	Q	A	P
H	D	I	G	Z	X	Z	T	O	O	K	A	W	T	K	Y	S	Q	G	J	V
M	P	L	J	G	D	O	O	J	C	T	T	E	H	A	V	R	Z	P	G	A
O	X	K	X	B	S	T	G	H	H	Z	I	A	A	P	T	U	P	R	A	B
H	L	S	B	Z	Y	L	U	X	G	W	A	L	M	I	D	A	E	R	B	S
J	V	D	S	Y	P	R	A	B	S	U	H	T	E	G	N	E	L	N	K	E
B	J	F	I	C	C	F	S	T	L	Z	O	H	H	W	N	C	F	L	R	S
E	S	N	G	Q	S	C	K	P	I	K	H	D	V	B	E	J	A	H	A	L
C	E	S	K	Z	S	H	P	N	O	P	S	H	A	P	Q	F	D	S	C	E
U	I	K	Q	F	O	M	I	Y	P	R	A	C	W	M	W	A	C	S	H	K
T	D	O	H	Z	P	O	E	U	S	P	K	C	F	H	M	R	J	D	Y	E
T	O	Y	A	W	T	G	E	L	T	S	E	K	H	O	A	C	B	E	G	H
E	O	M	U	L	A	T	V	J	O	N	E	R	O	T	G	K	L	E	A	S
L	G	S	L	B	G	Z	U	R	K	L	K	L	C	N	Z	Y	A	C	K	U
K	Q	U	B	H	P	O	H	U	S	H	A	H	S	U	N	T	U	O	P	M
O	C	A	B	C	N	F	X	V	R	H	T	U	T	W	L	N	H	R	L	I
S	C	A	O	H	L	Y	T	O	X	Y	C	N	E	R	R	U	C	P	U	S
G	D	Z	J	S	I	L	V	E	R	S	F	L	C	K	F	O	F	X	N	I
Z	S	N	I	P	O	H	P	G	U	T	A	R	Z	Z	I	B	X	Q	D	G
M	S	O	U	R	V	W	S	Q	F	E	O	Q	R	N	I	W	P	G	E	N
A	C	B	E	F	L	N	T	F	F	R	O	X	S	J	K	G	W	G	R	F
O	Q	N	Y	V	E	L	A	B	F	L	G	L	V	M	O	B	D	B	B	T
V	I	S	K	C	U	B	S	G	U	I	E	M	A	A	O	B	J	M	D	H
D	Y	W	V	T	Z	R	H	R	T	N	T	I	M	N	Y	G	K	Y	J	U
G	S	Q	G	R	H	C	S	N	S	G	C	K	F	N	Y	V	T	T	F	W

CRIMEBIT No. 3

The Son

YOUR RATING /100

Leanne Anderson

His mother is a liar. A good one. There is an element of truth within the lies she tells, and she commits, no hesitation or flinching. No tells. He can't help but admire the skilled delivery.

But he's not sure that lying at this precise moment is the best course of action.

They are standing outside the house. Now referred to as the crime scene. Like some macabre disco, the flashing lights from the two cop cars, parked haphazardly on the lawn, color their faces blue, red, then blue again.

A gurney, unwieldy like a late-night shopping trolley, is maneuvered out of the front door and along the footpath, then loaded into the back of a white van. The flesh and bones, the truth of what really happened inside the house, hidden beneath the black plastic shroud of the body bag.

'Did either of you know the deceased?' The cop's fierce gaze flicks between them.

'No,' they respond simultaneously. Simon's answer, the truth. His mother's response, another lie.

He knows this because he heard her shout the man's name and saw him turn towards her.

Just as she raised the gun and shot him in the head.

? DID YOU KNOW ?

Ötzi the Iceman is one of the oldest known murder victims, believed to have been killed 5,300 years ago. Discovered in the Alps between Austria and Italy in 1991, his well-preserved body revealed that he had been shot in the back with an arrow, which caused his death. Further examination indicated that he also suffered a head injury, suggesting a violent exchange between him and his killer.

PUZZLE No. 3

Lies, Lies, and More Lies

Across

1. Ply the needle
4. Shorten a plank
9. Confirms attendance
14. World Cup chant
15. Rome Beauty
16. Cause a ruckus
17. Lie
19. Kim of "True Grit"
20. Scrabble rack item
21. Squeak (by)
22. Saudi Arabian export
23. Erstwhile
25. Big lie
29. Get comfy
30. Hi-__ computer graphics
31. Cells that contain ooplasm
32. Cosmetics giant
34. Place for a skip
36. Lie
39. Ruling family
40. Getaway for Gandhi
41. "__ bin ein Berliner" (JFK quote)
42. Dir. from Beijing to Tianjin
43. "__ Spirit" (Noel Coward play)
47. Lancaster lie
50. Part of a plane's wing
51. End a fast
52. Letters in a deli order
53. Alluvial deposit
54. Staff members?
57. Lie or fib
59. Accept formally
60. Open a castle door
61. NATO member since 1990
62. Detect, as danger
63. They get hit on the head
64. Conversational hesitations

Down

1. Infatuated with
2. One of Seinfeld's friends
3. "Citizen Kane" portrayer
4. Singer Corinne Bailey __
5. Time-sensitive items
6. Gave a speech
7. Lip balm ingredient
8. Leave the single life
9. Transmitter
10. Hustle tickets outside the stadium
11. Telly accessory
12. Draft picks are made here
13. Double agent
18. Ends a suit
22. Cries of despair
24. "__ Lucy" (classic sitcom)
25. "Fantastic Voyage" actress
26. Olympic sport eliminated after 1936
27. Make level
28. Liotta of "GoodFellas"
30. Procure, as money
33. Delete from the hard drive
34. Even slightly

35. Most fertile, as soil
36. Little bit, in Spain
37. Its principal city is Essen
38. Judicial
39. Pants pocket's place
42. Take a load off, so to speak
44. Process for sorting the injured
45. Hoot partner
46. Makes an appearance
48. Castle strongholds
49. Wallpaper adhesive
50. Common defense
52. Eric of "Hulk"
54. Rapper Lil ___ X
55. Dedicated lines of poetry
56. "Bridgerton" society
57. Recreation
58. Time meas.

CRIMEBIT No. 4

Detective Doyle

YOUR RATING /100

Steven Axelrod

Doyle was still working on his sister's murder on the night they killed his wife.

Everyone else had given up on the case, even Maggie, who was his partner, too, in the Detective Bureau of the Boston PD. She knew the case better than anyone, from every angle – civic outrage, political scandal, law enforcement mess, family tragedy, personal obsession. And Doyle was obsessed, there was no denying that. The giant case-board on his living room wall had been spreading like the crabgrass on her family's lawn, taking over, ruining everything else while it thrived. Doyle worked the case on weekends, he dreamed about it at night. He had even started keeping a dream diary in case there was any clue lodged in his unconscious that his over-worked waking mind had missed.

PUZZLE No. 4

Murder in Beantown

Poor Detective Doyle! He won't be assigned to investigate his wife's murder, of course, but three new cases were just dropped on his desk. The victims were found in various locations around Boston, and each one was murdered in a different way. From the clues, determine ***who*** *was found and* ***where,*** *as well as* ***what*** *caused their deaths.*

The Victims

Charles Rivera - Attending Harvard on a rowing scholarship as he's good at sitting down and going backward.

Jack Hancock - No relation to Herbie Hancock.

Prudence Hyde - Horse veterinarian. All of her patients are in stable condition.

Cause of Death

Blunt force - A Louisville Slugger was found near the body.

Gunshot - Three bullets were collected at the scene.

Stabbing - A knife was found near the victim.

Locations

Back Bay - Their deeded parking spots are as valuable as their Victorian brownstones.

Beacon Hill - The most expensive neighborhood in Boston. You get less apartment for your money than anywhere else.

North End - Boston's oldest residential community. Dino's is still great, but getting pricey.

? CLUES ?

1. Charles Rivera's body was located in Back Bay.
2. Prudence Hyde was not a gunshot victim.
3. The stabbing victim was found in the North End.
4. Jack Hancock wasn't found in Beacon Hill.
5. The victim who was beaten to death was not Charles Rivera.

	Charles Rivera	Jack Hancock	Prudence Hyde	Blunt force	Gunshot	Stabbing
Back Bay						
Beacon Hill						
North End						
Blunt force						
Gunshot						
Stabbing						

Who? ______ ______ ______

Where? ______ ______ ______

What? ______ ______ ______

CRIMEBIT No. 5

Steel

YOUR RATING

/100

Cailey Barker

Blurs of color in a smudge of gray, muffled grunts and feral shouts. Twisted ugliness in a mass of swirling limbs. This is what fights are like. Real fights. Not costumed clowns in superhero poses and chop-socky dances. Shards of pain in a dreamy haze of red. A moment of madness, indelibly etched into memories of life.

We lock eyes, just for an instant. Dark pupils shrinking in a pool of white. Part pain, part surprise. Recognition. A whisper, barely a breath. Everything changed in those three words.

'The Big Bang . . .'

PUZZLE No. 5

Fight Club

Across

1. Booth shot
6. "Clueless" protagonist
10. Holes
14. Saab models
15. Money abroad
16. Andy Taylor's boy
17. Fight over some kitchen furniture?
19. Modern fencing weapon
20. Really, really bad
21. Basketball filler
22. Joins a contest
24. Lepidopterist's device
25. Bowl of greens
27. Irish actress Maureen
28. Angelic sort
30. Fight over a bit of shrubbery?
32. Alpine call
33. Vast land mass
34. GPS lines
35. Piece for two
37. Bluish hue
40. The Shirelles' "___-La-La"
43. End of a threatening phrase
45. Is deficient
49. Argument over camp accommodations?
52. Type of pill
53. "Star Wars" android, for short
54. Sounds of resignation
56. "Lo, How a Rose ___ Blooming"
57. Eliot's forte
59. Scot's "No way!"
60. Potent prefix?
61. Dust bunny component
62. Land dispute?
65. Feminizing suffix
66. Bumbling sorts
67. Final step in cleaning
68. Immoderately priced
69. Football officials, briefly
70. Cracks jokes

Down

1. Obviousness
2. Bum's rush
3. Revolved around
4. Ring, as a church bell
5. Saccharide suffix
6. The C in C.S. Forester
7. Good-natured cheers
8. Eventful years
9. Kids skip it
10. "Faust" dramatist
11. Is suddenly seen
12. Comic character in whiteface
13. Fluctuates wildly
18. Former Swedish automaker
23. Strong English ale
25. "Star Trek" helmsman
26. Clear a freezing windshield
29. Color on the Canadian flag
31. Calendar page
33. Cartographer's compilation
36. Sinuous sea dweller

38. "I'm sorry to say..."
39. Take captive
40. Bound, in a way
41. Katniss Everdeen or Merida
42. Dish alternative
44. "Dot's Story" or "Pat and Mo" to "EastEnders"
46. Twain's original surname
47. Most eager
48. Bitter quarrels
50. Lose stability
51. Not against
52. "That was ___, this is now!"
55. Magnetic flux unit
58. "The Ghost of Frankenstein" role
60. Stage award since 1956
63. Issa ___ of HBO's "Insecure"
64. Only player named MVP in the ABA and NBA

CRIMEBIT No. 6

Slow Bones

YOUR RATING
/100

Sacha Bissonnette

My daddy is my protector. He taught me that there are fast bones and slow bones and bones that will never heal. He taught me that in all cases, it's always the bones that will give you away.

'Last time,' he said. He said it quietly, and angrily, watching me like a railroad foreman, knowing that any one mistake will end in disaster. 'Faster and deeper,' he said, reaching over me, ripping the shovel from my limp grip.

My earliest memory is of Christmas. Ma was still in the picture. I knew she was sober because she bought me a gift: pajamas with these beautiful glow-in-the-dark green seahorses. I loved them. At night, if my room was pitch black, they would dance across the wall.

My daddy was making me breakfast when we heard the sirens. He knew they were coming for him but he still finished cooking my eggs. He said I could eat in my room this one time. He grabbed my plate in one hand and lifted me off my chair with the other. 'Sorry kid, this one's on me,' he said softly, and then spun me around twice. It was our first dance.

PUZZLE No. 6

Bad to the Bone

CARPAL
CLAVICLE
COCCYX
FEMUR
FIBULA
HUMERUS
MAXILLA
OCCIPITAL
OSSICLES
PARIETAL
RADIUS
RIB
SACRUM
SCAPULA
STERNUM
TARSAL
TIBIA
ULNA
ILIUM

V	A	P	I	M	H	X	Z	X	B	D	L	C	A	H	S	R	H	G	N	Y
M	E	N	B	Y	Y	B	I	O	M	X	Z	L	E	U	I	T	R	U	C	P
A	N	L	U	N	U	Q	G	J	J	A	F	B	A	V	I	F	P	D	F	M
F	S	A	C	R	U	M	R	W	D	J	E	W	Y	Q	G	I	Q	S	F	U
E	S	F	T	F	Y	R	Y	I	I	V	F	J	R	Y	U	Q	W	E	J	I
R	I	B	L	F	E	M	S	K	H	G	O	Y	Y	Y	H	A	X	L	S	W
B	M	B	A	I	U	I	M	J	G	Z	K	N	P	O	U	Y	O	C	G	K
Y	R	U	T	M	S	E	R	A	B	K	L	S	R	U	J	B	R	I	R	B
T	J	E	I	J	C	E	P	K	R	V	Z	S	I	N	P	V	H	S	C	O
A	M	L	P	L	A	N	I	X	F	I	X	P	I	S	C	U	Q	S	H	X
R	A	F	I	L	I	W	U	N	R	I	Z	G	T	X	Y	C	C	O	C	U
N	M	L	C	W	A	P	Y	T	P	Y	C	J	V	L	X	Q	F	Z	S	M
F	Z	S	C	X	X	S	C	B	P	J	Q	K	N	L	A	P	R	A	C	M
I	D	G	O	L	S	I	R	O	H	U	B	Y	C	F	M	F	B	D	A	B
B	U	K	Q	U	B	C	H	A	T	W	T	L	C	U	Y	T	R	X	S	A
U	K	W	Y	Z	P	P	A	T	T	G	R	A	Q	Z	M	D	I	M	D	C
L	Q	E	Q	B	G	K	L	P	X	U	R	K	M	U	L	L	Q	L	W	I
A	A	Y	U	N	T	Z	N	V	U	O	O	G	I	U	L	Q	B	T	V	S
S	A	N	Q	Z	K	H	V	Y	D	L	D	N	J	A	N	X	O	C	P	J
N	V	Y	O	F	F	A	F	J	T	I	A	M	B	N	M	R	O	H	W	A
Z	Z	V	E	B	X	O	M	T	U	T	L	K	S	E	E	C	E	W	T	I
Y	G	M	C	B	X	Q	Y	A	A	J	M	A	M	I	K	W	G	T	C	B
C	U	B	R	P	A	R	I	E	T	A	L	K	X	I	P	W	W	D	S	I
R	A	D	I	U	S	E	I	W	I	G	C	E	L	C	I	V	A	L	C	T
B	J	S	U	R	E	M	U	H	C	Z	R	P	R	C	G	Y	X	P	P	L

CRIMEBIT No. 7

The Tape

YOUR RATING /100

Jamie Brannan

'Play it again,' said the man who accompanied her, pointing at the machine. 'We have to be sure,' he said, and he was right. The last thing she wanted to do was have a bunch of polis traipsing around her properties, but she'd rationalize it as not wanting to waste valuable police time. After all, it was just a tape . . .

'You may sit there wondering why I recorded this, or indeed for whom, if not you. Amongst my earthly possessions, you will no doubt find many other audio tapes, much like this one, along with videos, even photographs of my candid moments, if you will. I like to think of it all as my portfolio in a way. And after partaking in them, you may label me a monster, certainly evil by most conventional standards at least, and truly utterly vile. For who am I but the foul stain at the bottom of the barrel that is humanity? I make no allusions otherwise, nor do I offer any excuses for who I am. But dear listener, I beg of you to endure our journey together until the very end. I promise it will be something truly spectacular.'

WRITING PROMPT
1

He should have known.

There should have been a sign.

A way of seeing what was about to happen.

He should have felt it.

It wouldn't have helped him.

The clock was ticking, the minutes and seconds passing by, without him realizing.

He would be dead in an hour and he wouldn't see it coming.

Scan to visit the
CrimeBits Writing Space

PUZZLE No. 7

Remix

Across

5. Enjoy to excess (9)

8. Expansive (4)

9. Pertaining to legal debate (8)

10. On a plane or train (6)

11. Arugula (6)

13. Sculpting tool (6)

15. Insect midsection (6)

16. Data seen by a jury (8)

18. Confess (4)

19. Giving an account of (9)

Down

1. Mathematical figures (8)

2. Breathed hard (6)

3. Looking-glass (6)

4. Benumb (4)

6. Conduct oneself improperly (9)

7. Wretched (9)

12. Coagulating, as blood (8)

14. Steam-ships (6)

15. One-fifth of 100 (6)

17. Immoderately priced (4)

1
2
3
4
5
6
7
8
9
10
11
12
13
14
15
16
17
18
19

CRIMEBIT No. 8

Shadows of Redemption

Jamie Brannan

I pulled the car off the road down a dirt track. The bump of the tires as they left the blacktop into the gravel jostled me inside the car. Pain tore through my abdomen, like I was being shot for a second time. I gritted my teeth together. The pain passed. I brought my hand up. It was wet, and I could see the blood in the low light of the dash. My poor job at stitching and bandaging the wound had come undone. Typical. I drove on into the darkness. I had to find a place to bury Mason. I continued for another two miles when the dirt track curved to the left, my lights dancing on the road, illuminating the rocks and holes and shrubs by the side of the track. I came to an area that was a little more secluded. I pulled over and got out, glancing in the back seat where Mason lay as I passed. Popping the trunk I grabbed a small shovel. Placed there no doubt by the rental companies, for emergencies, or just in case someone had to take a dump in the middle of the desert, or bury a body. Convenient.

PUZZLE No. 8

Desert Burial

*Mason's body isn't the only thing that's buried in this desert. In fact, three other people have buried things nearby. Each of them buried something precious to them, in three different locations. From the clues, determine **who** buried **what** and **where**.*

The Criminals

Ned Bundy - Never met a crime he didn't want to commit. His best asset is his lie ability.

Charlie Gambino - Shot a man with a paintball gun just to watch him dye.

Frankie Harvard - Whoever said "crime doesn't pay" must have worked with him.

What They Buried

Incriminating documents - Evidence, evidence and more evidence.

Loot from a bank heist - A million dollars in fifty dollar bills. You do the math.

Toxic waste - Just talking about decaying, radioactive material is enough to make someone go nuclear.

The Locations

Rock shaped like a face - From one angle, it looks at lot like Adrien Brody.

Between two mesas - Flat-topped mountains make good land-marks because they don't move.

Near a natural aquifer - Groundwater that dates back to the last Ice Age.

? CLUES ?

1. Ned Bundy buried his "treasure" near a rock shaped like a face.
2. Someone buried loot between two mesas so he'd be able to find it.
3. Charlie Gambino has a fear of water.
4. Frankie Harvard doesn't care about incriminating documents; he can't even read.
5. The person who buried the toxic waste was not Ned Bundy.

	Ned Bundy	***Charlie Gambino***	***Frankie Harvard***	*Incriminating documents*	*Loot from a bank heist*	*Toxic waste*
Rock shaped like a face						
Between two mesas						
Near an aquifer						
Incriminating documents						
Loot from a bank heist						
Toxic waste						

Who? ______ ______ ______

What? ______ ______ ______

Where? ______ ______ ______

CRIMEBIT No. 9

The Protocol

YOUR RATING
/100

Jamie Brannan

The whip of the silenced pistol echoed a short distance over the water following in the trail of a muzzle flash piercing the night. A man slumped against the console of the small boat. Shock contorting his face, his last breath escaping his lungs. The killer, still holding the silenced Beretta M9A3 aimed towards the dead man, released his own breath. It was over. Mission accomplished. Moving to holster the weapon, he heard the click of a safety catch. The man spun on his heels, raising his weapon to face down the barrel of another silenced weapon. This time, he was on the wrong end of an FNX-45 Tactical Pistol.

'It's not what it looks like,' the man behind the Beretta proclaimed, dropping the weapon with a thud as he raised his hands. 'He was an enemy asset. He had to be put down. The Tailor sanctioned this. The mission is over.'

'Funny, I was told the same thing about you.' The whip sound of a silenced weapon rang out over the water for a second time that night.

Two splashes soon followed, then the roar of the engine from the small vessel as it disappeared in the darkness.

PUZZLE No. 9

Tailor Swift

Across

1. Dressmaker's bolt
6. Shuttle, often
9. In front
14. "Jar of Hearts" singer Christina
15. Hard little worker
16. Tostitos dip
17. Mislaying tailoring supplies?
20. Info on an ID
21. Egg, in combinations
22. Little monsters
23. More illustrious
26. Bath additives
28. "Beowulf," for one
29. Tailoring step that comes after measure and mark?
35. Arachnid trap
36. Plans (out)
37. Observe Yom Kippur
38. Grade
40. Milky Way matter
42. Discolor
43. React to a twist
44. Bad way to start?
45. Stolen shirt fasteners?
48. "My Wild Irish __"
49. Wooley who sang "The Purple People Eater"
50. More foolish
52. Hacking it
56. "__ last requests?"
57. Rising star?
58. Forget to remove temporary basting?
64. Drinks with rice
65. Always, in verse
66. Biblical pronouns
67. Future signs
68. X or ultraviolet
69. "__ So Vain"

Down

1. Sgt.'s subordinate
2. Sign before Virgo
3. Alternative introductions
4. Court affairs
5. Door adjunct
6. Dracula, on occasion
7. Opens, in a way
8. Many-hit Wonder
9. Fire remains
10. Mata __
11. Basic abbr.
12. PDQ cousin
13. Some Boston pops
18. Leipzig language
19. Pinball taboo
23. Hardly used
24. Considering
25. Lynx variety
27. Cheddar type
30. Tarzan's "mum"
31. Sked entry
32. Ordinary
33. Disquietude
34. Bank employee
36. Disadvantage
39. Women's __
40. Preserve fruit
41. Umbrian hill town
43. Sail
46. Native of Rayong
47. Sawbuck
48. Vaquero's spread
51. Full of almonds
52. "Let me add..."

53. Radiant smile
54. Place to canoe
55. Odd opposite
59. Shower head?
60. Be the judge
61. A TX city, to British Airways
62. Grand Tour cont.
63. 157.5 deg. from N

CRIMEBIT No. 10

Assassins

YOUR RATING /100

WINNER
SELECTED BY LEE CHILD

Richard Burke

I stood in silence beside my sister as we waited for the police forensic team to arrive. Yellow crime scene tape surrounded an area of patchy grass and low shrubs located a few yards off the rutted woodland track. Sunlight cut through the branches of the surrounding trees, lighting the morning air with golden shafts of brightness. The muted drone of insects provided a sombre accompaniment.

'It's peaceful here, isn't it?' I said, glancing sideways at Cathy.

Her only acknowledgment was a slight frown as her eyes remained fixed on the scrubby ground.

'In some ways, it would be good if she could stay here,' I continued.

Cathy swung to face me. 'She deserves a proper burial,' she snapped, 'and a headstone.'

My sister's gaze lasered in on me. When I didn't reply, she turned back and resumed her silent vigil. My fingers closed around the confession letter in my pocket. The police had retained the original, but I made a photocopy before handing it over. The author of the note had committed suicide after posting it to me – or so the investigating officers believed. But I knew better, not that I had any intention of revealing the fact.

?

What's your writing process like?

Richard Burke: *'I'm somewhere between a plotter and a pantser. I like to plan the outline and the big events in a story, but I also want to give the characters space to breathe, and I only get that by allowing them a certain freedom from the plot. Some of my best twists have occurred to me while I was writing what I thought would be a well-planned chapter.'*

PUZZLE No. 10

Fancy Plants

AZALEA	HOLLY	NANDINA
BAYBERRY	HONEYSUCKLE	OAK
BOXWOOD	HYDRANGEA	PINE
CYPRESS	JASMINE	QUINCE
DOGWOOD	JUNIPER	SPIRAEA
FORSYTHIA	LILAC	SPRUCE
HAWTHORN	MAGNOLIA	WILLOW
	MAPLE	WISTERIA

S	E	J	L	K	I	Q	M	K	Z	Z	F	C	X	Z	K	E	X	T	U	D
N	J	A	L	Z	R	A	D	D	U	H	H	Y	M	G	Y	D	E	Q	O	A
E	L	S	Q	B	N	Q	C	R	A	X	J	A	L	J	Z	L	Y	O	E	E
D	B	R	W	I	H	P	G	X	M	I	P	Z	N	O	K	H	W	A	C	Z
C	G	N	D	E	S	U	K	Y	R	L	R	D	W	C	M	G	R	N	L	H
G	P	N	Q	D	N	P	X	C	E	D	D	E	U	L	O	I	U	B	T	Z
L	A	T	R	P	T	A	T	X	Z	T	X	S	T	D	P	F	T	T	E	C
N	P	G	G	L	P	T	E	J	R	X	Y	M	M	S	Y	G	G	A	Y	K
H	G	K	K	X	E	Y	J	G	Q	E	G	P	W	F	I	B	M	P	A	C
V	M	F	P	B	E	B	D	D	N	F	C	Y	V	I	C	W	R	O	W	W
A	N	A	G	Y	O	P	T	O	O	A	V	J	C	N	L	E	S	C	B	W
Y	V	R	G	X	Y	E	H	J	I	V	R	Y	O	V	S	L	K	L	G	C
Z	F	H	W	N	P	Y	J	J	E	E	Z	D	Q	S	G	D	O	W	V	U
O	B	O	W	G	O	A	R	C	H	C	Q	P	Y	T	W	S	Z	W	Y	I
Y	O	K	P	C	S	L	I	R	E	S	N	Y	A	H	K	Y	D	D	H	X
D	O	M	O	M	N	M	I	Z	E	I	E	I	Y	M	W	J	Q	F	R	Y
A	R	L	I	G	N	L	L	A	S	B	O	M	U	L	I	K	E	N	I	P
A	Y	N	O	M	R	W	Z	R	A	F	Y	T	Z	Q	N	E	D	R	Q	H
W	E	L	J	V	O	N	X	E	E	W	N	A	O	H	J	A	E	V	J	T
V	S	C	W	V	H	Z	S	M	Z	B	O	C	B	P	M	P	D	A	K	Y
K	J	A	Q	X	T	X	L	N	W	F	T	S	W	X	I	W	Q	L	G	X
Y	Y	L	H	Z	W	A	Z	C	L	V	G	F	Z	N	Y	L	Q	U	B	W
X	B	I	T	B	A	Q	A	N	K	Q	E	C	U	R	P	S	X	O	F	J
L	Y	L	L	O	H	A	Z	A	L	E	A	J	C	K	U	W	U	M	B	B
D	V	W	Z	L	Q	O	A	I	H	T	Y	S	R	O	F	D	N	X	F	V

DID YOU KNOW

Lee Child always begins writing a new Reacher novel on September 1st. One reason for this is to avoid procrastination and ensure he starts on time. Additionally, this date marks the anniversary of when he lost his job at Granada Television and subsequently wrote the first Reacher novel.

CRIMEBIT No.11

Rainfall

YOUR RATING /100

Tony Bury

He could feel the first drops of rain as they started to hit his face, it stopped him dead in his tracks. It was instinctive but he didn't know why his feet were suddenly rooted to the ground. Something else was happening, for an unknown reason it made him slowly close his eyes. As he did a calmness started to wash over him. Instantaneously he took a deep breath and breathed in the weather as if he was soaking up the atmosphere around him. The rain started to fall harder, it was bouncing off his clothes now and the wind was picking up bringing a chill in its tail. Somehow there was still a peace in the rain, a peace that he couldn't quite touch but he knew that they came hand in hand. He took a further two deep breaths until he could feel the rain on his tongue and the scent in the air, then he slowly opened his eyes.

Immediately he was rocked from where he was standing, almost falling backwards in the process.

The calmness of twenty seconds ago had disappeared and panic had suddenly set in.

HAVE YOUR SAY
What happens next?

Scan to visit the CrimeBits Writing Space

PUZZLE No. 11

Rain of Terror

Across

1. Death-feigning critter, slangily
7. Four doses?
11. Turned tail
14. Quite sharp
15. "In your dreams!"
16. Lemieux milieu
17. Highly localized rainfall?
19. This woman
20. Musk of business
21. Red, white or blue, to an American
22. Graze
23. Old photo hue
25. Junkyard deal
27. Small valley that's prone to freezing rain?
32. Chess pieces
35. Girl of the glen
36. Sling item
37. Writer Levin
38. "King ___" (1978 pop hit)
39. Rare dir. for hurricanes
41. Work onstage
42. Stowage
44. Heston's captors, in film
45. Jardin ___ Plantes
46. Like icy precipitation?
50. City in Denmark
51. Andante or allegro
55. Life of the party
58. Nap noisily
60. Post
61. "We ___ The World"
62. Reasons for rain?
64. Pro vote
65. "L' ___, c'est moi"
66. "___ Fidelis"
67. Assumed the lotus position
68. Ones in office
69. Andrea of ITV Daytime

Down

1. Acts restless
2. "___ Mio" (Caruso hit)
3. Barber's band
4. Those who belong to branch of Islam
5. ATV, briefly
6. SLR, for short
7. Factory stores
8. Fussy or finicky
9. "Yay, we did it!"
10. Electric unit
11. Pay increase
12. Aspirin target
13. Crave
18. Most annoyed
22. Fuzzy fabric
24. In sum
26. Comes undone
28. Filler of la mer
29. Put on board
30. In olden days
31. Saturates
32. Flaky rock
33. Notable times
34. Ultra-violent video game that was re-released in 2005
39. Planet
40. Shade of green
43. Beneficial

44. Puts in order
47. Spanish explorer of the Yucatan
48. Certain flower
49. Swift's Gulliver
52. High-stick pool shot
53. Work at St. Peter's
54. Elizabeth of Marvel films
55. Low coral reefs
56. Atlas factoid
57. Mark in music
59. Short test
62. Zip or zing
63. __ Group (British investment co.)

CRIMEBIT No. 12

Enrichment

YOUR RATING
/100

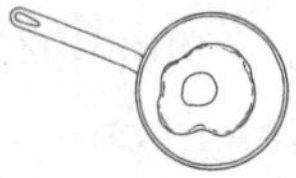

Victoria Chang

We were the best and the brightest.

We were hired for (according to Doreen the HR representative) 'our sibling vibes'.

Or in Doreen's more precise words:

'We want the students to not just feel that you are specialists in your fields, but that you are young. Approachable. Like an older sibling.'

Sarah had let out an inadvertent snort then. That was when I knew we would be friends. I also knew we would be friends when she drew a fried egg on paper when we were told to draw what most represented ourselves on orientation day.

Nearly everyone else had drawn a picture of a favorite novel. Mine was Murakami's *Hardboiled Wonderland and the End of the World*.

Sitting there that day in Tokyo 5, for the first time in my life, I realized: this is what it means to be included. I am amongst the best and the brightest. And now I am worthy of mentoring teens who want to know what it takes to reach the top. I thought I had finally made it.

That was, until we all saw Sarah lying in a pool of her own blood outside Malta 6.

PUZZLE No. 12

House of Tutors

Sarah and three other students, the best and brightest in their fields, were very excited to start their new jobs as tutors. Sadly, Sarah won't be joining them now. The remaining tutors each have a favorite author and are specialists in certain areas. From the clues determine which ***tutor*** *prefers what* ***author*** *and what* ***class*** *they'll be helping.*

The Tutors

Veronica - Sarah's best friend, briefly. Very briefly.

Louise - After Sarah's death, she wanted to go home. She still might.

Marianne - She thought Sarah's fried egg drawing was weird.

Their Favorite Authors

Neil Gaiman - British novelist who wrote *Coraline*.

Stieg Larsson - Swede who wrote the *Millennium* crime trilogy.

Haruki Murakami - He wrote the Tanizaki Prize-winning *Hard-Boiled Wonderland and the End of the World*.

Tutoring Classes

Chemistry - Dr. Jekyll's best subject, not Mr. Hyde's.

English Grammar - Linguistic rules and pitfalls.

Calculus - The math one, not the kidney stone one.

? CLUES ?

1. Veronica tutors English Grammar.
2. The tutor who prefers to read in Swedish is not Veronica.
3. The tutor who loves a British author is a Calculus whiz.
4. Louise doesn't tutor English Grammar. She doesn't speak English.
5. Marianne got a C in Chemistry. Tutors need to carry an A average to qualify.

	Louise	*Marianne*	*Veronica*	*Calculus*	*Chemistry*	*English Grammar*
Haruki Murakami						
Neil Gaiman						
Stieg Larsson						
Calculus						
Chemistry						
English Grammar						

Tutor	Favorite author	Class

CRIMEBIT No. 13

The Dirt Nap

YOUR RATING /100

Nathan Coon

In the darkness, a struggle can be heard. The sounds of dirt and gravel rustle in cycles with high-pitched air moving through pursed lips. Something is being dragged. Breathe – drag . . . And so on. The dragging comes to a pause. Heavy breathing fills the air. Steam thickens the molecules in the darkness.

The struggling sound of dragging continues a little longer and is finished with an intense exhaled grunt. Something tumbles downhill through dry grass and tinder sticks. The jingling of metal keys chimes closer to the tumbled object. Stabs of metal are heard prior to that of a key being pushed into its hole. The hinges of a heavy trunk squeak open. The dead weight is dropped into the trunk, its glowing bulb reveals a man wrapped like a baby in a flannel blanket. I awoke with a panicked gasp. My face was covered in dirt, or was it night soil? I raced to the bathroom and vomited. My brain was on fire. I walked to the freezer and plucked two ice cubes out and pressed them hard against my eye lids until everything above my nose went numb. I couldn't believe this was happening again.

PUZZLE No.13

Buried

Across

1. Captivate

7. Brushes up on

15. Made a dent in

16. Instantly

17. Cattle calls?

18. Geniality

19. Rhea relative

20. Darjeeling and pekoe

22. Lustrous fabric

23. Salon specialists

25. Outer arm bone

26. Word on bills

27. __ Eleison

29. __ Spiegel

32. Move unsteadily

35. Fleming or McKellen

36. Animal pelt

37. Dies __

38. "Skyfall" chanteuse

40. Desiccated

41. Fast friends

42. Luth. or Episc.

43. Spiced, in a way

45. Lemon head?

46. Desk site

48. __ hair day

49. Earth science eponym

50. Eternally young

54. Luton van users

57. First to putt

58. Strive (for)

59. Mental image

61. Lampoon

63. "Once upon a __ dreary..."

64. "Conviction" playwright Eve

65. To an extent

66. Balanced states

Down

1. "Blood Simple" star M. __ Walsh

2. Watts in pictures

3. It's not a pop-up

4. Vince's agent on "Entourage"

5. Profusely polite

6. Landscaping tool

7. Kids

8. Brian of rock fame

9. Cell alternatives

10. Gas used as a fuel

11. Bakery allure

12. "Green Mansions" girl

13. "JAG" spinoff

14. Nose around

21. Satisfy curiosity

24. Some pasta

25. Asian range

28. Road sign

29. Razor Vacs, for example

30. 2017 title role for Sheila Hancock

31. Sitcom star Foxx

32. Use a flannel

33. Administered by spoon

34. Capricorn, Taurus or Virgo

36. Fit to eat, to Muslims

39. God, to Gaius

44. Inactive

46. Bombing run

47. Twist in flight

49. Great wealth

51. Starry makeup

52. "Yes __, Bob!"

53. Those with vision
54. "Out Tonight" singer in "Rent"
55. King of Asgard
56. Ancient Hindu text
57. Poker stake
60. "I get it now" sounds
62. Org. founded by Lord Baden-Powell

CRIMEBIT No. 14

323 Calvert Street

YOUR RATING /100

Liz Correal

The day I became the owner of 323 Calvert Street was one of the strangest days of my life. There'd be stranger ones to come, but I didn't know that then. If I had, I would have stayed in bed. I wasn't one to linger between the sheets though and there was a good reason for that.

On the day in question, I'd been in Havre, Montana, for just over a year. The pittance of a salary I was paid to write for the *Havre Star* didn't stretch to much. Once I'd paid the monthly due on the studio I rented in a damp-stricken brownstone downtown there was next to nothing left.

While working for the *Havre Star* was my first reporting job, it wasn't the burning ambition to break a newsworthy story that woke me every day in the pre-dawn hours. That accomplishment could be credited to the hundred or so cockroaches residing in the rotten wood under the apartment's kitchen sink. Who knew the whispering rub of roach wings sounded so loud when the only other sound in the room was your own breathing? Not me or at least not me until I moved to Havre.

PUZZLE No.14

Post Production

*The owner of 323 Calvert Street has finally worked their way up to a reporting job, after years of taking any job offered at any newspaper, like writing obituaries. From the clues, determine **where** they worked, **what** job they were doing, and **why** they left each job.*

The Towns

Middletown - So small, the local daily newspaper was called Joe's Newspaper and Grill.

Bloomfield - You can tell the people from Bloomfield, but you can't tell them anything.

Lakeville - The city where the crosswalk signal is like a count-down to a race where nobody wins.

Reasons for Leaving

Toxic work environment - They had the highest disregard for all their hard work.

Bad hours - They didn't call it the "graveyard shift" for nothing.

Low wages - Unlimited doughnuts and coffee don't pay the bills.

Newspaper Job

Obituary writer - Just a few words in passing.

Copy editor - Telling other people they're wrong? Yes, please!

Restaurant reviewer - Next time, no double espresso for the baby.

? CLUES ?

1. The job writing restaurant reviews wasn't a toxic workplace.
2. The toxic work environment was the newspaper in Middletown.
3. They didn't leave the job writing obituaries for a better paying job.
4. They didn't leave Lakeville for a job with better hours. The copy editing job was in Bloomfield.

	Bad hours	*Low wages*	*Toxic work environment*	*Copy editor*	*Obituary writer*	*Restaurant reviewer*
Bloomfield						
Lakeville						
Middletown						
Copy editor						
Obituary writer						
Restaurant reviewer						

Where? **What?** **Why?**

CRIMEBIT No. 15

Lost in Translation

YOUR RATING /100

Daniel Cox-Howard

Some fool tried to kill my dad last summer in a Safeway parking lot in Culver City. He popped out from behind a parked car and swung a Bowie knife at my father's face, but my old man ducked and stepped in with his left foot and broke the guy's ankle.

Picture it: A hundred and two degrees in dead August air, the tweaker tries to hobble away but falls down, Dad takes a photo of him and calls the cops. While he's waiting, he calls me. 'Hey, remember that move you taught me?' I have no idea what he's talking about, what move?

We chatted for a bit and made plans to get together. He said there were some things I needed to know about his family, most of whom I had never met.

It was the last time I ever talked to him; three days later they found him at the bottom of a ravine in Malibu Canyon with a bullet in his head.

PUZZLE No. 15

Killing Dad

*The narrator's old man either has terribly bad luck or some determined enemies. He's been attacked five times, in five years, in different places around the Los Angeles area with a variety of weapons. From the clues, determine **when** the dad was attacked, **where** it happened, and **what** weapon almost killed him. The weapon that finally finished the job was the gun in Malibu Canyon.*

The Weapons	The Locations	The Years
Axe	Anaheim	2020
Car bomb	Culver City	2021
Knife	Glendale	2022
Machete	Long Beach	2023
Pipe wrench	Santa Ana	2024

? CLUES ?

1. The attack in Glendale was in an earlier year than the car bomb.
2. The attack in Anaheim wasn't in 2024.
3. The machete was not used in either 2023 or 2024. The axe wasn't used in 2024.
4. The attack in Long Beach was in an earlier year than the attack in Santa Ana but in a later year than both the pipe wrench attack and the car bomb.
5. The Santa Ana attacker didn't use a knife.

	Axe	Car bomb	Knife	Machete	Pipe wrench	2020	2021	2022	2023	2024
Anaheim										
Culver City										
Glendale										
Long Beach										
Santa Ana										
2020										
2021										
2022										
2023										
2024										

When?

Where?

What?

CRIMEBIT No. 16

Jackknifed

Alys Cummings

The M6 was where Ava felt most at home. Sweeping past the Pennines and towards Northumberland opened the country like a beautifully illustrated pop up book. The hills, the skies and, if you timed it right, the sunrise or sunset. Today, luck was not on her side. Sunday had only just turned into Monday and dawn was hours away.

Normally on this route she'd have pulled over by now to bunk up for the night in the back of her lorry cab. But tonight Ava was keeping her eyes on the road. She took one hand off the wheel to turn up her music. Miley Cyrus was singing about buying herself flowers. She sang along. Good for Miley. And although Ava couldn't remember the time she'd bought anyone flowers, she did own 7.5 tonnes of metal.

Overhead signs started flashing 50 somewhere among the Cumbrian hills, and Ava dropped down a gear as the traffic in front slowed. The dashboard clock showed 12.48am. She should have built more time into the journey. A delicate frond of fear grew inside her as she glanced up to where the fat packet of heroin was stashed in the compartment above the windscreen.

PUZZLE No. 16

Road Work

APPLEBY	CARLISLE	HEYSHAM	MORECAMBE	STAFFORD
BARROW	CARNFORTH	KENDAL	NEWCASTLE	STANDISH
BIRMINGHAM	COVENTRY	KESWICK	NEWTON	TEBAY
BLACKPOOL	CUMBRIA	LANCASTER	PENRITH	TODHILLS
BOLTON	FLEETWOOD	LEEDS	PRESTON	WALSALL
BROUGH	GARSTANG	LEIGH	RUGBY	WARRINGTON
BURNLEY	GRETNA	LEYLAND	SEDBERGH	WIGAN
CANNOCK	HEXHAM	LIVERPOOL	SKIPTON	WOLVERHAMPTON
			SOUTHPORT	MANCHESTER

D	R	Z	O	X	Q	E	F	N	O	T	L	O	B	W	U	C	U	B	O	R
M	A	H	S	Y	E	H	T	P	O	K	N	H	S	D	E	E	L	S	H	R
N	L	O	O	P	K	C	A	L	B	T	T	F	B	I	N	N	T	V	G	E
E	B	C	Y	Q	F	I	Q	B	I	S	P	P	K	J	X	A	A	S	I	T
W	W	P	S	M	R	W	W	U	R	E	A	I	J	D	F	W	P	L	E	S
C	J	M	T	B	X	O	P	R	M	D	Z	X	K	F	B	O	P	I	L	E
A	O	U	M	S	E	L	R	N	I	B	M	U	O	S	S	R	L	V	T	H
S	H	U	N	C	O	V	E	L	N	E	N	R	G	K	F	R	E	E	J	C
T	C	C	V	R	O	E	S	E	G	R	D	Z	R	L	K	A	B	R	L	N
L	I	R	U	O	N	R	T	Y	H	G	S	L	E	S	K	B	Y	P	A	A
E	U	G	C	J	W	H	O	W	A	H	A	E	T	B	V	E	V	O	N	M
Q	B	A	B	F	R	A	N	N	M	K	T	Y	N	C	A	N	N	O	C	K
Y	X	Q	N	W	C	M	L	S	S	W	Y	L	A	F	D	T	X	L	A	S
T	Q	T	N	R	A	P	U	S	O	G	N	A	T	S	R	A	G	Y	S	S
W	P	M	D	F	T	T	D	O	A	O	Y	N	U	N	A	G	I	W	T	L
H	A	O	B	Y	T	O	D	P	H	L	F	D	X	T	K	E	A	V	E	L
S	M	R	C	C	R	N	M	T	A	A	L	G	Y	S	V	N	G	L	R	I
I	B	E	R	F	G	T	I	D	H	R	A	C	A	R	N	F	O	R	T	H
D	B	C	G	I	W	R	N	C	A	R	L	I	S	L	E	T	J	M	E	D
N	V	A	R	X	N	E	P	E	H	E	K	C	I	W	S	E	K	X	B	O
A	U	M	S	E	K	G	W	X	V	G	V	O	J	I	J	B	H	N	R	T
T	C	B	P	S	O	U	T	H	P	O	R	T	W	Y	O	A	G	F	O	X
S	E	E	G	X	R	R	A	O	P	J	C	V	M	F	M	Y	Z	W	U	N
P	E	J	F	P	Q	U	J	O	N	E	P	Z	T	Z	Y	W	X	D	G	S
M	T	V	P	M	G	X	V	T	N	O	T	W	E	N	L	O	I	A	H	U

CRIMEBIT No.17

The Fixer

SHORTLISTED BY LEE CHILD

YOUR RATING /100

Alys Cummings

The windows were up and the air con on full blast, but the smell of death had found its way in.

Each side of the road were abandoned vehicles, doors left hanging open, a glimpse of a handbag on a dashboard as their car moved swiftly past. They turned off the smooth road, following the jeep ahead down a rocky path towards the settlement. The bodies were covered up now, white covers with blue writing in an alphabet that Kate couldn't read.

'What does the writing say? Is it names?' She asked the translator.

Dilek didn't even glance in her direction.

'Dead,' she said. 'Deceased. Dead.'

Kate bit the inside of her mouth in embarrassment as she realized the blue writing all said the same thing. She tasted blood. You are a fucking idiot Kate. She sensed Dilek brace herself as if for more inanities.

And then the world turned into a furious fire. As the jeep ahead disappeared, all Kate could hear was an incessant ringing.

The seatbelt tried to cut through to her heart and her fingers clenched on her biro.

Dilek turned, looked Kate in the eye, and smiled.

EDITOR'S NOTES

'The unerring sense of impending horror runs through this amazing opening from Alys Cummings. From its opening sentence, to the incongruous smile from Dilek at the end, this is a spectacular piece of descriptive writing. It draws the reader in instantly, which is difficult to execute. There is something about not wasting your time with unnecessary building – getting right to the heart (and blood) of the action straight away. Sublime.'

PUZZLE No. 17

Fixer Uppers

Across

1. Largo and presto
6. Letters before omegas
10. Numero after siete
14. Court star Shaq or movie star Tatum
15. Of a different sort
16. Hammerhead end
17. Plastic material
18. Caribou kin
19. Like some agreements
20. Do sum work
21. Apple variety
23. In a big way
25. Last
27. Takes the gold
28. Response to "Am too!"
30. Picasa uploads
34. Kind of acid
35. Practical value
36. Office message
37. Twitch
38. Hat-blocking machines
41. Peter with a fairy friend
42. "It all makes sense now!"
44. Palm Pilot, e.g.
45. Confer holy orders
47. Hotbed of corruption
49. In a flip way
50. Clock ticks, for short
51. Aesop's grasshopper, notably
52. Mineral vein
55. Parks in 1955 news and a "Doctor Who" episode
56. US campground company whose first word is deliberately misspelled
59. "__ Flux" (1990s MTV cartoon)
60. Work for Money, maybe
62. Armstrong and deGrasse Tyson
64. After-shower powder
65. Sandwich fish
66. Toys flown at the beach
67. __ Stanley Gardner
68. Rolls out a lawn
69. "Happy Days" actor Williams

Down

1. "L'Shana __" (Rosh Hashanah greeting)
2. Emma's role on "Wednesday"
3. Fix some yard boundaries?
4. Be profitable
5. US state where Bears and Cubs play
6. Tandem mover
7. Wooden coaster
8. Verb form suffix
9. Fix potholes and other highway hazards?
10. America's marsupial
11. Legal writ, for short
12. Cure
13. Exclusively

22. Fix cargo pants features?
24. Little red soldier
26. Overnight stop
27. Profound
28. Room at the very top of the house
29. Pull up
30. Of an insect stage
31. Fix first aid boxes?
32. Send without stamps
33. Valentine of "Hollyoaks"
39. Commotions
40. Country once called Ceylon
43. Quiddity
46. Cube's "Natural Born Killaz" rap partner
48. Green legume
51. Just jots
52. Fill to capacity
53. Make a mad dash
54. Sushi order
55. Produce skin
57. Margarine in old recipes
58. The A in BMA
61. Singing pair
63. Zwei preceder

CRIMEBIT No. 18

Pelgram's Progress

YOUR RATING
/100

John Cunningham

Anita Pelgram stood over the grave of her husband, John. He'd been shot in the line of duty, while investigating a county lines racket in their sleepy market town. Accompanied by her two children, she looked around at the weeping, mourning faces of his family, friends, and work colleagues. It wasn't meant to be like this, she thought. This time last year, they'd moved from the city, to escape its dirty grime and crime, to settle down and bring up their children in the heart of the countryside. It was meant to be a fresh start. He had seen the role advertised, applied and secured the position out of a number of worthy candidates. And here they were, burying her husband, the father of her children, in a cold, damp grave, on this rainy December day. A nice Christmas present for the kids, she thought, looking towards John's visibly grief stricken colleagues. Colleagues so properly solicitous, resolute in their desire to find her husband's killer. His partner, Eddie, short for Edwina Lark, suddenly looked at her from across the burial mound, and Anita knew instantly, something else was wrong.

PUZZLE No.18

The Police Secrets

Something is seriously wrong in Wexham. John Pelgram is the fourth police officer to be killed on duty in the last year. Wexham has a reputation for being a sleepy little market town, but it's now harboring an undercurrent of crime and violence. John was shot while investigating a county line racket. From the clues, determine ***who*** *was investigating* ***what****, and* ***where*** *their bodies were found.*

The Officers

Bobby Blue - Also played for the precinct volleyball team, serving and protecting.

Barney Piccolo - Owns a lawn maintenance company called "Lawn Order".

Ursula Kojak - Once gave a cat a ticket for littering.

The Investigations

Equipment theft - Never trust a thief. They take things literally.

Vandalism - Someone is painting hopscotch boards all over town.

Assault - You can't punch someone in the face, even if you think they deserve it.

The Locations

Behind the local store - A nostalgic relic of simpler times, a place where news is shared and friendships are forged.

Next to the fire station - With its bright red doors and spotless brick exterior, it stands as a beacon of safety and readiness.

The church parking lot - The small town church parking lot, bordered by neatly trimmed hedges, gravel and faded lines.

? CLUES ?

1. Barney Piccolo was a staunch atheist who wouldn't be caught dead near a church, not even while investigating a crime.
2. The officer who was investigating vandalism in the local cemetery was found next to the fire station.
3. The officer who specialized in assault cases was not Bobby Blue.
4. Ursula Kojak never investigated theft cases.
5. Bobby Blue's body was found behind the local store.

	Barney Piccolo	Bobby Blue	Ursula Kojak	Assault	Equipment theft	Vandalism
Church parking lot						
Fire station						
Behind the local store						
Assault						
Equipment theft						
Vandalism						

Who? ______________ **What?** ______________ **Where?** ______________

______________ ______________ ______________

______________ ______________ ______________

CRIMEBIT No.19

Sticks

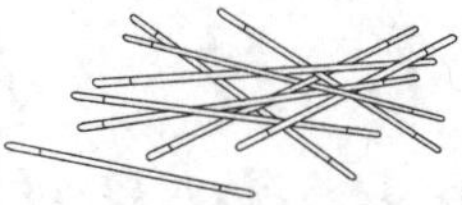

Catherine Darensbourg

How to halt global famine, collapse, and enslavement like a colorful jumble of sticks in a child's game? How to pick up the precariously balanced pieces? Rebuild?

There are Five Methods:

First – Go high stakes. Never compromise or accept small victories. End things quick.

Second – Stay low. Humble. Always accept loyal assistant's seat. Never lofty first.

Third – Swift opportunism. Blend absolute, popular success with public and approachable modest gain.

Fourth – Play for time, but play hard.

Fifth – Let your opponents win, think you're soft as they eventually show their flawed moves. Then shut them down as they smile.

Smile back. Wait. Watch them bow. Choose allies from among them.

Rebuild so every political party's faction feels safe. Secure enough so they beg you to lead.

Take your seat. Start quietly seeking your real enemies as you finally relax to pat yourself on the back . . .

Checking for knives.

PUZZLE No. 19

The Body Politic

Across

1. Pipe type
6. School basics
10. Signaled
14. Grand Canyon beast
15. Kauai keepsakes
16. Legendary brute
17. Empty ballot roster?
19. Gooey clump
20. Adventure story
21. Potent beginning?
22. Martini option
23. Herding dog
25. Shellac finish?
26. "Yes __!" ("You bet!")
29. Maritime-minded group of voters?
34. Beaut of a beau
36. Little woman
37. Connector with colored ends, for short
38. Fit nicely
40. Brandenburg capital
42. Future profs, maybe
43. Woosnam and Fleming
45. Shalimar Gardens locale
46. Election on Vulcan?
49. Folk histories
50. Glasgow's Argyle Street station code
51. Having seniority
53. Loses energy
56. Sierra Club founder
57. Miso soup cubes
61. Bun or stotty
62. Item in a swag bag at a US political convention?
64. Smooth
65. Jigsaw starting point
66. Another time
67. Son of Seth
68. Chatty twins?
69. Big Ben has four

Down

1. Tidal refluxes
2. "Be-Bop-A-__"
3. Crow
4. Holiday bauble
5. Taipei pan
6. Brothers who sang "Sweet Melissa"
7. Shapeless chair
8. __ Field (Queens ballpark)
9. It's at 5:00
10. Loft sight
11. Citrus fruit from Jamaica
12. Son of Aphrodite
13. Red ink, so to speak
18. Chip off the old block, often
22. Revelatory
24. Upper limits
25. Music for the present day?
26. Clara or Monica

27. Lofty goal
28. Portia de __
30. Mr. Big
31. "Ada or __: A Family Chronicle" (Nabokov)
32. Cause for alarm
33. Chair designer
35. Chars
39. Test material?
41. Scarcity
44. Cause of calamity
47. Golf scores
48. Exclusive groups
52. Wipe with a flannel
53. Without a date
54. Money deal
55. Plus
56. Prepared, as dinner
58. Pecan's shape
59. Disrupt, as an evil plot
60. Ornamental vases
62. Furry family member
63. It can follow "Ab" or precede "Four"

CRIMEBIT No. 20

Murder in Ecotopia

YOUR RATING /100

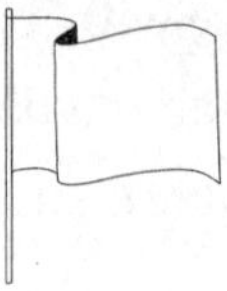

Lee Dawkins

Zuzu Bailey is enjoying a quiet midnight stroll along Main Street with Beyoncé. High above the photovoltaic cupolas crowning the four turrets of the Tower of London, a flag ripples in the breeze. It features a lion and a unicorn supporting a scroll bearing the legend, 'Less is More'. It's the leitmotif of a pioneering community, where less consumption, less waste, less stuff, equals more fulfillment, more contentment, more well-being. The visionary behind this post-growth model society has drawn inspiration from Stendhal's maxim that 'beauty is the promise of happiness', creating a magical island in the shape of Great Britain, filled with scaled-down replicas of iconic buildings, and picturesque vernacular housing.

Something in the narrow moat encircling the mock-Norman building attracts Beyoncé's attention. Zuzu tries to coax her away from the water, but the labradoodle won't listen. When Zuzu ventures over to investigate, her resulting coloratura scream can be heard from Dartmoor to the Lakes. Zuzu grabs hold of the man lying face down in the shallow water and rolls him onto his back. She lets out another operatic shriek – a soubrette soprano this time – when she sees his face. It's Sam Butler; the founder of this unique microcosmic eco-community.

DID YOU KNOW

The best-selling crime fiction novel of all time is *And Then There Were None* by Agatha Christie. With over 100 million copies sold, it ranks among the best-selling books ever published. Originally published in 1939, the novel follows 10 strangers who are invited to a secluded island mansion where the host is mysteriously absent. Each guest harbors a dark secret, and as they find themselves isolated from the outside world, they begin to share their stories. Soon, one by one, they start to die . . .

PUZZLE No. 20

Iconic Britain

BIG BEN
BLETCHLEY
BRIGHTON
BUCKINGHAM
CAMBRIDGE
CAMDEN
CANTERBURY
CARNABY
COLISEUM
COTSWOLDS
COVENT GARDEN
COVENTRY
DARTMOOR
DOVER
WESTMINSTER
GLOBE THEATRE
HADRIAN'S WALL
HAMPTON
HYDE PARK
KENSINGTON
KINGS CROSS
LIVERPOOL
LONDON EYE
MADAME TUSSAUDS
NOTTING HILL
OLD BAILEY
OXFORD
PICCADILLY
PORTOBELLO
PORTSMOUTH
ROMAN BATHS
ROYAL COURT
SHARD
SOHO
SOMERSET
ST PAUL'S
STONEHENGE
TATE
THAMES
TINTAGEL
TRAFALGAR
WEMBLEY
DURHAM
WINDSOR

L	O	N	D	O	N	E	Y	E	E	R	T	A	E	H	T	E	B	O	L	G
B	P	V	L	C	I	N	M	F	F	Y	N	O	T	G	N	I	S	N	E	K
B	O	S	L	L	A	W	S	N	A	I	R	D	A	H	E	C	Q	O	O	O
R	R	V	I	B	R	M	L	N	F	X	N	T	S	H	C	H	N	T	M	Y
I	T	M	H	U	T	E	D	F	G	Y	B	A	N	R	A	C	L	P	Q	J
G	O	S	G	C	E	Y	O	E	Y	R	T	D	H	E	U	T	C	M	M	B
H	B	H	N	K	S	L	S	Y	N	X	L	I	U	P	V	R	T	A	T	E
T	E	T	I	I	R	L	S	H	Y	D	E	P	A	R	K	O	M	H	R	E
O	L	A	T	N	E	I	O	L	D	B	A	I	L	E	Y	Y	C	W	O	D
N	L	B	T	G	M	D	R	J	D	E	I	L	B	I	G	B	E	N	S	K
L	O	N	O	H	O	A	C	S	X	B	L	E	T	C	H	L	E	Y	D	B
E	R	A	N	A	S	C	S	Y	O	T	Q	O	Y	I	M	O	P	O	N	M
C	R	M	C	M	Y	C	G	J	Y	H	T	P	O	A	N	Z	V	E	I	W
D	L	O	T	A	R	I	N	O	X	F	O	R	D	P	N	E	G	G	W	E
S	N	R	O	T	N	P	I	H	P	T	T	A	A	E	R	D	M	O	X	S
D	T	J	O	M	O	T	K	P	R	S	M	U	D	F	I	E	I	Z	J	T
L	T	P	C	K	T	M	E	U	G	E	E	R	R	R	A	L	V	F	X	M
O	F	I	A	O	E	R	O	R	T	Q	A	M	B	G	A	L	K	I	M	I
W	U	A	N	U	L	C	A	U	B	G	O	M	A	U	W	H	G	B	L	N
S	K	T	P	T	L	I	S	D	T	U	A	N	A	H	L	Z	S	A	I	S
T	O	N	O	A	A	S	S	N	H	C	R	H	M	I	T	L	X	B	R	T
O	W	F	Y	M	A	G	E	E	U	H	U	Y	E	L	B	M	E	W	D	E
C	X	O	Q	U	P	V	E	S	U	E	G	N	E	H	E	N	O	T	S	R
Y	R	A	D	C	O	C	G	L	J	M	M	R	Q	C	D	U	R	H	A	M
M	N	S	B	C	H	T	U	O	M	S	T	R	O	P	E	H	E	J	Z	O

CRIMEBIT No. 21

Savant Malignant

YOUR RATING /100

Jim DeFilippi

Eric DuBois was fifteen years old when his father died.

They had a sort of wake at the Malta Club after Father Abernathy said the Church didn't want to get involved. They served little frozen shrimp that still cracked with ice as you bit in. Masha tried to make the homemade gnocchi the old man used to roll off the fork with his thumb.

Everyone kept coming up to Eric and saying what a soldier his Dad had been. Those seven years away without a crack. Even a couple words could have sweetened the deal.

Eric didn't bother telling anyone that he was the one who killed him.

PUZZLE No. 21

Just Say Gnocchi

Across

1. Diamond unit
6. Scala and Carides
10. Arizona native
14. Abundant (with)
15. Dermal dilemma
16. Guffaw
17. Pasta dish made with arugula?
20. Use skillfully
21. Hefty herbivore
22. One of 5 beaches involved in Operation Overlord
23. In public view
24. Site with restaurant ratings
26. Pasta platter for piscatorial pursuits?
33. Watery expanse
34. 905-year-old of Genesis
35. Put on
36. Beyond racy
37. Gulps down
39. Pinochle coup
40. Bill stamp
41. Ice chunk
42. "Norwegian Wood" strings
43. Pasta dispensed from an aerosol?
47. "... __ any man should boast"
48. Artificial yellow spread
49. Central Florida city
52. "Siddhartha" novelist
54. Model material
57. Force generated by feather-shaped fare?
60. Rare blood type, briefly
61. Trombone insert
62. Diminish slowly
63. __ -majesté
64. Like Pollyanna
65. Boca __, Florida

Down

1. Find fault with
2. At large from Sarge
3. Not for prudes
4. Drill
5. Occupying that place
6. Playing Minecraft, say
7. "No prob!"
8. Pesky
9. Blue whale relative
10. Cue
11. Nitpicking amount
12. Summer class for US students?
13. Cantata solo
18. Segue starter
19. Pepsi and Coke
23. Migratory food fish
25. They're big among bigwigs
26. Makes origami
27. Become frozen
28. "Teenage Mutant Ninja Turtles" setting
29. Be in charge
30. Start of a tribute
31. "Oppenheimer" director
32. Lemur of Madagascar
37. "I'll only be a few __"
38. In high dudgeon
39. Parker or O'Shea
41. Way to play music

42. Unexpected hit
44. Charge
45. Grazed on goodies
46. Additionally
49. Beautiful form of silica
50. Bottom of a 99
51. Bowls over
53. James of R&B
54. Intricate problem
55. Asian prefix
56. Young person
58. "4 real?!?"
59. Page in history

CRIMEBIT No. 22

Nola Smoke

YOUR RATING /100

Meg E. Dobson

The assassin drove his ATV down a deep arroyo to the dry creek bed, dropping from sight. Images flashed across Nola's mind: sweet young Willow standing by the Salt River collecting the grasses and devil's claw, the image of the child's great-grandmother surrounded by the baskets made by her and ancient ancestors. All at risk. All innocent. Because she'd come into their lives.

When the ATV's driver with the rocket launcher strapped to his back rose into view, Nola sighted her old '86, released the memories from her mind, concentrated on the range to target, the faint breeze across her face, and emptied her lungs. She sweetly caressed the trigger. A heartbeat later, pink mist exploded as her shot struck.

Justified. His body fell from the ATV and bounced a bit. Justified. A second time she shot. Through the scope, she inspected the man's corpse looking for breath, movement. Nothing. Justified.

PUZZLE No. 22

Basket Cases

Nola, Willow and their friend Iva spent their youth gathering plants from the nearby Salt River and weaving them into decorative and useful baskets. Each of the basket weavers prefers a specific plant, and each weaves baskets for a specific purpose. From the clues, match the basket ***weaver*** *with their preferred* ***plant*** *and the type of* ***basket*** *they like to weave.*

The Weavers

Nola - Tough, determined, incorruptible and a darn good shot.

Willow - Shy, nerdy girl with a heart of gold.

Iva - Her skills are legendary; her fingers fly when she's weaving.

The Plants

Rabbitbrush - Not to be confused with sagebrush.

Dunebroom - Aromatic shrubs with slender stems.

Galleta grass - Shrub-like and woody, best gathered during the warm season.

The Baskets

Cooking basket - Tightly woven to be watertight, or loosely woven to use as a sieve.

Gathering basket - Handles make them easy to carry.

Storage basket - Some with lids, some with handles, but all are beautiful and practical.

? CLUES ?

1. The basket weaver who likes galleta grass was not Nola.
2. Willow doesn't make baskets for storage.
3. The basket weaver who prefers to use dunebroom makes baskets for gathering berries and herbs.
4. Iva is allergic to rabbitbrush; she doesn't go near the stuff.
5. Nola makes specialty baskets for cooking.

	Iva	**Nola**	**Willow**	*Dunebroom*	*Galleta grass*	*Rabbitbrush*
Cooking						
Gathering						
Storage						
Dunebroom						
Galleta grass						
Rabbitbrush						

Weaver	Plant	Basket

CRIMEBIT No. 23

Sharing

YOUR RATING
/100

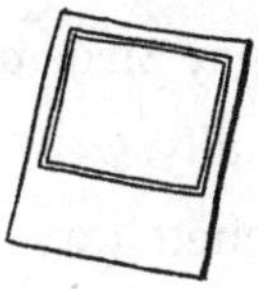

Niamh Donnellan

I was twenty-one when I found out how my father died. My Mam had decided it was best for me to grow up unburdened by such a dark thing. I see her point. Younger me would have ranted and raved, worn all the emotions like a badge of honor among my teenage friends desperate for drama. Now, it's still fucking dramatic, don't get me wrong, but I can cope with it now, at least I think I can.

Hang on, I'm getting ahead of myself. So basically, Mam got pregnant when she was my age. Of course, I wanted to know everything. Who was my father? Why didn't he want to be in my life? She never answered.

I left it there. It's hard to explain why. It was just me and Mam you see. I trusted her but there was also a little sliver of fear there. Fear of pushing her too far, of hurting her by poking and prying into her past. I know other people might not approach such a gaping hole in their life this way but there you go, it's what I did. Until a few weeks ago. Until I saw that photo.

PUZZLE No. 23

Sharing Is Caring

Across

1. Opposite of 55 Across
5. "Pretty slick!"
10. Some iTunes buys
14. Jack London hero
15. Shirley in early "Carry On" films
16. Sagan or Jung
17. Dessert served at Sylvia's and the Apollo Theater in NYC?
19. Beech or birch
20. "__ little teapot, short and stout"
21. "Wow, that's exciting!"
22. Capital of Samoa?
24. Hairy Hollywood heavy
25. Took to jail
27. Pint or pixel
28. Hole
29. Loose things to tie up?
30. Fundamental essence of the largest Channel Island?
33. Aries or Taurus
35. Hermit
36. Angry Birds birds, essentially
37. Pitched low
39. Lover of Euridice, in a Gluck opera
42. Makes up
46. PC peripherals at the cushion factory?
49. Brownish hue
50. Prefix equivalent to equi-
51. British Harness Racing Club gait
52. Barley or bulgur
53. "... __ the battle to the strong"
54. That girl
55. Lousy review
57. Twitter shares, informally
58. Celeb pair
60. "Fabian of Scotland Yard," perhaps?
63. "Great" East Frankish king
64. Neo's portrayer
65. American Jay who hosted a nighttime program
66. Funk sensor
67. Seasonal gift giver
68. Banjo feature

Down

1. Not-so-new work crew
2. Unshakable
3. Place for a wicker chair
4. Photo lab request
5. Film fish nicknamed "Shark Bait"
6. Excluding none
7. __ later date
8. Symbolic gifts
9. Easy-on baby outfit
10. Legal passage?
11. Peerless example
12. Ready
13. Railroad car
18. Wait in an A&E line, seemingly
23. Fashion fads

26. Neighbor of Jordan
27. Stone vessel
30. Hawkins of "Treasure Island"
31. I problem?
32. Office machine
34. Use a plane
37. Title for Pierre Perignon
38. A nanny has three
39. Gist of an editorial
40. Creamy dish made with arborio grains
41. Broccoli pieces
42. Hogwarts' Mrs. Norris is one
43. Less abundant
44. Music interval
45. Solar "blemish"
47. Inflicts, as havoc
48. Eye bank donation
52. Wildebeest
55. Pub purchase
56. Greenish-blue
59. Dunford who plays Aethelwulf on "Vikings"
61. Graphing calculator key
62. Galadriel, for one

CRIMEBIT No. 24

Mindhacker

YOUR RATING /100

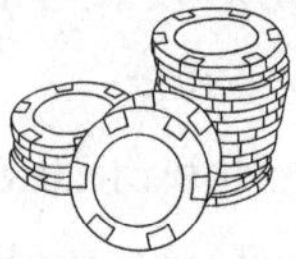

Mickey Dubrow

Some people fail at their jobs because they're not good enough, while others fail because they're too good. Mentalist Danny Rox was one of the latter. He was way too good. That was why he was performing at a casino in Cherokee, North Carolina instead of the Las Vegas Strip.

People wanted to be dazzled by Danny's performance, but they thought they knew it was an illusion. A trick. Part of the fun was waiting to see if he slipped up and revealed how he did it.

But Danny never slipped up, because it wasn't a trick.

Danny was telepathic.

PUZZLE No. 24

Uncommon Sense

ASTRAL PROJECTION
BILOCATION
CHANNELING
CLAIRVOYANCE
CRYOKINESIS
DOWSING
LEVITATION
MEDIUMSHIP
MIND CONTROL
PRECOGNITION
PREDICTION
PREMONITION
PROPHECY
PSYCHOMETRY
PYROKINESIS
REMOTE VIEWING
SHAPESHIFTING
TELEKINESIS
TELEPATHY
TELEPORTATION
TIME TRAVEL
TRANSFORMATION

S	C	S	Q	N	X	U	A	F	L	B	X	L	L	G	J	A	J	V	C	H
F	L	H	I	J	K	X	T	C	H	A	N	N	E	L	I	N	G	G	F	U
D	G	X	Z	B	I	L	O	C	A	T	I	O	N	X	M	P	N	Z	K	D
C	C	N	G	S	I	S	E	N	I	K	O	R	Y	P	N	I	P	L	K	T
C	P	D	N	E	P	X	Z	M	S	A	E	O	Q	W	S	L	I	Y	N	C
L	L	L	I	G	T	B	I	I	E	S	R	H	H	W	Q	K	H	S	N	L
U	H	S	W	G	E	R	G	N	N	T	M	H	O	J	V	Z	S	S	O	A
E	G	U	E	F	L	G	J	D	G	R	O	D	I	X	B	T	M	I	I	I
A	Z	Q	I	S	E	T	P	C	W	A	T	G	X	X	I	L	U	S	T	R
Y	J	E	V	F	K	E	J	O	S	L	P	Y	V	H	Y	N	I	E	I	V
I	H	P	E	Y	I	L	R	N	T	P	E	H	C	F	Q	E	D	N	N	O
E	J	X	T	C	N	E	V	T	E	R	Z	V	M	E	D	A	E	I	G	Y
A	C	I	O	P	E	P	A	R	E	O	O	I	A	S	H	S	M	K	O	A
N	I	C	M	R	S	A	Z	O	F	J	B	F	N	R	P	P	Z	O	C	N
Y	F	S	E	E	I	T	X	L	N	E	U	P	N	S	T	R	O	Y	E	C
H	F	M	R	M	S	H	L	O	L	C	T	Q	Y	I	C	E	V	R	R	E
H	P	D	Z	O	T	Y	I	W	N	T	R	C	C	O	A	A	M	C	P	G
Q	I	K	Q	N	N	T	V	J	T	I	H	C	J	E	F	I	I	I	I	K
X	R	Q	M	I	A	N	B	D	R	O	V	M	R	V	Q	T	T	L	T	N
V	H	X	H	T	X	H	J	Y	M	N	J	Y	L	R	E	W	X	G	H	W
U	A	Y	I	I	T	E	L	E	P	O	R	T	A	T	I	O	N	A	V	U
E	R	V	S	O	A	O	T	R	A	N	S	F	O	R	M	A	T	I	O	N
M	E	E	N	N	F	R	I	C	M	O	N	C	S	F	R	G	F	B	F	I
L	K	L	D	J	Y	A	C	B	N	O	I	T	C	I	D	E	R	P	Z	L
B	C	O	L	G	N	I	T	F	I	H	S	E	P	A	H	S	J	U	J	R

CRIMEBIT No. 25

The Slow Knife

YOUR RATING /100

Antony Dunford

Nigel had lived an average life. That was the best you could say about it. He'd cured no diseases, made no fortunes, fought in no wars. Sometimes kind and sometimes cruel, he'd made people cry and he'd made people smile. He thought about himself more than others, though he didn't have that high an opinion of himself. He knew very few people and disliked people he didn't know, and he wasn't that fond of those he did. The only person he'd ever really liked was his wife, and he'd made the mistake of never letting her know it. She'd left with their son, and Nigel hadn't seen them in years. He'd heard he had grandchildren.

It didn't matter now. Nigel lay and stared at the needle sticking into a vein in his arm. What a strange thing it was. Just a needle, held in place by tape, connected to a tube that carried the morphine, that kept the pain away. It didn't matter now. It wouldn't be long.

But one thing did matter now. He knew who had killed him, no mystery there. But he didn't know why. For some reason that mattered. Why mattered. Nigel scowled.

WRITING PROMPT
2

I wasn't there the moment Ella died.

I didn't see what he did.

I didn't know.

Not that it mattered to anyone out there. The gossips and the critics. They made their judgment of me the moment my name appeared on the front of the newspapers. Trending on social media. People hiding behind anonymity, saying what they thought should happen to me now.

I wasn't even there.

Scan to visit the
CrimeBits Writing Space

PUZZLE No. 25

Common, Man

Across

1. Carrying out successfully (13)
8. Activate, as a torpedo (3)
9. Patrick McGoohan's TV nemesis (6,3)
10. Narcotic pain reliever (8)
11. Faucet flaw (4)
13. Forbid to fly (6)
14. Dispatch once more (6)
16. Put to the proof (4)
17. Honoring, at a banquet (8)
20. Analgesic painkiller (9)
21. Body digit (3)
22. Sons' sons, say (13)

Down

1. Sudden terror (5)
2. Early projection device (6,7)
3. Eating eagerly (8)
4. Ovate yellow fruits (6)
5. Look as though (4)
6. One who intervenes between two parties (13)
7. Classified (7)
12. Confidential (8)
13. Obtaining (7)
15. Bather's exfoliant (6)
18. Color between blue and yellow in the spectrum (5)
19. Part of a crossword puzzle (4)

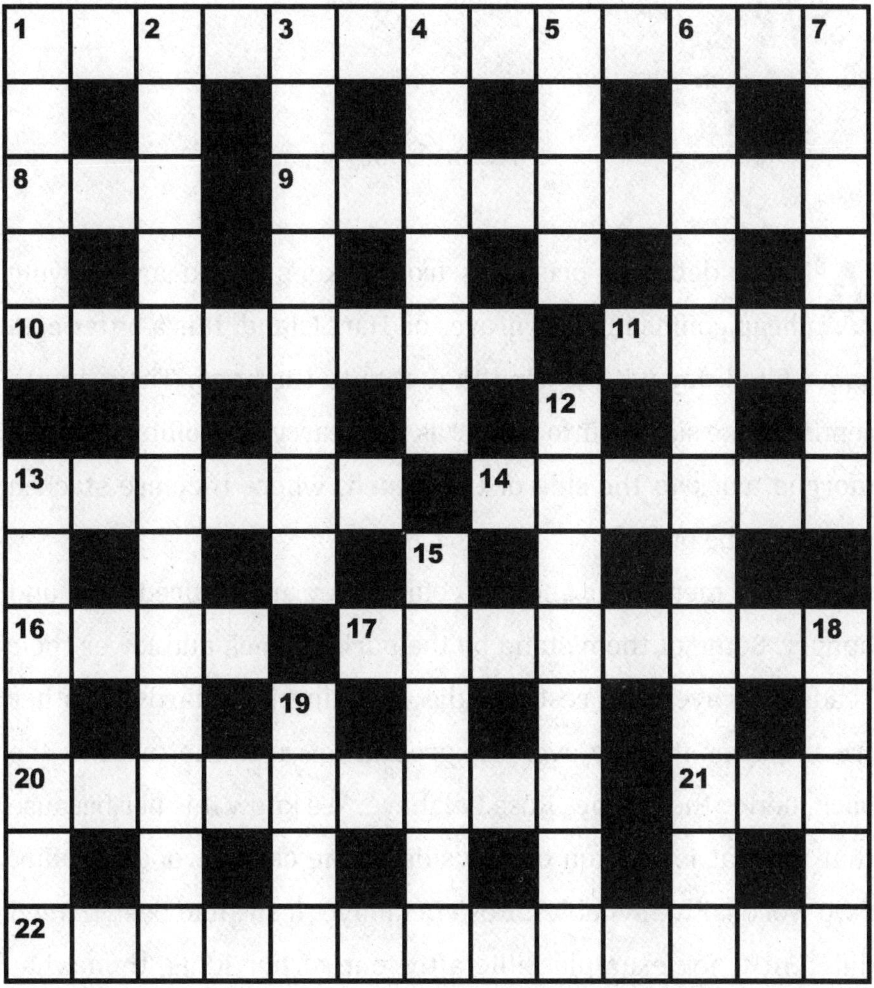

CRIMEBIT No. 26

Lost and Found

YOUR RATING /100

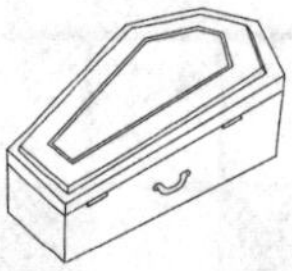

Helen East

A burial detail of prisoners from Riker's Island are burying cheap coffins in mass graves on Hart Island. It is a bitter cold snow-filled day with a wind that cuts to the bone. Their breath sends smoke signals into the air as they carry the coffins from the morgue truck to the side of the trench, where they are stacked waiting to be buried.

The men cover another coffin. They are all tired, cold and hungry. Some of them stand by the burial trench and lower their heads in prayer, the rest join the watching jail guards. Another truck bumps its way over the ground towards the men. In the back, under the pile lies Rosa Delahaye. We know it is her because that is what is written on the side of the cheap wooden coffin. Two words. Five syllables. Rosa Delahaye. If she had been named differently, for example Billie after one of her idols, then what happened next would not have happened, and February 22nd would have just been the day Rosa Delahaye was buried. Period. End of story. Except, it was just the start.

PUZZLE No. 26

Details, Details

*There are five men in the Riker's Island burial detail, each from a different neighborhood in New York City. They're all looking forward to their release dates, and each man is eligible for release in a different month. From the clues, determine **who** is from **where**, and **when** they're due to be released.*

The Prisoners

Brian
David
Don
Kevin
Mark

The Neighborhoods

Brighton Beach
Flushing
Greenpoint
Sheepshead Bay
Washington Heights

The Release Months

May June July August September

Who?	**Where?**	**When?**
______	______	______
______	______	______
______	______	______
______	______	______
______	______	______

?CLUES?

1. The man from Washington Heights is being released in an earlier month than the man from Sheepshead Bay (who isn't David) but in later month than both Mark and Don.
2. Brian isn't being released in either August or September.
3. The man from Flushing isn't getting out in September.
4. The man from Brighton Beach will be released in an earlier month than Mark.
5. September isn't the month that Kevin is being released.

	Brian	*David*	*Don*	*Kevin*	*Mark*	*Brighton Beach*	*Flushing*	*Greenpoint*	*Sheepshead Bay*	*Washington Heights*
May										
June										
July										
August										
September										
Brighton Beach										
Flushing										
Greenpoint										
Sheepshead Bay										
Washington Heights										

CRIMEBIT No. 27

On the Knife Edge

YOUR RATING /100

Lucy Edwards

Quick, heavy footsteps followed the sandblasted tarmac path down towards the beach. The man's head tucked deep into the collar of his jacket, eyes squinted against the wind, thick with dust and grit. Old fashioned streetlamps, designed to please the tourists, were set at intervals along the way, casting a dim, yellowish glow that failed to reach the path. Staggering, the man paused beneath the nearest lamp to catch his breath. He wiped his face and turned to peer back up towards the house. It was hard to tell through the gloom but he thought he had lost them. He walked on, focused on the steady sound of his steps, trying to block out the threatening roar of the waves below and the pain in his side.

Almost there.

At the foot of the cliffs, a figure hid behind a rocky outcrop. Although shielded from the worst of the weather it shivered wildly, not from the night's chill but from anticipation. Unlike the man on the path, it was ready for what would happen next.

PUZZLE No. 27

Sticking Points

Across

1. Pool exercise
5. US state where "The Book of Mormon" begins
9. Nation of Hispaniola
14. Subordinate
15. Grandmother, to some
16. PC key
17. Aromatic herb
19. Narrow platform
20. Audible dance step
21. Family nickname
22. Voice of Spider-Woman in "Spider-Man: Across the Spider-Verse"
25. Master-at-___
29. Work on a road
32. One of many on a kilt or a cheerleader's skirt
34. Lyrical poets
36. Older PC screens
37. A little past due?
38. Reaper's wake
39. "Doctor ___"
40. Dry white wine
42. Epithet
43. Making waves?
45. Unwise
46. The CW franchise that sometimes includes "The Flash" and "Supergirl"
49. Hamilton's bills
50. Seepage
51. Evokes affection
53. Literary Rand
55. Had to admit an error
59. Music pace
62. Tourist destination in Devon
64. Go bad
65. Garden party?
66. Formal ceremony
67. Small shop in King's Cross Station
68. "Bro!"
69. Sufficient, once

Down

1. Scout badge holder
2. Erase, as memory
3. ___ fixe
4. Most crumbly
5. Exposes
6. Clavell novel
7. Massachusetts cape
8. Uniform part
9. Captain Sir Tom Moore, for one
10. Chinese zodiac sign
11. "___ up to you"
12. Tomorrow's leader?
13. Discount tag abbr.
18. Twitter shares
21. Keep a date
23. Crusading king
24. Classic Diana Ross hairdo
26. Do over, as a TV show
27. Cartoon alien whose dog is called K-9
28. Mounts
29. Pertaining to mail
30. Cause of pop-ups
31. Sildenafil brand
33. Surreptitious signal
35. Relax
39. "Push th' Little Daisies" band

41. Leave your tennis opponent with love?
44. Swedish film shooter Nykvist
45. Rainy city where "Frasier" is set
47. Congolese giraffids
48. Browned quickly
52. "Shiny Happy People" band
54. Mayonnaise component, often
56. Wreck
57. ___ Octavius AKA Doctor Octopus
58. Exclamation of relief
59. "Naughty, naughty!"
60. Outer prefix
61. Hereford howdy
62. Word before bod or joke
63. Aladdin's monkey pal

CRIMEBIT No. 28

The Fall of the Watchers

YOUR RATING /100

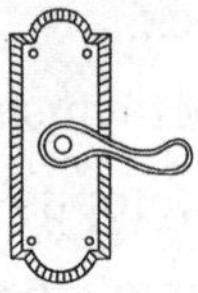

Susie Ellis

Surrey, 2010

Holly Raymond is holding a gun.

It's some kind of handgun, made of black metal with a hard rubber grip. Holly isn't sure how to use it, but she likes the cold weight of it in her hand. She doesn't even know if it's loaded, but she's hoping that the man in front of her doesn't know that either. He tilts his head to one side and slowly raises his hands in surrender. Fear ripples through his oily gaze. Holly likes that too.

She was looking for cash and had found the weapon instead. Just as she was sliding it into the pocket of her dressing gown, there was a click behind her as the bedroom door was unlocked. Holly had whirled around, pulling the gun back out at the same time. Taking aim, she planted her feet apart and locked her elbow, like she had seen on TV.

'Are you going to shoot me Holly?' His accent made her name roll thick and wet from his tongue like a slug. 'After everything I do for you.' He shakes his head and takes a step towards her.

PUZZLE No. 28

Watch Out!

CHECK OUT
CLOCK
CONTEMPLATE
EYEBALL
FOLLOW
GAZE AT
LOOK AFTER
MARK
MIND
MONITOR
NOTE
OBSERVE
PAY ATTENTION
PROTECT
REGARD
SAFEGUARD
SCRUTINIZE
SEE
SHELTER
SPY ON
STAKE OUT
STARE
SURVEY
TEND
TRACK
VIEW

O	D	L	U	S	M	Q	H	G	Q	K	L	T	O	N	X	E	E	M	H	O
U	N	N	M	B	Q	T	N	V	O	L	T	U	X	A	T	E	A	O	A	O
G	B	Z	I	B	Z	D	U	B	A	N	F	G	D	X	S	G	N	M	H	K
S	X	N	B	M	K	X	J	B	E	K	G	S	U	R	V	E	Y	J	N	S
P	Q	L	W	N	H	M	E	U	R	E	V	R	E	S	B	O	C	D	L	T
C	U	S	W	X	Q	Y	Q	N	A	G	G	P	K	R	A	M	B	P	P	I
T	H	N	H	X	E	O	G	U	T	V	R	J	F	R	I	K	K	U	A	Y
B	O	G	W	O	N	C	Y	X	S	B	S	Y	W	G	J	R	B	E	Z	P
U	N	Z	E	B	E	B	R	E	T	L	E	H	S	Q	P	N	G	B	P	M
Z	P	P	Z	R	C	Y	V	M	S	E	G	O	H	P	L	K	Y	O	E	S
Y	D	X	U	T	U	E	C	S	E	O	I	S	V	Y	D	V	J	J	Z	S
X	B	C	H	B	Y	V	E	C	U	Y	M	G	O	R	O	F	Z	R	I	V
G	C	R	P	O	S	H	H	G	W	Q	T	R	A	J	E	F	P	C	N	W
K	U	H	R	D	A	M	I	U	O	I	K	G	S	T	X	H	O	Y	I	E
C	U	V	Q	U	R	W	I	L	T	C	E	T	O	R	P	N	A	D	T	S
T	U	O	K	C	E	H	C	Q	O	R	A	N	K	S	T	W	Z	R	U	W
D	R	U	X	T	U	B	B	O	M	K	W	Q	H	E	P	E	R	A	R	E
M	X	N	K	H	A	B	U	F	E	O	U	T	M	O	N	E	K	U	C	I
O	Z	N	C	T	E	N	D	O	L	J	C	P	J	C	T	G	E	G	S	V
N	R	A	A	I	Q	E	U	L	P	C	L	O	O	K	A	F	T	E	R	F
I	I	I	R	J	K	T	O	C	G	A	B	Y	F	Y	E	X	J	F	J	C
T	N	S	T	G	I	F	H	C	T	L	Y	V	R	M	Z	G	S	A	O	Q
O	J	P	A	Y	A	T	T	E	N	T	I	O	N	L	A	C	A	S	H	F
R	U	P	M	U	C	T	L	X	D	M	J	F	L	C	G	C	L	O	C	K
K	B	R	M	I	D	Q	I	R	U	L	N	O	Y	P	S	W	B	N	Q	V

CRIMEBIT No. 29

The Cellphone

YOUR RATING /100

Alan Evans

Has this ever happened to you?

I was walking down the street in Quebec City – the old part – when I heard an unfamiliar ringtone behind me but nobody answered. It was annoying. Why didn't they answer?

Maybe they were a little deaf. I turned around . . . only to find no one was behind me. The sound was coming from my backpack. In an outside pocket, I found a cell phone. It rang again.

'Hello?'

'Rasha. Don't hang up.' A woman's voice. There was something in the tone . . .

'Who's this?'

'Promise me you won't hang up.'

'I'm not promising anything. I don't know you.'

'Good for you! No commitment till you have the facts.'

'Damn right!' I was angry but my curiosity overruled it. I knew I wouldn't hang up. She did too. 'Who are you?'

I guessed the answer as she said: 'It's your mother.'

My mother. I hadn't heard from her since I was five years

old. We thought she'd died. My mother. We had a memorial service for her and grieved for months, years. She'd faked her suicide by disappearing into the sea.

That was when we learned she was a wanted terrorist.

EDITOR'S NOTES

'As a reader, you're part of this story from its first line. Alan Evans is talking to us directly. An interesting way to open a novel. There is a lot of information to take in during its final few lines, which leaves the reader with questions they will want answered as they read on.'

PUZZLE No. 29

Québécoise

Across

1. What Watt was
5. Covered passage
11. Bouncy Jamaican music
14. Idris in the movies
15. Rang
16. Outer edge
17. Means of becoming a Québécois god?
19. Psychic initials
20. "Jaws" town
21. Without delay
22. __ en scène
23. Helpers for profs
24. Indicated a choice, in a way
26. Riddle
28. Editor's abbr.
30. One who shares water in Québec?
33. Gloss
35. Feed an infant
36. Spanish 101 verb
37. Mo. when Trafalgar Day was celebrated
38. Hair curlers
42. Nugget of wisdom
44. Military commission
45. "Now, this is fromage!"
49. Sweetheart
50. Mexican folk hero
51. Off-road transport, for short
53. Irish broadcaster
54. "L' __ de Siege"
55. Low reef
57. Feels concern
59. Fish & chips fish
60. Result of a Québec dairy farm disaster?
63. Gradation of color
64. Theatrical opening
65. Fencer's blade
66. GPS data
67. Items
68. Some displays, briefly

Down

1. Sleep aid
2. Weather conditions
3. Reverential
4. Loose antonym
5. Mo. when William and Catherine got married
6. "Help Me, __"
7. 2017 film set on the Day of the Dead
8. Again from the start
9. ...cole __ Beaux-Arts, Paris
10. Davey and Miliband
11. Santa's vehicle
12. "Pucker up!"
13. Pop up
18. Eucharist box
22. Beveled for joining, to a Yank
25. "If __ he loved, 'twas her alone"
26. Make a faux pas
27. "I disagree, Major!"
29. Eagerly accepted
31. __ Albert ("Only Fools and Horses" character)
32. "However..."
34. Not hunched over
37. Pitchblende, to uranium
39. Like black bananas

40. Made tidy
41. Pressures
43. "I see it now!"
44. Enter the pot
45. People from Prague
46. Patronize a pizzeria
47. Black suit
48. Adage
52. PAL tape player
55. __ Field (NYC ballpark)
56. Whole gobs
58. "Clan of the Cave Bear" novelist
60. GPS fig.
61. "__ du Lieber!"
62. "Super Mario Bros." console

CRIMEBIT No. 30

Red Elvis

YOUR RATING /100

Peter Everett

February 4th 1957

There were eighteen men in the basement room, sitting at attention on stackable chairs. They wore neatly-pressed two-piece suits in charcoal or navy blue, white shirts and dark ties. None of them was old enough to have fought in the Second World War, and some were too young even to have been in Korea, but there was about each of them the look of a junior officer in the military. The girls up on the second floor called them 'the crew-cuts' and knew nothing else about them.

Their leader entered the room and the murmured conversation ceased instantly. He took his place in the front row and nodded to the man on his right, who stood, placed a manila folder on the table by the blackboard, picked up a stick of chalk and wrote 'EP'.

'It begins with routine,' he said. He was comfortable at the front of a classroom, might once have been a schoolteacher or a college lecturer. The voice was Ivy League, Boston-patrician.

'The usual checks. The paper trail. Legwork. Same old

thing . . .'

A wry grin and, in the room, quiet appreciation like a breeze across a pond. *We've been there, brother.*

? DID YOU KNOW ?

The first person to be convicted using telecommunications technology was John Tawell, a British murderer, in 1845. Police used a newly installed telegraph machine to send a message to Paddington train station, while on the hunt for a man seen leaving a crime scene. They sent a description, which was picked up by police, who were able to apprehend Tawell after following him for a short while after he arrived at Paddington.

PUZZLE No. 30

The King

*The day after Elvis Presley died, a man resembling him gave the name "Jon Burrows" at Memphis Airport, which was the same name Elvis used when booking hotels. Since then, a series of alleged sightings have taken place. From the clues, determine **when** and **where** he was spotted, and **what** he was doing.*

$ The Odd Jobs

Dishwasher - Maybe at the Heartbreak Hotel.
Drywall installer - Had a job putting up jailhouse sheetrock.
Handyman - Fixing things was always on his mind.
Lawn maintenance - Don't be cruel; he cleaned up a lot of backyards.
Truck driver - "Return to Sender" meant a two-way trip.

The Locations

Arlington, Kentucky - Famous for its cold Kentucky rain.
Clinton, Iowa - Next door to a little sister and her teddy bear.
Franklin, Indiana - Elvis celebrated a Blue Christmas here.
Madison, Virginia - Rumor has it Elvis had a pet hound dog.
Newport, Tennessee - Working for the devil in disguise.

The Years

2019 2020 2021 2022 2023

When?	**Where?**	**What?**
________	________	________
________	________	________
________	________	________
________	________	________
________	________	________

? CLUES ?

1. Elvis wasn't installing drywall in 2023.
2. Elvis was spotted in Arlington in an earlier year than the year he was spotted in Franklin (where he wasn't a handyman) but in a later year than both his truck driving and dishwashing jobs.
3. Elvis wasn't doing lawn maintenance in either 2022 or 2023.
4. Elvis was spotted in Madison earlier than when he drove a truck.
5. Elvis wasn't spotted in Clinton, Iowa in 2023.

	Dishwasher	*Drywall installer*	*Handyman*	*Lawn maintenance*	*Truck driver*	*Arlington*	*Clinton*	*Franklin*	*Madison*	*Newport*
2019										
2020										
2021										
2022										
2023										
Arlington										
Clinton										
Franklin										
Madison										
Newport										

CRIMEBIT No. 31

Undercover Mother

YOUR RATING /100

Tracy Falenwolfe

In the wild, motherly instincts run the gamut. Bears will attack to protect their cubs, bald eagles spend weeks sitting on eggs, yet stand by idly when one hatched eaglet sibling pecks the other to death, and wolf spiders have been known to eat their young. At Bower Academy, the private high school my kids attend, things aren't much different.

Of course, I didn't know that when I enrolled Sam and Jenny at Bower. I thought I was doing a good thing. The right thing. Hell, I thought I'd be in the running for mother of the year given all I'd sacrificed to scrape together the outrageous tuition. But I didn't do it for the accolades. I did it for Sam and Jenny. For their futures.

I chose Bower Academy for my kids because Bower graduates earn more full-tuition college scholarships than the graduates of any other private high school in all of Pennsylvania. That and the fact that the public school they'd go to in our new town had a rape, a knife fight, and a drug bust all in the first week of school last year.

Bower seemed so much more civilized in comparison. At least at first.

HAVE YOUR SAY

What happens next?

Scan to visit the
CrimeBits Writing Space

PUZZLE No. 31

School Daze

Across

1. Sounds scared
6. Scoop (out)
10. Bit of cricket equipment
14. Lauder of the beauty biz
15. ___ regni
16. Trapezoid measure
17. Business involving amulets and talismans?
19. Purple haze
20. Musical levers
21. European financial concern
22. Insect with a stinger
24. ___ buco
25. Coin in circulation since 2002
27. Capital that's home to the Potala Palace
31. Uneventful plane journey?
34. Ancient polytheist
37. Bodies with arms
38. Versatile vehicle, for short
39. Pistol, in old slang
42. Little refresher
43. That lad
44. Like a shooting star?
47. Character who underwent "The Metamorphosis"
49. Lodestone that's free for anyone to use?
52. Investigate, perhaps
53. First name in courtroom fiction writing
54. Advice from pros
58. Drivers' org.?
60. Go a round?
61. Invention impetus
62. Asia's Trans-___ Range
65. Regulations concerning boat and bus hiring?
68. "Mystic River" Oscar winner
69. Rhodes of "Planet of the Apes"
70. Silly people
71. Gang
72. Pulitzer winner Ferber
73. Quirkier

Down

1. Small lizard
2. Grateful?
3. Lingers
4. Outward image
5. Aspiring minister's sch.
6. Bailey's circus partner
7. Course for Crusoe?
8. Ballot abbr.
9. "Stay (I Missed You)" singer
10. Perfect baseball game spoiler
11. Supply with weapons
12. Feline in the sky
13. Audio problem
18. Part of Wembley Stadium
23. Oval in maths
26. Lena who was nominated for a BAFTA for "Chocolat"

28. AARP concern
29. Powerful Persians
30. Out with the buoys
32. In progress
33. UK consumer credit group
34. Some heels
35. Believed gullibly
36. Barely survive
40. Javelin path
41. A metronome keeps it
45. Running for one's wife?
46. Parking shelter
48. Decked out
50. Price on "Coronation Street"
51. Counter word?
55. Scrimshanked
56. Porridge type
57. Carpenter, at times
59. Reason to whinge
62. Mo. when Shakespeare was born
63. Don Ho's neckwear
64. Elliot in Jane Austen's "Persuasion"
66. Ate or owned
67. I trouble?

CRIMEBIT No. 32

Timor Estates

SHORTLISTED BY LEE CHILD

YOUR RATING /100

Dahlia Fisher

Mallory's pudgy little hands pressed against the window from inside the bedroom where she was told to stay. But the night's deep black void called to her in a whistle from the forest behind the house. Pushing the glass pane ajar, she poked her head through the slender crack and listened to the wind navigate between branches of naked trees and fallen leaves. She heard sweeps of debris slap the wooden fence and shutters, catching along the climbing ivy that clung to the whitewashed brick. There was music in it.

Singing with the melody, 'Lala la, lala la,' Mallory patted down the winding stairs without so much as a creak. Her light feet let no relative sleeping in Timor Estates be the wiser that she was about to disappear.

By morning alarms would sound, 'Six-year-old from Wells Cottage vanishes during family vacation.' Mallory's mother would sit in the kitchen with detectives and police, hysterical and screaming, chain smoking while apologizing that she had meant to give them up but now she was feeling too guilty for leaving her only daughter to sleep alone in this strange place.

And what a strange place it was.

EDITOR'S NOTES

'An eerie opening, with a glorious sense of place that resonates with the reader. We're thrust into a situation that feels off-kilter. Uncomfortable. There is a lyrical quality to the writing, that really shines through from Dahlia Fisher. I want to read more about the strange place that is described here. And I certainly want to know what happened to the child who has vanished.'

PUZZLE No. 32

Grand Children

BABY
BAIRN
BAMBINO
BUSTER
IMP
INFANT
JUVENILE
KID
KINDERGARTNER
MINOR
MONKEY
NESTLING
NIPPER
OFFSPRING
PRESCHOOLER
PROGENY
RAPSCALLION
RASCAL
SCALAWAG
SCAMP
SHAVER
SMALL FRY
TODDLER
TOT
TYKE
WAIF
YOUNGSTER

B	I	U	Q	S	C	A	L	A	W	A	G	U	V	U	T	C	Q	L	G	W
A	G	Q	B	Z	U	D	B	S	Q	A	A	X	J	V	Z	P	K	H	V	H
T	N	J	A	J	N	D	G	Z	K	J	U	V	E	N	I	L	E	G	M	I
W	I	F	I	V	P	D	P	D	A	J	U	G	C	N	Y	Z	I	Q	F	P
Z	R	Q	R	K	P	U	M	S	C	H	I	P	B	S	E	T	T	K	M	E
H	P	H	N	Z	D	I	W	I	U	M	Y	M	Y	K	W	O	D	I	O	V
W	S	G	R	W	N	A	E	M	R	S	L	S	S	L	V	T	Z	R	Z	Y
B	F	R	O	O	I	O	K	A	T	S	P	J	Q	F	E	P	D	G	A	O
E	F	A	R	F	U	O	M	G	C	N	M	E	U	H	B	K	B	M	N	U
Y	O	S	N	V	F	F	Q	W	O	H	C	K	K	G	Q	N	Y	U	D	N
K	P	C	K	Y	T	S	F	I	G	Q	W	I	M	Q	A	J	R	T	J	G
D	E	A	L	I	H	I	L	I	F	N	N	W	Q	O	R	X	K	W	K	S
X	T	L	A	Z	Q	L	G	P	N	P	Y	F	N	P	N	K	Z	T	J	T
K	S	G	P	N	A	P	L	M	W	F	F	Y	N	A	I	K	R	S	U	E
C	J	U	B	C	K	D	Q	F	S	Y	A	E	P	H	Q	Y	E	A	D	R
J	O	B	S	T	Y	E	U	Q	M	Z	S	N	F	F	B	K	L	Y	W	K
F	X	P	A	K	D	K	L	Z	A	T	I	X	T	A	R	Y	D	U	B	P
H	A	U	S	M	U	V	I	M	L	D	I	K	B	C	Z	U	D	Q	D	C
R	A	W	C	N	B	B	J	I	L	N	H	E	V	R	D	U	O	N	S	R
R	E	V	A	H	S	I	N	I	F	Z	Z	I	C	C	E	U	T	X	L	E
E	Y	P	M	X	B	G	N	V	R	N	Z	M	I	I	K	T	T	G	F	P
R	Q	A	P	D	A	Q	O	O	Y	R	E	L	O	O	H	C	S	E	R	P
C	V	G	W	J	F	R	W	X	L	Q	U	Y	Q	Z	T	Q	P	U	H	I
Q	H	Q	I	D	V	N	P	Z	U	P	R	O	G	E	N	Y	T	O	B	N
K	I	N	D	E	R	G	A	R	T	N	E	R	E	G	U	Q	A	A	V	E

CRIMEBIT No. 33

The Myth of Fingerprints

YOUR RATING /100

Dónal Fogarty

It's said empathy is the defining characteristic of successful crime writers and detectives alike. Both professions require a strong intuition for what people are thinking and feeling if they are to piece together a plot or divine the motivations for a crime. From my vantage point looking back on the day's events, I'd say that, in the case of the most successful crime writers, a hint of psychopathy is probably a more common characteristic.

Now I'm not suggesting that they all act out the vicious and brutal crimes they dream up, it just happened to be my misfortune to bump into one of the ones that does.

PUZZLE No. 33

Lit Detectives

Across

1. White gemstone
5. Fixed points, in geometry
9. Ignominy
14. Pram pusher
15. Soon after
16. Martini & __
17. Podcast about a James Patterson detective?
19. Gut
20. "Downton Abbey" daughter
21. Make enquiries
23. "Dolorous" character in "A Song of Ice and Fire"
24. Bank holiday day, briefly
25. Bournemouth Beach display
28. What's left behind
31. Can.'s most populous province
32. Frisbee toss from a Mickey Spillane detective?
35. Atoll component
37. More spacious
38. Proofreader's catch
40. Japanese pond fish
41. Supermarket section
45. Fixes a shoe
48. "ER" actor LaSalle
49. Dessert for a Janet Evanovich detective?
53. Water of Oise
54. Classroom delivery
55. Eggs __ suisse
56. Shola who sang "You Might Need Somebody"
57. H, as in Hera
58. Draw even
61. Showy bird
63. Chance to swing
66. Case for a Dashiell Hammett detective?
69. Patty Bouvier's sister on "The Simpsons"
70. Actress Virna
71. "Garfield" pooch
72. Build a building
73. Mimic exactly
74. Take first steps?

Down

1. All over again
2. Queen Elizabeth II, to Alan Turing
3. Holy oil sprinkler
4. Least likely
5. Dieter's dread
6. Urizen's daughter
7. Bar mixer
8. Tattoo parlor supplies
9. Global sphere
10. Scooby-__
11. "Honestly!"
12. Familiar with
13. Damp growth
18. Reza Pahlavi, once
22. Russell of "The Diplomat" and "The Americans"
26. Sand ridge
27. Like some hams
29. Flower stalk
30. Haiku line count
33. Hit a low note?
34. Clarke of "Game of Thrones"
36. Questionnaires

39. Seized vehicle, slangily
42. One of 11 for Los Angeles
43. Jamaican coffee liqueur
44. Screeched like a parrot
46. Safari
47. Tina Fey's old show, briefly
49. Tickle pink
50. Piece of mail
51. Not totally ruined
52. Parcheesi or polo
59. Capri or Man
60. Absolutely awesome
62. Missing from the Royal Marines, e.g.
64. Lloyds subsidiary since 1993
65. Low quality goods
67. Yggdrasil, for one
68. Ronnie James band

CRIMEBIT No. 34

Double Blind

YOUR RATING /100

Dónal Fogarty

'You driving mate?'

Hindsight has taught me a hundred and one correct answers to that question. But how was I to know that him and his mates had been banned from all the town pubs and that's why they were lowering the tone of this quaint little country inn.

'You driving mate?'

All the correct answers began with the word 'No'. With 'No mate' or 'Nah mate, just skint' being up there among the many non-life changing alternatives.

'You driving mate?'

'Yeah,' I said, inflecting that single syllable with a tone that meant everything from 'What's it to you' to 'I might be drinking a half, but you need to step the fuck away from me right now.'

'Give us a lift?'

Again, in retrospect, there were better answers to that question. A 'Soz bud, not much room on my push bike' or a 'Me moped ain't got the oomph for a pillion' would have made this a very short story.

Except this wasn't happening in retrospect.

'Give us a lift?'

'No,' I said with a derisive laugh and doubled down on the confrontational tone with a straightening of the shoulders and a not-backing-down stare.

? DID YOU KNOW ?

In 2019, Lee Child collaborated with the group Naked Blue on an album of music which explored the character of Jack Reacher. He provided vocals to the track "Reacher Said Nothing."

PUZZLE No. 34

Hoods in the Hood

*How was our intrepid hero to know that they had all been barred from the town pubs? Who could have predicted that each of them was banned for a different kind of bad behavior? From the clues, determine **who** was banned from **where** and **why**.*

The Hoodlums

Freddie -A smooth-talking con artist, with a silver tongue

Jack - A firebrand with a temper to match his crimson hair.

Leo - Tall and wiry, with a knack for breaking and entering.

Reasons for Ban

Fighting

Mean to staff

Stealing liquor

Locations

The Cat and Custard - A dimly lit joint with creaky floors and a bar that's seen more secrets than a confession booth.

The Drunken Duck - A rough-and-tumble dive on the wrong side of the tracks, where the whiskey flows like water.

The Queen's Arms - A shadowy establishment where deals are made in hushed tones.

? CLUES ?

1. The person who stole bottles of liquor was not Jack.
2. Leo has never been to the Cat and Custard.
3. Jack's local pub was the Drunken Duck.
4. One hoodlum was mean to the staff at the Queen's Arms.
5. Freddie doesn't fight.

	Jack	***Leo***	***Freddie***	*Fighting*	*Mean to staff*	*Stealing liquor*
The Cat and Custard						
The Drunken Duck						
The Queen's Arms						
Fighting						
Mean to staff						
Stealing liquor						

Who? ____________ ____________ ____________

Where? ____________ ____________ ____________

Why? ____________ ____________ ____________

CRIMEBIT No. 35

Snatch

Peter Fryer

The blonde woman didn't stand a chance. She was out of the SUV and two steps up the pavement, crouched down with a big smile and arms out, ready to hug her daughter running towards her from the school gate.

The white van mounted the curb next to her, side door already open. A man in work overalls leapt out, grabbed the woman and threw her headlong through the open door. In the same movement, he turned round to snatch the daughter.

Lisa Lyons saw it from the bus stop, laden down with shopping bags and arms already aching. She dropped the lot and ran, a shapeless scream-yell coming from her throat. It was only twenty yards and she made it just as the man's hands seized the little girl by the shoulders.

'Let go!'

She swung at him, both hands together as if she were holding a pistol. It caught him across the face and he fell backwards, kicking at her as he went. The blow hit her square on the sternum, knocking the breath out of her. As she went down, she grabbed at the girl's legs and hung on. Not going anywhere if she could help it.

HAVE YOUR SAY
What happens next?

Scan to visit the
CrimeBits Writing Space

PUZZLE No. 35

Shopping Spree

Across

1. They played Phillies in the 2024 London Series
5. Texas shrine in a 1960 John Wayne film
10. __ of the d'Urbervilles
14. Post-run feeling
15. Kyoto's country
16. Pay to get in
17. Mealy McIntosh?
19. Social unit
20. Patch, perhaps
21. Citizens of London and Manchester in US
23. Adjust, as the wheels
24. Order of columns
26. Univ. once known as the Government Sch. of Design
27. Bit of a dust bunny
28. Wile E. Coyote, more often than not?
30. Nottingham duo
31. Tanya's fiancé on "EastEnders"
32. Witherspoon with a BAFTA
33. Ways of escaping
34. Heidi on the runway
36. Joe who won a BAFTA for "Raging Bull"
39. "The Two Towers" tree herders
40. Sheffield-to-Nottingham dir.
43. Perform perfectly in Paper Fastener class?
46. Groovy places?
47. Child's sack
48. Sign symbol
49. Mark above a 6
50. Implement, in a way
52. Offer enticingly
53. "Downton Abbey" mother
54. Valley where female warriors live?
57. From the US
58. Backless furniture
59. Transmitted verbally
60. Livestock feed grains
61. Meticulous
62. Dame __ Hess

Down

1. It's tied up in knots
2. Corporate level
3. Awful, slangily
4. Waste
5. Not quite closed
6. Pool workout unit
7. Instagram, e.g.
8. Tina of "Brookside" and "Shameless"
9. All that some wonders ever had
10. Filled tortilla
11. Expand
12. Batting positions
13. Perceived by feeling
18. Chinese principle
22. The hot wings weren't good for him
24. Summery desserts
25. "Srsly?!"
28. Serious hang-ups?
29. __ sleep
31. Instrument for Clapton or Page
33. "Moseley Shoals" band, for short
34. Was acquainted with

35. Some RMAS grads
36. "Safety" vehicle during a yellow flag
37. Budget
38. Liberate
39. "Don't Bring Me Down" band, briefly
40. Physician's office
41. Heavenly
42. "Great Expectations" miss
44. Roofed passageway
45. Blend first
46. Chosen by chance
49. Corn unit, perhaps
51. Hydrodynamic duo
52. Word of warning
55. Robot in "Ex Machina"
56. MacGuire in a love triangle "Home and Away"

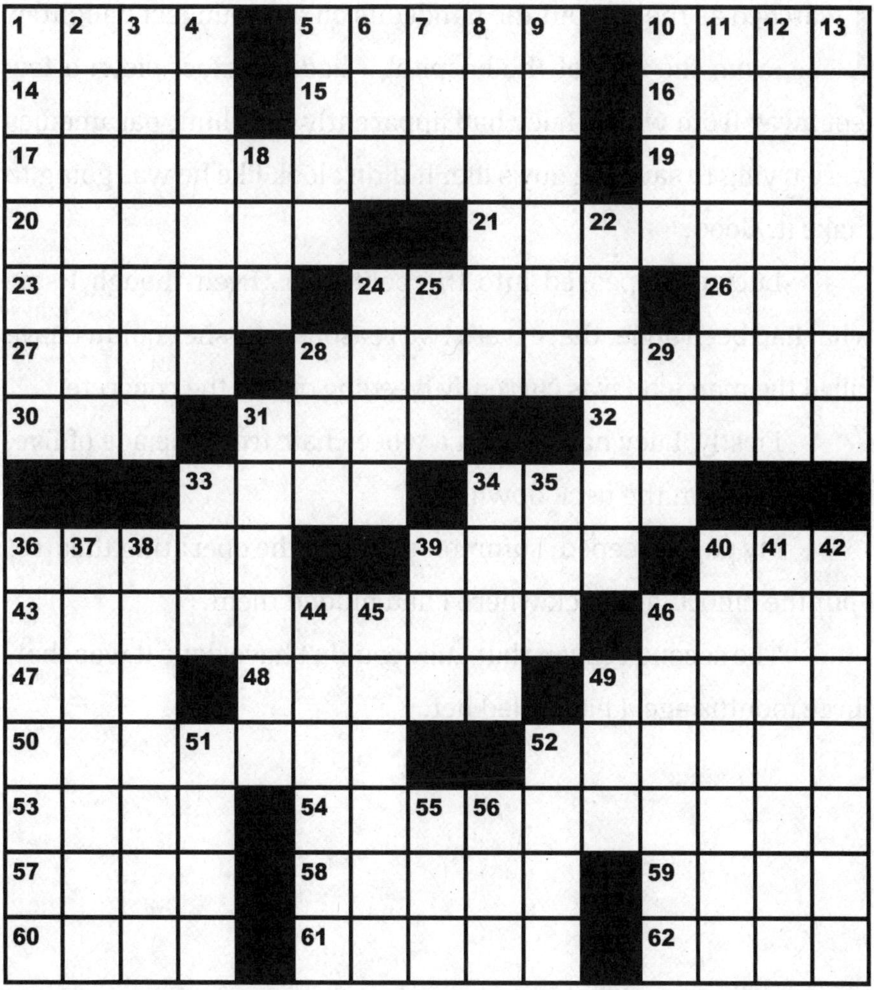

CRIMEBIT No. 36

Surgical Precision

YOUR RATING /100

C. A. Fulwell

I watched as the cop put the handcuffs on my youngest daughter.

From the roof of the hospital, I had a perfect view: a few feet away from where Lucy had apparently shot him, paramedics were trying to save the guy's life. It didn't look like he was going to make it. Good.

Lucy disappeared into the police car. Even though I saw what had been done, there were two reasons why she couldn't have killed the man who was currently bleeding out on the concrete.

Firstly, Lucy had been in a wheelchair from the age of five, paralyzed from the neck down.

My pager beeped, summoning me to the operating theatre. I put the binoculars back where I had hidden them.

The second reason that Lucy couldn't have done it was that, three months ago, I had killed her.

WRITING PROMPT 3

The old guy was sat on the same bench most days at around two o'clock in the afternoon. I first noticed him around a month ago. Always well dressed, suit and tie, polished shoes, the works. Always the same bench. After the first few times, he started nodding at me in a polite greeting as I passed him. I was always told to respect my elders, so I always reciprocated the nod. It's not often you see that these days. Everyone seems to be in their own little bubble, ignorant of other people around them. But this old guy was still espousing the social orders of old. He interested me. Always sat on the same bench most days. Not every day though. I walk through the park Monday to Friday at the same time, going home after the six am to two pm shifts I work. I'd say he was there at least three days out of those five.

Scan to visit the CrimeBits Writing Space

PUZZLE No. 36

I Didn't Do It

Across

1. 1973 "Battle of the Sexes" loser
6. Serves well done?
10. Ascorbic __
14. "You can tell me"
15. Facebook button
16. Spiel
17. Floppy topper
18. Contacted online
19. __ B'rith
20. "Must have been someone else!"
23. Start of an idea
24. Unlimited amount
25. "And __ off!"
28. Like Bollywood films
30. REM's "Lisa __"
31. Ewe'll be there?
32. Jarvis or Peacock on "EastEnders"
35. "Smokey __ Cafe"
36. "Must have been someone else!"
41. Dahlia or Agatha in P.G. Wodehouse fiction
42. Native of Cleveland or Columbus
43. UK merchant navy vessel
44. Kitchen cooker
46. Aft locations
50. Metro entrances
52. Cigar remains
54. Quite an achievement
55. "Must have been someone else!"
58. "When Irish __ are smiling..."
60. Extraordinary
61. Place in the log
62. Greedy person's demand
63. Tract
64. "Skyfall" vocalist
65. Attempt at a carnival booth
66. Diane who won a BAFTA for "Alice Doesn't Live Here Anymore"
67. St. __ University, Twickenham

Down

1. "Avatar" actor Giovanni or his twin Marissa
2. Old block deliverers
3. Decked out
4. Most miserly
5. "Who's out there?" org.
6. Calibrate
7. Broken in
8. Penultimate fairy tale word
9. Imperturbable
10. "Who's Afraid of Virginia Woolf?" playwright Edward
11. Dr. Seuss's young Miss Who
12. "Barefoot Contessa" chef Garten
13. "Agnus __"
21. Loveable older relatives
22. Freq. unit
26. Spool of film
27. One end of London
29. "Aladdin" alter ego
30. Game before the final

33. Part of, as a plot
34. Ultimate degree
35. She won BAFTAs for "Julia" and "The China Syndrome"
36. "H.M.S. Pinafore" characters
37. Ailing
38. First to hear the news
39. Dinosaur character in Nintendo games
40. What Jack Sprat eschews
44. Shoat shelter
45. Like the stars
47. Flat figure?
48. Strictly speaking
49. Metric measures
51. Blows the game
52. Hung on the clothesline
53. Golfer who said "Never concede a putt"
56. Legal prefix?
57. Cricket group
58. Chest thumper, for short?
59. "__ hoo!"

CRIMEBIT No. 37

Atticus

YOUR RATING /100

Vicky Garforth

The day that Lydia Brown lost her child, was the day that Atticus Brown gained a mother and his life began. Seventeen years later, Atticus came home from school to find his house burned to the ground, lights and sirens piercing the afternoon silence and his stepmother, Lydia, dead in the embers. And now his life really began.

PUZZLE No. 37

Atticus Brown

ALMOND	CARAMEL	DUN	RUST	TAWNY
AUBURN	CHESTNUT	ECRU	SAND	UMBER
BEIGE	CHOCOLATE	FAWN	SAND	WALNUT
BONE	COCOA	KHAKI	SEPIA	WHEAT
BRONZE	COFFEE	MAHOGANY	SIENNA	
BUFF	COPPER	OCHRE	TAN	
CAMEL	COYOTE	RUSSET	TAUPE	

M	W	I	N	A	L	M	O	N	D	O	B	W	Z	Z	O	Y	P	F	I	W
C	C	A	E	G	A	N	U	L	M	J	R	R	E	B	M	U	B	N	J	F
V	L	A	L	A	Y	B	X	E	P	B	O	B	U	Q	N	S	P	N	U	K
P	M	F	M	N	U	X	S	J	V	X	N	B	X	H	T	A	W	N	Y	D
X	A	W	S	E	U	L	L	N	L	P	Z	A	U	B	U	R	N	U	H	F
G	T	C	O	T	L	T	L	H	B	P	E	Q	N	W	R	H	N	O	S	S
A	P	V	Y	O	Z	S	S	O	L	W	Q	J	P	Y	E	R	J	U	T	F
F	Q	C	R	J	Z	J	X	A	G	S	W	W	C	I	S	E	L	E	A	B
E	B	B	T	R	U	S	T	O	L	R	W	W	A	E	E	P	Z	W	K	Q
V	T	T	O	M	J	U	U	C	T	L	L	G	N	D	P	P	N	X	T	L
A	U	O	H	N	A	Z	N	O	E	S	H	M	I	O	I	O	K	H	D	L
I	V	G	Y	T	E	J	T	C	X	U	S	E	U	H	A	C	K	H	O	D
L	X	I	Y	O	A	D	S	K	K	E	Z	J	K	T	T	Y	E	V	I	H
B	E	N	J	V	C	U	E	F	U	X	A	V	W	M	R	K	E	E	E	C
P	U	M	L	V	X	V	H	Z	X	X	J	U	G	G	E	V	W	C	I	W
A	C	F	A	Y	U	T	C	L	R	V	S	D	T	K	F	G	V	R	Y	R
Z	E	I	F	R	D	H	R	J	H	I	Y	T	F	T	V	A	I	U	W	K
Q	T	X	W	Y	A	C	A	K	E	D	H	K	W	B	Z	D	N	E	N	F
X	A	J	K	X	N	C	G	N	H	R	V	B	B	F	M	H	A	M	B	R
G	L	X	U	O	G	A	N	T	H	X	W	J	A	O	E	O	T	U	E	T
T	O	P	D	I	I	A	G	L	V	W	K	O	G	O	G	A	F	E	E	H
J	C	B	K	B	N	L	B	O	W	B	Y	Q	C	D	U	Z	F	S	X	S
X	O	A	Z	T	U	O	Y	A	H	I	P	H	K	P	X	F	S	Y	A	X
W	H	E	A	T	G	S	K	N	Q	A	R	I	E	H	O	U	S	N	I	W
K	C	D	E	L	W	C	C	T	S	E	M	O	O	C	R	P	D	I	B	L

CRIMEBIT No. 38

Tracking the Wolf

YOUR RATING /100

David Goodlett

First came the flash of light. Harold stepped closer to the glass front doors only to witness through the dense falling snow an expanding flame. Twenty seconds later, the air exploded.

To protect his eyes from the glare and stop his ears from ringing, he scrunched down as far as someone nicknamed Kong could manage. The wind and the snow had already become almost blinding, and now it was even worse. When he could finally make out anything, however faintly, what the security guard saw in the front of the plant's parking lot was a woman and another woman or girl struggling toward the offices, the older woman with her arm around the younger one, holding her up. In response, as almost anyone he knew could have predicted, he froze.

The woman began pounding on the doors with her fist, and, when there was no response, she shielded her eyes to peer inside, seeking any sign of life. Having backed up out of habit when he saw them running toward the front, he knew the woman couldn't see him. She looked desperate, but he hadn't been taught what to do if anything like this happened. His fear was paralyzing.

EDITOR'S NOTES

'A powerful opening few sentences that intrigue the reader instantly. We're thrust straight into the action and the stall is set from the get-go. We know we're in for a thrill ride. The character is set – we know it's a big guy, someone with an imposing size, but from the final line we know we're not in Reacher territory here – he's scared. His fear is palpable. We're told a lot about this character in very short prose, something that connects with the reader. I like the way the writer does this.'

PUZZLE No. 38

Blow Up

Across

1. Early open-reel device, for short
4. Dish of mixed greens
9. Oyster cracker?
14. Nest egg for some
15. Pancho's pal
16. Rebuke
17. Sound caused by shock waves
19. Puts up
20. Start work
21. Wood of the Rolling Stones
22. Pole staff?
23. Part of a razor
26. Shrewd
27. Lagoon barrier
28. Thunderous event
30. Southwest gully
32. First letter in the NATO phonetic alphabet
33. Cousins of aves.
34. Mohair source
36. Skipped town
38. "__, du lieber!"
41. Flood (the market)
43. Islands near Portugal
47. Explosive theory?
50. Halliday of Curve
51. Show worry
52. Where Bhutan is
53. Two, in a deck
54. Makes a debut
56. Seafood dishes
58. Whiskey __ (Hollywood rock club)
59. Loudest volume
61. Large asteroid
62. "Can you __ in a sentence?"
63. Think Global charity
64. Messy pair?
65. Noteless places
66. Sheeran and Skrein

Down

1. Innards
2. Piscatory rover
3. Exceeded
4. Plunders
5. Both, for openers
6. Geoffrey's role in "As Time Goes By"
7. Gone by
8. __ Perignon
9. Cinco + tres
10. 1998 song by Alanis Morrisette
11. Some smiths
12. Most jittery
13. Gets huffy
18. Arctic mist
21. Sign of trouble
24. 1949 film noir classic
25. Split
28. Heating fuel
29. "Joe Hill" singer Joan
31. Spiritual leader
35. Spots for soaks
37. "This I gotta hear"
38. Relaxed
39. David Bowie classic
40. Browbeats
42. __ Chi
44. Filled meat
45. Boxed in
46. Tijuana time-outs
48. Barry Gibb, for one
49. Campania's capital
53. Arrears

55. Diana who sang "Baby Love"
57. Hit terra firma
59. What a Sphynx cat lacks
60. Function

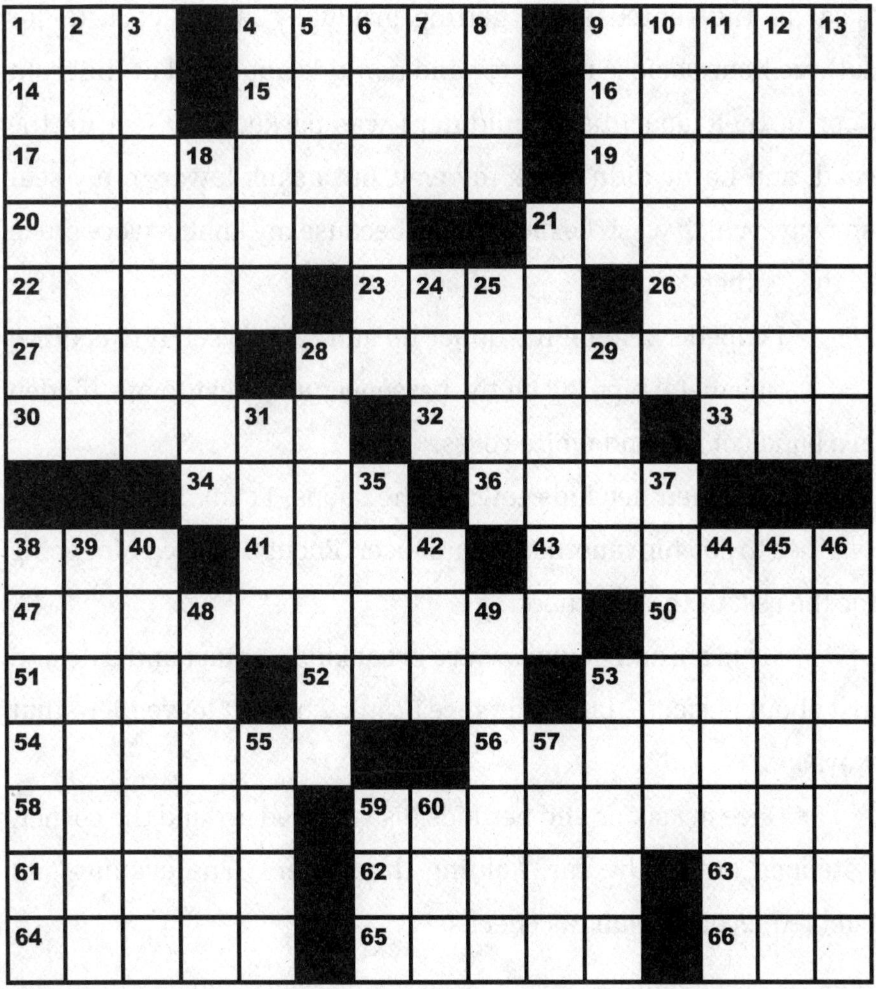

CRIMEBIT No. 39

I Am Karma

YOUR RATING
/100

Alan Peter Gorevan

I sat in the rented Ford, getting gradually steam-cooked, for three hours before my sister and her kids appeared at the front door of their apartment building. I was parked fifty feet up the road, and Kathy didn't look my way, but I sank lower in my seat anyway. Which wasn't exactly easy, because my khakis were stuck to the leather.

I wiped sweat off my upper lip and told myself it was time.

The metal pipe lay on the passenger seat next to me, hidden in a bunch of red and white roses.

Kathy led her kids toward the shops. Frank had probably sent her to buy him another sixer of beer. Enough to keep him going for the rest of the afternoon.

My niece and nephew were great kids – smart and cute and just about perfect – but I was sure Frank wouldn't leave them that way.

Once my sister and her kids disappeared around the corner, I stepped out of the car, holding the flowers. The evening sun bubbled feverishly on my cheeks.

I felt no guilt at the thought of killing my brother-in-law. None whatsoever.

? DID YOU KNOW ?

The earliest example of a detective story is considered to be Edgar Allan Poe's "The Murders in the Rue Morgue" (1841). Wilkie Collins's novel *The Moonstone* (1868), is also cited as one of the first police procedural novels, the tale of a Scotland Yard detective investigating the theft of a valuable diamond.

PUZZLE No. 39

Tricks and Treats

While Kathy's brother is committing a crime, she and her children are enjoying a welcome respite at the corner store. Each of them has a favorite treat, and Kathy has just enough change left over from buying Frank a six-pack of beer. Identify ***who*** *likes* ***what*** *candy, and* ***where*** *the treats are located.*

The Family

Kathy - Poor, beleaguered wife of the infamously abusive Frank.

Nella - She's the same age as her twin brother, Nicky, but that's where the resemblance ends.

Nicky - He's not like his father, and he doesn't like his father either.

The Candies

Caramel creme - Chewy caramel candy with a cream center.

Corn chips - Noodle-shaped snack food made from cornmeal fried in oil or baked.

Chocolate kisses - Conical bite-sized pieces of chocolatey goodness.

Locations

Top shelf

Behind the counter

End cap

? CLUES ?

1. Kathy's favorite treat was located on the top shelf.
2. The person with a taste for chocolate was not Kathy.
3. Nicky doesn't like caramel.
4. The person who likes corn chips spotted them behind the counter.
5. Nella never bothers to look at the end cap.

	Kathy	Nella	Nicky	Caramel creme	Chocolate kisses	Corn chips
Behind the counter						
End cap						
Top shelf						
Caramel creme						
Chocolate kisses						
Corn chips						

Who?	What?	Where?

CRIMEBIT No. 40

Portmagic

YOUR RATING /100

S. D. W. Hamilton

Finn slowed as he approached the roundabout on the outskirts of the town. The first exit would have taken him towards his old school, less than a mile up the road. The second would take him home.

Home.

It was funny he still thought of Portrush as home. There was a time when he had never wanted to leave but somehow he was the one who had stayed away.

He drove on, past acres of green fields and ancient stone walls until he was sure he could smell the salt in the air. A gentle curve on the road opened up to reveal a sweeping view of the Atlantic, dangerous and brooding, buffeting against the rocks of the Skerries.

The rain had eased but the November chill carried a bite as dark clouds rolled slowly over a tumultuous canvas of gray.

It was a perfect day for a funeral.

HAVE YOUR SAY

What happens next?

Scan to visit the
CrimeBits Writing Space

PUZZLE No. 40

Home Sweet Home

Across

1. Sadness caused by longing for one's family (12)

8. Sugarcane molasses syrup (5,7)

9. Burdening with a task (8)

10. Sandpaper coating (4)

12. Prepare for a second crop (6)

14. Decanter (6)

16. Pull asunder by force (4)

17. Amounts outstanding (8)

20. Large river mammal (12)

21. Obstructing parliamentary business (12)

Down

2. Applied lubricant (5)

3. Was superior in performance (8)

4. Purpose (6)

5. Joint between the thigh and lower leg (4)

6. Passage quoted (7)

7. Quality of sugar (9)

9. Slight linear abrasions

11. Never (3,2,3)

13. Hair wash (7)

15. Asian temple (6)

18. Machine for making butter (5)

19. Having no companions (4)

1
2
3
4
5
6
7
8
9
10
11
12
13
14
15
16
17
18
19
20
21

CRIMEBIT No. 41

Beat

YOUR RATING /100

Katt Hansen

Rap tap
Rap tap
Tappety tappet
Tappet-

Kyle stopped abruptly, catching himself doing it again. Now wasn't the time. Or the place. Or anything. Dammit, he needed to keep his fucking hands to himself and quit it, just quit it, just QUIT IT –

'You OK, bro?'

He gave a terse nod. Stared at the house across the street. Willed the light to go out. Feeling that if he just stared long enough they'd go to bed for God's sake, and he could MOVE.

He felt his shoulders bunch, too tense. His fingers twitched. Wanting to make noise, wanting to find the beat, the rhythm of the night. To drum until the world made sense again.

He clenched his hands into fists, pressed them tight against battered vinyl. Waited.

'We can do it another night.'

The whisper came from behind him, to the left. Weasel. How did he always know? Didn't matter. Weasel probably knew that too, that he would refuse. They'd put this off too long already.

'Easy man.' The words were punctuated by the snick of a cigarette lighter. Dirk's profile was etched in the soft glow at the end of a cigarette. 'It'll all be over soon.'

EDITOR'S NOTES

'Short, staccato sentences, which leave the reader breathless in this opening. Really effective, in putting you in mind of who this character might be. The way they think and act. It makes you concentrate, despite the writer almost daring you to try and skip words. Repetition in the opening is a brave way of introducing the story and works really well here.'

PUZZLE No. 41

Tap Dancing

Across

1. Turn over
5. Belief system
8. Pretentious talk
14. Turner or Del Rey
15. ___-Jet (alpine transport)
16. Fly by
17. 1998 Ian McKellen film
19. Plague
20. Collect bit by bit
21. By way of
23. "Hurry!" in the OR
24. Busts a move
26. Indefinite number
29. CPA suggestion, maybe
30. Mayberry sheriff
31. "Love Is a Battlefield" rocker
34. Dash meas.
35. Brief moments of time?
36. Avenue
37. Has claim to
38. Implements
39. Showed relief
42. Fight (over)
43. Airport uniform abbr. at JFK
46. After-school conference
48. Uzbek border sea
49. Fed. rule
50. Precalc subject
51. Defunct autos
53. OS X runner
55. Boat pronoun
57. Refrain on the farm
58. Intemperate speech
61. Drink that's a freebie
63. Internet reading material
64. Superlative ending
65. Batty in "Last of the Summer Wine"
66. Smell and sight
67. Poor start?
68. "Wheel of Fortune" turn

Down

1. June 14
2. Province in northern Finland
3. Aims to
4. Holy office
5. AOL, for instance
6. Trimming sound
7. Annoys continually
8. Nervous bit of laughter
9. Suffix with pay or boff
10. Coal derivatives
11. Mineral that geologists hunger for?
12. Star of HBO's "Insecure"
13. Boot up again
18. One for Jacques
22. Stick up
25. Extravagant one
27. Bit of voice mail
28. Start
32. Window boxes, for short?
33. Horace's "__ Poetica"
35. Like baklava
37. Electrical unit
38. Student identifier in the NPD
39. Brownies

40. Detail
41. First human in space
42. Discovered
43. Cradle location, in verse
44. His opera opened La Scala
45. Concession speech giver
47. "'__ the season to be jolly"
48. Koreans and Laotians
52. Morning beads
54. Preserves, as food
56. Hardly challenging
59. River near Balmoral Castle
60. Beginning of spring?
62. Score amts.

CRIMEBIT No.42

Dontrell Calling

YOUR RATING /100

Kathryn Hatfield

Jenny Crane was about to gatecrash another party. Although gatecrash was not quite the right word to describe her attendance. Gatecrash implied that she wanted to go. It did also suggest, however, that the other guests didn't want her there – and that part was true. She imagined it would be the usual scene. She had been to so many now that she could have written the script for this upcoming one. There were five common elements to the gatherings. One – the same five people attended, her cousin Toni being one of them. Two – Jenny would spend the evening observing the group's interactions. Three – before the group became completely inebriated, Jenny would escape early to a downstairs guest bedroom. Four – there would be an argument, normally later on in the night, about why Jenny was there. And five – Jenny always left the next morning feeling slightly happier about her life. But there was something different about this particular party. She couldn't put her finger on it but something made her think the script was going to change and it left her feeling, dare she say it, somewhat excited.

PUZZLE No. 42

Party Crasher

Jenny Crane has been gatecrashing the same party for years. Every year, the party guests take turns providing the liquor. Each of them has a different preference, though none of them prefer water. From the clues, determine ***who*** *brought* ***what*** *kind of booze, and* ***when****.*

The Party People

Jenny Crane
Cousin Toni
Uncle Joe
Aunt Laura
Cousin Ralph

The Beverages

Rum and Coke
Tequila Shots
White Wine
Vodka and Ginger Ale
Beer

The Years

2018 2019 2020 2021 2022

Who?	What?	When?

? CLUES ?

1. Aunt Laura wasn't in charge of the booze in 2022.

2. Cousin Ralph didn't provide the drinks in either 2021 or 2022.

3. The person who brought white wine provided beverages in an earlier year than Cousin Toni.

4. Nobody brought tequila shots in 2022.

5. Rum and coke were provided in an earlier year than the vodka and ginger ale (not by Jenny Crane) but in a later year than the drinks provided by both Cousin Toni and Uncle Joe.

	Beer	*Rum and coke*	*Tequila shots*	*Vodka and Ginger ale*	*White wine*	*2018*	*2019*	*2020*	*2021*	*2022*
Jenny Crane										
Cousin Toni										
Cousin Ralph										
Aunt Laura										
Uncle Joe										
2018										
2019										
2020										
2021										
2022										

CRIMEBIT No. 43

Sidewinder Café

YOUR RATING /100

Anne Hewling

Right now I'm cold. Really cold. The pealing church bells tell me I have been here for hours. I want to lie down and sleep, but my body won't do it anymore. I think about going home, but I fled my father's house and family because of fear and found safety with Cory. 'I am safe with Cory.' That was what I knew then. I mutter the words over and over to convince myself that I do not want to hear the other words, the ones I'm trying to unhear which echo ever louder,

'Come and live with me before he kills you.'

I am no longer sure where I am going. Nor whom I should be going with. Just where do you go when you really don't know where to go, because you can't trust your own instincts anymore, let alone take your own advice to quit while you can? I'm not safe with Cory, but he needs me, even more so after this latest escapade. How can I let him need me if I am not actually safe with him? If he only needs me to harm me, then why can't I just go where I am safe?

PUZZLE No. 43

"I Am Safe With Cory"

AIRSHAFT
AROMATIC
ARTIFICE
CAMSHAFT
CERAMIST
CHARIOTS
CHARISMA
CHRISTIE
COMFIEST
COWRITES
CRAWFISH
FORECAST
HAIRIEST
HISTORIC
HOTWIRES
MARIACHI
MATRICES
MISCHIEF
RATIFIES
SCIMITAR
SEACRAFT
SHOWTIME
SOFTWARE
SOMEWHAT
SWITCHER
WISTERIA
WITCHIER

I	Z	J	F	X	S	K	T	X	A	Q	D	M	E	S	Q	H	E	U	L	Q
S	F	D	Z	V	E	C	H	S	D	I	N	X	M	M	Z	Z	S	R	V	R
S	C	W	Z	W	C	Z	W	I	Z	D	Z	W	K	W	P	G	O	E	C	V
T	O	N	I	Z	I	U	X	P	S	E	I	F	I	T	A	R	M	I	T	P
C	W	E	Q	S	R	S	R	C	O	T	T	L	W	H	Z	I	E	H	V	O
G	R	E	M	I	T	W	O	H	S	S	O	W	P	E	G	Y	W	C	A	B
E	I	X	J	D	A	E	U	S	E	O	B	R	Z	F	F	D	H	T	U	G
A	T	H	K	O	M	Q	R	I	E	F	B	U	I	M	Z	B	A	I	H	X
J	E	W	A	S	D	U	R	I	R	T	O	X	J	C	P	R	T	W	K	Y
G	S	Z	O	S	E	I	A	Q	A	W	X	T	F	A	H	S	R	I	A	R
N	Y	Z	E	M	A	A	O	T	W	A	S	G	K	R	Q	M	M	K	R	E
U	Q	H	I	H	Z	X	C	P	G	R	H	A	C	T	Q	O	E	Y	O	H
H	F	T	T	N	S	H	A	R	W	E	C	F	E	I	H	C	S	I	M	C
S	T	A	S	Z	V	P	U	Y	A	J	E	R	P	F	J	O	T	J	A	T
A	C	U	I	C	A	M	S	H	A	F	T	F	B	I	I	S	I	S	T	I
Q	U	C	R	H	G	C	V	T	W	S	T	F	L	C	H	C	A	J	I	W
F	C	E	H	T	V	W	I	Q	O	H	D	V	G	E	C	N	C	B	C	S
S	E	L	C	S	C	E	R	A	M	I	S	T	S	P	A	S	F	N	P	W
R	Q	A	R	A	T	I	M	I	C	S	R	W	M	E	I	V	Q	M	C	P
Y	R	O	D	C	K	Z	T	X	K	B	P	A	Z	F	R	S	H	C	K	C
O	O	M	S	E	V	C	R	A	W	F	I	S	H	U	A	I	X	C	M	T
D	J	H	C	R	A	W	T	Y	I	N	W	R	S	C	M	R	W	U	Y	I
Q	R	A	K	O	R	R	J	G	C	L	R	O	M	X	F	A	Z	T	Y	A
B	J	P	S	F	F	F	R	E	T	S	E	I	F	M	O	C	R	I	O	O
U	E	M	C	A	U	Z	C	K	M	C	H	A	R	I	S	M	A	S	A	H

CRIMEBIT No. 44

No Amount of Botox Can Fix This

YOUR RATING
/100

Nikki HoSang

None of us got much out of the funeral except a terrible sense that everything was final: Deirdre was dead and we were not. We milled around in the parking lot, blinking in the sunlight until we felt alive enough for lunch. Someone remembered a reservation at Mimi's. The aunts drove ahead to secure a table while I drove Deirdre's parents and her ancient grandmother.

We circled the lot a few times, looking for parking. We weren't the only ones. We passed a woman with a white coat and bright pink nails standing in an empty space, then circled again and parked where she had been standing.

'Should we buy her dessert later?' Deirdre's dad joked.

The hostess led us to a long table in the back. One of the aunts jerked her head towards a third figure sitting at the head of the table. White coat, bright pink nails, too much filler in the face. Totally engrossed in her phone.

She looked up.

'Frederique Kim?' the woman screeched. 'It's me, Margot-Tina Duong – I'm Dr. Tina Trinh-Long now. On Instagram?' She air-kissed me, pressing her nails into my skin.

How could I forget? I thought. *You're the reason Deirdre's dead.*

PUZZLE No. 44

Diner Wars

Across

5. Eating places (11)

7. Inquires (4)

8. Welcoming ones (8)

9. British pastime (7)

11. Titan (5)

13. Substance in the sea (5)

14. Mauled (7)

16. Sobriquet (8)

17. Flow slowly (4)

18. In spite of that (11)

Down

1. Brings to bear (4)

2. Chortled (7)

3. Forest growths (5)

4. Aught (8)

5. Confirmation - uncertainty (11)

6. Quality of being uncommon (11)

10. Attacking the opponent's King (8)

12. Purveyor of provisions (7)

15. Festive occasion (5)

17. Look as though (4)

1
2
3
4
5
6
7
8
9
10
11
12
13
14
15
16
17
18

CRIMEBIT No. 45

The Secret

YOUR RATING

/100

Iqbal Hussain

'Can you hear me, love? You're safe now.'

The policewoman crouches down, peering at me, brow creased. Barely older than me, she pats my hands awkwardly, as though they're hot to the touch.

I blink and the room snaps back into focus. White-clad figures rustle around in paper boiler suits with cinched hoods. They look like oversized toddlers. I stifle a giggle.

I'm sweating. Did I forget to turn the heating down? The room also smells strange – something metallic. I look around. Every surface is spattered in red, including the ceiling. By the fireplace, a body, covered in a sheet. Blood leaches through, like a monstrous bloom. My mouth drops open. The policewoman squeezes my arm.

She has no idea. She thinks I'm in shock. Maybe I am, but not how she imagines. The truth is, I want to jump up and dance and shout. Lucy shouldn't have threatened me once she found out. They never learn.

I clench my fist – the hand that, only an hour earlier, had

wielded the knife that now juts up like a tent pole under the sheet.

Stick to the plan, I remind myself. On a count of three, I burst into tears.

? *DID YOU KNOW* ?

The hard-boiled detective genre, known for its gritty and realistic style, originated in the 1920s with writers like Dashiell Hammett, whose character Sam Spade in *The Maltese Falcon* became an archetype for tough, cynical detectives. Hammett and other authors such as Raymond Chandler had their work serialized in *Black Mask*, a publication instrumental in popularizing hard-boiled fiction.

PUZZLE No. 45

Blood Types

Across

1. Literary matchmaker
5. Plumbing woe
9. Ancient Israeli port
14. Maria's husband on "Sesame Street"
15. Holiday log
16. __ Island, NY
17. Without accompaniment
19. Duel props
20. Blood type abbr.
21. Less experienced
23. Modern art?
24. Diploma word of honor
26. Heater
27. First stuff to learn
28. Genesis redhead
29. Juice sources known as HT in the UK
32. Bantam
34. Crib toy
35. Imposing
38. Informal conferences
39. Procrastinator's word
40. Patch of woods
41. Stomach strengtheners
43. Room in a casa
47. Ride with runners
48. Stick in a rack
49. Poplar tree
50. Stags and stallions
51. Elude capture
54. Shar-__
55. Make a sound
57. 1913 novel whose title ends with an exclamation point
59. Bay on the English Channel
60. Plant with spores
61. Patella's locale
62. Floral ornament
63. Loose or loosen
64. PhDs in the UK

Down

1. Run its course
2. __ membrane
3. Effluvium
4. Racer's cousin
5. "__ Maker"
6. Render a decision
7. Bootleg
8. Triviality
9. Give a hoot?
10. "Heidi" peak
11. Pet peeve?
12. In an ardent way
13. Evaluates
18. BMW __ Championship
22. Snags
25. Dark yellow
27. Uncultured
29. Even out
30. Essex setting for "The Turn of the Screw"
31. Pinnae are parts of them
33. Dinner table?
35. Wrecks
36. Makeshift desk
37. George VI or Victoria, to King Charles
38. Edgar Allan __
40. Not so dear
42. End date
44. Place after
45. Looked like a cad

46. Liqueur flavors
49. Name on the cover of "Atlas Shrugged"
51. "Diary of a Wimpy Kid" kid
52. Secreted mike
53. Unrivaled
56. "__, the Barrow Boy"
58. Make do

CRIMEBIT No. 46

Avenging the Ghost

YOUR RATING

/100

Lorah Jaiyn

Tree bark from the massive oak tree dug into Reilynn Sloane's back as she struggled to slow her breaths. Rivulets tickled the back of her neck, but whether it was the humid Florida heat or the light rain that had picked up, she could not tell. Storm clouds masked any light from the moon, and shadows from the towering trees and thick brush leapt at her with each flash of lightning. Thunder rolled on the wind.

If she moved, she was dead.

Jacob Friendly, a name in complete betrayal of his dark heart, waited for her to make another mistake. An ex-Navy Seal himself, Jacob had sold his soul and murdered her partner and two others of their unit. And now he lurked somewhere close by. Sharp mental kicks kept her alert. Her skills matched his under normal circumstances, but blind warfare in the pitch black of wilderness was Jacob's specialty. To chase him into his element had been a reckless reaction on her part.

A silent prayer to whoever would listen permeated through her mind as her fingers cramped around the Glock pressed into her stomach.

HAVE YOUR SAY

What happens next?

Scan to visit the
CrimeBits Writing Space

PUZZLE No. 46

The Ghost

Across

1. Plant afresh
6. Affixes
10. Furry red Muppet
14. One of the crowd?
15. Gander, so to speak
16. Abstruse
17. Carry off secretly (2 wds)
19. 1953 Pulitzer winner for drama
20. Comfort from mum, briefly
21. Agitate
22. __ Thee Stallion
23. In fine fettle
24. Kitzbuhel attraction
27. Two past Tue.
28. Little Italian number
29. The Flying Dutchman or the Mary Celeste
31. Causing heebie-jeebies
33. "Don't bug me!"
34. "The Land Before Time" triceratops
37. Chicken chow __
38. Killarney's country
41. Letter after November
45. Yard that receives little direct sunlight
48. Prime minister appointed by Akihito
49. Former Saturn model
50. Engage, as counsel
51. Tear up
52. Cover group?
54. Low heels?
56. They sang "Evil Woman"
57. Something to pitch
58. 2011 sports biopic
61. "¿Cómo __ usted?"
62. Not even slightly busy
63. Take a tally
64. Look for truffles
65. Dare to interpret
66. Darn them!

Down

1. Put another way
2. Look into
3. Decal
4. "Catch-22" bomber pilot
5. "Cool your jets!"
6. Where Nome is home
7. Looking for water
8. Doomed to failure, slangily
9. "Lucy in the __ with Diamonds"
10. Brickell who sang "What I Am"
11. Race units
12. "Titanic" or "Star Wars," e.g.
13. Unfold
18. British rubbish
22. "Quantum of Solace" introducer
25. Couple, in tabloids
26. Brief reminder
29. Kitchen gadgets
30. Some children
32. Sealed, as a deal
35. Heated state
36. Body work, for short?

38. "Fingers crossed!"
39. Met
40. Lily Munster's maiden name
42. Painstaking
43. Where Eileen lives, in "All My Ex's Live in Texas"
44. Dispatches
45. Convent address
46. Phoned
47. At loose __
53. "Moi," to Louis XIV
55. Thusly
58. Title given to Galahad or Gielgud
59. Work by Horace
60. Outback hopper, for short

CRIMEBIT No. 47

The Scout Hall

YOUR RATING /100

Anwen John

'There's a body outside the scout hall on Acresfield Road.'

The call ended abruptly, before the handler could take any details.

'Me and Amir are about 4 minutes away. We'll attend and report back,' radioed Jim Stewart, a veteran police constable. He looked at his partner, whose eyebrows were hitting his fringe. Amir Patel had only been on the beat for six months but he was ambitious, and grabbed every new experience eagerly.

'Don't get too excited, son. Most of the bodies we find died of natural causes. There are very few murders in Dukesford,' said Jim.

As they rounded the corner and saw the scout hall, they knew instantly that this was not a case of natural causes. The elderly man's body was naked and had been positioned to look like da Vinci's Vitruvian Man.

The words 'I'm Sorry' had been carved into his chest.

PUZZLE No. 47

Vitruvian Man

AERIAL SCREW
ARCHITECT
ARMORED CAR
BORGIA
CALCULATOR
CANNON
CROSSBOW
ENGINEER
FLORENCE
FLYWHEEL
FRESCO
HANG GLIDER
INVENTOR
ITALY
LAST SUPPER
MEDUSA
MONA LISA
ORNITHOPTER
PAINTER
PARACHUTE
PATRON
PERSPECTIVE
QUATTROCENTO
RENAISSANCE
ROBOT
SCIENTIST
SCULPTOR
SFUMATO
TANK
TUSCANY
VITRUVIAN

E	K	I	L	L	C	L	A	R	M	O	R	E	D	C	A	R	I	Y	H	A
T	T	N	R	G	M	X	J	F	H	R	M	A	A	O	R	I	N	K	L	T
F	K	V	F	N	P	N	P	Q	V	N	X	P	E	E	C	P	E	X	A	A
T	A	E	L	U	Y	I	C	F	H	I	I	N	B	M	N	G	I	X	S	L
M	H	N	O	V	R	Q	A	B	I	T	T	E	N	D	X	W	Q	U	T	U
Z	C	T	R	Z	E	L	N	N	T	H	J	R	W	K	O	Y	D	R	S	Z
S	A	O	E	X	N	C	N	H	A	O	P	T	U	B	T	E	N	A	U	X
R	L	R	N	P	A	C	O	U	L	P	V	D	S	V	M	Z	D	K	P	G
R	C	E	C	N	I	R	N	B	Y	T	O	S	F	R	I	O	U	E	P	W
H	U	C	E	U	S	P	W	X	O	E	O	B	F	R	T	A	B	Y	E	V
A	L	C	E	J	S	U	E	S	Q	R	X	V	U	L	E	G	N	M	R	E
N	A	F	N	R	A	O	L	R	C	I	G	X	X	X	Y	S	F	V	M	A
G	T	A	Y	U	N	G	E	A	S	U	S	I	B	T	Q	W	C	W	S	W
G	O	B	U	I	C	X	S	N	R	P	L	E	A	P	F	U	H	O	C	U
L	R	E	P	T	E	I	U	X	G	T	E	P	I	Q	I	F	P	E	I	V
I	N	Y	T	I	L	L	U	C	D	I	S	C	T	T	V	J	A	T	E	G
D	C	W	B	A	M	P	A	T	R	O	N	U	T	O	C	H	I	U	N	L
E	H	D	N	J	Y	A	A	H	V	N	I	E	V	I	R	Q	N	S	T	V
R	W	O	R	S	D	P	W	M	V	C	J	W	E	D	V	D	T	C	I	F
Z	M	R	F	N	A	P	S	F	U	M	A	T	O	R	R	E	E	A	S	I
V	I	I	P	A	R	A	C	H	U	T	E	I	W	Q	Q	O	R	N	T	J
F	L	L	N	M	F	A	R	C	H	I	T	E	C	T	R	T	B	Y	R	N
U	A	E	R	I	A	L	S	C	R	E	W	E	I	P	C	P	A	O	O	L
D	O	M	U	K	E	K	W	T	F	H	G	G	O	K	V	E	A	N	T	B
Q	U	A	T	T	R	O	C	E	N	T	O	T	N	Y	L	A	N	Y	K	S

CRIMEBIT No.48

Never Look Back

YOUR RATING /100

Jason Kerrigan

Every day I dream up a new way to kill someone. Today's fantasy is more horrific than usual – pushing them under a train as my method of choice. I want it to be messy.

Having just missed an earlier train, I remain stood for the past six minutes, shivering, hunched over, positioned exactly where the doors will eventually open. It should be obvious to all the other commuters filing onto the platform; I was here first. Does this idiot think I haven't noticed him, or that he deserves to board the train before me? He is at my shoulder; hovering, waiting for a moment of weakness before pouncing. Why should I let him jump the queue? The tracks crackle as the train approaches, and right on cue, I feel him trying to slide his way around me. It is not fair, I have been here, stood on the yellow line the longest, the permitted limit of encroachment, the space beyond which is out of bounds. I have played by the rules, and he knows he is in the wrong and shouldn't be at the front, yet plans to push in and get a seat ahead of me?

No chance.

WRITING PROMPT 4

It's happening again.

I keep hearing them. Scratching behind the skirting board. I know they're there. No one else believes me though. They say it's all in my head. I know I'm right though. That's all that matters. Mum came round to visit. She brought some food with her, but I can't eat it. Don't know what's in it. I need to check everything again. No tins, no frozen foods. Fresh meat, fresh veg. Even that is risky.

Brush teeth for one minute. Wash hands three times. Face twice. Repeat once. Keeps them away for a few hours.

It's been over a year since I'd heard them. They were just waiting for me to feel a little normal for a while. They know when to come back.

I've heard the clicks on the phone. They're listening to my conversations so I can't even tell Mum about them.

Scan to visit the CrimeBits Writing Space

PUZZLE No. 48

Crazy Train

Across

1. Most elementary
9. Washington city
15. Cherub
16. Animals with striped legs
17. Those who shout "All aboard!" in a most excellent way?
19. Bug, say
20. "Be patient!"
21. Place to curl up and hibernate
22. Pirate's leg, often
24. At large
27. City transit
30. Business attire at Amtrak?
35. City between Turin and Genoa
37. Attempt
38. Approximately, as a date
39. Insulting one
41. More indistinct
43. Caste member
44. Rabid rooter
45. Turn at roulette
46. Impediment to a locomotive?
50. They're between ems and ohs
51. National emblem
52. Household pest
54. "Right there. Don't stop."
57. Pushes off
59. About the city
63. Danger for some train passengers?
67. Garment for an obi
68. Fences in
69. Grasping
70. Appraise again

Down

1. Get smart
2. Morning mumble
3. Glum
4. Hosp. area
5. "My Fair Lady" lyricist
6. "And so forth"
7. Put in a hold
8. In a melodic sense
9. "Have a good day!" reply
10. Award from KCL
11. Kit __ Club
12. Music player that was new in 2001
13. Swampy tract
14. The A in BSA
18. Big name in French fashion
23. Slalom course marker
25. Pouches
26. Gets to work on Time?
27. Clean in a tub
28. Bolt at great speed
29. Smarted
31. Not std.
32. Utter nonsense
33. Isolate during winter
34. Gets the hard way
36. Low-budget film, briefly
40. Toro, in sushi bars
41. "Nixon in China" tenor

42. Sun worshiper of Peru
44. Scam artist
47. New Year's drink
48. Post pieces
49. Knots in wood
53. Sextet halves
54. Quizzes
55. French date, often
56. Chrome button
58. Balanced
60. Ignoble
61. An eternity, seemingly
62. Alleged monster's loch
64. Japanese swimmer
65. Rural rest stop
66. Former Sony rival

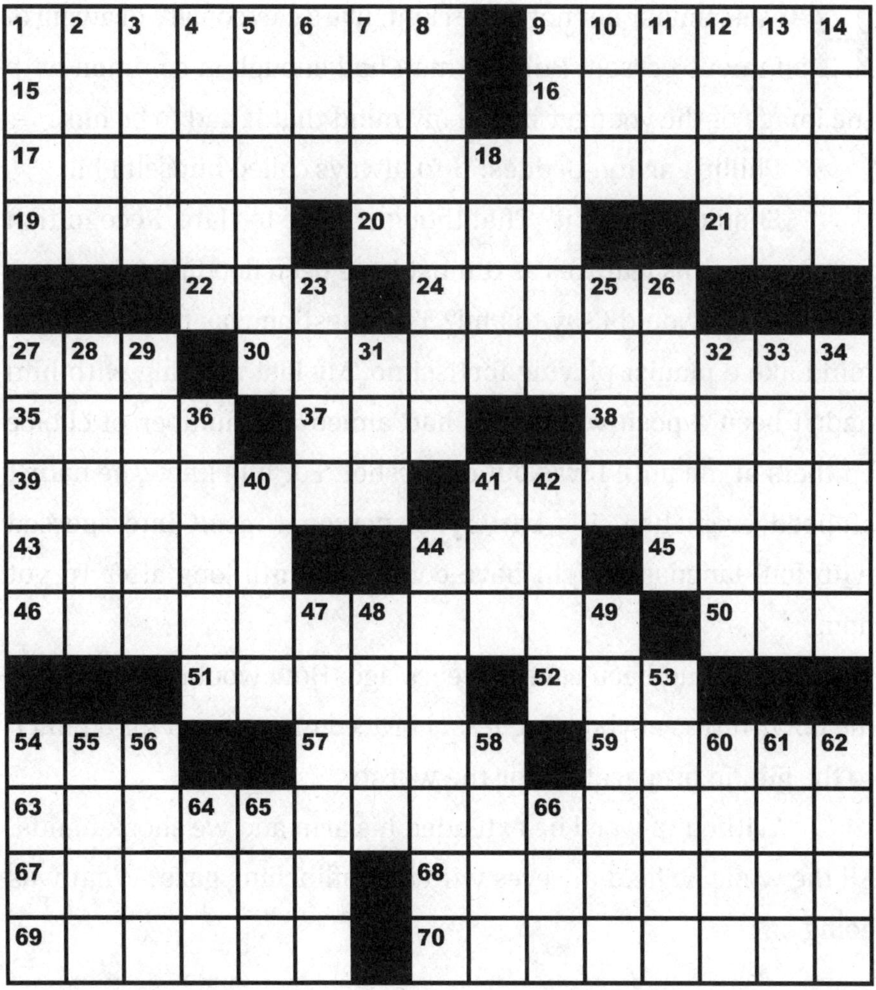

CRIMEBIT No. 49

The Covert Memoir

YOUR RATING
/100

Andrew Komarnyckyj

He was familiar but not quite right, like a cartoonist's drawing of a famous person. But this man had enough in common with the image of the younger one in my mind that it had to be him.

Phillip Carlton Geddes. He'd always called himself Phil.

Should I run for it? That thought came too late. Recognition was flooding his features as it must have been flooding mine.

What would I say to Phil? The question was playing on my mind like a pianist playing fortissimo. My last meeting with him hadn't been a positive one. He had aimed any number of choice epithets at me until I was out of earshot. For all I knew, he hadn't stopped even then. His battery of personal insult interspersed with foul language might have continued until long after I'd got home.

That had been several years ago. How would Phil react to me now? It was anybody's guess. I braced myself, as if for a punch to the gut, in preparation for the worst.

Without a word he extended his arm and we shook hands. All the while he held my eyes with an unflinching gaze. What was going on?

? DID YOU KNOW ?

The Motion Picture Production Code (Hays Code) of the 1930s to 1950s was a set of industry guidelines for film content in the US, imposing restrictions on things such as sexual content, profanity and violence. Filmmakers were forced to explore darker themes and moral ambiguity in more creative and subtle ways, contributing to the rise of film noir; it's shadowy visuals and nuanced storytelling adhering to the Code's moralistic requirements.

PUZZLE No. 49

Phil in the Blanks

Across

1. Beaker material
6. __ Nui (Easter Island)
10. Calendar entry
14. Having a twang
15. Choose not to use
16. Lemon juice, e.g.
17. Battle of Shephelah warrior
19. Bushy rug
20. Ladybug's lunch, at times
21. The nearby items
22. "Harlem Nights" actor Foxx
25. More or less
28. Kamoze who sang "Here Comes the Hot-stepper"
29. Where Tagalog is spoken
34. Computer button
36. In spite of every-thing
37. Most debonair
40. Star of the HBO series "Insecure"
41. Turns gruesome
43. Able to creep you out
44. Stamp collector
47. CN Tower's prov.
48. Juárez of Mexico
49. Blows away
50. Air traveler's choice
54. Artificial waterway
56. Speak irrationally
57. David Hume's specialty
62. "Hold __ your dreams"
63. All, in combinations
64. Film fest film, often
65. Barely audible sound
66. Roman garment worn over a tunic
67. Colorful ornamental stone

Down

1. Econ. measure for a country
2. "Well, __-di-dah!"
3. "__ was going to St. Ives..."
4. Cold course
5. Berth place
6. Edible helixes
7. Queen in the "Star Wars" movies
8. Fastener with a sharp point
9. "I can't believe I __ the whole thing!"
10. Bit of salt
11. Rue the run, perhaps
12. Alejandro's aunts
13. On__ (anxious)
18. __ Tzu
21. Prepare for printing, once
22. Tears to pieces
23. "Knock it off!"
24. Hindu festival of lights
26. Signal in many homes, nowadays
27. Flats in NYC or LA
29. Quickie buildings
30. "Of wrath," in a requiem
31. Intolerant

32. Paige who sang "Memory" in "Cats"
33. Comes down in icy drops
35. Pernicious or perfidious
38. Builder's purchase
39. "My Mad Fat Diary" extra
42. Preparing, as lunch meats
45. Venezia's country
46. Prefix in acoustics
49. Parallel to
50. Clip, as a photo
51. Brick or Penny
52. A chip for a kitty
53. Standstill
55. Tian Shan locale
57. Prize at the table
58. US medical insurance group
59. Multi-purpose mobile device, for short
60. Popular show
61. "__-haw!" (cowboy's shout)

CRIMEBIT No.50

Daisy Blue

YOUR RATING /100

John Lau

I finally find Renata at a Popeyes on Cahuenga. She's with her boyfriend Jimmer who's seven years older, which is still only 22. Renata had left a note for her mum when she and Jimmer ran off, saying she was in love. Five weeks into their romantic getaway, it seems clear to me that the honeymoon's over.

She goes to the Ladies and I follow her in. Judging by the way Jimmer kept his arm around her neck, Renata didn't get out of his sight too often. Jimmer's a hulking beast and he's not going to like what I have to say, so I'm happy I don't have to taze him to get to Renata.

She's puffier than she was in her Tenth Grade photo and her skin's broken out. That's what happens when you live on take-out and dumpster diving for a month. She catches me staring at her in the mirror and shrinks into herself like the defense mechanism of a tiny animal.

'Renata, don't be afraid,' I tell her. 'My name is Daisy Blue. Your mum hired me to find you. Would you like to go home?'

Soon as she stops crying, I tell her the plan.

PUZZLE No. 50

Child Finder

*Daisy Blue is a professional child finder with a knack for locating runaway teenagers. Her secret? They almost always end up at a fast food restaurant. And she knows every single fast food place in Los Angeles. This week alone, Daisy Blue found three runaways. From the clues, determine which **runaway** was found in what **restaurant**, and in which **hiding place**.*

The Runaways

Renata - Thought she was in love with Jimmer; realized she didn't even really like him.

Loretta - Ran away with her BFF; BFF dumped her and ran off with someone else.

Diana - She was hot in Phoenix, but not hot enough for Hollywood.

Fast Food Restaurants

Popeyes in West Hollywood

McDonald's in Melrose Hill

Taco Bell near University Park

Hiding Places

Bathrooms

Outdoor dining area

Back booth

? CLUES ?

1. Diana has never been to Popeyes and doesn't even like chicken.
2. Loretta doesn't like to sit in booths.
3. The teen found at McDonald's was in the outdoor dining area.
4. The teen with a taste for tacos was not Renata.
5. Renata was located in the bathroom.

	Diana	***Loretta***	***Renata***	*Popeyes*	*McDonald's*	*Taco Bell*
Bathroom						
Back booth						
Outdoor dining area						
Popeyes						
McDonald's						
Taco Bell						

Runaway	**Restaurant**	**Hiding Place**
______________	______________	______________
______________	______________	______________
______________	______________	______________

CRIMEBIT No. 51

Gray Ghost

YOUR RATING
/100

Allen Learst

The Gray Ghost stood at the edge of a marsh: cattails, sedge grasses, and algae slime thawing at the shoreline. Detroit's skyline downriver from Belle Isle: Buhl Building, the Guardian, and the Penobscot rising above a morning fog, covering the city like a cloak. A testimony to modern day sophistication and wealth. One day he would be part of it, but for now he must focus, not on the dead kid, whose arm dangled from a truck window, his head lolled to one side, a bullet hole through his temple, but on thievery and intelligence. Be smart, he tells himself as he loads cases of stolen whiskey into his boat, its keel resting in muck and gravel. He didn't want to shoot him, but when the kid pulled a knife and cut the Ghost's arm, he didn't have a choice, didn't really think about it except as an act of survival. The kid, maybe twenty-years-old, faster than a bat out of hell, would have cut his throat if he hadn't shot him. Fool kid, the Ghost thought, I had the drop on him. Now he's dead and someone will have to pay for the booze.

PUZZLE No. 51

Whiskey Delivery

*Fortunately for the Gray Ghost, Detroit hosts a whole lot of dive bars. He didn't have any trouble unloading all those cases of whiskey. In fact, each of the three bar owners who bought his stash owned a different bar. They all wanted a different brand of whiskey. From the clues, determine **who** ended up with **what** kind of whiskey, and **where**.*

The People

Phil McCup - A no-nonsense bartender with a quick wit.

Holden Cole-Brues - A retired trucker with a heart of gold.

Jen N. Tawnick - A former lounge singer, with a touch of class.

The Whiskey

Johnnie Walker - The spirit that makes spirits soar.

Jack Daniel's - Life happens. Jack Daniel's helps.

Jameson - Because no good story ever started with a salad.

Locations

Abick's Bar - Owned by the same family since 1907 with the ancient cash register to prove it.

LJ's Lounge - Wood paneling, a mirrored back bar, beer and Jell-O shots.

Bronx Bar - Teetering on the brink of respectability, the burgers are stellar.

? CLUES ?

1. Jen N. Tawnick didn't buy the Johnnie Walker.
2. Holden Cole-Brues is not the owner of the Bronx Bar.
3. The customer who was bought cases of Jack Daniel's owns LJ's Lounge.
4. The customer who bought Jameson was not Phil McCup.
5. Phil McCup owns Abick's Bar.

	Holden	***Jen***	***Phil***	*Jack Daniel's*	*Jameson*	*Johnnie Walker*
Abick's Bar						
Bronx Bar						
LJ's Lounge						
Jack Daniel's						
Jameson						
Johnnie Walker						

Who?

What?

Where?

CRIMEBIT No. 52

A Murder in Nowhere

YOUR RATING /100

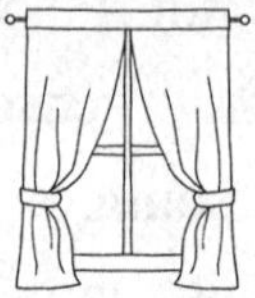

Jennifer Leeper

Detective Lou Becker watched a tumbleweed's erratic path down Main Street in Frontera, Colorado. It was a madman's dance. For Lou, it seemed appropriate that the only thing moving in a town that had been dead for more than four decades was itself technically dead. The plant's false reanimation echoed an illusion of life in the town itself – an illusion ironically conjured by the discovery of Reyna Mercado's body.

Even more ironic, it was the first murder in a ghost town – at least during Lou's tenure – on the Eastern Colorado plains. It was also a first for Lou, who was accustomed to suburban crime – which was plentiful and diverse across the Front Range. There had been a smattering of rural casework, but dwindling populations all over Colorado's Eastern plains also meant dwindling crime.

That meant the high, southeastern Colorado plains were dead enough without murders in ghost towns to send home the message, Lou thought as she squatted down in the pale, dusty earth of an alley to get a closer look at Reyna – the young woman's body cold as winter. Reyna's neck was tattooed by the marks of death.

EDITOR'S NOTES

'This is a descriptive and somewhat cinematic opening, relaying setting, character, and plot, in less than two hundred words. This is more like the old-school type of crime novels we'd see in decades past. This tallies really well with the setting of a ghost town, somewhere that may have been bustling and vibrant before, but is now dead to the world. Great imagery and stands out in the crime fiction world we now live in.'

PUZZLE No. 52

Tumble Weed

Across

1. Bogus deal
5. Adobe ingredient
10. Hanks of "Shameless"
14. Alan who was born Alphonso D'Abruzzo
15. Mimi of "After Everything"
16. Lamarr who helped invent a radio guidance system
17. Herbicide
19. Skillet stuff
20. Knack
21. Mat word
23. A third of 111?
24. Seemingly forever
27. "Wait, what?"
28. System used in libraries
33. Relating to eight
36. FAQ checker
37. Lacto-___ diet
38. Sartorial aide
40. Part of a boa
43. Go-to sushi fish
44. Duet
46. Joe of "GoodFellas"
47. Moon Unit's brother
51. Charlotte to George, informally
52. Thornfield Hall governess
53. Actor known for wearing gold
56. Express
60. Less puzzling
62. Zone
63. She played the mum in "Cujo" and "E.T. the Extra-Terrestrial"
66. William H. ___ ("Shameless" star)
67. Newton or Asimov
68. Second of a Latin 101 trio
69. Wild buglers
70. Cold sign
71. Track info

Down

1. Handled
2. All washed up?
3. She released "21" in 2011
4. ___-to-measure
5. Bunny slope conveyance
6. ___ el Amarna, Egypt
7. Theologian's subj.
8. From the jump
9. Visitors' announcement
10. Overly stylish
11. Jack Reacher, famously
12. Biblical kingdom near Moab
13. River to the North Sea
18. Shows homage
22. Filmdom's Jean-___ Godard
25. Anatomy adjective
26. Part of GPS
28. "___ Kapital"
29. Cover, as costs
30. Maker of a scale of hardness
31. Sans opposite
32. Petty or Singer
33. Slanted column?

34. "Titanic" extras
35. Prompter prelude
39. Like sitcoms
41. Supplication
42. It's measured in spots?
45. Verb-forming suffix
48. School papers
49. Oxy-5 target
50. Evangelize
53. Florida city in a Nicki Minaj song title
54. Hit the high points, briefly
55. Lock, of sorts
56. Tag line?
57. Like a campfire story
58. Hourglass part
59. Philippine money
61. Lobster pot part
64. Evian water?
65. Droll sort

CRIMEBIT No. 53

Bad Decisions

YOUR RATING /100

Marti Leimbach

Through the window, Gloria sees her neighbor, Annie, barely in her twenties and with a powerful beauty that cannot go unnoticed. Gloria can imagine her being 'discovered', as in the old Hollywood tale of Lana Turner, sipping an iced Coke at a soda fountain after school and being spotted by a famous movie director. Not that Annie should sit on a stool and wait for a man. Who needs that?

The morning air smells fresh, clean of the wastewater odor that permeates much of Burbank. It's quiet, only the robins singing. But last night, across the thin strip of land that separates their two houses, Gloria heard the husband shouting, a crash of glass, then the soprano sound of Annie's girlish tears. It's not the first time.

Gloria could walk over to Annie, tell her that there is a future ahead, and that she could lead her to it. Long ago, Lana Turner drank a cold soda on a hot afternoon in LA and someone took notice of her, plucking her out of one life and setting her down in another. Together, they could take care of the husband problem. Gloria knows how to arrange such matters, after all.

PUZZLE No. 53

Witness Protection

Gloria knows all about plucking someone out of one life and setting them down in another. That was her job with the U.S. Marshall's Witness Security Program. Tasked with the security, safety and health of government witnesses and their authorized family members, Gloria placed five people into witness protection. Identify ***who*** *moved* ***where****, and* ***when****.*

The Witnesses

Holly Johnson
Mary Ellen Froelich
Francis X. Quinn
James Barr
Susan Turner

The Towns

Margrave, Georgia
Key West, Florida
Hope, Colorado
Bolton, South Dakota
Carter's Crossing, Mississippi

The Years

2019 2020 2021 2022 2023

Who?	**Where?**	**When?**
______	______	______
______	______	______
______	______	______
______	______	______
______	______	______

? CLUES ?

1. Susan Turner didn't disappear in either 2022 or 2023.
2. One of the witnesses relocated to Hope, Colorado in an earlier year than Mary Ellen Froelich.
3. Neither the witness who relocated to Key West nor James Barr moved in 2023.
4. A witness moved to Margrave, Georgia in an earlier year than the person who relocated to Bolton, South Dakota (who isn't Holly Johnson) but in a later year than both Mary Ellen Froelich and Francis X. Quinn.

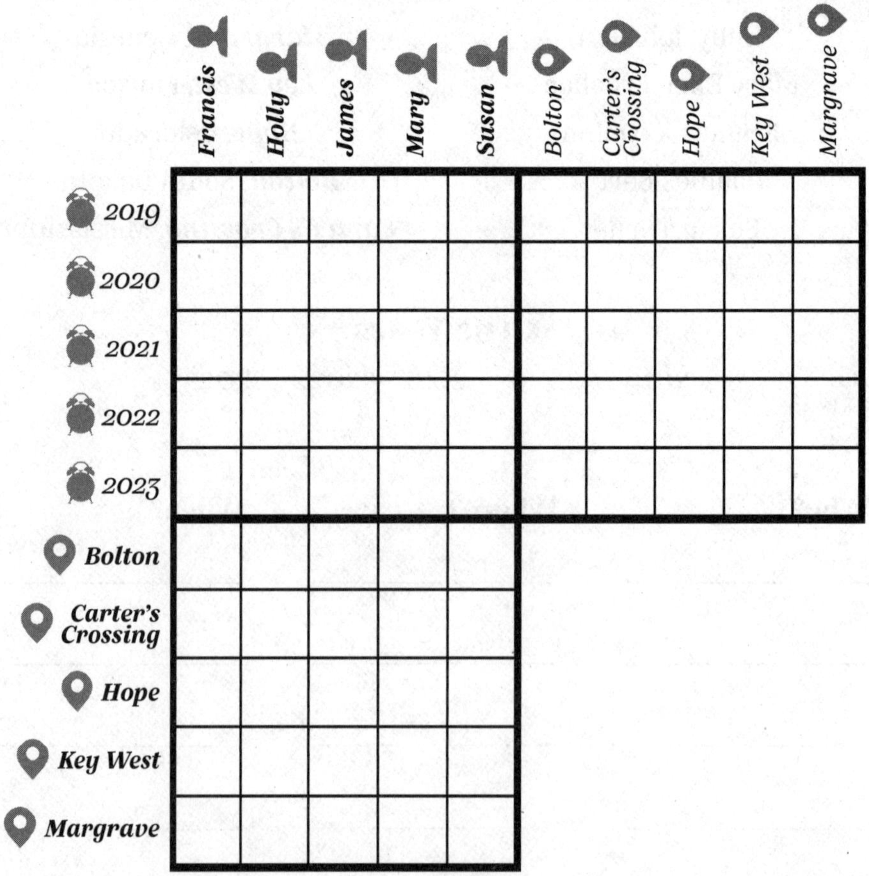

CRIMEBIT No. 54

Caliope

YOUR RATING /100

Amy Lyn

Rust falls from the sky, the landscape a patchwork quilt of vibrant orange, red, and yellow. Manic wind shakes branches, whispering dark thoughts to the velvet sky, as stars pepper the tooth-grinding river.

Memories rattle around her head like a tin can tumbling down the sidewalk in the wind. Most nights she rode on the back of regret, her bed a harbinger of pain, flooding the backs of her eyes with visions of revenge.

The moment he entered her shop her skin crackled with that familiar prickly feeling. She forced a smile and turned her eyes on the new customer. The burning feeling became a flame thrower.

With a navy and white, back-to-school outfit draped over her arm, Caliope said 'Welcome to the Orange Moose.' The 40-something man stared intently into her eyes with a lopsided grin she was sure he thought was charming. He nodded and made a beeline for the rack labeled Tweens, where he started fingering the skirts and dresses.

It had been years since allowing her chimera to uncoil and creep back into her consciousness. She'd satiated her twin with murderous bedtime stories, but now it clearly wasn't enough.

PUZZLE No. 54

Clothes Lines

Across

1. Avoid extinction, say
6. They play at work
10. Crème ___ crème (elite)
14. Ma makes a living with it
15. Think piece?
16. LHR stats.
17. Garb for a formal cricket game?
19. Philosophical questions
20. "A Clockwork ___," Burgess book
21. The Beatles' Pepper, briefly
23. Lea lady?
24. Really cool, in slang
25. US Centre for Cryptologic History org.
28. Carmichael and Donnelly
30. Something brewing?
31. Frock for an Amazon warrior?
33. Mouth watering?
34. Concert receipts, collectively
35. Not indoor
38. Sang alpine songs
41. Lingerie company named for an island
42. One generating a lot of interest?
44. Origami undergarment?
47. Professor X's power
50. "Imperium" character
51. ISP connection
52. Word on a cornerstone
53. Bi halved
54. Almost forever
56. Parlor purchase
58. Photogravure process, for short
60. Garment that's designed to hide legs?
63. Site of a Biblical plot
64. Shed light
65. Sniggler's quarry
66. Beatty film of '81
67. Trophy rooms
68. Like a dive bar

Down

1. Confront boldly
2. Honey substitute?
3. Silky wool source
4. Bad thing to have to walk
5. Serve sugar cubes
6. Popular, so to speak
7. Wasteful bother
8. Nightly broadcast
9. Hang around, say
10. Lawn cover?
11. Delicate
12. Depredate
13. Gauged

18. Alaska Range peak
22. Just a smidgen
26. Arouse
27. Four-wheeler, for short
29. His forte is to exhort
31. Ewe can say that again!
32. Easy basketball shots
33. Take verbal potshots
35. Even less famous
36. Formal retraction
37. Drew forth
39. "... and I mean it!"
40. The, to Hamburgers
43. Full of tears, say
45. Some metal bands?
46. Paid, as the bill
47. Curly-leaved salad green
48. Caught with a rope
49. Frost lines?
52. Tarsus location
55. Christen
57. Plays like a fiddle
59. Come-___
61. Rubbish receptacle
62. Ranks below cpts.

CRIMEBIT No. 55

Dutch Courage

YOUR RATING

/100

Camilla Macpherson

The Hague, April 1940

Down on the beach, two uniformed policemen bent to take one end of the canvas stretcher each. They began to trudge steadily towards the shore road, swinging the stretcher between them on metal poles. Their heavy, booted feet crunched against the sand as they trampled through the sharp marram grass. They passed directly below the veranda. On the stretcher, covered by a gray blanket, was the unmistakable shape of a body.

Clem de Vries leaned over the veranda railing, the breeze tugging at her blonde hair and little felt hat. She caught the faintest scent of honeysuckle in the air. A sweet note, above the salt tang sweeping in from the Noordzee. But death wasn't meant to smell of honeysuckle. There was too much activity for it to have been an accident. There were still three men standing around. Two of them, in uniform, doing nothing. The third pointing at the ground, then gesticulating wildly.

There was something familiar about his tall, rangy frame. As she watched, he turned towards her. Even from a distance, his face looked fierce and focused. Clem recognized that look.

Ralf. Ralf de Jong. After all these years.

PUZZLE No. 55

Dutch Treat

BEEMSTER
BOERENKAAS
EDAM
GOUDA
GRASKAAS
KANTERKAAS
LEERDAMMER
LEYDEN
LIMBURGER
MAASDAM
MAASLANDER
NAGELKAAS
PARRANO
PRIMA DONNA
ROOMANO
ROTTERDAMSCHE OUDE
VLASKAAS

G	G	E	Z	S	X	V	Q	O	Y	A	F	R	I	Q	J	K	N	H	P	G
N	Q	H	J	U	S	B	D	Z	V	X	F	N	A	G	E	L	K	A	A	S
E	E	W	C	Y	N	X	W	C	U	A	G	T	X	I	V	H	K	Z	L	S
D	M	D	W	S	Y	V	Z	A	R	R	Z	P	A	R	R	A	N	O	M	N
U	A	A	Y	Q	Y	N	N	J	L	H	R	S	A	B	N	Q	D	Y	E	K
O	A	C	N	E	L	S	Z	R	B	R	D	I	V	T	C	R	R	M	O	R
E	S	R	W	C	L	D	R	T	W	Z	V	Q	E	O	Q	E	G	A	Y	F
H	L	R	D	W	Z	A	E	A	N	S	I	R	U	T	O	V	A	H	Z	Z
C	A	G	A	T	X	B	G	B	H	A	K	U	G	T	E	S	P	J	E	H
S	N	U	G	O	M	E	R	M	P	A	V	V	F	D	W	A	G	I	I	R
M	D	C	V	B	R	E	U	D	A	K	S	V	R	I	Z	A	W	U	B	N
A	E	V	G	K	B	M	B	S	O	N	Y	I	Y	U	C	K	M	Z	T	Z
D	R	H	W	Y	K	S	M	A	U	E	V	C	V	C	A	S	K	O	B	N
R	T	B	T	H	J	T	I	S	Y	R	J	G	Z	O	E	A	D	X	H	R
E	Q	F	P	M	F	E	L	R	A	E	P	H	L	W	E	R	O	E	V	S
T	S	L	E	W	D	R	B	M	L	O	Z	R	U	B	A	G	P	X	Y	R
T	B	W	E	Y	E	R	U	V	A	B	Y	P	I	G	D	Q	D	F	S	Z
O	A	W	I	E	O	D	C	J	F	D	N	D	T	M	G	O	U	D	A	K
R	Q	Z	Y	O	R	O	A	A	X	B	S	T	R	H	A	A	W	X	M	H
S	Y	E	M	I	A	D	A	M	S	A	T	A	D	A	A	D	W	D	D	V
S	U	A	X	O	L	V	A	S	A	A	K	S	A	L	V	W	O	T	G	G
X	N	S	T	G	S	H	T	M	Z	Q	V	P	J	M	I	R	R	N	E	L
O	J	M	Z	C	O	M	Z	F	M	S	M	T	E	S	N	B	L	H	N	S
F	T	A	B	P	E	J	K	B	Z	E	L	Z	D	M	T	M	R	H	P	A
E	N	R	N	O	B	V	G	O	Y	X	R	B	Z	D	K	V	I	S	Q	M

CRIMEBIT No. 56

How To Get Published

YOUR RATING /100

Camilla Macpherson

The bargain between author and literary agent is well-established. The author's job is to craft 100,000 words of elegant yet page-turning prose. The agent's job is to reject the same on the basis of the difficult, unbelievably tough, or downright impossible publishing market.

It's ironic that the nearest thing to a bite I got for my manuscript *All The Love We Can Get* (a will-they-won't-they romance with the usual tragic ending) was also the straw that broke the camel's back. One particular agent described it as 'wonderful', 'compelling' and a 'must-read'. I immediately cracked open the champagne (OK, prosecco). Then she asked me to tell her all about myself. I emailed back eagerly. I live in Kent. I'm an accountant. Forty-something. Studied English at Cambridge. Hobbies reading and gardening. To which she replied – eventually, after two chasers – that although the story was top notch, she just wasn't sure I was quite what she was looking for.

I was too ordinary, that's what she meant.

Frankly, I felt like killing her. And that, Lee, is where it started.

WRITING PROMPT
5

I'm waiting.

Minutes have turned into hours, hours into days, days into weeks. I don't know how long anymore. I'm not that good at counting that many. Just sat next to the window, waiting for her to come back.

Dad has been drinking that strange glass of light brown stuff a lot more lately. I tried some once. Didn't like it though. Made me go all shivery inside. My mate Ben said it was probably beer. His Dad drinks that as well.

I don't mind waiting. Because I know she'll come back. She always said I was her 'Special little man'. I liked it when she called me that. Made me feel all warm and toasty.

I love my mum.

She's the best mum in the world. She makes special cakes and lets me lick the spoon when she's done with the mixing.

So I'll wait for her. As long as it takes. Have to keep my eyes peeled, just in case she can't find the house anymore. It's been a while, and sometimes I forget where things are, so maybe she might as well. So I best keep sitting here next to the window.

Yesterday, Dad didn't come home.

PUZZLE No. 56

A Bit of a Reacher

Across

1. Pocket full of food
5. Clumsy clod
11. Comic's performance
14. Olympian battler
15. Cook up
16. Sense of pitch
17. Lee Child novel where Reacher hikes through campgrounds?
19. Honest __ (pomegranate product)
20. In a muddle
21. Annual Mass book
22. "If that doesn't work..."
23. Google, say
25. "Stop stressing"
27. Lee Child novel in which Reacher joins a diet group?
32. Iguana on "Dora the Explorer"
35. Broadcast
36. Comedian Wise who partnered with Eric Morecambe
37. Broadway show set in Cob County
40. Appoint beforehand
42. Part of a telecast
43. Dip bread in gravy, say
44. Keep time, in a way
45. Lee Child novel featuring Reacher learning how to joust?
50. Lei Day greeting
51. It's an anagram of itself
55. Surgery souvenir
58. Composer of "Le Roi d'Ys"
60. Pack with pentacles
61. Time's 2006 Person of the Year
62. Lee Child novel in which Reacher learns to avoid a certain German composer?
64. She wrote "Trapeze"
65. Hans Christian Andersen's hometown
66. Suzanne Vega smash
67. Tolkien creature with bark
68. Happened
69. Plot of Genesis?

Down

1. Family members
2. Cross
3. Hadley who wrote "Clever Girl" and "The Past"
4. Say for sure
5. "The butler __ it"
6. Wise about
7. Infested
8. Splash guard
9. Never revealed
10. Urban grid abbrs.
11. Regal imprint
12. "CSI" actor George
13. Bird house?
18. Unit price word
22. Go all out
24. At this point
26. Stuns
28. 1963 film for which Patricia Neal won BAFTA
29. Pt. of a monogram
30. Lollobrigida once called "the most beautiful woman in the world"
31. Dickens villain
32. Meryl's role in "Out of Africa"

33. Disavow
34. Allroad Quattro maker
38. Cuban export
39. Cleopatra's eye makeup
40. [Facepalm!]
41. Body of majestic poetry
43. Far from equilateral
46. Home of El Greco
47. Free of stubble
48. Black ball in an Italian pool hall
49. Exposed
52. Certain cybercrime
53. "Father of Liberalism" philosopher
54. Frome of literature
55. Last word of the year?
56. Slot insert
57. Betsey Trotwood of "David Copperfield"
59. Amount qualifier
62. Drink garnished with nutmeg
63. Army off.

CRIMEBIT No. 57

The Space Between

YOUR RATING /100

Oliver Marlow

It starts with a line of tiny black shapes crossing a vast expanse of white.

Zoom down and you're with a convoy of black vehicles traveling across a desolate snow-covered landscape. Two black land rovers at the front, two black juggernauts behind and a third black land rover bringing up the rear.

Inside the back of the second land rover a young woman is sitting next to a young man. The woman is wearing a fur hat, the man a woolen hat with ear flaps. Their black overcoats are both undone at the front. The woman is looking out of her window. The man has his hand on a metal briefcase lying on the seat between them.

A set of headlights appears on the horizon coming towards them, and a minute later a lorry laden with gas pipes hurtles past in the opposite direction.

Then nothing but emptiness and white again.

A gray sky, with some soft red lines showing in the west.

It's dusk, and you're traveling through the Yamal Peninsula

in northern Siberia.

Yamal means 'the end of the world'.

And that's about right, thinks the young man to himself.

? DID YOU KNOW ?

The character of Sherlock Holmes first appeared in *A Study in Scarlet* in 1887, but he gained popularity through the short stories published in *The Strand Magazine* starting with "A Scandal in Bohemia" in 1891.

PUZZLE No. 57

End of the World

Across

1. Pascoe on "Taskmaster"
5. Poke into
10. Beer, casually
14. Winnerless games
15. Where to hear "Capital London"
16. "I'm __, boss!"
17. Final battle between good and evil
19. The Beatles' "Back in the __"
20. "Frankenfood" letters
21. Agitate
22. The Jetsons' pooch
23. "Downton Abbey" extras
25. Day of doom, in Scandinavian mythology
27. Milanese rice dish
30. Centre of many an orbit
31. Lincoln or Burrows
32. Offed, as a dragon
33. "Now __ seen everything!"
35. Nickname for Michigander from the Upper Peninsula
37. Human history's conclusion
40. Ancient amulet
43. Spam holder
44. Bib and tucker
48. Aurora, to the Greeks
49. Muscle spasm
51. Cap in a joint
53. Doomsday
56. Dallied (with)
57. Take the wrong way?
58. Mint product
61. Ready for an asylum
62. Trail markings
63. Catastrophic disaster
65. Discharge, as photons
66. Dr. Salk
67. Celine on CDs
68. 1920s art style
69. Evaluate
70. __ souci

Down

1. They get houses ready for showing
2. Kind of postage
3. Bitter regret
4. Quick __ flash
5. Cram for an exam
6. Radioactivity units
7. Less regular
8. Ecologists' concerns
9. Millennia
10. March king
11. Loosen
12. Prepare to streak
13. "__ Ace" (Burt Reynolds film)
18. Squall
22. Disturb
24. Bring down
26. Neighbor of Suriname
28. Morsel
29. Ab __: initially
34. Direct deposit abbr.
36. Bone head?
38. Concerning birth
39. Appetizer bowlful
40. Gets angry

41. Fancy dress garb
42. Religious recluse
45. Liverpool theatre
46. "Into the Woods" Tony winner Joanna
47. Dispirits
50. Non __ mentis
52. Texter's ta-ta
54. Can't say no
55. Lunchtimes, often
59. Org. with Spartans and Trojans
60. Like pie?
63. Grammy-winning Steely Dan album
64. They are 3 ft. long

CRIMEBIT No. 58

The Lure

YOUR RATING /100

Deirdre Mcauley

To be good at this takes patience. To be one of those rape and stab individuals was a waste. Unenjoyable. Like rushing junk food because you know someone's going to judge you for it. Those guys always get caught. Those guys are described in newspapers as 'Always a weirdo.' No, to be good at this takes tenacity. Fortitude. Get to know your subject, become an expert. That way there's a thrill every time you saw them; the baiting, the lure, finally reeling them in. The wait is the cherry. Most people who do this, don't know that, rushing to get to an anti-climax.

If you've enjoyed the battle, well, sometimes you let your catch go. Let it live to struggle another day. Sometimes that's more satisfying, knowing that just one little tug can send someone over the edge, one late night vibration from a caller unknown. A little gift with a baby pink ribbon on the top step for their eye to fall on, brings all that control flooding back. You don't always let go of course. But sometimes. Then, when you catch sight of them, it's like finding a ten-pound note in an old pair of jeans.

? DID YOU KNOW ?

The first known literary female detective is considered to be Mrs. Gladden, created by Andrew Forrester in *The Female Detective* (1864). Set in Victorian England, the novel follows Mrs. Gladden as she employs her wit and observational skills to solve mysteries, challenging traditional gender roles and pioneering the depiction of women as capable investigators in fiction.

PUZZLE No. 58

Hunt Down

Across

1. Shortened word or phrase (12)

8. One's spouse's parents (7-2-3)

9. Trumpet flourishes (8)

10. Assistance (4)

12. Niche (6)

14. Groundless rumor (6)

16. Little devils (4)

17. Purchaser of goods (8)

20. Contemporary folklore (5,7)

21. Capability of winning a political race (12)

Down

2. Composite color (5)

3. Practice (8)

4. Diversified (6)

5. Medium having a pH less than 7 (4)

6. Affliction (7)

7. "The Guardian" or "Evening Standard" (9)

9. Physical strength (9)

11. Largest city in Quebec (8)

13. Up to the task (7)

15. Magnificent (6)

18. Centered among (5)

19. Complicated problem (4)

1
2
3
4
5
6
7
8
9
10
11
12
13
14
15
16
17
18
19
20
21

CRIMEBIT No. 59

Loser Come Back

YOUR RATING /100

Alexandra McDermott

On the twenty-seventh of February, 1951, Stephen Kenward vowed never to return to Austria. On the twelfth of December, 1956, he boarded a late Vienna-bound flight from Ciampino Airport in Rome with a light carry-on and a heavy heart.

It would be all right, he told himself. Six years is a long time. Things change; people move on. He probably wouldn't even recognize the place.

When he landed, the airport was encouraging. In his time, it had still been RAF Schwechat, Allied troops and occupation blues. Since being handed back to the civilian authorities, it had been transformed, like so much else in Austria: all things bright and shiny, post-war optimism in rising glass and concrete.

Such visible change was an illusion. Cosmetics. At the British consulate, the receptionist greeted him by name. In the taxi rank outside, the first driver's face he saw was the indomitable Herr Barragan, provider of many late-night rides back to his barracks. Stephen bypassed the rank and walked to the bus stop instead.

Six years. A long time in a man's life, but nothing in the lifespan of a grand old city.

Vienna, city of dreams. But some dreams are nightmares.

PUZZLE No. 59

People of Vienna

ALBAN BERG
ANTON WEBERN
ARNOLD SCHÖNBERG
BORIS KODJOE
CARL JULIUS HAIDVOGEL
CHRISTIANE HÖRBIGER
CHRISTINE BUCHEGGER
CHRISTINE OSTERMAYER
CHRISTOPH WALTZ
ERIC POHLMANN
FALCO
FRANZ SCHUBERT
FRITZ KREISLER
HEDY LAMARR
JOE ZAWINUL
JOHANN STRAUSS
JOHN BANNER
JOSEPH LANNER
KARL LEOPOLD VON MÖLLER
LILY GREENHAM
LOUIE AUSTEN
MISCHA HAUSSERMAN
SENTA BERGER
STEFAN ZWEIG

G	A	R	D	A	L	B	A	N	B	E	R	G	F	Z	C	N	G	C	B	V
O	N	L	I	L	Y	G	R	E	E	N	H	A	M	T	F	H	L	H	R	P
S	T	P	G	W	K	Q	M	C	K	S	L	A	Y	L	H	N	E	R	E	E
U	O	C	W	Z	N	L	Q	J	E	C	L	U	O	A	E	N	G	I	L	D
Z	N	D	H	E	Q	U	V	P	O	Q	B	Z	J	W	C	A	O	S	S	R
R	W	A	U	R	A	W	F	U	Q	R	L	P	O	H	H	M	V	T	I	E
G	E	E	M	O	I	Z	H	F	R	L	E	O	E	P	R	L	D	I	E	L
J	B	G	M	R	Y	S	L	F	M	T	J	A	Z	O	I	H	I	N	R	L
B	E	T	R	E	E	F	T	P	W	O	N	R	A	T	S	O	A	E	K	O
F	R	D	R	E	S	S	V	I	S	T	B	N	W	S	T	P	H	B	Z	M
V	N	K	V	H	B	H	S	E	N	O	B	O	I	I	I	C	S	U	T	N
F	L	W	E	M	K	A	P	U	R	E	D	L	N	R	A	I	U	C	I	O
C	R	W	N	J	T	H	T	I	A	C	O	D	U	H	N	R	I	H	R	V
X	Y	A	K	D	L	Q	S	N	W	H	S	S	L	C	E	E	L	E	F	D
O	V	I	N	A	P	K	M	Q	E	T	A	C	T	G	H	U	U	G	N	L
U	V	A	N	Z	O	I	Y	K	E	S	R	H	Z	E	O	M	J	G	E	O
G	K	N	J	D	S	Y	Y	F	F	R	V	O	C	E	R	H	L	E	T	P
Y	E	G	J	M	G	C	A	P	A	F	G	N	H	S	B	M	R	R	S	O
R	N	O	B	O	V	N	H	M	Z	S	G	B	B	T	I	Q	A	C	U	E
E	E	P	S	F	Z	H	A	U	E	F	K	E	H	O	G	M	C	Y	A	L
B	E	A	C	W	O	L	V	B	B	L	Z	R	P	J	E	Z	P	B	E	L
V	B	S	E	G	Y	Q	V	Y	F	E	J	G	F	R	R	H	Q	U	I	R
P	L	I	M	D	N	G	B	Z	C	T	R	V	G	N	Z	Z	G	R	U	A
X	G	R	E	N	N	A	B	N	H	O	J	T	R	H	L	A	F	J	O	K
F	T	H	I	J	O	H	A	N	N	S	T	R	A	U	S	S	Z	U	L	G

CRIMEBIT No.60

Fun House Murder

YOUR RATING /100

Cate McDermott

Here's a piece of free, unsolicited advice for you: if you're ever faced with the problem of how to get rid of a body you have somehow acquired, never mind how, do not, I repeat, do not, throw the corpse down the back of the Dark Smoky Mountains roller coaster.

I know, I know, it seems like the perfect cover. It could so easily be an unfortunate accident. Someone just slipped their seat belt and plummeted to their death, right? No one else has to be involved. But it just doesn't work out that way.

Especially if said corpse is still clutching a carnival games dart between his fingers.

WRITING PROMPT 6

'Do you believe in fate? Some guiding force which brings us all together, so that we may share certain moments together? A lot of people do, you know. I do . . . to a point.'

The man, known as "The Cutter", by most of the tabloids in the country, surveyed the man currently laid on his table. Stood to the man's left side and spread his arms wide over the stricken body. 'I'm going to remove the tape now. You may scream if you want. I'd enjoy that immensely in fact.'

He didn't like the name they'd given him. Probably started on social media by some scrote in his mother's basement. He wasn't a "cutter".

He was much more than just a "cutter".

They didn't know that, of course.

They would soon.

Scan to visit the CrimeBits Writing Space

PUZZLE No. 60

Drop Down

Across

1. Bodhrán beaters
8. Firm no
15. Very much
16. Arthur Sullivan opera
17. Armored contestant
18. Frosty's fear
19. Hide ___ hair
20. Photo ___
22. Actors speak them
23. Turtle-to-be
25. He was also known as Edom
27. Store in casks, as wine
28. "Jeopardy!" host Alex
30. Dessert list
32. Jacuzzi site
35. ___ Nui
36. Like a fair ball
38. A, as in Arles
39. Dodge
41. Arabian Nights name
42. "The Metamorphosis" hero
44. ___ volente
45. "Time to find out if you're bluffing!"
48. Above, in Bavaria
49. July third?
50. Big name in set theory
51. Did some fishing
53. Rest area?
54. Slalom obstacle
56. Many a "Star Trek" extra, briefly
57. Rich man
60. Digital lang.
61. Rook's cry
63. Bright green
65. Knack
69. No longer minding one's business?
70. Most fastidious
71. Sheath and shift
72. Takes steps

Down

1. Luxury hotel chain with an Indian name
2. S&P debut
3. Post-sauna refresher
4. Coin in Acapulco
5. Main meal
6. US West Coast's US 101, e.g.
7. Turkey abuts it
8. Opposite of hubs
9. Big day preceder
10. Scapegoats
11. Pull strings?
12. Commonly bruised bone
13. Super rating
14. A decapod has ten
21. Boiled dough balls
23. Internet brokerage company
24. Rock group?
26. Alpine runner?
27. Santa ___ winds
29. "The Crow" actress Ling
31. Original Olympics site
32. Windblown vegetation
33. Covert
34. Facial disguises
37. Bread with vindaloo
40. Seedy pubs
43. Summer mo.

46. Fez color
47. Finish the course?
52. Ambrosia
53. Former PM Johnson
55. Ritchson and Rickman
57. Dorkmeister
58. Abbr. after N. or S.
59. Belle's compagnon
60. Contributes
62. Negative one
64. __-on-the-Solent, Hampshire
66. Furry adoptee
67. Not quite S
68. Ave. crossings, sometimes

CRIMEBIT No. 61

Latency

YOUR RATING /100

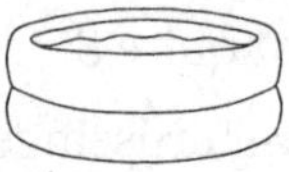

Samantha Metcalfe

Lawnmowers, birds chirping, delighted squeals from children in paddling pools. The sweet smell of cut grass in the air. This neighborhood was ideal, the house was perfect too. Admittedly, it was stretching their budget but they would make it work.

'I'll leave you to think about it and give you a call tomorrow.' The estate agent smiled warmly at them. 'I'm running late for another appointment, if you'll excuse me?'

'No need, we'll happily pay the asking price.'

'Excellent! We'll be in touch.' The family made their way down the drive, beaming as they took in the rest of the houses on the street. After strapping their daughter into her car seat, they started the engine.

He was watching from the window. Hidden behind the nicotine stained net curtains. He looked the type. Greasy comb-over, overhanging belly strained against a filthy t-shirt. Eyes fixed on them, he lit another cigarette and took a long satisfying drag. Licking his lips before exhaling slowly. He knew what he had to do.

PUZZLE No. 61

Hummingbird Lane

*He knew that side of the street like the back of his hand. He knew all six houses and who lived in them. He knew every family's name. From the clues, determine which **family** lived in what **number** house, as well as the **style** and **color** of the house.*

The Families

Gagnon - The picture-perfect family in a picture-perfect suburb.

Johnson - A neat two-story affair with white picket fences.

Lee - A couple that seemed too perfect, polished to a high gloss.

Martin - New kids on the block.

Tremblay - The type who mow the lawn in straight lines.

Wilson - They watched the world from behind lace curtains.

The Styles of Houses

Craftsman - A popular 20th century American home style.

Modern - Modernism is a spirit as much as it is a style.

Ranch - Popular with the booming post-war middle class.

Split-Level - Multiple levels separated by half-flights of stairs.

Tudor - Pitched gable roofs, elegant masonry and beams.

Victorian - Tiled roofs, painted brick and bay windows.

The Colors of Houses

Blue   Brown   Grey   Green   Pink   White

The House Numbers

104   106   108   110   112   114

? CLUES ?

1. The gray house is to the immediate right of the Victorian home but to the immediate left of the split-level.
2. The blue house is to the immediate right of the Johnson place.
3. The ranch-style home is to the immediate right of the brown house but to the left of at least one other house.
4. The Martins live to the immediate right of the green house but to the immediate left of the Craftsman-style house.
5. The Tudor is to the immediate right of the Wilson home but to the immediate left of the Lee house.
6. The modern house is somewhere to the right of the pink house but somewhere to the left of the Gagnon family's home.

	104	106	108	110	112	114	
Left							*Right*
Color							
Type							

Family	**Number**	**House style**	**House color**

CRIMEBIT No.62

The Eye of the Needle Stitching Club

YOUR RATING /100

Linda Millington

Five to three on a Monday afternoon may not appear to be the most obvious time for a murder, but that's when Barbara meets her untimely end. She is comfortably settled on her sofa, propped up on a large scatter cushion, purchased by her daughter, Steph, at one of her trips to the local car boot. The neighbor's tom cat purrs with contentment at her feet. Barbara's latest knitting venture, a winter scarf for some distant cousin, slips from her hands as she gently drifts off to dreams of happier times. The pensioner isn't the heaviest of sleepers; her night time slumbers are increasingly punctuated with violent bursts of coughing that burn her throat as if she's swallowed a razor.

The squeak of the back door is almost inaudible but it is enough to disturb her from her sleep. The moggy's flicking tail on his surrogate owner's feet alert her to the danger. The soon to be victim quickly realizes that the trespasser isn't there for a pleasant chat over a brew and slice of lemon drizzle.

'Now, let's not be hasty. Have you really thought through what you're going to do?'

PUZZLE No. 62

Knit Wit

Across

1. Country fellow from the Southern US
5. Diacritical mark
11. Army noncom
14. NYC stadium named after a tennis great
15. Place near each other
16. Salaried athlete
17. Knitting class thug?
19. South American river?
20. Schussing sites
21. Least restrained
23. Breeze of a class
24. Welcome token
26. Route
27. Irish public service broadcaster
28. Implement used by the Galactica knitting club?
32. Southern European
34. Short hopper?
35. Cleared off
36. Some stars have inflated ones
38. Kelly Clarkson's "All I __ Wanted"
39. Bowlers pick them up
42. "__ seen worse"
43. Beneficiaries of primogeniture
47. Really fine knitted goods?
50. Parasite's egg
51. Italian bubbly source
52. Symbol for element 172
53. Accepted procedure
55. It's in the stratosphere
58. Band boss
59. Antonym of downs
60. A tale of some knitting supplies?
63. Turned on, as a bulb
64. Kind of musical wonder
65. Battle of Lake __ (War of 1812 conflict)
66. French years
67. Periods of inactivity, as a ship in winter
68. Rise on hind legs

Down

1. Heavy-duty ropes
2. Put into quarantine
3. Picky person?
4. Rife with seaweed
5. Spring months
6. "Calling all cars" alert
7. PC part, for short
8. Hand-rolled cigarette, slangily
9. Port city of Norway
10. "Because of You" singer
11. Bed coverings
12. Steak throwaway
13. Dentate
18. Places where black-eyed Susans grow
22. Obsolete weaponry
24. Indochinese land
25. "Foucault's Pendulum" author
29. Dull and boring

30. "Not happening"
31. "... ___ he drove out of sight"
33. Checkpoint Charlie locale
37. Prizm manufacturer
38. Hardly bumpy
39. Egg flipper
40. Alternative to a thumbtack
41. Agent's clientele, perhaps
42. "___ complicated"
44. Impetuously, in a way
45. Nation of West Africa
46. Less compromising
48. County bordered by Kent and Hampshire
49. Engaged in litigation
54. Pop singer Leo
56. GI chased down by Jack Reacher
57. Island in the Inner Hebrides
58. Do-overs, in tennis
61. Mu ___ pork
62. Iceberg summit

CRIMEBIT No.63

Knit One Pearl One

YOUR RATING /100

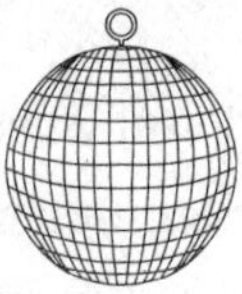

Donna Moore

'Four and two, forty-two . . . Seven and nine, seventy-nine . . .' Sylvia Abercrombie gave a deep sigh and spun her wheelchair expertly round to face the door. She couldn't bear Death Bingo a moment longer. The tiny squares of dancing brightness from the huge glitterball in the ceiling and the cheery sunshine yellow of the walls did nothing to lift her mood. Besides, if she had to watch Effie McCallum in her winceyette goonie and curlers prancing up to the front to pick up yet another prize, she wouldn't be able to hold her tongue. The woman had the luck of the devil. Sylvia tucked her own turquoise silk dressing gown more closely around herself and started to wheel herself over to the door.

'Legs . . . eleven.' The lugubrious voice of Albie Stark was drowned out by a chorus of half-hearted whistles. Sylvia smacked the big metal button that opened the automatic doors. 'Two and three, twenty-three.'

'House!'

Even if Sylvia hadn't recognized the cackling voice, the accusatory whispers would have given it away.

'Well done, Effie, hen. That's a wee tin of gravy granules for Effie, there. Now, we're on the pink card. Eyes down, look in. A line for a bottle of shampoo.'

EDITOR'S NOTES

'I love this opening. Something quite different than many of the entries to this competition and all the more appealing for it. "Death Bingo'" is a startling term and the only indication that something is amiss, set against the "glitterball" and the "cheery sunshine yellow of the walls." A clever uneasiness is created here by Donna Moore.'

PUZZLE No. 63

Death Bingo

*Maybe Sylvia Abercrombie is sick and tired of playing Death Bingo, but Effie McCallum and her friends are having a wonderful time! Players can win by completing lines of numbers on their boards. From the clues, determine which **player** won which **prize** with which bingo card **line**.*

The Players

Effie McCallum - She traded in gossip, her whispers carrying more weight than the local paper.

Clara Boyd - A regal figure who has been a war nurse, they said, and her stories of the Blitz were as riveting as they were chilling.

Agatha Davies - Quiet and unassuming, her life an open book of simple pleasures and long-forgotten dreams.

$ The Prizes

Bottle of HP Sauce - Named after London's Houses of Parliament, it's often referred to as "brown sauce."

Box of Barry's Tea - A golden color tea with a deep aroma and full bodied taste.

Jar of Branston Pickles - A sweet pickle first made in 1922 in the village of Branston near Burton upon Trent, Staffordshire.

Winning Line

Top Line Middle Line Bottom Line

? CLUES ?

1. The winner of the box of Barry's tea won on the middle line.
2. Clara Boyd didn't get a bingo on the bottom line.
3. The winner of the Branston Pickles was not Effie McCallum.
4. Agatha Davies didn't win the HP Sauce.
5. Effie McCallum won on the top line.

	Agatha	**Clara**	**Effie**	*Barry's Tea*	*Branston*	*HP Sauce*
Top Line						
Middle Line						
Bottom Line						
Barry's Tea						
Branston						
HP Sauce						

Player	**Prize**	**Winning Line**
________________	________________	________________
________________	________________	________________
________________	________________	________________

CRIMEBIT No. 64

Secret Bones

YOUR RATING
/100

Laurel Nicholson

His bones floated beneath the murky basement drain in my childhood house. My parents knew the bones were there too, but it was never mentioned or acknowledged. A silent understanding existed between us. A ghostly pact.

Years later I am haunted by a dream where I am the killer. Standing alone in my little-girl pajamas, I clutch a small gun in both hands. A tall stranger reaches out to grab me and I shoot him – for I am certain those bones are a man's.

PUZZLE No. 64

"Secret Bones"

BERETS	ENCORE	RECENT	SCENTS	SNEERS	STEREO
BRONCS	ENROBE	RECESS	SCONES	SNORES	STONES
CENSOR	ENTERS	RECONS	SCORES	SNORTS	STORES
CENTER	ENTREE	RESECT	SCORNS	SOBERS	STROBE
CORNET	ERECTS	RESENT	SCREEN	SORBET	TENORS
CORSET	ESCORT	RESETS	SECTOR	SOREST	TENSES
CRESTS	NESTER	RETCON	SENSOR	STEERS	TONERS
CRONES	ONSETS	SCENES	SERENE	STENOS	TOSSER

I	X	P	V	Q	Y	E	H	V	W	T	M	S	V	S	E	R	O	T	S	S
G	R	E	D	B	S	W	H	I	O	L	R	X	Y	J	R	U	W	D	Q	S
S	I	F	N	R	B	R	S	M	W	I	O	P	J	U	C	F	B	P	E	A
T	H	Y	F	E	E	O	W	U	Z	S	S	C	E	N	T	E	R	R	N	M
E	D	L	R	C	R	Q	T	K	E	S	N	O	R	T	S	Q	O	C	N	E
E	G	E	H	E	K	E	W	C	Z	Z	E	Q	K	C	M	C	S	R	I	U
R	T	M	S	S	S	H	S	L	S	B	S	X	O	S	S	E	H	E	D	W
S	X	T	E	S	E	Y	S	H	Q	E	O	R	D	Z	C	Z	N	S	A	G
A	M	V	M	P	G	N	Z	C	S	T	N	D	O	T	U	E	Q	T	G	B
J	N	X	X	G	I	F	O	N	E	S	Y	O	O	N	S	R	N	S	S	T
S	H	L	L	D	S	H	E	C	I	N	Y	R	R	O	E	R	E	T	S	G
E	R	C	U	C	T	T	W	D	S	O	E	B	T	C	N	T	E	C	S	U
N	E	O	K	D	M	I	E	K	H	R	Q	S	O	X	C	N	N	V	L	D
O	T	A	T	V	E	R	M	H	E	E	J	N	N	W	O	O	C	X	S	A
T	S	P	M	N	I	E	M	C	Y	S	S	E	E	S	R	E	S	E	C	T
S	E	L	T	X	E	S	S	I	S	O	A	E	R	B	E	K	R	M	O	Y
Y	N	R	X	S	X	S	X	T	F	D	R	R	S	N	O	R	F	G	R	S
O	E	Q	I	F	Q	O	E	K	C	M	A	S	P	S	Q	R	J	O	N	D
E	S	U	M	E	L	T	V	R	F	E	R	T	E	V	X	W	N	L	E	M
T	B	T	A	G	Q	N	O	C	T	E	R	N	T	R	O	C	S	E	T	T
K	N	O	E	C	E	N	S	O	R	T	A	E	U	I	S	R	E	T	N	E
U	T	W	R	S	B	Z	B	V	M	L	Q	C	C	F	I	W	A	H	L	S
Z	O	K	P	T	E	X	H	S	O	R	B	E	T	N	E	E	R	C	S	R
D	R	U	U	C	S	R	E	B	O	S	T	R	M	U	U	F	L	E	Y	O
J	B	O	L	F	H	B	B	M	T	P	R	U	O	N	S	E	T	S	U	C

CRIMEBIT No.65

Ms Fairchild

YOUR RATING /100

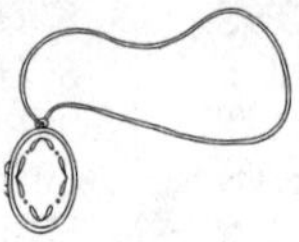

James Nisbet

Ms. Fairchild pushed open the ancient oak door. It swung smoothly open on silent hinges, exposing the body of Mrs. Billinghurst.

She was quite dead.

Her neck had been torn open, like a rotten tomato. There was a thick, red mulch spreading underneath her head and shoulders, and the tinny-sweet smell of spilled gore forced Ms. Fairchild to take small, shallow breaths through her mouth.

She looked up at the door, where her hand was resting and pulled it back with a snap. She reached into the pocket of her coat and took out her handkerchief, and rubbed away at where her hand had touched the wood, then she took out her white cotton gloves and slipped them on.

She knelt down by the body, careful not let the end of her scarf drop into the scarlet quagmire soaking through the beautiful Persian rug.

There was no need to check for a pulse, so instead she rifled through Mrs. Billinghurst's pockets.

One of them revealed a small pewter locket, and as Ms. Fairchild took it out to examine it, she heard a loud, male voice behind her.

'Don't move! This is the police!'

'Of course it is,' she sighed.

? DID YOU KNOW ?

One of the earliest crime films ever produced is *The Great Train Robbery* (1903), directed by Edwin S. Porter, following a gang of bandits who rob a steam train in the American West. It is also one of the earliest narrative films, using cross-cutting and other techniques to tell a cohesive story.

PUZZLE No. 65

Body Parts

Across

1. MP's quarry
5. "Divine" showbiz nickname
10. Company whose business is picking up
14. Bartok or Lugosi
15. Carey who won a BSA for "Doctors"
16. Ridiculously Photogenic Guy, for one
17. Penelope Bridgerton's pinkie?
19. Too proper
20. Father of scholasticism
21. Big Pharma's wares
23. Standing invitation?
24. Part of the queen's parure
25. DJ's noggin?
27. Brief blowup
28. Bath tissue layer
30. Bonn bakery buy
31. The Beatles' __ Pepper
32. Grasshopper's critic
34. Foreign currency
35. British Red Cross donation from Papa Smurf?
38. Dealt in antiques
41. Star closer than Alpha Centauri
42. PC inserts
45. Common acid
46. Vim
48. This guy
49. Noel Fielding's humerus?
53. Citrus center in the US state of 55 Across
55. "Scarface" setting, for short
56. Valley
57. Wind god in "The Lost Hero"
58. Trellis piece
60. Rocket scientist's piehole?
62. "Sommes" is a form of it
63. Flap
64. Activity that involves touching
65. Sewer's union?
66. Fall shade with an American spelling
67. Many T-ball coaches

Down

1. Wears thin
2. Gradually with-drawing
3. Savvy sailor
4. Piece of cake?
5. Mangle
6. "Tales of a Wayside __"
7. Sum symbol, in math
8. Rosinante or Bucephalus
9. __ Gras
10. Person behind a strike?
11. Crazed
12. Sharjah or Fujairah
13. Modernize
18. Beat the air
22. Bantu language
25. "High School Musical" star Sanborn

26. Whacked weeds
29. Acclaim
33. Court TV sister station
34. It's under a foot
35. Rhine port
36. "EastEnders" role for Garey Bridges
37. Bound along
38. School fundraisers
39. Be like
40. "That's Life" singer Frank
42. Tostada platter in Mexican cuisine
43. Watered down
44. Breaks up
47. Donne deed?
50. Buffo or cantante
51. Ancient Mexican people
52. "__ the spreading chestnut tree"
54. Acted lovey-dovey
57. Suffix for a doer
59. Finished edge
61. Map abbr.

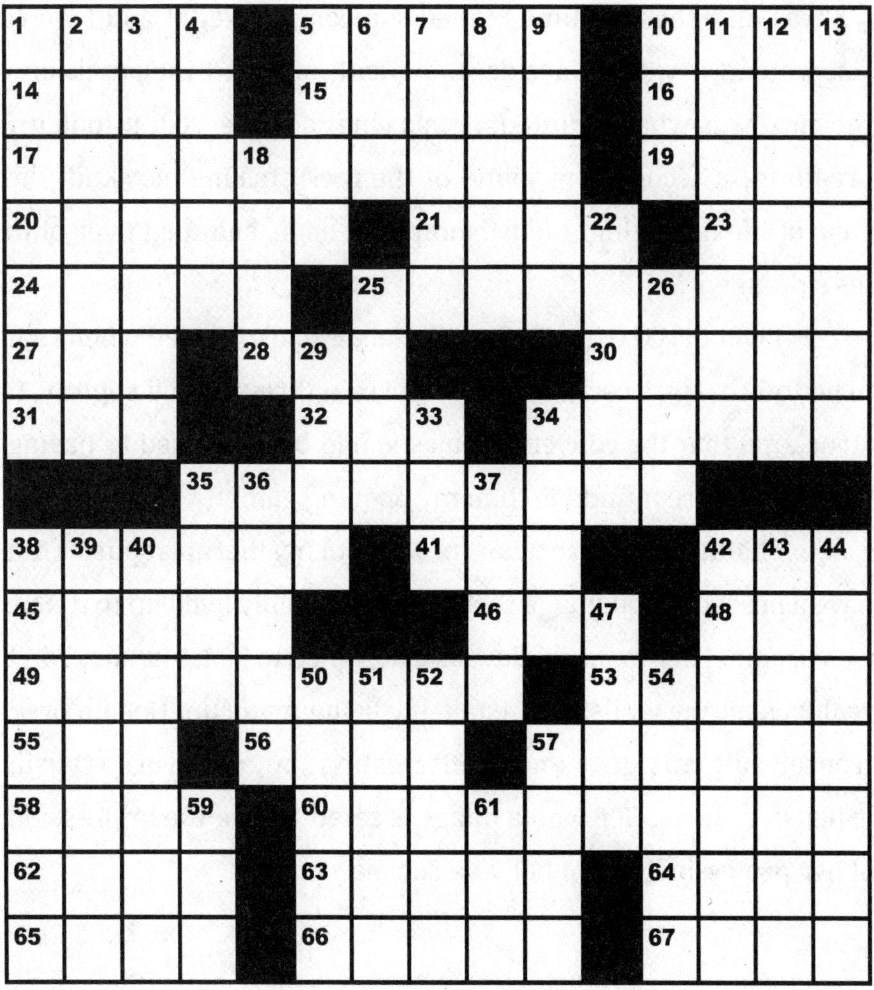

CRIMEBIT No.66

Bad Deads

YOUR RATING /100

Angela Nurse

'I was nine the first time I killed someone. I liked it and I won't pretend it was an accident. When I launched that rock into the air it was what I wanted, it was what he deserved. It took my breath for a second, the sound of the rock striking his skull, the gasp of life departing. I felt triumphant as he slumped over onto his side, silent.'

I wondered what Dr Evelyn Stalker had expected when I sat in her office. I was certain that what I said threw her off slightly. It struck me that the conversations she had become used to having were a lot more mundane than my opening gambit.

I hadn't been sure what to expect of my therapist but if I did have a preconceived image then Evelyn certainly lived up to it. She was pristine, her make up flawless, designed to look like she didn't really wear any whilst unmistakably being made up. Her tailored trouser suit was gray and uninteresting, but she wore stylish, expensive shoes. Her whole image created to give the impression of her profession, not of her as a real person.

HAVE YOUR SAY

What happens next?

Scan to visit the CrimeBits Writing Space

PUZZLE No. 66

Abnormal Psychology

Across

1. Twelfth month (8)
5. Edible kernel (4)
9. Onwards (5)
10. Legislator (7)
11. Unintentionally (12)
13. Post anew (6)
14. Decorous (6)
17. Interview - voices rant on (anag) (12)
20. Melodious (7)
21. Vast body of water (5)
22. Garden center item (4)
23. Fireproof material (8)

Down

1. Make a sketch (4)
2. Options (7)
3. Splendor (12)
4. Cricket team (6)
6. Up to the time (5)
7. Garden hose attachments (8)
8. Outstanding skillful act (12)
12. Ornamental band (8)
15. Guard (7)
16. Old Testament book (6)
18. Sensory receptor (5)
19. Connectives (4)

1
2
3
4
5
6
7
8
9
10
11
12
13
14
15
16
17
18
19
20
21
22
23

CRIMEBIT No. 67

Shadowland

YOUR RATING /100

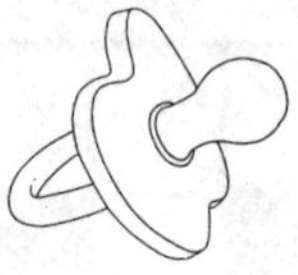

Randy O'Brien

Lach stared at the miracle in his hands.

The baby's eyes were round, and its toothless mouth moved silently in a sucking reflex. Lach assumed it was a girl, but the bald head and tight blanket left the detective clueless. He'd based his guess on the bracelet on the infant's wrist. The sparkle from the gold caught Lach's eye. He touched the small gold cross attached to the clasp and sighed. He knew how the next 24 hours would likely play out for the battling couple and this child. The investigation and possible outcome could affect the family for years.

Lach felt his blood rapidly pulsing through his body, and he was still breathing hard. His adrenal glands had dumped its powerful drug into his bloodstream and allowed him to move quickly enough to make the catch.

It had all happened so fast.

PUZZLE No. 67

Baby, Baby

BELL	BUNTING	DRIVER	OIL	TALK
BLUE	CAKES	FACE	POWDER	TOOTH
BOOK	CARRIAGE	FOOD	SHARK	
BOOM	CLOTHES	GRAND	SHOWER	
BOUNCER	CORN	JOGGER	SITTER	
BOY	DADDY	KISSER	SPLIT	
BUGGY	DOLL	LOVE	STEP	

K	H	N	J	X	C	A	R	R	I	A	G	E	L	U	I	K	T	I	J	G
E	K	E	U	L	B	K	U	L	G	S	S	E	Y	L	R	R	O	W	C	S
W	I	R	V	E	Q	Q	D	Y	I	B	K	Y	O	C	E	Q	J	O	J	K
N	V	D	A	Z	Q	R	O	T	V	D	I	D	I	E	C	B	R	H	B	R
P	Z	H	E	H	X	B	T	A	J	M	S	D	Y	R	N	N	N	I	J	N
W	M	O	J	J	S	E	A	N	K	A	S	A	R	P	U	Z	H	G	O	B
N	W	Z	B	X	R	D	R	O	F	P	E	D	V	E	O	S	K	J	H	D
Y	W	K	S	P	E	P	J	Y	U	U	R	Q	F	L	B	R	P	B	B	S
N	O	B	I	D	U	K	Z	W	N	C	P	C	D	V	N	H	T	L	L	H
C	T	B	B	N	R	O	F	R	R	S	C	T	T	Z	U	Q	P	M	I	R
J	C	H	Y	C	U	X	X	H	I	Z	V	Z	A	K	Q	L	P	L	W	T
L	M	P	P	F	C	K	U	U	Q	V	J	R	R	O	D	D	M	T	G	O
N	I	S	F	P	N	K	N	C	C	J	X	R	O	R	T	S	P	S	B	O
C	J	O	P	L	Z	D	G	A	Z	S	A	M	I	W	E	B	T	W	C	T
B	O	O	V	Y	O	X	X	G	L	R	H	V	O	U	R	D	E	N	L	H
D	U	D	G	L	L	O	D	S	W	F	E	R	O	E	W	P	W	T	J	Z
K	S	N	V	G	W	T	K	M	H	R	O	N	W	K	J	L	T	O	H	B
T	G	P	T	A	E	I	Y	S	I	C	L	O	T	H	E	S	M	Z	P	I
H	R	X	Z	I	F	R	P	E	T	S	H	Z	M	J	Y	C	V	N	C	E
U	A	G	F	G	N	U	I	K	Q	S	P	O	F	R	M	B	R	A	U	E
Y	N	G	Y	D	P	G	B	A	S	L	Y	D	E	T	O	C	K	S	C	B
Y	D	B	F	Y	Y	I	M	N	T	O	Q	X	V	O	S	E	T	A	P	U
Q	P	G	R	D	P	V	G	C	K	V	T	Y	M	C	S	A	F	Z	D	G
O	M	Q	O	T	A	O	Z	U	X	E	B	G	K	E	L	U	A	K	W	G
K	J	D	Y	G	K	G	Q	Y	R	R	W	Z	R	K	T	L	E	A	T	Y

CRIMEBIT No. 68

Turn Left For Eggs

YOUR RATING /100

Barry Penfold

It was a Wednesday and Eric had an itch. An itch that compelled him to resurrect his sign.

Stepping back, white paint and brush in hand, he determined that there should be a few touch ups. He got to work. Ten minutes later he was satisfied.

TURN LEFT FOR EGGS.

It looked good. Surely it would bring them in and allow his itch to be satisfied.

Approximately one hour later, he heard the crackle of vehicle tires on the gravel driveway. His sign was working. A collection of knives had been sharpened. Ropes ready. The smile on his face was for the new arrivals and his itch. It would be a killing day after all.

WRITING PROMPT
7

There's something about being eleven years old and having no real say over what you do with your life. You can scream IT'S NOT FAIR all you like, but it means nothing to your parents. Strike that, she only has one parent now. No matter what her mum thinks, there's no way she's calling him dad. He can't just show up when she's aged nine and expect to replace her real dad.

It doesn't matter that she doesn't see him anymore. That he doesn't seem interested. He's still her real dad.

Only, she can't find him now.

She's scared she never will.

Scan to visit the CrimeBits Writing Space

PUZZLE No. 68

Get Ova It

Across

1. Trinidad and __
7. Kinda
10. Java can be found in it
14. Graphics machine
15. Surname for the Scottish King of the Gypsies
16. What trotters do
17. Bluff
18. Easily donned jumper
20. First part of an ovular quip
22. Lifted
23. Fiesta food
24. Debate sides
27. Call on
29. "Chicago" star Richard
33. Dreamland acronym
34. Posh party
36. Cardboard tube, say
38. Second part of an ovular quip
41. Manga series about gaming
42. Lady Catherine de Bourgh, to Mr. Darcy
43. Boxing Day's mo.
44. Hindrance
45. Radio Times staff
46. Last name shared by Hedley of the navy and Henry of the clergy
47. Penury
50. When compared to
53. Last part of a hilarious ovular quip
59. Fraternity members
60. Lilliputian
61. __ Beach, Florida
62. Means to excommunication
63. Achieve
64. Peppa Pig or Kipper, for short
65. Demolitionist's letters
66. Crimson garments worn by Foot Guards

Down

1. Petty clash?
2. Khayyam of Persia
3. Make quiche, e.g.
4. Active causes
5. American insurance giant
6. Prefix meaning "straight" or "correct"
7. "Based on that..."
8. Private response?
9. Bay of Acre port
10. Augustine's "The City of God," e.g.
11. Lay by
12. Fruity desserts
13. __ Lingus
19. Hampshire team nicknamed "Pompey"
21. Brain holder
24. Appeals to a higher authority?
25. Repeat showing of a program
26. Alpha's opposite
28. Chef's mix-up?
30. Get away
31. Sega Mega Drive button

32. Vertical
34. Non-___ (food label)
35. "That's nice!"
36. Pieces on a chess-board
37. Do a part?
39. Joined up
40. John Donne Memorial, et al.
45. Fit, but just barely
46. ___ Berry Farm of Buena Park, California
48. Hosp. diagnostic tool
49. Antonym for absorb
51. Luau performances
52. West of "Blue Peter" or Carey of "Coronation Street"
53. Pseudo butter
54. Claudius' successor
55. Fails to exist
56. Johnny ___ ("Point Break" character played by Keanu Reeves)
57. ___ and Earlsferry, Fife, Scotland
58. Bogs
59. Lowest army rank

CRIMEBIT No. 69

The Copycat Murder

YOUR RATING
/100

David Potter

No one needed to force down-to-earth Doreen Ramsbottom to concede that finding a dead body in her rhubarb patch was not an everyday occurrence. She always suspected there must have been a good reason why her crop was so lush it won a special prize in the annual village show. But discovering the source of her unusually fertile soil had been a bit of a shock, even if she remained unmoved by the identity of the owner of the remains. Indeed, the retired librarian was more concerned about the possibility of her win being declared null and void by the organizing committee for a technical breach of the rules. For the question being asked was whether she was responsible for growing the rhubarb, or if the credit should go to the late, but very nutritious, Jack Armitage.

PUZZLE No.69

Garden Parties

Doreen Ramsbottom was stunned to discover the body of Jack Armitage in her rhubarb patch. Even more shocking were the five other bodies found in five other gardens in Bognor-on-the-Sea. Five souls, bound by their love for gardening, hid behind pruned hedges and well-tended plots. From the clues, identify which ***gardener*** *found which* ***victim*** *among what* ***plants****.*

The Gardeners	**The Victims**	**The Plants**
Nigel Cardiff	Cressida Bertram	Lavender
Agatha Grimsby	Archibald Dover	Roses
Asda Swindon	Rafe Laurence	Phlox
Bernie Camden	Edmund Lysander	Geraniums
Brixton Kensington	Fraser Digby	Delphinium

Gardener	**Victim**	**Plant**
____________	____________	____________
____________	____________	____________
____________	____________	____________
____________	____________	____________
____________	____________	____________

? CLUES ?

1. The five murder victims are: the one who was in the phlox (who wasn't Archibald Dover), Rafe Laurence, the one found in Nigel Cardiff's garden, the one who was found in the roses, and Fraser Digby.

2. Edmund Lysander was found in Bernie Camden's garden. Archibald Dover's body was found in Asda Swindon's garden.

3. Brixton Kensington didn't grow the geraniums.

4. Nigel Cardiff grew neither geraniums nor lavender. Frasier Digby was not found in Agatha Grimsby's garden.

	Agatha	*Asda*	*Bernie*	*Brixton*	*Nigel*	*Delphinium*	*Geraniums*	*Lavender*	*Phlox*	*Roses*
Archibald										
Cressida										
Edmund										
Fraser										
Rafe										
Delphinium										
Geraniums										
Lavender										
Phlox										
Roses										

CRIMEBIT No.70

Dead to the World

YOUR RATING /100

David Potter

Christmas Day; 7.30am

'Police. What is the nature of your emergency?'

'Someone's been stalking me,' said the caller, his voice quavering on the edge of panic. 'And now there's a car I don't recognize parked in my drive with the headlights full on and the engine running.'

'Is there anyone with the car?'

'What? Please send someone,' said the man, his voice now reduced to little more than a pleading whine. 'I've got a bad feeling about this.'

There was a loud bang like the sound of a car or motorbike backfiring.

'Oh God, no!' he moaned.

Then silence.

'Caller? What's happening caller?'

PUZZLE No.70

Bang Galore

BANG	CLANK	DRIP	HISS	MUMBLE	RATTLE	SNIFF	WHAM
BEEP	CLATTER	FIZZ	HONK	PLINK	RING	SPLAT	ZING
BURBLE	CLICK	GROAN	HOOT	PLOP	ROAR	SQUEAK	ZIP
BUZZ	CLINK	GROWL	HOWL	POOF	RUMBLE	SWOOSH	ZOOM
CACKLE	CRACKLE	GULP	HUSH	POP	SCREECH	THUD	
CHATTER	CRASH	GURGLE	JINGLE	POW	SHUFFLE	THUMP	
CHIRP	CREAK	GUSH	KNOCK	PUFF	SIZZLE	TOOT	
CHUG	CRUNCH	HICCUP	MOAN	PURR	SLURP	VROOM	

Y	J	V	C	B	C	L	I	N	K	P	Q	V	D	W	E	L	K	C	A	C
M	Q	E	L	Z	L	E	Y	J	F	S	N	X	S	E	H	P	U	F	F	Y
O	K	B	A	U	I	L	K	X	X	J	G	X	T	P	V	D	M	G	A	E
A	U	E	T	F	C	K	R	A	O	R	S	F	A	O	U	N	I	W	U	F
N	X	B	T	O	K	C	G	S	L	E	M	G	E	L	F	C	Z	W	U	P
R	J	A	E	I	Y	A	N	X	X	C	O	A	L	P	O	U	I	I	H	L
B	L	N	R	T	V	R	I	S	G	S	O	J	Z	I	N	G	V	Y	P	I
E	L	G	R	U	G	C	R	I	O	C	R	H	Z	N	S	P	L	A	T	N
C	Y	F	F	I	N	S	G	F	Y	Z	V	T	I	H	P	L	U	G	O	K
C	R	M	D	I	G	W	U	R	M	D	Z	H	S	Z	M	Z	P	R	A	K
R	B	A	V	A	E	S	A	T	O	O	T	U	B	C	Y	I	X	O	T	X
U	Y	H	S	U	H	T	F	M	U	A	G	D	B	U	R	L	J	W	S	M
N	T	W	F	H	T	I	N	N	P	U	N	S	Z	D	M	U	L	L	U	S
C	X	I	H	L	Q	G	S	D	H	L	M	L	C	Z	G	T	M	I	V	Y
H	Z	P	E	I	P	P	D	C	L	O	D	W	X	R	S	Q	N	B	R	H
Z	K	A	E	R	C	A	I	A	M	U	D	O	W	Q	E	P	Q	W	L	I
I	N	H	M	O	O	Z	T	E	W	D	C	H	U	B	P	E	O	T	D	E
S	O	D	B	I	S	U	K	E	D	H	H	E	M	O	K	C	C	H	N	D
X	C	H	N	N	D	N	L	W	I	D	A	H	W	T	P	D	A	H	E	E
I	K	S	Q	K	X	G	I	R	M	K	T	I	G	Y	T	L	A	L	L	K
W	I	O	N	X	N	L	P	U	P	S	T	C	H	V	U	L	F	B	Z	H
F	O	O	P	I	K	A	M	B	E	L	E	C	Q	O	F	F	R	V	Y	T
A	H	W	J	Y	Q	B	L	S	E	U	R	U	Y	O	U	U	C	R	O	P
H	I	S	S	I	L	T	E	C	B	R	G	P	R	H	B	S	H	O	U	O
E	Q	P	L	E	E	F	V	S	L	P	L	I	S	J	A	T	H	U	M	P

CRIMEBIT No. 71

The Violent Rain

YOUR RATING /100

Fiona Quinn

Developing your mask is a breeze. The trick, however, is holding it in place. If other inmates or, God forbid, the wardens see your face, then you are buggered. Shafted. Ask me how I know. Well, only last Tuesday, Didier slumped on the dirt in the soft April rain, his massive ham arms clasped around his legs, sobs shuddering his body as grief enveloped him, advertising his soft underbelly to everyone in the exercise yard, despite my attempts to haul him upright.

'Get up. Keep vigilant, like a meerkat, eyes and ears working overtime.' But maybe my French wasn't as good as I thought, because he sure as hell didn't take it in. Souls don't hang around here; not even ghosts choose to haunt this prison, so you must protect yours always.

Didier didn't stay sharp and guard his soul. The storm ensured the yard was empty. Big, heavy splats fired down, bouncing back up, carrying red mud with every drop. He lay pounded by the rain, shanked with a filed down chunk of plaster from the wall in B corridor. Shafted. They killed my one friend. But don't worry, I've got my mask in place and a plan.

PUZZLE No. 71

Stormy Weather

Across

1. Imprisonment (13)
8. 1479 meters (4)
9. Allowed in (8)
10. Indoor court sport (10)
12. "Monsters, Inc." job (6)
14. Reply (6)
15. Lexicon (10)
19. Enquiry (8)
20. Require (4)
21. Extremely pale (5,2,1,5)

Down

2. Annoyance (8)
3. Every seven days (1-4)
4. Book division (7)
5. Caribbean dance (5)
6. Gives away (7)
7. Roasting appliance (4)
11. Proximity (8)
13. Examine afresh (7)
14. Balkan republic (7)
16. Porcelain (5)
17. Daily meal (5)
18. Impetus (4)

1
2
3
4
5
6
7
8
9
10
11
12
13
14
15
16
17
18
19
20
21

CRIMEBIT No.72

When Death is the Day Job

YOUR RATING /100

Deborah Rayner

The sex was, at best, sub-optimal, and Louise Jepson felt cheated. What was the point of the bloke being hung like the ox tongue in Brannigan's Butcher's window when he didn't have the first clue what to do with it? The guy looked like Harry Styles and gave off all the right vibes, but he was just as useless as the rest of them. It was a trade description travesty of the worst kind. She'd been had and not in a good way.

Louise re-read the WhatsApp message Diane sent to the St. Michael's Church choir group:

'Just seen Louise Jepson heading into the boys' toilets with the new caretaker. She's old enough to be his mother. Is this the kind of person that should have the solo soprano spot?'

Louise couldn't dispute the facts Diane laid out. To be truthful, she didn't want to. At forty-two and with more than a passing resemblance to Kylie, Louise relished being the new cougar on the block. It wasn't just the sex that was a bad idea. Killing him afterwards wasn't her best plan either. Still, when death is the day job, getting away with murder should be easy.

PUZZLE No. 72

St. Michael's Choir

The St. Michael's church choir has been practicing for their upcoming spring concert. Five of the choir members will be performing five different solos. Each choir member sits in a different section of the choir. From the clues, determine which ***choir member*** *will perform which* ***hymn****, singing in which* ***part****.*

The Choir Members

Cadence Capricio
Scherzo Molto
Harmony Courante
Melody Barcarolle
Rubato Fudge

The Hymns

"Adoro Te Devote"
"Come, Holy Ghost"
"Salve Regina"
"Parce Domine"
"Lo, How a Rose E'er Blooming"

The Vocal Parts

Soprano Bass Alto Tenor Second Soprano

Choir Member	Hymn	Vocal Part
______	______	______
______	______	______
______	______	______
______	______	______
______	______	______

? CLUES ?

1. Melody Barcarolle will perform the solo in "Parce Domine" and Harmony Courante has the "Come, Holy Ghost" solo.
2. Rubato Fudge isn't a tenor.
3. The five choir members are: an alto (who won't be singing "Come, Holy Ghost"), someone who will sing "Salve Regina", Cadence Capricio, a bass, and someone who will perform "Lo, How a Rose E'er Blooming."
4. Cadence Capricio is not the tenor or the soprano. Scherzo Molto isn't the member who will sing "Lo, How a Rose E'er Blooming."

	Cadence	*Harmony*	*Melody*	*Rubato*	*Scherzo*	*Alto*	*Bass*	*2nd Sop.*	*Soprano*	*Tenor*
"Adoro"										
"Come"										
"Lo,"										
"Parce"										
"Salve"										

	Cadence	*Harmony*	*Melody*	*Rubato*	*Scherzo*
Alto					
Bass					
2nd Sop.					
Soprano					
Tenor					

CRIMEBIT No.73

Cut Swiftly

YOUR RATING /100

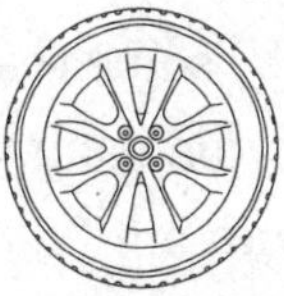

Callum Reid

Friday night started with a teenager being thrown into traffic. A sequence of startling noises – one following immediately after the other – cut through the ambient buzz of the street.

The explosive, far-too-late blast of a car horn.

Tires screeching against tarmac.

The sharp whack of bone on bonnet.

Finally, the screaming.

PUZZLE No. 73

Traffic Jam

Across

1. Acrobat's wear
8. Celebrated a birthday
15. Very far from
16. One of the Twelve Peers of Charlemagne's court
17. Where inconsiderate chauffeurs drive?
19. "Fifteen Miles on the __ Canal" (Pete Seeger song)
20. __ Lanka
21. "__ made a huge mistake"
22. Prepare to drive
24. Prime time?
26. Les Coker's wife on "EastEnders"
29. Financial gain from sales of a highway divider?
33. Appley Bridge railway station code
36. Hairstyle
37. Ne __ ultra
38. "__: The Story of Father Damien" (1999 biopic)
40. Like some seals
43. Leyton band, __ Maiden
44. Bolivia's capital
46. King of Castile
47. The act of clearing up a traffic jam?
51. Miliband and Sheeran
52. Lanchester of "Bride of Frankenstein" and "Willard"
53. "Cosmos" creator Carl
57. Sacha Baron Cohen's __ G
58. End of a theory
61. Roman known as "Sapiens"
62. Where to pull a car over and have a bawl?
67. More like a lion's pelt
68. Shakespearean lady killer?
69. Nuns
70. Rascals

Down

1. Not yet fulfilled
2. Bete __
3. Art film, often
4. Ancient hymn
5. 2006 coming-of-age rap film
6. Shad delicacies
7. Way in or way out
8. Seemly
9. Falafel condiment
10. David Llewellyn novel of '06
11. Assiduous attention
12. Bustle or fuss
13. South Korean automaker
14. Adjourn
18. Absolute
23. Quarter of a bushel
25. Everyday pest
26. Raft operator
27. Make smile
28. Rumpled
30. English-Albanian singer __ Lipa
31. Frequent Van Gogh subjects
32. Sgt.'s inferior
33. Ammonia derivative

34. Read studiously
35. Unions
39. She sang "Imagine" on her album "Warzone"
41. "Thank U, Next" singer Grande, for short
42. Some 100-year-old autos
45. American carrier name until 1997
48. Dame __ Melba of opera
49. Engineless plane
50. Mother-of-pearl sources
54. Rankin who plays Sheila the She-Wolf in "GLOW"
55. Maldives feature
56. Bad ideas
57. Dahlia in Wodehouse novels, e.g.
59. Hide
60. Speck of dust
62. Aaron, Alban and Julius, briefly
63. Yes, in Japan
64. Plaints of pain
65. Hospital depts.
66. __ -ching!

CRIMEBIT No.74

Lady Killer

YOUR RATING /100

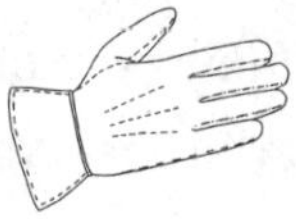

Reilly Reaghan

As she exits the subway, the draft slides icy fingers down her neck. Pulling her scarf over her nose and yanking her leather gloves from her pockets, she leaps backwards as a double decker rushing home to the depot splashes freezing puddle water at her.

Ducking her head, she strides off in the opposite direction. Sharp rain needles the street. A gaslit sign promising 'alcohol' fizzles and goes out. An unseen shutter rattles and clangs into its housing.

A sudden lull of the wind as she approaches the corner sends the stench of burning cigarette ends into her scarf. She holds her breath till she's past the pub. All she hears are her heels clicking on the uneven pavement.

And the hollow quickstep of a second pair of feet.

Flat shoes. Quick. Sneaky. Following her.

Following her?

The wind picks up. She strains to hear, won't risk looking back. A side glance into the wing mirror of a car, parked at the curb, confirms it.

There's a man.

And he's closing the gap.

EDITOR'S NOTES

'A gentle sense of foreboding in this opening. The action is slow at first, but we're building to something. I want to get there quicker, but the writer isn't going to give me that satisfaction. I have to work and wait for what's coming. I like that. We can picture the scene, place ourselves in the character's shoes, as the writer is allowing us to.'

PUZZLE No. 74

Trail Boss

Across

1. Fergie's first name
6. Employ a Singer?
9. Detective Arsène
14. Make a copy
15. "Alice in Wonderland" party drink
16. Habituate
17. Trail Toto and Lassie?
19. Mass units
20. Radiation, for one
21. Introduce
23. Tribute
24. Females that may be fleeced
26. Benefit from
27. Trail Lonsdale Belt competitors?
32. Delivery person?
35. Deposit eggs
36. Mange curer
37. Belgian bun topper
38. Dreidel, for one
39. River seen from the Eiffel Tower
41. G-man or T-man
42. Wrap for RuPaul
43. Dormitory weapon
44. Follow the money trail?
48. Article for a señorita
49. Arboretum specimen
50. Route-finding gizmo
53. Country band with the 1985 album "40-Hour Week"
57. Sand in "A Song of Ice and Fire"
59. Blues, for example
60. Trail a brown delivery truck?
62. Light metallic sound
63. Londontown trio
64. Appellations
65. Wastes produced from refining ores
66. Little, like laddies
67. "Everything's Coming Up Roses" show

Down

1. Poor sap
2. Meant to be heard
3. Busman's beat
4. Sister of Dido in myth
5. Mr. Pricklepants in "Toy Story 3," e.g.
6. Paved, in a way
7. Skull session?
8. Mud dauber, for one
9. "Just watch me"
10. Like Calvin Klein's CK One
11. Childish whine
12. Laundry room appliance
13. Grass house
18. Big name in Scotch
22. Red variety of corundum
25. Helpless performance?
27. Be a glutton, say
28. Customary manner
29. Dark forces
30. Jean of "The Da Vinci Code"
31. Agitated state
32. Go through carefully
33. Taiwanese PC maker
34. "Mi __ Loca"

38. Site of the phalanx bone
39. Like indirect glances
40. Level edges?
42. Gothic novelist Stoker
43. American shampoo brand that was once pearl-green
45. Exponential operation
46. Natural gifts
47. Blackmailer's words
50. Crotchety sort
51. Speaks (up)
52. Out of line
53. Tour bus gear
54. Breather
55. 17+ million square miles of the earth
56. Several
58. Gone
61. Gender-neutral pronoun

CRIMEBIT No.75

Gilding the Lizard

YOUR RATING /100

Robin Richards

They wouldn't let me wash her blood from off my body.

I was forced to sit in that overheated room feeling stained and grubby. Contaminated, violated even. If I'd even known the woman it might not have been quite so bad.

They'd taken my clothes away. All of them. Evidence they said. But they returned my trainers, minus the laces of course. There were no drops of blood on them to spoil their pristine whiteness. Of course not, I'd been barefoot when she died.

PUZZLE No. 75

True Blood

BANK
BATH
BROTHER
CELL
CLOT
COVENANT
CULTURE
CURDLING
DIAMOND
DONOR
DROP
FEUD
GROUP
HOUND
LINE
MONEY
OATH
ORANGE
PLASMA
PLATELET
PRESSURE
PUDDING
RED
RELATIVE
ROOT
SAMPLE
SAUSAGE
SHOT
SIMPLE
SPORT
STAIN
STONE
STREAM
SUCKER
SUGAR
TEST
TIES
TYPE
VESSEL
WORM

J	R	A	Z	P	R	E	D	V	B	W	H	B	L	S	S	S	G	Q	F	E
C	S	T	N	A	N	E	V	O	C	A	T	H	K	S	E	I	T	L	Z	L
I	D	R	K	A	S	M	T	S	H	O	T	O	J	Z	H	E	T	S	Y	L
L	R	O	Q	A	R	Y	V	H	D	M	S	H	D	E	V	O	I	C	G	N
G	O	P	I	P	K	V	E	A	Z	Z	Y	P	J	I	O	M	S	U	A	I
Q	P	S	U	H	P	X	H	G	G	Z	U	X	V	R	P	Z	A	L	P	A
G	N	O	O	Y	S	A	X	B	K	F	Y	R	W	L	U	R	U	T	Q	T
Q	R	U	F	I	F	N	T	V	Z	M	A	U	E	P	Q	W	S	U	T	S
G	N	P	N	J	J	A	K	T	R	E	U	M	Y	K	K	Y	A	R	X	N
D	F	M	Y	Z	X	Q	X	O	Q	I	L	P	I	N	N	I	G	E	E	P
X	B	I	C	K	P	N	W	R	H	W	Q	P	J	M	M	A	E	Z	I	L
Q	H	I	H	G	Z	P	W	L	Y	E	N	O	M	W	X	X	B	S	R	A
P	L	S	F	O	A	T	H	E	L	O	K	E	Y	A	P	T	Y	P	E	T
U	H	Q	H	Y	R	B	D	J	O	R	K	F	E	F	S	T	A	T	L	E
H	U	F	A	E	D	M	L	G	I	A	J	T	O	R	M	O	W	S	A	L
B	H	D	K	U	L	O	M	P	Z	N	C	Y	E	A	U	H	W	E	T	E
P	R	C	H	C	Z	E	N	A	W	G	G	N	I	A	L	S	M	T	I	T
H	U	O	R	N	J	C	S	O	G	E	I	Z	G	J	R	K	S	C	V	F
S	T	D	T	R	M	S	U	S	R	L	T	I	O	D	J	N	E	E	E	L
A	L	J	D	H	A	S	T	R	E	A	M	T	C	W	N	N	W	U	R	S
T	O	L	C	I	E	M	I	O	D	V	R	L	M	G	D	O	D	E	C	P
K	E	V	L	S	N	R	S	V	N	L	M	N	K	N	Q	C	M	M	Z	F
M	G	E	P	E	L	G	B	A	R	E	I	W	S	U	G	A	R	A	K	L
O	N	Q	Q	H	C	W	P	E	L	T	J	N	G	Y	Y	W	M	F	I	I
X	T	K	A	B	R	B	D	M	C	P	B	L	G	R	R	R	P	Y	H	D

CRIMEBIT No.76

And Then We Sever

YOUR RATING /100

May Rinaldi

His cologne invades my senses. My hands are bound. Not silk ties or satin cords; rough sisal rope. The constraints on my wrists tighten, biting into the flesh as I am hauled up until I swing freely, my shoulders wrenched; pain surges through my brain and blackness overwhelms me. I hear my screams echo round the room, no need for a gag, no-one to hear.

HAVE YOUR SAY

What happens next?

Scan to visit the CrimeBits Writing Space

PUZZLE No. 76

Fit to Be Tied

Across

1. Adoring Biblical trio
5. ___ around
11. Blobby substance
14. Partridge portrayed by Steve Coogan
15. "Absolutely, monsieur!"
16. One of a chair pair
17. Canceling a cable subscription
19. Red snapper on a sushi menu
20. Landing area
21. Nation bordering Lake Titicaca
22. Orion's ___
23. Motorcar
25. Off-the-wall remark?
27. Mr. Tumnus of Narnia, e.g.
30. Closet item featured in "Mommie Dearest"
35. "Dog Day Afternoon" BAFTA winner
37. "30 Rock" producer Michaels
38. Slugger?
39. Get tangled
42. "All for ___ ..."
43. Mug, say
45. Mammoth
47. Climbing device
50. Friend of Nancy?
51. Sensitive spot
52. Ship stowaways
54. Throw a line out
57. "The Big Fat Quiz of the Year" host
59. Pasture units
63. "Right you ___!"
64. It's in the hundreds for most sheets
66. Quilting gathering
67. Like an Arnold Palmer drink
68. Current event?
69. Dark
70. Hilltops
71. Cold shower?

Down

1. Apples, informally
2. "Thanks ___!'
3. Teri from "Tootsie"
4. Professor Jones in "Raiders of the Lost Ark"
5. Code for a Greater London sta.
6. Score more than
7. Practice
8. Quite the party
9. Castrato, e.g.
10. Understand, slangily
11. It's sometimes crashed
12. Administered by swallowing
13. Ignore
18. PC brain
22. Singer born Paul Hewson
24. One's double
26. Heartier
27. "Animal House" college
28. One place to hire a car at Heathrow Airport
29. "Gimme five!"
31. Stroked, in a way
32. Altar ego

33. Existential fatigue
34. Witherspoon who played Elle in "Legally Blonde"
36. Green with Grammys and a Brit Award
40. Flawless
41. Swinburne of "The Forsyte Saga"
44. Screen __
46. Pudsey Bear and Oscar Puffin
48. Quiver carrier
49. "Oh, goodness!"
53. Part of OOO or XXX
54. Many have meters
55. Flooring measure
56. Babe in the woods?
58. Vintage Olds motorcars
60. Totally botch
61. It means "within"
62. Bouillabaisse or burgoo
64. "No Scrubs" group
65. "Bad" from the start?

CRIMEBIT No.77

Time Keepers

YOUR RATING /100

Leslie Roberts

Martyn pulled up the collar on his tired old winter coat and trudged on even though he felt like the biting wind and teeming rain were cutting straight through to his very core. He was cold, wet and hungry but he pushed on regardless because he was a man on a mission. He needed credits, and he needed them now. And then he saw it up ahead, looming through the thick fog that shrouded the run-down city streets. A large tower block on the corner of Fourth Street, with only the lower floors lit up. Above the door he saw the familiar flickering fluorescent sign he'd seen so often before on other blocks. It read 'Time Bank'. He approached the huge timber door with trepidation and knocked firmly three times. A short second later a slot in the door at eye height slid sharply back and a pair of dark inquisitive eyes appeared. 'Whatdya want? If it's a hand out just clear off!' came the harsh shout. 'I'm here to sell my time,' Martyn replied immediately. The slot then firmly shut and the door swung abruptly open. Martyn found himself faced by a burly man.

? DID YOU KNOW ?

***Cain's Jawbone*, written by Edward Powys Mathers** under the pseudonym Torquemada in 1934, is one of the most challenging literary puzzles ever created. It consists of 100 pages that can be read in any order, and the reader must determine the correct sequence to solve six murders.

PUZZLE No. 77

Losing Time

Across

1. Like most people on Earth
6. Tasteless
11. Part of SNAFU
14. LuPone or LaBelle
15. Joby on "Strictly Come Dancing"
16. Bull session remark?
17. Jam on the way to see a Canadian prog rock band? (2 wds)
19. Permit no more
20. Huge star
21. Gold digger's quest?
22. Using a skillet
24. 2018 Christina Aguilera song
26. Red Hot Chili Peppers bassist
27. Last in a score of auditioners for Tails in "Sonic the Hedgehog"? (2 wds)
32. YouTube offering
35. Brief words?
36. Pronoun for two
37. Major load
38. Instruments of yore
40. Bit
41. Abbr. in division
42. Second Greek letter
43. Jittery
44. Result of a "Magnificent" ensemble cast getting poison ivy? (3 wds)
48. "Whiffenpoof" singers
49. Principal's staff
53. Pass along, as a present
56. "The X-Files" subjects
57. Something extra
58. "___ paid my dues"
59. Excellent mark for Royal Ascot contender? (4 wds)
62. For every
63. Mexico's Oaxaca, e.g.
64. Totally absurd
65. It has biceps
66. An American in Plano
67. Canasta holdings

Down

1. Easter month, at times
2. Iraqi's neighbor
3. "Don't fret!"
4. Team GB at the Olympics
5. Picayune point to pick
6. Ferryman of myth
7. "Life of Pi" actor Spall
8. "Bowwow" equivalent
9. ___ Mom ("American Pie" character)
10. Conceal
11. Prefix for both
12. Do a bank job?
13. Hanker after
18. Razzed or ribbed
23. Repeated word in "Fargo"
25. "Sands of ___ Jima"
26. Dandy mate?
28. Offspring of Uranus and Gaea
29. Espadrille insert

30. Things bowlers want
31. Penetrating look?
32. Chevy hybrid
33. Go way slow
34. Surfer guy
38. Float in air
39. People for whom a state was named
40. Cruel
42. City of Ulster
43. __ Liverpool (multi-purpose complex)
45. Balaenoptera borealis
46. Kind of proposition, in logic
47. Subdue with a stun
50. Union branch
51. Vogue
52. Some survey answers
53. Kelly on the telly
54. Oft-repeated modifier in a Taylor Swift hit
55. Tiny invader
56. James who sang "Mystery Lady"
60. Assessment
61. Top of a cup

CRIMEBIT No.78

Tommy's Art

YOUR RATING /100

Rodney Rogers

I'm drawing this dead dog, it's pit bull or Rottweiler, whatever it's a lot of dog. It's just this bloated mass – guts hanging out that's slumped up against the curb across the street from Suzy's American Dream Car lot, downtown Los Angles. All I got is this Burger King wrapper and a golf pencil to sketch with. But it's pretty good. Somebody found it thirty years from now, they might say the kid had some talent. They'll never see anything else with my name on it. Sometimes time, place, and talent don't match up. That's what my Pop always used to say. That and 'The cream don't rise to the top.' Seems a pretty bleak thought on my 30th birthday. But there we are. My birthday presents are this bullshit drawing of this dead ass dog, "Cum on Feel the Noise" by Quiet Riot playing low on my radio – a throwback from '83 – released, you guessed it on my sixteenth birthday. The kismet is getting thick. Present number three and ruining the first two is my boss – husband of the boss, that'd be Suzy, circling the car like a shark. He just bought this fabulous feast and is now taking a cigarette break. I knew I was in trouble when he sprung for it. That's when the lump in my stomach started. Now it's all mixed up with a Whopper with cheese. He laid out the plan before he took this dramatic pause of a cigarette break. Like he forgot this is how he taught me – 'Step three – put the customer on ice.' Dan's the kind of asshole you'd find selling used cars anywhere, but in LA, he's a special kind of brand. An aging never-was that's given up on acting class, but not plastic surgery. His big theory is that he's too tall to get work with the likes of barely 5 foot superstars. Inject the name here. Mel Gibson, Tom Cruise, Bruce Willis – though I've seen Bruce. He's tall. Everybody in the town's got a plan, and when their big movie dreams dry up they tend to move toward even more desperate fare. Now after *Pulp Fiction* came out, everybody thinks they're good at being a criminal. Fucking car salesman. Guess I'm one of them.

PUZZLE No.78

The Car Lot

Across

1. Lunch-counter specialty (12)

8. Relating to a country's leader (12)

9. Underground chambers (8)

10. Outer limit (4)

12. Short or moderate time (6)

14. Aden resident (6)

16. One of 24 in a day (4)

17. Made an exit (3,5)

20. Ones whose opinions are based on reasoning (12)

21. Certain drawing (6,6)

Down

2. Long-legged wading bird (5)

3. Towards sunrise (8)

4. Conclusion (6)

5. Earthenware vessels (4)

6. Crumpet cooker (7)

7. Making less burdesome (9)

9. Potentially lethal vehicle (5-4)

11. Sanction (8)

13. Largest city in Texas (7)

15. Cold dishes (6)

18. Eye nerve (5)

19. Indian ascetic (4)

1
2
3
4
5
6
7
8
9
10
11
12
13
14
15
16
17
18
19
20
21

CRIMEBIT No. 79

Billie Joe's Story

YOUR RATING /100

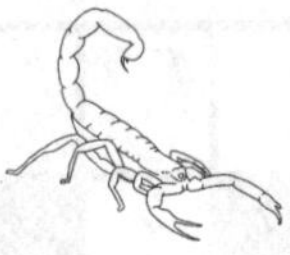

Claire Rozario

Eight-year-old Billie Joe Morton studied the scorpion on his desk. He flipped it onto its back with a pencil and moved it closer to the trap of sunlight, exposing an iridescent pale blue underbelly. He gently prodded its abdomen and then with the magnifying glass from his science kit, scanned its deadly black stinger. Billie Joe pushed the pencil underneath and lifted it above the plastic container. As he did so, its tail gave a sudden, violent jolt and the scorpion fell to the floor. 'Mum, the scorpion's alive!' he yelled, eyes fixed on the scorpion's cold body as it scuttled across his foot. It began sweeping its stinger back and forth and then turned anti-clockwise and crawled up the inside leg of his jeans; it settled just below his knee. Billie Joe wanted to scream now but he couldn't hear his mother padding around any more and the radio had gotten louder. He badly needed her now. She would know what to do. She would take care of it.

His mother would not be coming. Today or any other day. Billie Joe heard the gunshot before he felt the sharp sting, and just before he went into anaphylactic shock.

WRITING PROMPT 8

He hadn't been born bad. He didn't think so, not now. He'd had plenty of time to think about his life and there wasn't anything he could pinpoint as a child. He'd been a little different, maybe, but not overly so. It wasn't like he would torture animals, or bully other kids.

He'd been . . . normal. That's all. Just a normal kid.

As normal as you can be anyway. Ordinary, nothing special. He wasn't bottom of his class, but he wasn't top of it either. He was, like seemingly everyone else he knew as kid, in the middle. Just drifting by.

When he'd met her, he'd been the same. He was sure of it.

She was the one who had changed him.

Scan to visit the
CrimeBits Writing Space

PUZZLE No.79

Sting

Across

1. Charted
7. Publisher's imprint, on a US newspaper
15. Pleistocene epoch
16. "It's a Wonderful Life" role
17. Sting
19. Carries
20. Coffee blend
21. Rise
22. States
23. Grab onto
28. Make the cut?
30. Folks
31. Any aunt
34. Get back to work?
38. Cantata highlight
39. Sting
42. Old newspaper section, for short
43. Mercury's atomic number
44. "Au Revoir __ Enfants"
45. Clue category
47. Taste
49. Kingdom divisions
50. Where Al Yankovic bought a "Dukes of Hazzard" ashtray, in song
53. Idris of "Luther"
57. Fibula neighbor
59. Hot dog topping
60. Sting
65. Baloney
66. Formality
67. Southwest Florida home to Clown College
68. Outlaw hunters

Down

1. Hands, slangily
2. Sternutatory sound
3. "The Hunger Games" boy
4. Proof of pedigree
5. Flattery feeds them
6. Actor Benicio __ Toro
7. "I'm a doctor, not a bricklayer" doctor of "Star Trek"
8. Guinness and Douglas-Home
9. Waist wear
10. A&E system
11. Layer on a farm?
12. London lang.
13. Air hero
14. "__ Spiegel"
18. "__ Believer"
22. Bergman and Borg
24. Thunderous noise
25. "The cruelest month"
26. Hook's counterpart
27. Blanc and Rainier
29. One of mine Minecraft heroes
30. Comely
31. Reject
32. Rotgut liquor
33. Diary writing
35. I.M. who won a Royal Gold Medal in 2010
36. Lee in a director's chair
37. Einstein's "I"
40. Sap
41. Odin's heroic son
46. Some woodland deities
48. Meddling types

50. T.S. who said 25 Down
51. Rhymes of rap
52. Bat tree?
54. Mythomaniacs
55. Italian lawn game
56. Egyptian amulets
58. Jackson Five hairstyle
59. Harbach or Klemperer
60. Au __ (in gravy)
61. Inbound flight approx.
62. 8 1/2 x 11, for short
63. Thompson in "Fish Don't Blink"
64. Egyptian adder

CRIMEBIT No. 80

Mum, Unknown

YOUR RATING /100

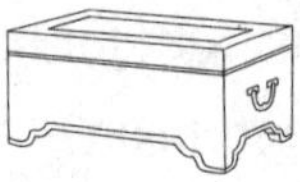

Sabine Sapia

'Such a tragic loss! Your mother was a pillar of our community.' The reverend's slimy voice was accompanied by his meaty hand on Sam's shoulder as if he did not want to support but weigh her down.

Like a warm embrace, her mother's voice floated through her mind, calling him a liar. Despair followed as unstoppable as the tide. Sam slipped away, snippets of whispered dialogue following her like vultures.

'. . . car . . . drunk . . .'

'. . . ran away with her money . . .'

'. . . orphans now . . . Kate only ten . . .'

The door to mother's study cut them off, and Sam stumbled towards the overstuffed armchair, sank to her knees in front of it and pressed her head into the pillow. She screamed and boxed until her throat was too hoarse, and her arms burned with exhaustion.

Sam slid to the floor, resting her cheek on the polished wood. Only then did she notice the box, dislodged from her mishandling of the chair. Inside rested a key on velvet.

A note, written on a torn map, nestled beneath: 'Friday, midnight, or your daughters will pay.'

? *DID YOU KNOW* ?

S.S. Van Dine, an American art critic and author, published *Twenty Rules for Writing Detective Stories* in 1928. These rules were intended to be guidelines for writing fair-play mysteries, where the reader has a fair chance to solve the crime along with the detective.

PUZZLE No. 80
Found Keys

Across

1. Kabuki props
5. Frets
11. "__ Brown You've Got a Lovely Daughter" (#1 hit of 1965)
14. Footnote word
15. Things squirreled away?
16. "__ never can tell"
17. Gloomy convention speech?
19. Stage help
20. Pioneering
21. __ generis
22. Fodder
23. Last film directed by Howard Hawks
26. Toast vessel
28. Headliner at the computer peripherals show?
32. "Black gold"
35. Certainly not often
36. Common basket filler
37. Air show stunt
39. Assuages
42. Bits and bytes
43. Pool covering, perhaps
45. Respected Smurf
47. Vote to kill?
48. Jingling attachment that holds Tinker Bell's car fob?
52. Length of yarn
53. Thankless one
57. Stinging insects
59. Ms. Piggy's one-word question
61. Stickpin site
62. Hawaii's __ Day
63. Part of Stuart Little's ATM?
66. Eyebrow shape
67. '60s Ford model in the UK
68. "Anybody __?"
69. Urgent call at sea
70. Bach or Strauss
71. A couple of bucks?

Down

1. Bran substance
2. US ambassador to the UN, 1961-65
3. Nervy prefix
4. Notices in the kitchen?
5. Canadian singer Carly __ Jepsen
6. Subzero, maybe
7. Dresses
8. Bellyache
9. Being
10. Compass dir.
11. Prehistoric Greek
12. Rakish fellow
13. Kept a lawyer fed
18. Japanese cultural center
22. Coastal gorge
24. En __ (in full court)
25. Mammal seen on Alaska cruises
27. Wane
29. Abounding in sea-weed
30. Pro __
31. "Dunkirk" event

32. One of five Norwegian kings
33. Evans in "Choose or Die"
34. Military science
38. Puts on the spot?
40. Husband, in Paris
41. Board game turn
44. Shadow site?
46. Acute or right
49. "Mikado" costume
50. "I quit!"
51. Got silver, as hair
54. Tell tale target?
55. Build a beehive?
56. Octogenarian, for one
57. "Ah, 'twas not to be"
58. "__ and Zero" (comic strip)
60. Puerto Rico, por ejemplo
63. Mil. officer
64. Article in a famous JFK quote
65. "The Wizard of Oz" state abbr.

CRIMEBIT No. 81

Time Waits for No Guy

YOUR RATING /100

Paul Smitham

He left the apartment and stood outside, looking left and right. He chose neither, he never chose. Surrounded by nothings and nobodies, he walked with his head in the clouds of a clear blue sky and acknowledged everyone and no-one, he smiled at a passing 'friend' and the shards pierced deeper and his heart wept tears that his soul would devour. An impossibly wide grin behind the mask, that was not him but something else, whispered in his ear.

'Keep walking, I will look after everything, I've always been here for you, I am your only friend, I will always take care of you, just keep on walking and I will keep on watching . . . I love you.'

His smile faltered and slipped but only for a moment, not enough to be noticed by those who ghosted by on their way to wherever their way was. He had a purpose now, he felt something shift within him, he was different, it was time again. He tried not to cry but a single tear defied him and left his cheek with a kiss.

HAVE YOUR SAY

What happens next?

Scan to visit the CrimeBits Writing Space

PUZZLE No. 81

Split Personality

Across

1. Rehearse (8)

5. Take a hike (4)

9. Caterpillar or grub (5)

10. Social position (7)

11. Individual characters (12)

13. As a matter of fact (6)

14. Aboriginal (6)

17. Sunny day feature (5,4,3)

20. British actor in "Sparticus" (7)

21. Brain output (5)

22. Negligible (4)

23. Up to Camelot standards (8)

Down

1. Heap (4)

2. Ditzy type (7)

3. Conveying from one place to another (12)

4. Ballistics shell (6)

6. Proof of innocence, maybe (5)

7. BAFTA winner for "Gandhi" (8)

8. Covering the interior of a room (12)

12. Ballot-box bungle (8)

15. Most pitch-black (7)

16. Nine and two (6)

18. All finished, as dinner (5)

19. Cinderlike (4)

1
2
3
4
5
6
7
8
9
10
11
12
13
14
15
16
17
18
19
20
21
22
23

CRIMEBIT No. 82

The Past Giveth. The Past Taketh Away

YOUR RATING /100

Rosie Sorenson

Here's the thing. You didn't do it on purpose. You're pretty sure about that.

But who would have faulted you if you had?

You'll never know.

What you do know is that they might be on to you. Thirty-seven years later – how is that even possible?

Your mum is no longer alive. She didn't want you to go to jail then; she'd hate it for you now.

Your beloved older brother, no longer alive, figured it out and felt bad for his part.

Who will protect you?

The remains were found three weeks ago at the bottom of the old quarry six miles out of town on a deserted oak-lined road where you kids used to swim in the summers. Recently drained to free up space for a new shopping center.

Cause of death? Questionable shotgun blast to the head, they said, though difficult to say.

Your brother had left it lying around.

He felt guilty about that for the rest of his life.

Only you know where it's been for the past 37 years.

PUZZLE No. 82

Shopping Centre

APOTHECARY
BAKERY
BAZAAR
FLORIST
BIG BOX
BODEGA
BOOKSHOP
BOOTH
BOUTIQUE
BUTCHER
CANTEEN
GARDEN CENTER
GROCERY
HABERDASHERY
HARDWARE
HOME IMPROVEMENT
LUXURY BRANDS
MERCANTILE
MILLINERY
OUTLET
PATISSERIE
PAWNBROKER
CHAIN
CLEANERS
COLLECTIBLES
COMMISSARY
CONFECTIONERY
DELI
DISCOUNT
DIY
ELECTRONICS
EMPORIUM
BEAUTY SALON
PERFUMERY
PIZZERIA
SOUVENIR
SPORTING GOODS
SUPERMARKET
SURPLUS
TOY STORE
WAREHOUSE

L	U	X	U	R	Y	B	R	A	N	D	S	E	H	J	G	S	X	D	X	X
W	U	G	D	B	X	U	V	L	P	Q	L	Q	M	C	E	P	V	Z	H	M
J	Y	H	A	Y	S	J	V	Z	H	I	N	C	F	L	M	I	Y	B	M	I
H	V	S	U	R	P	L	U	S	T	E	I	Q	B	I	L	R	U	T	E	N
K	P	D	C	F	D	H	W	N	E	G	Z	I	L	O	E	T	J	S	Q	O
A	I	X	X	L	M	E	A	T	M	O	T	L	T	C	C	Q	U	B	D	L
Y	Z	L	Z	H	L	C	N	B	S	C	I	E	O	H	X	O	I	K	R	A
T	Z	N	K	I	R	A	N	C	E	N	K	R	E	M	H	G	D	Y	W	S
S	E	K	T	E	C	I	V	L	E	R	G	R	A	E	B	K	T	R	T	Y
I	R	R	M	E	A	L	L	R	A	N	D	H	R	O	A	W	Z	E	S	T
R	I	A	I	H	L	O	Y	M	D	I	T	A	X	P	R	Z	I	M	D	U
O	A	A	C	U	C	T	R	U	S	I	W	E	S	F	F	V	F	U	O	A
L	H	Z	U	Q	D	E	U	C	D	P	J	X	R	H	J	N	F	F	O	E
F	L	A	C	I	P	Z	O	O	R	S	R	E	N	A	E	L	C	R	G	B
K	N	B	Z	U	L	U	F	P	P	A	T	I	S	S	E	R	I	E	G	A
S	G	M	S	J	N	P	L	G	O	I	D	P	I	L	K	R	Y	P	N	T
S	B	O	U	T	I	Q	U	E	T	H	U	N	E	R	W	M	P	M	I	O
E	C	H	E	M	P	O	R	I	U	M	S	C	H	V	G	A	L	P	T	Y
A	P	O	T	H	E	C	A	R	Y	Y	T	K	T	P	S	X	U	I	R	S
P	A	W	N	B	R	O	K	E	R	R	Y	B	O	D	E	G	A	E	O	T
H	A	R	D	W	A	R	E	U	O	Z	N	X	O	O	Y	H	K	D	P	O
S	O	U	V	E	N	I	R	N	K	V	G	X	B	G	B	A	E	S	S	R
C	O	N	F	E	C	T	I	O	N	E	R	Y	X	P	B	L	Y	Y	K	E
I	M	V	N	E	B	C	V	M	A	A	C	O	M	M	I	S	S	A	R	Y
L	L	D	N	I	S	H	O	M	E	I	M	P	R	O	V	E	M	E	N	T

CRIMEBIT No.83

Only Criminals

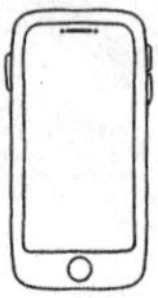

Daniel Stewart

'Like OnlyFans?'

'Yeah.'

'But for criminals?'

Sian watched his Malachai's eyes do the three-drink drift. Flying from her face and off out to the balcony with the shiny ones. The better to look down on the alien spaceship below. The Hydro, a fetching shade of fluorescent red tonight.

And back. 'Not for criminals, though they can pay too if they want. OnlyFans of Criminals. Forget just watch cop shows, go in through the windows with the actual robbers.'

'Pay how, exactly?'

His fingers mimed a blur of activity on a keyboard, the beginnings of a smile on his lips. 'On the beige web, let's say.'

'Where would we get the criminals?' The question out of her mouth before she could drag it back.

'I think we both know the answer to that,' said Mal slowly, the grin now turned up to ten, the burn and churn in her gut confirming the truth of his words.

PUZZLE No. 83

OnlyCriminals

In the underbelly of the digital world, where shadows dance and secrets lurk, there exists a platform unlike any other: OnlyCriminals. On OnlyCriminals, users aren't selling glimpses of their bodies; they're auctioning off glimpses of their crimes. From the clues, determine which ***criminal*** *committed what* ***crime,*** *their* ***username****, and in what* ***prison*** *they've most recently served time.*

The Criminals

Bruno Cadaveretta
Redd Blue
Roger Payne
Sal Minella

The Usernames

Mr. Warmth
Merchant of Venom
Tick-Tock
The Mastermind

The Crimes

Tax Fraud
Counterfeiting
Embezzlement
Bribery

The Prisons

Allenwood, Pennsylvania
Atwater, California
Beaumont, Texas
Big Sandy, Kentucky

Criminal	Username	Crime	Prison

? CLUES ?

1. Roger Payne, who committed bribery, is nicknamed Mr. Warmth.
2. Redd Blue is incarcerated in Atwater, California.
3. Tick-Tock is in prison for embezzlement.
4. Bruno Cadaveretta is not in Allenwood, Pennsylvania.
5. The Mastermind is in prison in Beaumont, Texas.

	Bruno Cadaveretta	**Redd Blue**	**Roger Payne**	**Sal Minella**	*Bribery*	*Counterfeiting*	*Embezzlement*	*Tax Fraud*	**Merchant of Venom**	**Mr. Warmth**	**Tick-Tock**	**The Mastermind**
Allenwood												
Atwater												
Beaumont												
Big Sandy												
Merchant of Venom												
Mr. Warmth												
Tick-Tock												
The Mastermind												
Bribery												
Counterfeiting												
Embezzlement												
Tax Fraud												

CRIMEBIT No. 84

Murder Party

YOUR RATING /100

Lorelai Tarlow

If Cam weren't dead, she'd have a cow right now. Vincent Donovan (I told her he'd be trouble, but no, she insisted we needed his business) is ruining the Persian rug she brought back from Turkey with an expanding pool of blood seeping from an ugly stab wound in his back.

'That's a terrific effect,' a voice says from behind my shoulder. The guests at our latest Murder for Dinner event had dispersed into the maze of Cam's giant and suitably spooky Victorian home, but half have drifted back to the parlor. This is Vincent's party, after all, and he is now the main attraction, his eyes wide, pupils blown, mouth open against the floor. He's drooled on the carpet, too.

I wonder if I can quietly call 911 and keep the still-living guests calm and clueless until the police arrive.

A small body slips past me. 'I don't think it's an effect.' Ori leans over Vincent. 'Why isn't Cam here, Tilly?'

'You were supposed to stay upstairs,' I say through clenched teeth, cursing Cam for stepping in front of that Yukon. I've inherited Cam's cousin and her Alzheimer's, which sucks. And a dead body on the carpet. That also sucks.

PUZZLE No. 84

Knives Out

*In this crazy twist on murder mystery parties, everyone's a killer! From the clues, determine **who** killed their victim using **what** kind of weapon **where** in the Victorian house.*

The Killers

Bach Stabber - Tall and lean, he moves with a predator's grace.

Blade Boggs - A ghostly figure with a deadly purpose.

Cookie Cutter - His knife is a symphony of silence and death.

Mick Dagger - His face is shrouded in perpetual shadow.

Slash Gordon - He moves with a lethal elegance.

The Weapons

Athame - A ritual knife used in ceremonial magic traditions.

Bowie Knife - Fixed-blade fighting knife created by Rezin Bowie.

Dirk - Long-bladed thrusting dagger, the knife of a Highlander.

Scalpel - A sharp bladed instrument used for dissection.

Switchblade - Pocketknife with a sliding or pivoting blade.

The Locations

Dining Room Kitchen Library Bedroom Parlor

Who?	**What?**	**Where?**
____________	____________	____________
____________	____________	____________
____________	____________	____________
____________	____________	____________
____________	____________	____________

? CLUES ?

1. Mick Dagger is the owner of the scalpel. Cookie Cutter has the Bowie Knife. Slash Gordon wasn't anywhere near the bedroom.
2. The five murderers are: someone who was in the library (who didn't use the Bowie Knife), the owner of the dirk, Bach Stabber, someone who murdered his victim in the kitchen, and someone who used a switchblade.
3. Bach Stabber was neither in the bedroom nor the dining room.
4. Blade Boggs isn't the murderer who used a switchblade.

	Bach Stabber	***Blade Boggs***	***Cookie Cutter***	***Mick Dagger***	***Slash Gordon***	*Dining Room*	*Kitchen*	*Library*	*Bedroom*	*Parlor*
Athame										
Bowie Knife										
Dirk										
Scalpel										
Switch-blade										
Dining Room										
Kitchen										
Library										
Bedroom										
Parlor										

CRIMEBIT No. 85

Web of Scars

YOUR RATING
/100

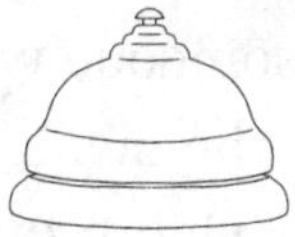

Michael Telfer

Jake had protested when his sister had signed him up for speed dating. Forty minutes in, he was wishing he'd pushed back harder.

A bell dinged and number 17 smiled thinly and stood, her attention already on the guy at the next table who was trying very hard to look like he played rugby. Another woman sat down opposite Jake, her hair obscuring her number badge. She was about his age he thought, but with fewer miles on the clock.

She smiled as the bell sounded to start the next round.

'You don't look thrilled to be here?'

'My big sister's idea,' Jake replied, suddenly self-conscious.

She laughed and he blushed hard.

'Divorced or widowed?'

He told her he was separated, which was a lie.

Talking came easily, for the first time that night. She liked triathlons, Indian food and was looking to meet somebody outside her work and friendship circles. He loved curry, thought he owned a bike and wasn't really sure what he was looking for.

Which was the truth.

The bell dinged again.

He smiled, 'That was . . .'

'I'm who you're looking for,' she said.

He laughed without thinking and looked up at her.

'I killed your wife.'

DID YOU KNOW

Lee Child cites several influences on his writing, including John D. MacDonald, the creator of the *Travis McGee* series, and Alistair MacLean, known for his adventure novels such as *The Guns of Navarone*.

PUZZLE No. 85

Dating Pairs

Across

1. Erma Franklin's sister
7. Surface muck
11. "Get away from my squeaky toy!"
14. Magic trick's climax
15. Best of the best
16. "Jungle Fever" director Spike
17. Budget-friendly banquet?
19. "A Wrinkle in Time" director DuVernay
20. "Hardy" follower, in a mock laugh
21. Maker of Fairy washing-up liquid
22. Secret, as a message
24. Time piece?
26. North or Irish
28. Comic Yashere or actress Bellman
29. Bar measure
30. Passengers on a maiden voyage?
32. Invalidates, as a ticket
34. Hole to receive a shoelace
35. __ Ben Canaan of "Exodus"
38. Two-part composition on Miles Davis' "Dark Magus"
39. Word after armored or cable
40. HMRC in the USA
41. AKA Mount McKinley, Alaska
43. Citrus flavor
45. Summer beach read, maybe?
47. Not __ (zilch)
51. Masked dueler's blade
52. Unusually large
53. 1970s US sitcom that included Carlton the Doorman
54. Pick up, as a vibe
56. Florida's "Cruise Capital of the World"
58. The bottom line in sewing class?
59. Part of the Home Office replaced by the BIA
60. Two nightmares in one evening?
63. Honker configuration
64. Beach scavenger
65. Becoming
66. Byrnes who played Vince Fontaine in "Grease"
67. Palindromic suffix
68. Rate or evaluate

Down

1. McDonald's sign pair
2. Discuss again
3. To a great degree
4. Reception with scones
5. Grumpy co-worker?
6. Pierce player on "M*A*S*H"
7. Carpenters, at times
8. Dances with one person after another?
9. Article in "Le Monde"?
10. Carnaby Street maker of harrington jackets
11. Flowers with sword-shaped leaves
12. Poteen maker's adversary

13. Conforms again
18. Where to be on a rainy day
23. Shrek, famously
25. CIT, once
27. Full of passion
30. Coat with varnish or lacquer
31. Sandwich served with tzatziki
33. One's partner?
35. Sticky
36. Back in business
37. Bride-to-be
39. Breakfast bowlful
42. Distorted room
43. Easy on the eyes?
44. "Ain't gonna happen"
46. Garboil
48. "La __" (Puccini classic)
49. Archetypes
50. Grimes and Wynette
53. Disneyland delights
55. Bono's bandmate, with "The"
57. Large, flat-topped hill
61. Not in
62. Hi-__ (finely detailed)

CRIMEBIT No. 86

Poacher

YOUR RATING /100

Lorraine Thomson

Jimi lifted the gun bag from its hiding place in the loft. Tonight they would come for her and she would be ready for them. They'd win in the end, but she wouldn't make it easy.

She carried the bag downstairs and opened it on the kitchen table. The rifle, a Remington 700, had once belonged to her grandfather, and now it was hers. A secret, hidden by her father when the firearms amnesty came in.

If the police had any inkling, they'd have taken it when they arrested Jimi along with the .22 her father used for killing sheep and the .243 rifle they used on the hill.

She glanced around the kitchen, the room familiar yet not, like a loved one when the life leaves their eyes. They had the same face, same hair, same clothes, but in that moment of death everything changed. The old croft house was like that now. Everything that mattered had gone. Even so, she wasn't giving it up without a fight.

HAVE YOUR SAY

What happens next?

Scan to visit the CrimeBits Writing Space

PUZZLE No. 86

Last Stand

Across

1. Flavoring for Japanese soups
5. Daytime drop-offs?
9. Blood designation
14. Desiccated sea
15. Giant who's not jolly
16. American TV's "Uncle Miltie"
17. What call center customers frequently hear
19. Vacation isle near Venezuela
20. Condor variety
21. Royal ball?
23. Polka __
24. Glittery wear
25. "Wait until you hear this!"
28. Many adults
29. American feminist writer Rita __ Brown
31. Formulaic rule
32. "Right away," in memos
34. Sleazy tabloid
36. Glasgow banks holding
37. Next day delivery
41. Saxon leader?
44. John's "Pulp Fiction" dance partner
45. American sports channel
49. Lying in ambush
52. Paranormal talent, briefly
54. Edgar Allan who wrote "Israfel"
55. Fiber optic transmission, e.g.
57. Clapton title woman
59. When the flight's due, for short
60. Class of wine
61. Oilman's hope
62. Like barely cooked eggs
65. Perfect living space
67. In a difficult spot
68. Biblical pottage buyer
69. James who performs stand-up in English and Welsh
70. Nestlé bars filled with tiny bubbles
71. Eggheady sort, in stereotypes
72. Clan

Down

1. Epithet for Gandhi
2. American writer O. Henry plot devices
3. Uhura portrayer
4. Marlon Dingle, compared to Eli Dingle
5. This may be a subject
6. Law Officers of the UK
7. Monastic officer
8. Unrevealed
9. Sked abbr.
10. "So's __ ol' lady!"
11. Excessive modesty
12. Muscled through, as a crowd
13. "No clue"
18. Word of address to a queen
22. "A Christmas Carol" expression
25. Landing equipment
26. Hardware repairer

27. "The Prince of Tides" star Nick
30. "What __ the odds?"
33. Dance of Bohemian origin
35. Migratory African critter
38. Abyss
39. Pinged, in a way
40. Shell sells it
41. Banff National Park locale
42. Help grow
43. Bad pun, for one
46. Peeping Tom's spot
47. Diatribe
48. Companion of dearest
50. America's "Peacock" network
51. Flower plot
53. Sweet bonus
56. Bring back to health
58. Some timber trees
61. Cheap trinket
63. "The Matrix" role
64. American football meas.
66. Vase handle

CRIMEBIT No. 87

Skin of a Cop

SHORTLISTED BY LEE CHILD

YOUR RATING /100

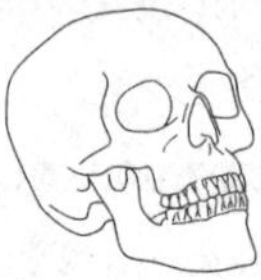

Marek Turner

The guy burned quicker than his wife. That surprised John. She had a bouffant hair style that reminded him of an eighties pop star, and clothing that was more processed than a Twinkie. Same color too.

Still, they had taken them from a room that stank of sweat, cheap liquor and even cheaper aftershave. The type from a market stall with a spelling mistake on the label. Highly flammable, no doubt.

With a sniff of the acrid night air, Frank choked down the bile in his throat and stared absently at the wilted bodies, which were propped up only by the remnants of scorched wood in a cleared patch of moorland.

He closed his eyes to block out their contorted faces, but their silent screams continued on a loop inside his skull. Biting his bottom lip, he shook his head and willed his cortex to save him. To remind him of why he was here. To vindicate him.

It was nearly Christmas, and he had a kid on the way.

EDITOR'S NOTES

'A horrifying opening sentence, that really shocks on second reading. A reader will go back and read that again, just to be sure they've read it right. Wonderful imagery and use of language in the descriptions, that only portray the horror more. Compare the first line to the last – a brilliant entry from Marek Turner.'

PUZZLE No. 87

Firestorm

Across

1. Bear mascot of the 1980 Moscow Olympics
6. "Vidi," in English
10. Engine sound
14. Peru natives
15. Without a partner
16. Air
17. Garage supply
19. Golfer's bane
20. Beverage brewed naturally
21. Fouls
23. The Pennines, e.g.
24. Relic site
26. Antique cars for which a classic rock band is named
27. Waste time, metaphorically
32. Pop up again
35. "Listen up, Luis!"
36. "Indeed!"
37. Complete doofus
40. "To the __ of the Earth"
41. Passing fancy
42. Certain statistics
44. Source of the dragon's sound in "Sleeping Beauty"
49. Countess on "Downton Abbey"
50. Vegan milk ingredient
51. "Starpeace" performer
54. Childish
58. Lucidity
60. Back at square one
61. Burlesque actress played by Lolita Davidovich 1989 (2 wds)
63. Border crosser's stamp
64. Relating to planes
65. Sweet rich wine
66. Mail routing abbr.
67. "Cowboy Man" singer Lovett
68. Digging tool

Down

1. "The Divine __" (Midler)
2. Opinions
3. Checks out
4. Mature male red deer
5. Invited in, in a way
6. Not well
7. Alternative to salad
8. Goat with silky hair
9. Beverly Crusher's son on "Star Trek"
10. Mashed Potato alternative
11. Grieved
12. "Dies __"
13. T-Pain and Ice-T output
18. Bigeminal
22. IRC chuckle
25. Be a busy beaver
27. A&E vitals
28. Joyless, poetically
29. Ringside ringer
30. "Strange Case" title character
31. Daly of "Strictly Come Dancing"
32. Bit of jazz
33. And others, in brief

34. Its first performance was in Cairo
38. Cooking acronym used by American TV chef Rachael Ray
39. Start of a dog owner's sign
40. Abalone shape
43. Checks to make sure
45. "Atonement" author Ian
46. A thousand ages
47. Of nomadic bands
48. British astronomer with a comet named after him
51. Major port of Japan
52. Annual US tracker of Santa's flight
53. Pastrami's place, often
54. Barista's offering, slangily
55. Single component
56. Prom garment, maybe
57. British noble
59. Straddling, maybe
62. "Sunshine on a Rainy Day" singer

CRIMEBIT No.88

An Illustrious Corpse

YOUR RATING /100

Marek Turner

Frank grabbed the spare keys off the hook, their ridges digging into his palm, and yanked open the front door of the mock Tudor mansion.

He paused, watching as his primary set of keys swung limply from the outside lock.

'Stupid cow. Must have left them there last night,' he muttered under his breath, resisting the urge to go back and admonish her. These late night shopping sprees with the girls, none of which he knew, were becoming more frequent and boozy.

A saccharine stench filled the car, causing his nose to wrinkle. He lowered the window and considered his wife's new-found lease of life. It all started two months ago when, in the heat of an argument, he told her she was a trophy wife, so she should polish herself up. He smiled at the memory, shoved the car into drive, and headed down the gravel driveway.

Within seconds, the boot warning light flashed. His jaw clenched and his foot slammed down on the brake. He cursed loudly. Hand on the door handle, he paused.

A text message from a withheld number flashed up on the car's touch screen. His eyes narrowed.

'There's a gift for you in the boot.'

? DID YOU KNOW ?

Arthur Conan Doyle once helped solve a real crime. He became involved in the case of George Edalji in 1907, a solicitor wrongly accused of mutilating animals. Doyle's investigation helped exonerate Edalji and highlighted flaws in the British justice system.

PUZZLE No. 88

Tyre Rotation

Across

1. Tender stuff
5. Design
10. Blew a save
14. Antioxidant berry
15. Bar for prying
16. Concerned with
17. Lousy replacement fender for a Bentley?
19. Fret (over)
20. "As You Like It" locale
21. Address abbrs.
22. Alternatives to sunroofs
23. Kenya capital
25. Precaution
27. Hood on a Hillman Imp?
32. Cranberries source
35. One working in a row
36. __ Dan
37. "No need to wake me!"
39. Stuff and nonsense!
41. Freeway exit
42. Sherwood __
45. Bedford who wrote "Yoruba Girl Dancing"
48. Agatha Christie's "A Pocket Full of __"
49. Last in a quartet of British station wagons?
52. Hammer or hacksaw
53. Intercept
57. Easy on the wallet
60. Elevenses beverage
62. Bibliothèque item
63. Mystical person
64. Trunk of John Wayne's Aston Martin?
66. Soon, to Spenser
67. Spoken exams
68. Toe the __
69. Al Capone's pursuer, Eliot __
70. Panhandler, often
71. PhDs in the UK

Down

1. Settlers of __
2. North American Honda whose current models all end in "X"
3. New York restaurateur Vincent
4. Peripatetic ones
5. One way to travel
6. Script doctor?
7. Hardly indifferent
8. Person of integrity and honor
9. Wee bit of work
10. Eavesdropper
11. Enlightened about
12. Gradation
13. Pulls behind
18. Adam's grandson
22. Fairly brisk pace
24. Frightening sound?
26. Things in a sixpack?
28. "Sailing" singer Christopher
29. Just steps away
30. Abounding in shade trees
31. Bang the keyboard
32. Word that appears out of thin air when Batman hits someone
33. "Typee" successor

34. Advisor of a sort
38. Relates (to)
40. Liable to regular payments
43. "Enough!"
44. "Sweet is true love __ given in vain": Tennyson
46. "If We Ever Broke Up" singer Stephens
47. Dante's land
50. Barcelona bull
51. Suitable as food
54. Not quite spherical
55. Palm piece
56. Honors grandly
57. Blue hue in a printer
58. Improve an edge
59. Some are inflated
61. McGregor of "Big Fish" with an OBE
64. Atlantic fish
65. Sugar name suffix

CRIMEBIT No. 89

No Sleep for the Dead

YOUR RATING
/100

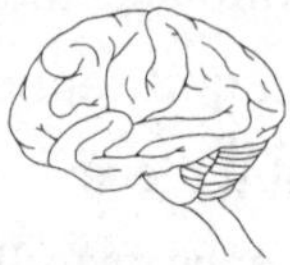

Marek Turner

Frank Turner stood on the grass bank watching as the flames from the car licked the night sky. The black smoke disappeared into the nothingness above.

Beads of sweat trickled down his forehead as the heat intensified and the acrid stench of burning rubber filled his nostrils. He ran a grubby hand down his face and exhaled, knowing that the gas tank would soon blow, and with it, any hope that the investigators would identify the driver.

It didn't matter, though. Max was already dead. A single bullet through the windscreen and into his cranium. While Frank's continued existence implied that either the shooter was ignorant of him or had fled. An amateur.

A deafening blast roared. The inferno consumed his brother's body.

Frank remained stone-faced as the fire reflected in his eyes. He nodded and contemplated his promise. The reason they were in the vehicle. He turned to look at the shattered crash barrier. It was at least ten feet up. Too high to climb.

A shrill beep stole his attention, and a dim glow emerged in a nearby patch of scrubland. He strode toward the source. Max's phone. Its cracked screen displayed a one-word message: 'Sorry.'

? *DID YOU KNOW* ?

Before creating James Bond, Ian Fleming wrote a true crime piece called *The Diamond Smugglers* (1957). The book details the activities of real-life diamond smuggling operations and was based on interviews with a former MI5 agent.

PUZZLE No. 89

Sleeping Beauties

Across

1. Support for a bridge
6. Where the cubs play
9. Ball
14. Oscar de la __
15. Centre front?
16. Humbled
17. Checked
18. Score unlikely letters on America's "Wheel of Fortune"?
20. Rocker Ronnie James __
21. Buy a round
22. Loos' Lorelei __
23. Overshadow
26. Besides
29. Off?
32. Swift
33. Bad way to play
34. Given food
35. Most of Jack Reacher's 110th MP Special Investigations Unit
37. Health org.
40. Dinnerware
42. MTV cartoon with the show-within-a-show "Sick, Sad World"
44. End-of-the-day chore for Little Bo-Peep?
47. Operating system in the Linux family
49. Most greasy
50. Grouper grabber
51. Isn't a pinball wizard
54. "Rock It Out" singer Zadora
55. Take out one's anger on a barn bale?
58. "Scary Movie" actress Cheri
60. Cooler brand
61. Low digit
62. Televised again
63. See 64 Across
64. With 63 Across, bugbear
65. Abates

Down

1. Quid pro quo, sometimes
2. Grandmama's purse
3. Opened, as a door
4. Place to see a sched.
5. "Here's an idea..."
6. Commencement award
7. Event on a piste
8. "Brother Bear 2" girl
9. Sporty Pontiac in a Ronny & the Daytonas song
10. Hasty getaway
11. Brunch order
12. Gemstone mounting
13. '50s Ford fiasco
19. Access to the attic
21. "For shame!"
24. Paris' __ de la Cité
25. Mango seed
27. The S in T/DS
28. Kid's inquiry
30. First name associated with 4 Stevensons in US politics
31. Mendacity
35. Clock hand
36. Aesop critter

37. Vines, e.g.
38. Hymn about the Day of Judgment
39. Hook and Cook
40. Bamboozle
41. Not exactly a palace
42. Alternative to cable internet
43. Big Polynesian fish
44. Ned in "Dombey and Son"
45. Soon, perhaps
46. American soldiers, for short
47. Not plugged in
48. Earth tone
52. American breakfast eatery chain, initially
53. "Daily Planet" employee Lois ___
56. "Mazel ___!"
57. Furrow maker
58. Bauxite or malachite
59. Afternoon cupful, say

CRIMEBIT No.90

The Missing Heart

YOUR RATING
/100

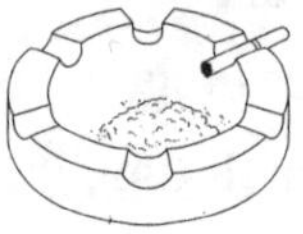

Richard Valanga

The Londonderry, Sunderland

The Londonderry pub was lively and full, the raucous noise level had been steadily rising since opening time which was usual for a Friday night in the town center. People were singing their favorite songs but the woman that was singing the loudest was now beginning to irritate the man who was sitting in the corner opposite the bar. He had come into the pub with his workmate but his friend had now left leaving him alone with his beer and his memories, memories he could only face at the bottom of a bottle.

The lonely man lit up another cigarette even though there was one still burning in the ashtray next to his brown Derby hat. The smoke above hovered over him like a dark depressive cloud as he stared at the beer bottle on the table which was now empty. He knew it was time for another and he really wanted to tell that irritable singing woman to shut the fuck up but this was what he wanted though, why he was there; the hustle and bustle, the noise and chatter, the need for alcohol, it was always a way to forget.

PUZZLE No. 90

Pub Singers

In the Londonderry pub, where the notes of fiddles and the trill of tin whistles fill the air, five spirited souls are brought together by a love for Irish music that runs deeper than the River Liffey. From the clues, determine which ***singer*** *will perform what* ***song****, and if a grateful patron chooses to buy them a* ***drink****, what their order is.*

The Singers

Niamh - A mezzo-soprano with a fierce passion for her heritage.
Siobhan - A soprano with a spirit as wild as the cliffs of Moher.
Cillian - The baritone with a voice smooth like aged whiskey.
Declan - The tenor with a knack for storytelling.
Fiona - A soprano whose voice dances like a faerie on the wind.

The Songs	The Drinks
"Whiskey in the Jar"	Smithwick's Ale
"The Black Velvet Band"	Hot Whiskey
"Seven Drunken Nights"	Jameson
"Finnegan's Wake"	Cider
"The Wild Rover"	Guinness

Singer	Song	Drink
________	________	________
________	________	________
________	________	________
________	________	________
________	________	________

? CLUES ?

1. The five singers are: the one who performed "Seven Drunken Nights" (who isn't drinking the hot whiskey), the singer who is drinking Jameson, Niamh, the one who is drinking Guinness, and the singer who performed "The Black Velvet Band."
2. Declan is drinking the cider. Cillian is drinking hot whiskey.
3. Niamh didn't sing "Finnegan's Wake" or "Whiskey in the Jar."
4. Fiona didn't sing "Finnegan's Wake" and Siobhan isn't drinking Guinness.

	Cillian	Declan	Fioana	Niamh	Siobhan	Black Velvet	Finnegan's Wake	7 Drunken Nights	Whiskey in the Jar	Wild Rover
Cider										
Guinness										
Hot Whiskey										
Jameson										
Smithwick's										
Black Velvet										
Finnegan's Wake										
7 Drunken Nights										
Whiskey in the Jar										
Wild Rover										

CRIMEBIT No.91

Kill You First

YOUR RATING /100

Graham Wall

Brett slipped into Cantina's comfortable interior, the West 8th Street bar's gentle hum and warm, scented air a sharp contrast to the quiet chill outside.

Pausing in the shadows of the doorway, his practiced eye analyzed all around him.

Brass pendant lights hung from the ceiling, their soft golden glow turned low to create an intimate atmosphere for the few people still drinking despite the lateness of the hour.

Dotted along the edge of each wall, brown leather booths ran the room's length to its famed 35-foot granite bar, which caught and reflected the backbar's thin strip of blue lighting.

Standing at the center of the bar, three traders slammed their shot glasses in unison against the polished granite. The heavyset man in the middle, the trio's alpha, shrugged off the jacket of his five-thousand-dollar suit, then waved at the barman, pointed at the glasses and held up three thick fingers.

But Brett wasn't interested in the alpha or the other two hanging off his every word. So he dismissed them and shifted his focus to a couple sitting in a booth against the right-hand wall.

PUZZLE No. 91

Bar Hopping

Across

1. Corkboard holders
6. UK charity with a red star logo
9. Slinkies
14. Take up
15. Stagewear for Madonna
16. Ready at the bar
17. Maine resort town in Rick Riordan's "The Titan's Curse"
19. "Boss!"
20. "Long __ in a galaxy far..."
21. Java dispenser
22. Flatter, as beer
23. Jalopy
26. Conveyance for skiers
28. More husky
30. One __ time
31. Capital of Canada?
32. Stock in trade
33. US country music venue, Grand Ole __
35. New to you
36. Expelled, in a way
39. Finishes off a bun?
42. With the skills
43. "Farewell, amigo!"
47. Night deity
48. Pablo Neruda's "__ to My Socks"
49. Energize, as a party
51. Large semiaquatic rodent in "Encanto"
54. It comes before first, in maths
55. Most cool, in slang
56. Unreasonably
58. Highway with a no.
59. Got illegally
60. Certain mustache shape
63. Some aristocrats
64. Not go straight?
65. Identical
66. Boutique buy
67. Super Bowl impossibility
68. Fast snacks

Down

1. Coffey who wrote "It's Not Really About the Hair"
2. Slow compositions
3. Celestial rings
4. Canadian speed meas.
5. Short stop?
6. St., ave., or blvd.
7. Leading edge
8. Bentley or Jaguar
9. Not in accord with
10. "Love Story" star Ryan
11. Emphatic letters
12. Fine, in a sense
13. Showed off
18. Letter to Odin?
22. Maenad chaser
24. Street reps
25. Piedmont wine area
27. Rifle part
29. Crook
34. American mate
35. Milk dispenser?
37. Third president of Egypt

38. Wasp's nest location, perhaps
39. Engraved
40. Dye source
41. Plumb
44. Like a satellite
45. Blooper, often
46. Round solids
48. Lose sleep over
50. Shirt maker with an alligator mascot
52. Cries out
53. "Space Invaders" video game
57. Aforetime
60. Toque or kepi
61. Chocolate companion?
62. Marlon Dingle's younger brother on "Emmerdale"

CRIMEBIT No. 92

Souls on Board

YOUR RATING /100

Rachael Warecki

We blew Del's face off the second the cherry bombs exploded. There was a hell of a mess everywhere, as far as Del's remaining eye could see if it had still been in the blinking business. Columns of dust rose skyward like God leading Moses across the desert, flames licked at a wingless fuselage, men and women sprawled across an acre of tamped-down Southern California dirt, moaning at the third-degree burns on their hands and faces. To the emergency workers leaning against their semicircle of cop cars and fire trucks, grinding their wads of gum, the scene probably seemed like a hard morning's work. To Mac and Louie and me, it looked like a job well done.

EDITOR'S NOTES

'A scene that is difficult to imagine for long. I'm interested in why the writer decided to open with this – another writer may have taken their time, but Warecki plows straight into the horror. Brave and unrelenting. That's a writer I can get on board with.'

PUZZLE No. 92

Crash

Across

1. Bone in a cage?
4. GIF or JPEG alternative
10. Like many radios
14. "Star Trek: Deep Space Nine" changeling
15. Po Valley product
16. "Deck the Halls" syllables
17. Prefix like atmo-
18. "If I Had a Hammer" composer Pete
19. Clare in "Bleak House" and Lovelace of computing
20. __ Carta
22. It may be used at a red light
24. Audio lab name
26. Carpenter's tool
27. Innermost
29. Calls it quits
32. Python's slayer
34. Teatro __ Scala
35. "Balderdash!"
38. Lowish pinochle card
39. Certain hormone
41. She played Beatrix in "Kill Bill"
42. Pindaric output
43. Sacked
44. Bingo blotter
46. Drop in the ocean?
48. Recipe abbr.
49. Danny of "Moonstruck" and "Do the Right Thing"
52. Bold choice
54. Widespread outbreaks
57. Danger for a king
60. "Smooth Operator" chanteuse
61. God with four faces
63. First mo.
64. White bills in Monopoly
65. Begin gently
66. Barely squeeze by
67. Share
68. Fix a second draft
69. What starts tomorrow?

Down

1. Ape buffalo?
2. "I had no __!"
3. Seven of Nine, formerly
4. Intrinsic
5. Verb suffix
6. Fabric coloring method
7. Astrologers of yore
8. Times of your life?
9. Swing seat alternative
10. Bank devices
11. Lady's title
12. Blizzard minutia
13. Electromagnetic amplifier
21. "Frosty" air?
23. Chunky Monkey flavor
25. Joltin' Joe DiMaggio's nickname
27. Roman statesman
28. Kind of commentary
30. Jordanian neighbor
31. "__ be back!"
33. Likely
35. Laser alternative

36. Singing brothers of '50s music

37. Image on an Irish euro

40. Play area

45. Normandy landing site

46. First among progeny

47. Ran 100 yards, perhaps

49. "Sour grapes" fabulist

50. Old toothpaste brand sold by Bucky Beaver

51. Duck down?

53. "Count me out"

55. "Of wrath," in a requiem

56. Carrier

58. Baba au rhum, e.g.

59. Femur and tibia connector

62. Nintendo Wii avatar

CRIMEBIT No. 93

Beneath the Surface

YOUR RATING /100

Joanne Watkinson

Sometimes I think I hear your cry. I hold you in my arms and I believe I can see you, smell you. I look down and realize I am holding a blanket tight, close to my heart because that is all that I have left of you. It is still bloodied from the day you were born, which reminds me you were real and that the accusations of my delusion are unfounded. I could not forget holding you, however short that moment may have been. Was your life cut short that day? Tossed away like rubbish! It burns me inside thinking such awful things. I need to believe you are alive, happy. Maybe you feel me, a space in your heart needing filling, but you don't know by who, or why. If I didn't talk to you there would be no point to my existence. I have lost track of time and have no idea how long I have been kept here. The scratching of the wall is less about marking the passing of time and more about causing my fingertips to bleed, so that I feel pain, so that I feel something.

PUZZLE No. 93

Beneath the Surface

ARROWROOT	GALANGAL	LEEK	PARSNIP	TANNIA
BEET	GARLIC	MACA	PEANUTS	YAM
BONIATO	GINGER	MALANGA	POTATO	TURMERIC
CARROT	HORSERADISH	MASHUA	RUTABAGA	TURNIP
CASSAVA	JICAMA	ÑAME	SALSIFY	UBE
CELERIAC	KOHLRABI	OCA	SHALLOT	WASABI
DAIKON	KONJAC	ONION	SKIRRET	YACON

Q	Y	S	J	P	S	T	L	M	C	X	D	R	D	B	R	E	G	N	I	G
C	A	Z	J	J	G	H	S	I	D	A	R	E	S	R	O	H	S	Q	E	B
T	C	A	M	T	C	R	B	S	H	W	R	P	U	W	D	A	I	K	O	N
U	A	I	K	T	N	A	J	F	I	E	Y	R	E	F	G	W	X	W	X	G
R	M	T	A	D	A	K	J	W	G	Q	T	T	O	A	Z	A	W	N	Y	X
M	M	R	L	N	Y	U	Y	N	O	M	X	B	S	T	N	Y	E	P	A	A
E	O	A	X	Z	B	G	A	M	O	V	P	D	I	S	V	U	R	F	I	D
R	T	X	S	N	L	M	K	E	A	K	P	D	B	K	L	G	T	M	H	C
I	K	B	H	H	E	S	O	K	V	M	Y	E	A	I	O	O	A	S	H	J
C	Q	Z	A	K	U	M	Y	S	A	M	J	H	R	R	G	K	W	K	A	K
X	H	X	L	V	E	A	M	Z	S	U	P	O	L	R	R	H	C	N	V	P
G	I	V	L	Q	D	E	O	N	S	C	W	Z	H	E	Y	N	U	Z	P	V
Z	I	S	O	B	Q	U	L	W	A	N	J	T	O	T	V	J	Q	D	I	H
C	Q	B	T	I	J	F	J	M	C	Q	R	Z	K	M	S	H	A	J	N	D
G	D	C	A	A	S	A	L	S	I	F	Y	N	G	K	A	B	P	J	S	J
W	A	O	Z	S	N	I	G	N	K	G	W	Z	T	V	I	M	P	R	R	B
N	N	U	T	D	A	N	O	N	O	C	E	Q	P	G	R	H	A	S	A	D
A	S	B	V	A	T	W	I	N	O	C	I	E	A	Z	Y	A	M	C	P	H
G	O	E	K	G	T	C	I	A	D	T	A	L	Y	C	T	U	R	N	I	P
A	R	R	O	W	R	O	O	T	N	W	A	Y	R	N	G	E	M	F	G	J
B	L	F	W	W	N	M	P	X	R	N	I	I	O	A	M	W	G	J	Z	B
A	T	T	W	F	I	V	J	R	G	S	K	X	N	Z	G	F	U	Z	E	A
T	R	X	L	F	M	A	L	A	N	G	A	A	Z	O	S	K	D	E	C	Z
U	T	C	A	I	R	E	L	E	C	O	K	U	N	L	B	L	T	O	R	J
R	F	Q	P	G	H	V	Y	C	I	E	X	Y	W	O	T	H	S	G	H	P

CRIMEBIT No. 94

The Vermin Below

YOUR RATING /100

Joanne Watkinson

Gazing at the view through the sash window with a blank expression, she rocked gently in her chair. Back and forth in a rhythm like the ticking of a clock monitoring the length of time she had been sat there. Her mind blank, seemingly unfazed by what had gone on only an hour before. She wasn't heartless, she had feelings, but in this moment, it was easier to feel nothing. Perhaps in shock, she maintained this trancelike state for some time, the floorboards creaking beneath her breaking the deathly silence, until the rocking chair came to an abrupt stop and just like that hysteria took over. She put her head in her hands leaving a blood stain streak across her face and let out a guttural sound reflective of a beast. She had acted like an animal; they had treated her like one.

The bodies were face down, she didn't want to see their faces. She didn't want to see their faces ever again, the need to erase their existence was real. She pulled herself together and stepped over the bodies one by one, reaching for the phone. The line was dead. They were dead. She was dead inside.

HAVE YOUR SAY

What happens next?

Scan to visit the CrimeBits Writing Space

PUZZLE No. 94

Infestation

Across

1. Breads to dip in hummus
6. 56 Down car
10. A former Spice Girl
14. Harry's Hogwarts rival
15. Strong enough
16. Drury __ Theatre
17. Ray in "The Princess and the Frog"?
20. Stocking stuffer?
21. New York restauranteur
22. Part of Ceylon's new name
24. Computer lab inventory
26. Not totally worthless
30. Bit of ice in a cup of coffee?
33. Band instrument
34. US version of the HMRC
35. "__ Mio"
36. Clear a frozen windshield
37. Split and toasted treat
39. Seizer
41. Buenos __
42. California, for example
44. "Brokeback Mountain" director Lee
45. Byte beginning
46. Villainous intent shown while walking the dog?
48. Contemporary of Etta
50. Cone or Cat prefix
51. Choice word
52. Attire for an abbess
54. Easter fleur
56. "Dude! That is one fine grissino!"
63. Electric guitar sound effect
64. "Downton Abbey" nobleman
65. __ of duty
66. "Brown __ Girl"
67. Musical intermission?
68. Contribute

Down

1. File that may be read-only
2. Flawed clothing abbr.
3. Red __ (sushi fish)
4. Like vinegar
5. Baby's first pic?
6. Khan Academy's Khan
7. Like a chasm
8. Bravo preceder
9. Mideast capital
10. Cluster in Taurus
11. Bumbling bungling buffoon
12. US comedy show since '75
13. "Hold on there!"
18. Deprive of office
19. Travel rtes.
22. More contrite
23. Rise anew
25. Spinner of myth
27. Where Lee Child is from
28. Clearness
29. Break out
30. Tuber also known as a Mexican Turnip
31. "How klutzy of me!"

32. F = ma formulator
36. Rio __ Plata
38. "All in the Family" nickname
40. Cast over
43. Edible mollusks
46. Chatter, in Queensland
47. Survived
49. Bean cover?
53. End of a hymn title
55. Rae who created "The Misadventures of Awkward Black Girl"
56. Nor. neighbor
57. One word on an arrow?
58. Pecorino Romano source
59. Prefix in music genres
60. Unaffiliated pol's abbr.
61. Nuffield College, Oxford research gp.
62. Role for Ryan Gosling, Simu Liu and John Cena

CRIMEBIT No. 95

Five Out of Nine

YOUR RATING /100

Rachael Watson

It had been 3 minutes and 25 seconds since Ellen had left the university chemistry lab. A strand of her short black hair lay abandoned on the sterilized steel counter. When she shoved her stool back, shaking Ivan's glass beakers as she did, the hair had escaped, landing on his workspace. She had slung her backpack on her shoulder, yelling goodbye, before slamming the door. A few seconds later, she raced back in for her phone that she'd forgotten, brushing his shoulder as she retrieved it, reminding him that he was the only one staying late and not going out for drinks at the pub. She slammed the door again on her way out, ordering him not to stay late as she went.

She did not come back for her hair.

It had been 4 minutes and 25 seconds since Ellen had first left the lab. Ivan extended one blue-gloved hand forward, reaching into his pocket with the other, withdrawing a clear plastic bag. Carefully, reverentially, he transferred the hair from his workspace into the bag, counting its contents. He tucked the valuables away, then discarded his disposable gloves.

'That's five hairs now,' Ivan said.

WRITING PROMPT 9

I don't remember exactly when I realized I loved him. I just know I blurted it out in the middle of a nightclub. Having to repeat myself, as he didn't hear me the first time. Shouting into his ear, struggling to be heard over the music.

'I said, I love you.'

That grin of his. No teeth showing, just his lips widening and spreading across his face.

'I love you too, babe.'

That had been it. A quick kiss to seal the deal and that was the end of the conversation. Back to whatever we had been doing before that. We'd been out in a group and I'd managed to sidle us away from them, but we'd quickly rejoined the others and carried on into the night.

It had been the same night I'd seen how quickly that grin could turn.

Not on me, not then.

Scan to visit the CrimeBits Writing Space

PUZZLE No. 95

Chemical Reactions

Across

1. Some secretaries
6. Subdivision of India
11. Wait for it
14. Low interest rate?
15. Ends of the Earth?
16. It's of miner concern
17. Royal unit of electrical energy?
19. "National Velvet" horse, with "The"
20. Chef Cat __
21. Certain somethings
22. Peanut butter amt.
23. Like contrarians
24. "The __ Effect" (unreasonable expectations of real-life forensics held by juries)
25. RR structure
26. Steals acetylenes from a lab?
32. They hit #1 with "To Be With You"
35. Adhesive
36. Where the utricle is
37. Germann in "Gen V"
40. "Fireside chats" US presidential monogram
41. "Fat chance!"
42. Hosts, initially
45. Multi-campus university of Boston, Amherst, Lowell, etc.
47. "I'm not detecting any ammonia derivative"?
50. Animals, in taxonomy
51. Trumpeter's asset
52. Boss Tweed lampooner Thomas
56. Time span
58. Assiduous care
60. Mindful of
61. "Left turn, Dobbin!"
62. Own a charged atom?
64. "Hot Right Now" Rita
65. Diva's gig
66. "Coming of Age in __" (Margaret Mead book)
67. Insidious
68. Didn't go out
69. Tortoise topper

Down

1. Beatles-snubbing label
2. "Conspiracy of Fools" topic
3. Quick drink
4. Certain Persian Gulf native
5. Do the wrong thing
6. Joint filer
7. Hawaii's largest industry
8. Spaghetti __ puttanesca
9. They make beer better
10. Loser at heart?
11. Bigwig
12. Showy purple bloom
13. Cry for worms
18. Universal tradesman?
22. "K bai"
25. Slippery slope
27. "The Mousetrap" playwright Christie
28. "__ Wiedersehen!"
29. Flat-panel TV type
30. Negotiation obstacles

31. Works on a broken radius
32. Ryan and Tilly
33. Like holographic Charizard, in Pokémon
34. House-garage connection
38. Home to many schools
39. Are in the Bible?
43. Hairy sci-fi critter
44. "Amadeus" narrator
46. Ceremonial candelabrum
48. Quorum
49. ___ jure
53. "My Neighbor Totoro" genre
54. Ottoman
55. Having a key
56. "___ asking?"
57. Man addressed as "My Lord"
58. Haydn's sobriquet
59. Rarae ___
62. Scientific inquiry?
63. Abbr. before American ship names

CRIMEBIT No. 96

I Killed a Man

SHORTLISTED BY LEE CHILD

YOUR RATING /100

Lucy Wetherall

I was a profoundly lonely child. I didn't ask for anything; I didn't cry often. I learned to look after myself. I knew I was brilliant at a very young age. Maybe that's how I ended up here, in the Bedford Hills Correctional Facility for Women. You see, I killed my husband. I shot him in the head while he was sleeping. Finally, being able to say those sentences out loud feels like the heavy boulder I've been carrying has broken into pebbles. It is a secret that I have kept for over ten years. So why am I saying these words out loud now, after all these years?

EDITOR'S NOTES

'This is incredibly powerful. I love the way we're drawn into this character's mindset in a single paragraph. We know we want to learn about them, who they are, all that good stuff. The central question of what is to follow ends the paragraph. I would possibly open with the line 'I killed my husband' and follow on from there, but that's all I would want to change. It's such a good line.'

PUZZLE No. 96

Break It Down

Across

1. Nursery rhyme eloper?
5. Mishandle
10. Riff, vocally
14. Ellery's contemporary
15. Jury list
16. Lincoln who played Tarzan
17. Lake Mead holder in Colorado, originally
19. Mug lips
20. Jet, to a Shark
21. Lab or peke
22. Early phone fees in America
23. Dress up
25. Home for a hamster
27. Got into a pickle?
28. Earlier than
29. B-52's song with the lyric "Watch out for that piranha"
32. Man of Belgrade
34. Existed
35. Con artists
36. Encourage bad behavior
38. Olympics glider
39. "Monsters, Inc." job
42. __ Shop Boys
43. Far from naked
47. California golf locale
50. Caesarean salute
51. DVR brand
52. What comes to mind
53. Actress Anjelica
55. "__ Meenie" (2010 hit)
57. __ poetica
59. Court claims
60. "Fantasy" singer Nova
61. Bed trimming
63. Singer of "The Wanderer"
64. Pub quaff
65. They may be broken by drivers
66. Lacking, in Le Mans
67. Paul who sings "Kids" in "Bye Bye Birdie"
68. East anagram

Down

1. Campaign clashes
2. Goethite, for one
3. Batman?
4. __ Kitty
5. Siamang, for one
6. Avon product?
7. Casts off, as a boat
8. "Fire Down Below" star Steven
9. One throwing shade?
10. Golf pro Pak
11. Air condition?
12. Electric gauge
13. Folks having fun with a Frisbee
18. Grumpy
22. Clear of glitches
24. Loomed (over)
26. Split with one's boyfriend, perhaps?
30. Smilodon was one
31. On __
33. Hook part
37. Misrepresent
38. __ & Perrins
39. Holiday meals

40. Titular woman of a Simon & Garfunkel hit
41. Leave
42. Toronto airport
44. Visa problem
45. "Anne of Green Gables" town
46. Most compact
48. Drugstore section
49. "The Handmaid's Tale" airer
54. Processes flour
56. Some atomic particles
58. Wall board?
61. Speedy WWW hookup
62. Travel plan abbr.

CRIMEBIT No. 97

Seven Sins

YOUR RATING /100

Jill Whitehouse

Dan is carving the meat as if everything is normal. At moments like this, I almost believe it is. I still kiss him goodbye in the morning, welcome him home with dinner in the evening. Sleep next to him. Have sex with him, though that is hard. But I keep imagining her. Wondering if his face is the same when he comes as when he's with me. That look's mine. Not hers.

A bead of sweat trickles down my face. My hand trembles as I wipe it away. Each time these thoughts hit, I'm overwhelmed by the enormity of what my discovery might mean. But I won't let her destroy this. My life. Our life.

Flora snaffles a piece of crackling and Dan laughs. 'You'll turn into a little piglet.'

She snorts, and scampers round the kitchen on all fours. Her brother copies. 'Look Mummy,' he says. 'We're baby pigs.'

'You're right barmpots, that's what you are.' I tell my face to smile, but my head's somewhere else. I pour a bag of peas into a saucepan of water and turn on the hob.

'Can you make sure these don't boil over?' I say to Dan. 'I need the loo.'

PUZZLE No. 97

Hog Wild

BABE	HANS	OLD MAJOR	PIGLING BLAND	ROSITA
BEBOP	HAWK	OLIVIA	PIGNITE	SIR OINKSALOT
BOTAN	HEN WEN	OPAL	PORCO ROSSO	SNOWBALL
GALA	HUXLEY	ORSON	ARNOLD ZIFFEL	SPIDER-HAM
GORDY	IGGY ARBUCKLE	PEPPA	GULLINBURSTI	SQUEALER
GUNTER	MADAME OINK	PETUNIA	PORKY	TOOT
HAMILTON	MCMUG	PIGGLEY	PUA	WILBUR
HAMM	MISS PIGGY	WINKS	PUDDLE	
HAMTON	NAPOLEON	PIGLET	PUMBAA	

B	E	B	O	P	Q	G	G	D	U	X	H	O	E	M	R	M	P	P	A	T
J	B	D	N	N	U	V	U	R	O	O	Y	I	P	B	F	U	S	R	I	O
A	I	F	G	I	T	X	O	L	U	S	S	G	O	R	D	Y	N	E	P	L
K	U	S	T	Y	D	Y	U	O	L	A	S	Y	E	D	J	O	O	T	I	A
F	R	P	B	O	E	C	R	V	Q	I	M	O	L	E	L	O	W	N	G	S
I	Y	Y	V	J	E	C	F	B	P	W	N	E	R	D	H	B	B	U	N	K
U	P	L	F	P	L	F	E	G	I	M	S	B	Z	O	P	O	A	G	I	N
G	I	J	T	H	F	O	X	A	I	B	Z	I	U	O	C	N	L	N	T	I
K	G	Z	E	Q	H	L	P	L	X	N	F	N	Y	R	E	R	L	R	E	O
D	G	E	L	A	X	P	S	A	I	F	H	A	Q	W	S	Z	O	T	C	R
N	L	M	W	E	E	H	G	Q	E	D	S	U	N	F	Y	T	M	P	T	I
A	E	K	N	P	P	A	K	L	U	P	E	E	O	X	B	A	I	N	P	S
L	Y	T	F	O	E	M	I	O	A	E	H	H	Z	P	W	P	O	R	K	Y
B	W	O	A	I	T	M	P	T	P	N	A	O	L	D	M	A	J	O	R	S
G	I	S	K	N	T	L	I	K	U	O	T	L	L	T	V	Y	J	Z	O	P
N	N	X	N	D	P	S	I	B	M	T	X	U	E	I	E	E	T	W	N	I
I	K	N	I	W	O	A	K	M	B	M	R	A	H	R	L	L	Y	E	W	D
L	S	E	O	R	Y	Z	U	W	A	A	I	W	I	T	I	X	G	Q	M	E
G	D	X	E	S	J	G	H	R	A	H	I	B	O	V	H	U	T	I	H	R
I	Y	T	M	Z	R	N	A	P	O	L	E	O	N	S	I	H	L	A	P	H
P	W	P	A	A	W	O	F	O	B	G	T	T	Y	A	K	L	N	A	N	A
W	Z	N	D	W	P	E	T	U	N	I	A	A	B	B	N	S	O	L	P	M
Y	F	Z	A	S	E	Y	R	F	I	T	U	N	A	J	X	I	Z	A	K	O
D	C	S	M	Y	G	G	I	P	S	S	I	M	B	G	U	M	C	M	G	V
I	G	G	Y	A	R	B	U	C	K	L	E	U	E	Q	D	P	L	G	B	W

CRIMEBIT No.98

Get Here Now or I'll Kill You

YOUR RATING /100

Judith Wilson

'Get here now or I will kill you.'

The short message flashed on the phone for half a second before fading away leaving Maggie jabbing at the screen.

It wasn't her phone. It wasn't her life being threatened, but that wasn't going to stop her trying to find out who was going to be killed. And who was going to kill them.

She pressed the power switch and gasped. There was no password. Everything was on display. And she could see why. The row of default icons along the bottom led nowhere. There was no email or social media. This was a device for quick messages. And there were only two of them.

The first from Tommy.

'Where's the bracelet? Bishop is angry.'

And thirty minutes later the one she'd just seen, from an angry Bishop.

Her fingers shook as she ran through the short list of contacts and looked for anybody who might be able to help.

Andrew. Maybe.

Bishop. Definitely not.

Maggie. Interesting. How many people had a Maggie in their lives?

With her phone number.

? DID YOU KNOW ?

Edgar Allan Poe had a keen interest in cryptography and wrote several cryptograms and ciphers throughout his life. His fascination with codes and puzzles is reflected in some of his stories, such as "The Gold-Bug", where a hidden treasure is deciphered using a code.

PUZZLE No. 98

Contact List

The contacts in the phone Maggie found don't provide a lot of information. Each one has a first name, a photograph of a Star Wars character, and a New York City area code. It's not much to go on! From the clues, determine which ***contact*** *in the phone is associated with which Star Wars* ***character*** *and what their* ***area code*** *is.*

The Contacts

Andrew

Bishop

Tommy

Star Wars Characters

Luke Skywalker

Mace Windu

Obi-Wan Kenobi

The Area Codes

212

718

917

? CLUES ?

1. Tommy is located in 212 area.
2. Luke Skywalker's picture isn't Bishop's.
3. The Mace Windu contact's area code is 917.
4. Andrew's area code isn't 718.
5. Tommy doesn't have the Obi-Wan Kenobi picture.

	Andrew	*Bishop*	*Tommy*	*Luke Skywalker*	*Mace Windu*	*Obi-Wan Kenobi*
212						
718						
917						
Luke Skywalker						
Mace Windu						
Obi-Wan Kenobi						

Contact	Character	Area Code

CRIMEBIT No. 99

The Habitat of the Dartford Warbler

YOUR RATING /100

Marcia Woolf

At six-fifteen a.m. on 19th April, Robert Kenney set off on his bicycle along the Brighton Road. Later, his wife said this was the last time she'd seen him alive. The phone rang at nine. She dried her hands and picked up the receiver, thinking it was the school, complaining that Toby hadn't arrived, but it was Carl.

'Hi, Veronica. Is Rob okay? He's not turned up. There's a customer waiting.'

'He's not here.'

Carl started making excuses to the customer even before he'd hung up. Veronica looked out, both ways along the street. Nobody. Rob had left the gate open. She'd been asleep when he'd clicked the front door shut and swung his leg over the crossbar of the bike. She hadn't seen when he looked up at the closed bedroom curtains before turning onto the main road and beginning to pedal slowly towards the junction. Veronica was heading upstairs when she caught sight of herself in the mirror. Truth to tell, she hadn't seen her husband since the night before, when she'd switched off the bedside lamp. He'd been sleeping; curled up like a child, facing away from her. That was what she'd have to tell the police.

HAVE YOUR SAY
What happens next?

Scan to visit the CrimeBits Writing Space

PUZZLE No. 99

Cycling

Across

1. Vividness (10)
7. Annual tennis team event (5,3)
8. Uncle's counterpart (4)
9. Sups (4)
10. Canada or Mexico (7)
12. It prevents pants from catching in the 5 Down (7,4)
14. Tested (7)
16. Bisque or borscht (4)
19. Accessory on the handlebars (4)
20. Subjects of some sea tales (8)
21. Relating to betrayal of one's country (10)

Down

1. Slow down (5)
2. Daft (7)
3. Security device (4)
4. Sanctions (8)
5. Sprockets linker (5)
6. Catch cunningly (6)
11. One who sings in shrill piercing tones (8)
12. Hit on the head (6)
13. Ferocious cat (7)
15. Lively folk dance (5)
17. Propel a tandem (5)
18. Aquatic reptile (abbr) (4)

1
2
3
4
5
6
7
8
9
10
11
12
13
14
15
16
17
18
19
20
21

CRIMEBIT No.100

Rock Bottom

YOUR RATING /100

Rebecca Wurth

A person's home can tell you almost everything you need to know about someone. Belinda's home for instance, alerts any visiting entrants that the occupier is a middle-aged woman who has hit rock bottom. The stench of week-old kitty litter hits you before you ever lay eyes on the assortment of empty wine bottles left as decorative ornaments on any patch of hard surface not already occupied by half-empty tuna cans. The dust motes twirl through the air frantically trying to escape the confines of the dreary room which is well overdue for a clean. Which is ironic because what this house doesn't tell you about Belinda is that she is a cleaner.

Belinda absent-mindedly plaits her long, tangled hair, trying to subtly brush the knots with her fingers and avoid Pat's eyes as he thunders down the corridor towards her. 'You're late again.' He calls to her as he advances. 'Save your apologies for your own time, Lucy is sick again and I need you to take her place on the trauma clean and I needed you there 20 minutes ago.' Trauma clean? That can only mean one thing, someone has died.

WRITING PROMPT 10

The handler sighed heavily, looked me in the eyes and said, 'Are you sure you want to do this? I don't have to give you this one you know.'

Looking back, all I can think about that moment was what was running through my mind. One thought over and over.

I said, 'This happens today.'

Thinking . . . am I sure?

* * *

It didn't take long to find him. After receiving the tip I'd been waiting for, I found him within a week. Almost as if he hadn't been hiding at all. Took me longer to find that drifter on the west coast last year. It was three months before I discovered him working in the kitchen of a truck stop diner. Waited outside for him and followed the guy home. Poor bastard never saw me coming. This old man was no different. Had no idea I'd been following him for a week.

Scan to visit the
CrimeBits Writing Space

PUZZLE No. 100

Clean Slate

Across

1. Brest friend
5. Conservative
10. 3-D pic
14. __ fide (in good faith)
15. Ambiguous dating term
16. Mystery author?
17. One covering a big story?
19. Chocolate units
20. East German currency, once
21. Dinner-and-a-show venue
23. __ lemon (hybrid citrus fruit)
24. Grassy glade
26. 2020 Millie Bobby Brown role
27. Goethe's "The _-King"
28. Kreese's direction to Johnny in "The Karate Kid"
31. Tiny amt. of time
33. Misspeak or misdo
34. AI in a '72 Nebula-winning novel
35. Swiss watch company
37. Furlan or Sorvino
38. "The Good Body" playwright
41. One little piggy
42. Flopsy's tail
46. Mike's pets in an '80s BBC show
49. Hairy anthropoid
50. Jejune
51. They're rated in BTUs
52. Pacific or Atlantic
54. Instance of unfairness
56. Fencing moves
58. Dermatology topic
59. Component of early computers
61. Amphitheater level
62. Old Spanish card game
63. Time pieces?
64. Cousins of PhDs
65. Smartens (up)
66. "Round and Round" rockers

Down

1. Navel setting
2. Cats on the prowl
3. Trendy
4. Message on a Wonderland cake
5. Sign of injury
6. Rib-__ (jokes)
7. Craft built from gopher wood
8. Polar formation
9. Spreadsheet content
10. Cuban dances
11. Hot, hot, hot!
12. Rhineland siren
13. Behind the proscenium
18. Array in the pickle aisle
22. Howard of Starbucks or Sasha on "Coronation Street"
25. "As wicked dew as __ my mother brush'd": "The Tempest"
29. Al Yankovic's moniker

30. One taking things badly?
32. Drainers and strainers
36. Rapp or Zellweger
37. What humidity measures
38. Dubai or Kuwait
39. Basic, chemically
40. Created a video game character
41. US film buff's cable network
43. Breathing pause, in music
44. Getting ready to hit, in cricket
45. Most edgy
47. Antipasto ingredient
48. Compose
53. More cuddly, say
55. Solemnly declare
57. Swatch assortment
60. Paramount+ network in the US

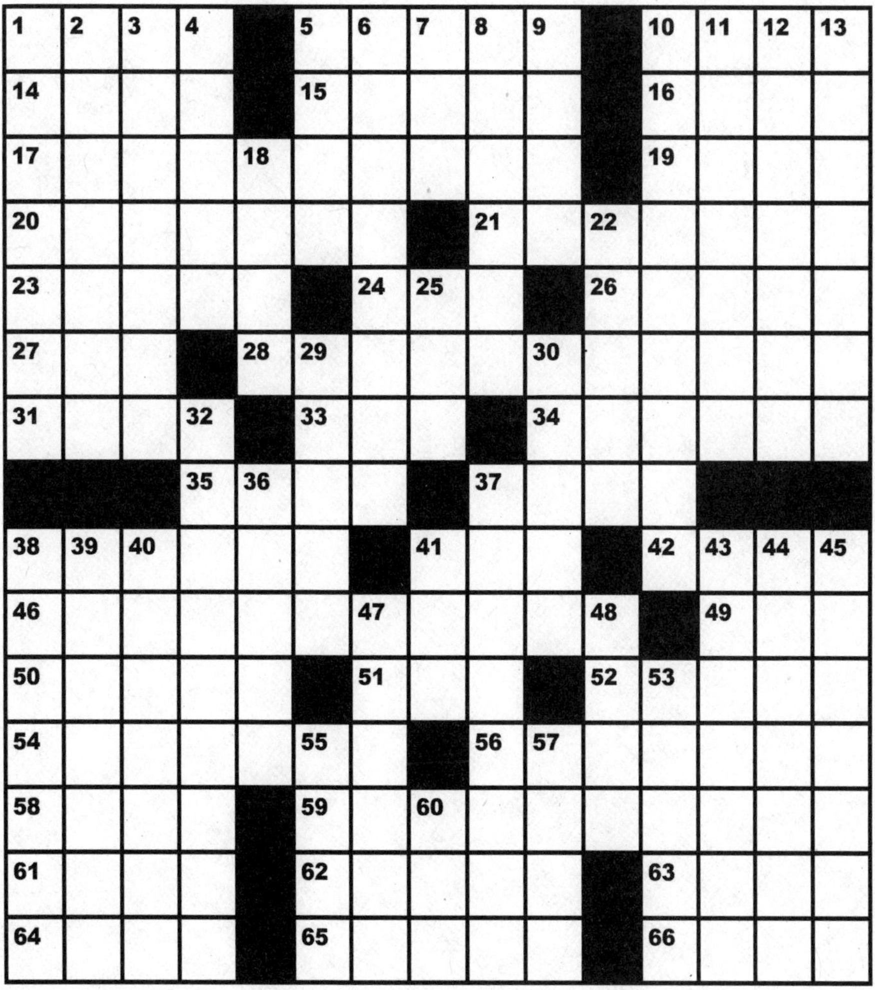

AFTERWORD
by LUCA VESTE

There is something about opening a new book for the first time. There's no way of knowing what lies inside, before you turn that cover over and start flipping through the pages. Absorbing the words, becoming immersed in a story. It's a hidden world, waiting to be discovered.

Only, there is a multitude of things desperately trying to take your attention. Maybe that's a mobile phone sitting next to you, pinging with notifications. The entire world at your fingertips. Social media, the world's town square, with a wealth of shared opinions waiting to be heard. The constant rolling nature of news. Videos to be watched. Then, there's the television in the corner of the room, with its constant barrage of entertainment. Hundreds of channels, all with different types of programs. Streaming services, with films, documentaries, comedies, all sitting there waiting for you to press play.

It's perhaps the most difficult time in human history to sit down and lose yourself in a good read.

I remember being a child and discovering the joy of reading. Of being five or six years old and entering a library for the first time. Being told that there was all this free entertainment, just waiting for me to check out. It seemed a ridiculous thing to child me – that you could walk into a building and take something for free. That you could be just given entertainment, with nothing expected in exchange.

Even back then, I was fascinated by the mechanics of it all. How could some books draw me in, gripping tightly and never letting go. Then others, that were more difficult to get into – a slow burn, that I wasn't racing through as I did so many others. I was far too young to understand it, of course, but that didn't stop me trying.

Of course, there are a multitude of things going on when you pick up a story. No doubt you'll have read the blurb on the back (or inside flap) and worked out if it's the type of novel you're interested in. You've read the author before, so you kind of know what to expect maybe. Or, the cover has drawn your attention enough to pick it up from a shelf – piqued your interest to want to find out more. Then, you start reading.

Picture this – you go out to a restaurant. A meal is prepared for you and is placed on the table. You take a first bite and think, 'Hmm – I'm not sure about this.' You take another and feel the same way, maybe even more so now. You're sitting there wondering if you've made the right decision. You're not enjoying the taste of this food, it's not something you were expecting when you ordered, or you had something similar a while ago and this isn't as good. Do you continue eating? Do you finish the whole meal? Do you ask the server if there's something wrong with the dish? Many different possibilities here. Now, compare that to a novel. You open the first page. The first line, the second. A paragraph, a page. How long do you give it before you stop? A few pages, ten, twenty? Do you persevere, hoping your taste will change, that you'll eventually end up liking this book? Or, do you give up quickly?

Every reader is different.

One thing I've begun to really take notice of when writing novels is how novels open. I know what I'm competing against, because I'm a reader too. I'm distracted by all the same things my readers are, so over the years, I've concentrated much more on the openings of my stories.

Take my first novel, *Dead Gone*. Over ten years old now, written in 2012. It opens with an extract from a psychology review paper (that I made up). It talks about society's fascination with death, setting the tone of the novel. It goes on for around 250-300 words, a little over a page. Then, a reader would turn the page and be confronted with the chapter heading . . .

Experiment Two

Now, instantly the reader is made to question a few things – why isn't it 'Chapter One' for a start. It's an odd chapter heading. Then, you start examining it more closely – 'Experiment Two' . . . what happened to the first experiment?

Then, the first line.

She hadn't been afraid of the dark.

More questions. She hadn't been, but now she is? Why?

It continues.

Not before. Not before it entered her life without her knowing – enveloping her like a second skin. Becoming a part of her.

(I'd like to add here that reading over something that you wrote twelve years ago is horrible for a writer – you want to change every word!)

Now, the reader is hopefully drawn in and wants to know more. About this character, the situation they're in and how it happened.

Unfortunately, I've opened the book with that one and half page, very dry psychology review paper. Have I already lost them by that point?

If I was writing *Dead Gone* today, I would have opened

immediately with the 'Experiment Two' chapter. I would have gone with the part that was more likely to draw the reader in and hope to keep hold of them.

What would you prefer as a reader?

Now, if you're a writer, this is a moment for you to pause and think about this yourself. What would you do in this situation?

Think of an opening to a novel which starts with an odd chapter heading. Something that will make a reader question what they're about to enter.

What can you come up with?

My second novel, *The Dying Place*, opens differently. Chapter heading . . .

Now

First line . . .

No one believes you.

I'm personalizing the read. I'm making the reader part of the story instantly. I'm doing something here that is intentional – I want to draw you in and make you forget about the outside world for a moment.

The page goes on to talk about a certain type of character – one that will feel very familiar to a lot of people.

My sixth novel, imaginatively titled *The Six* for very good reasons, opens with a single page, with no chapter heading.

When it was over, there was silence.

It wasn't a calm type of quiet. Peaceful or tranquil. It was a suffocating stillness, as reality settled over us all.

On me.

No turning back now. No changing our minds. No fixing our mistake.

I can still feel the mud under my fingernails. I could feel the blood that didn't belong to me on my skin. The smell of sweat and fear.

I could scrub myself clean over and over and it would never be enough.

It would still be there. Ground down, seeping into my skin. Turning my blood black and cold.

The dirt.

The pain.

The evil.

This was my mistake.

My fault.

Now, if you're looking for a final writing prompt, use this opening page. Tell me who this character is and what they'd done. Write out the scene that immediately precedes this one. What happened to this person and what did they do?

I guarantee that everyone will write something different. Especially to what I wrote next.

That's the beauty of storytelling – we all have our own way.

By my ninth novel, *Trust In Me*, its opening line is stark, impactful I hope.

The children were quiet.

Nothing more, nothing less.

I've become much more conscious of the openings to my novels over the years, because I want to give the reader the same feeling I get when I pick up a book. I want to immerse myself in a read. I want to be drawn in, gripped tightly, and not let go.

What has been incredible about the competition we ran was the breadth of different styles of openings. Some are character led, some are about a situation. All of them draw you in and wonder . . .

What happens next?

I know I've been intrigued by many of them since reading. They've made me think and wonder about those characters and situations and how I might continue the story. And that means they've done their job right! They've drawn me in as a reader and made me want to know how the story continues. That's the beauty of storytelling and in this fast-paced society in which we live, that's a difficult thing for a writer to do.

Crime fiction is an amazing genre. I came to it early, reading Enid Blyton as so many kids do and did back in the eighties and nineties. I remember staring at the shelves in my local library (now sadly no longer in existence) and being blown away by just how many books I could read. *The Famous Five, The Secret Seven* . . . even my secret favorite series *Malory Towers.* So many books, that would lead me to a lifetime of reading within that genre.

What I love about the genre is different sub-genres within it. Police procedurals, action thrillers, psychological thrillers, domestic noir, historical, the list goes on and on. There is something for everyone it seems! I've been fortunate enough to have had the chance to write a number of different styles of books. *Dead Gone* and the next three books were police procedurals, before I moved into a crime/horror crossover with *The Bone Keeper*. Then, a more psychological horror crime novel with *The Six*, another police procedural with *The Game*, before my novels *You Never Said Goodbye* and *Trust In Me* became straight thrillers – in the mold of ordinary people in extraordinary circumstances. The genre has given me the ability to tell very different types of story, in very different types of ways, but what is always important to me is drawing a reader in from those first few pages.

I am delighted to have been involved in *CrimeBits*, which is a delightful collection of opening gambits, puzzles, and so much more. What it shows more than anything is the different strands of crime fiction and all the stories that can be told within it. A glorious display of the many different facets to my favorite genre.

Luca Veste

2024

AUTHORS

John Adamcik
Leanne Anderson
Steven Axelrod
Cailey Barker
Sacha Bissonnette
Jamie Brannan
Richard Burke
Tony Bury
Victoria Chang
Nathan Coon
Liz Correal
Daniel Cox-Howard
Alys Cummings
John Cunningham
Catherine Darensbourg
Lee Dawkins
Jim DeFillippi
Meg E. Dobson
Niamh Donnellan
Mickey Dubrow
Antony Dunford
Helen East
Lucy Edwards
Susie Ellis
Alan Evans
Peter Everett
Tracy Falenwolfe
Dahlia Fisher
Dónal Fogarty
Peter Fryer
C. A. Fulwell
Vicky Garforth
David Goodlett
Alan Peter Gorevan
S.D.W. Hamilton
Katt Hansen
Kathryn Hatfield
Anne Hewling
Nikki HoSang
Iqbal Hussain
Lorah Jaiyn
Anwen John
Jason Kerrigan
Andrew Komarnyckyj
John Lau
Allen Learst
Jennifer Leeper
Marti Leimbach

Amy Lyn
Camilla Macpherson
Oliver Marlow
Deirdre Mcauley
Alexandra McDermott
Cate McDermott
Samantha Metcalfe
Linda Millington
Donna Moore
Laurel Nicholson
James Nisbet
Angela Nurse
Randy O'Brien
Barry Penfold
David Potter
Fiona Quinn
Deborah Rayner
Callum Reid
Reaghan Reilly
Robin Richards
May Rinaldi
Leslie Roberts
Rodney Rogers
Claire Rozario
Sabine Sapia
Paul Smitham
Rosie Sorenson
Daniel Stewart
Lorelai Tarlow
Michael Telfer
Lorraine Thomson
Marek Turner
Richard Valanga
Graham Wall
Rachael Warecki
Joanne Watkinson
Rachael Watson
Lucy Wetherall
Jill Whitehouse
Judith Wilson
Marcia Woolf
Rebecca Wurth

Scan here to read more about our authors

SOLUTIONS

Crosswords

1

L	I	B	E	L		O	W	L	S		M	O	E	S
A	R	E	N	A		T	O	I	L		I	N	T	O
D	A	D	D	Y	S	H	O	M	E		R	E	A	D
E	N	S	U	I	T	E		O	D	O	R			
			S	N	A	R	L			P	O	L	O	S
P	O	M	E			S	I	S	T	E	R	A	C	T
A	R	A	R	A	T		D	E	A	N		T	A	E
J	A	N	S	S	E	N		P	R	E	P	O	S	E
A	T	E		C	A	T	S		P	R	A	Y	E	R
M	O	T	H	E	R	H	E	N			R	A	Y	S
A	R	S	O	N			T	U	N	E	R			
			S	T	A	R		M	O	R	O	C	C	O
A	M	B	I		B	I	G	B	R	O	T	H	E	R
L	O	A	N		E	P	E	E		D	E	U	C	E
L	O	N	G		D	E	E	R		E	D	G	E	S

3

S	E	W		R	E	S	A	W		R	S	V	P	S
O	L	E		A	P	P	L	E		A	C	T	U	P
F	A	L	S	E	H	O	O	D		D	A	R	B	Y
T	I	L	E		E	K	E		O	I	L			
O	N	E	T	I	M	E		W	H	O	P	P	E	R
N	E	S	T	L	E		R	E	S			O	V	A
			L	O	R	E	A	L		A	L	L	E	Y
	P	R	E	V	A	R	I	C	A	T	I	O	N	
H	O	U	S	E		A	S	H	R	A	M			
I	C	H			S	S	E		B	L	I	T	H	E
P	O	R	K	P	I	E		A	I	L	E	R	O	N
			E	A	T		B	L	T		S	I	L	T
N	O	T	E	S		F	A	I	R	Y	T	A	L	E
A	D	O	P	T		U	N	B	A	R		G	E	R
S	E	N	S	E		N	A	I	L	S		E	R	S

5

P	H	O	T	O		C	H	E	R		G	A	P	S
A	E	R	O	S		E	U	R	O		O	P	I	E
T	A	B	L	E	S	C	R	A	P		E	P	E	E
E	V	I	L		A	I	R		E	N	T	E	R	S
N	E	T		S	A	L	A	D		O	H	A	R	A
C	H	E	R	U	B		H	E	D	G	E	R	O	W
Y	O	D	E	L		A	S	I	A			S	T	S
			D	U	E	T		C	Y	A	N			
S	H	A			E	L	S	E		L	A	C	K	S
T	E	N	T	F	L	A	P		T	A	B	L	E	T
A	R	T	O	O		S	I	G	H	S		E	E	R
P	O	E	T	R	Y		N	A	E		O	M	N	I
L	I	N	T		G	R	O	U	N	D	B	E	E	F
E	N	N	E		O	A	F	S		R	I	N	S	E
D	E	A	R		R	E	F	S		J	E	S	T	S

7

			N		P		M		S			
		L	U	X	U	R	I	A	T	E		
	M		M		F		R		U		M	
W	I	D	E		F	O	R	E	N	S	I	C
	S		R		E		O				S	
A	B	O	A	R	D		R	O	C	K	E	T
	E		L						L		R	
C	H	I	S	E	L		T	H	O	R	A	X
	A				I		W		T		B	
E	V	I	D	E	N	C	E		T	A	L	K
	E		E		E		N		I		E	
		N	A	R	R	A	T	I	N	G		
			R		S		Y		G			

9

C	L	O	T	H		B	U	S		A	H	E	A	D
P	E	R	R	I		A	N	T		S	A	L	S	A
L	O	S	I	N	G	T	H	E	T	H	R	E	A	D
			A	G	E		O	V	I		I	M	P	S
N	O	B	L	E	R		O	I	L	S				
E	P	O	S		M	A	K	E	T	H	E	C	U	T
W	E	B		M	A	P	S			A	T	O	N	E
I	N	C	L	I	N	E		C	A	R	A	M	E	L
S	T	A	I	N			G	A	S	P		M	A	L
H	O	T	B	U	T	T	O	N	S		R	O	S	E
				S	H	E	B		I	N	A	N	E	R
A	B	L	E		A	N	Y		S	U	N			
L	E	A	V	E	I	N	S	T	I	T	C	H	E	S
S	A	K	E	S		E	E	R		T	H	O	U	S
O	M	E	N	S		R	A	Y		Y	O	U	R	E

11

P	O	S	S	U	M		O	C	H	O		R	A	N
A	S	T	U	T	E		U	H	U	H		I	C	E
C	O	R	N	E	R	S	T	O	R	M		S	H	E
E	L	O	N		C	O	L	O	R		F	E	E	D
S	E	P	I	A		R	E	S	A	L	E			
			S	L	E	E	T	Y	H	O	L	L	O	W
M	E	N		L	A	S	S			S	T	O	N	E
I	R	A		T	U	T		S	S	E		A	C	T
C	A	R	G	O			A	P	E	S		D	E	S
A	S	C	O	L	D	A	S	H	A	I	L			
			O	D	E	N	S	E		T	E	M	P	O
C	A	R	D		S	N	O	R	E		M	A	I	L
A	R	E		P	O	U	R	E	X	C	U	S	E	S
Y	E	S		E	T	A	T		A	D	E	S	T	E
S	A	T		P	O	L	S		M	C	L	E	A	N

13

E	N	G	A	G	E		R	E	L	E	A	R	N	S
M	A	R	R	E	D		I	N	A	T	R	I	C	E
M	O	O	I	N	G		B	O	N	H	O	M	I	E
E	M	U		T	E	A	S		D	A	M	A	S	K
T	I	N	T	E	R	S		U	L	N	A			
		D	U	E		K	Y	R	I	E		D	E	R
W	O	B	B	L	E		I	A	N		H	I	D	E
I	R	A	E		A	D	E	L	E		A	R	I	D
P	A	L	S		R	E	L		S	A	L	T	E	D
E	L	L		S	T	U	D	Y		B	A	D		
			M	O	H	S		A	G	E	L	E	S	S
M	O	V	E	R	S		A	W	A	Y		V	I	E
I	D	E	A	T	I	O	N		S	A	T	I	R	E
M	I	D	N	I	G	H	T		E	N	S	L	E	R
I	N	A	S	E	N	S	E		S	T	A	S	E	S

17

T	E	M	P	I		P	S	I	S		O	C	H	O
O	N	E	A	L		E	L	S	E		P	E	E	N
V	I	N	Y	L		D	E	E	R		O	R	A	L
A	D	D		I	P	A	D		V	A	S	T	L	Y
		F	I	N	A	L		W	I	N	S			
A	R	E	N	O	T		P	I	C	T	U	R	E	S
T	A	N	N	I	C		U	S	E		M	E	M	O
T	I	C		S	H	A	P	E	R	S		P	A	N
I	S	E	E		P	D	A		O	R	D	A	I	N
C	E	S	S	P	O	O	L		A	I	R	I	L	Y
			S	E	C	S		I	D	L	E	R		
S	T	R	E	A	K		R	O	S	A		K	O	A
A	E	O	N		E	D	I	T		N	E	I	L	S
T	A	L	C		T	U	N	A		K	I	T	E	S
E	R	L	E		S	O	D	S		A	N	S	O	N

19

E	L	B	O	W		A	B	C	S		C	U	E	D
B	U	R	R	O		L	E	I	S		O	G	R	E
B	L	A	N	K	S	L	A	T	E		B	L	O	B
S	A	G	A		O	M	N	I		T	W	I	S	T
			M	C	N	A	B		C	E	E			
S	I	R	E	E		N	A	V	A	L	B	A	S	E
A	D	O	N	I	S		G	I	R	L		R	C	A
N	E	S	T	L	E	D		P	O	T	S	D	A	M
T	A	S		I	A	N	S		L	A	H	O	R	E
A	L	I	E	N	R	A	C	E		L	O	R	E	S
			A	G	S		O	L	D	E	R			
F	L	A	G	S		M	U	I	R		T	O	F	U
R	O	L	L		P	A	R	T	Y	F	A	V	O	R
E	A	S	E		E	D	G	E		A	G	A	I	N
E	N	O	S		T	E	E	S		B	E	L	L	S

21

C	A	R	A	T		G	I	A	S		P	I	M	A
A	W	A	S	H		A	C	N	E		R	O	A	R
R	O	C	K	E	T	M	A	N	I	C	O	T	T	I
P	L	Y		R	H	I	N	O		O	M	A	H	A
			S	E	E	N		Y	E	L	P			
F	I	S	H	I	N	G	R	I	G	A	T	O	N	I
O	C	E	A	N			E	N	O	S		D	O	N
L	E	W	D		S	W	I	G	S		M	E	L	D
D	U	E		B	E	R	G			S	I	T	A	R
S	P	R	A	Y	C	A	N	N	E	L	L	O	N	I
			L	E	S	T		O	L	E	O			
O	C	A	L	A		H	E	S	S	E		K	I	T
P	O	W	E	R	O	F	T	H	E	P	E	N	N	E
A	N	E	G		M	U	T	E		E	R	O	D	E
L	E	S	E		G	L	A	D		R	A	T	O	N

23

R	A	V	E		N	E	A	T	O		A	P	P	S
E	D	E	N		E	A	T	O	N		C	A	R	L
H	A	R	L	E	M	C	A	K	E		T	R	E	E
I	M	A		O	O	H		E	S	S		A	P	E
R	A	N	I	N			U	N	I	T		G	A	P
E	N	D	S		J	E	R	S	E	Y	C	O	R	E
S	T	A	R	S	I	G	N			L	O	N	E	R
			A	M	M	O		D	E	E	P			
O	R	F	E	O			C	O	N	S	I	S	T	S
P	I	L	L	O	W	C	A	M	S		E	C	R	U
I	S	O		T	R	O	T			G	R	A	I	N
N	O	R		H	E	R		P	A	N		R	T	S
I	T	E	M		A	N	T	I	Q	U	E	C	O	P
O	T	T	O		K	E	A	N	U		L	E	N	O
N	O	S	E		S	A	N	T	A		F	R	E	T

25

A	C	C	O	M	P	L	I	S	H	I	N	G
L		A		U		E		E		N		R
A	R	M		N	U	M	B	E	R	T	W	O
R		E		C		O		M		E		U
M	O	R	P	H	I	N	E		D	R	I	P
		A		I		S		P		M		E
G	R	O	U	N	D		R	E	S	E	N	D
E		B		G		L		R		D		
T	E	S	T		T	O	A	S	T	I	N	G
T		C		G		O		O		A		R
I	B	U	P	R	O	F	E	N		T	O	E
N		R		I		A		A		O		E
G	R	A	N	D	C	H	I	L	D	R	E	N

27

S	W	I	M	■	U	T	A	H	■	H	A	I	T	I
A	I	D	E	■	N	A	N	A	■	E	N	T	E	R
S	P	E	A	R	M	I	N	T	■	R	I	S	E	R
H	E	E	L	T	A	P	■	■	M	O	M	■	■	■
■	■	■	I	S	S	A	R	A	E	■	A	R	M	S
P	A	V	E	■	K	N	I	F	E	P	L	E	A	T
O	D	I	S	T	S	■	C	R	T	S	■	T	R	E
S	W	A	T	H	■	W	H	O	■	S	O	A	V	E
T	A	G	■	A	S	E	A	■	S	T	U	P	I	D
A	R	R	O	W	V	E	R	S	E	■	T	E	N	S
L	E	A	K	■	E	N	D	E	A	R	S	■	■	■
■	■	■	A	Y	N	■	■	A	T	E	C	R	O	W
T	E	M	P	O	■	D	A	R	T	M	O	U	T	H
S	P	O	I	L	■	A	B	E	L	■	R	I	T	E
K	I	O	S	K	■	D	U	D	E	■	E	N	O	W

29

S	C	O	T	■	A	R	C	A	D	E	■	S	K	A
E	L	B	A	■	P	H	O	N	E	D	■	L	I	P
D	I	E	U	P	R	O	C	E	S	S	■	E	S	P
A	M	I	T	Y	■	N	O	W	■	■	M	I	S	E
T	A	S	■	X	E	D	■	■	E	N	I	G	M	A
I	T	A	L	■	E	A	U	B	R	O	T	H	E	R
V	E	N	E	E	R	■	N	U	R	S	E	■	■	■
E	S	T	A	R	■	O	C	T	■	I	R	O	N	S
■	■	■	P	E	A	R	L	■	B	R	E	V	E	T
C	E	S	T	C	H	E	E	S	E	■	D	E	A	R
Z	A	P	A	T	A	■	■	A	T	V	■	R	T	E
E	T	A	T	■	■	C	A	Y	■	C	A	R	E	S
C	O	D	■	L	A	I	T	I	N	R	U	I	N	S
H	U	E	■	A	C	T	O	N	E	■	E	P	E	E
S	T	S	■	T	H	I	N	G	S	■	L	E	D	S

31

G	A	S	P	S	■	B	A	I	L	■	B	A	L	L
E	S	T	E	E	■	A	N	N	O	■	A	R	E	A
C	H	A	R	M	T	R	A	D	E	■	S	M	O	G
K	E	Y	S	■	I	N	G	■	B	E	E	■	■	■
O	S	S	O	■	E	U	R	O	■	L	H	A	S	A
■	■	■	N	O	R	M	A	L	F	L	I	G	H	T
P	A	G	A	N	■	■	M	I	L	I	T	I	A	S
U	T	E	■	G	A	T	■	N	A	P	■	S	H	E
M	E	T	E	O	R	I	C	■	■	S	A	M	S	A
P	U	B	L	I	C	M	A	G	N	E	T	■	■	■
S	P	Y	O	N	■	E	R	L	E	■	T	I	P	S
■	■	■	P	G	A	■	B	O	X	■	I	D	E	A
A	L	A	I	■	C	H	A	R	T	E	R	L	A	W
P	E	N	N	■	H	A	R	I	■	G	E	E	S	E
R	I	N	G	■	E	D	N	A	■	O	D	D	E	R

33

O	P	A	L	■	F	O	C	I	■	O	D	I	U	M
N	A	N	A	■	A	N	O	N	■	R	O	S	S	I
C	R	O	S	S	T	A	L	K	■	B	O	W	E	L
E	D	I	T	H	■	■	A	S	K	■	■	E	D	D
M	O	N	■	A	B	S	■	■	E	S	T	A	T	E
O	N	T	■	H	A	M	M	E	R	T	H	R	O	W
R	E	E	F	■	R	O	O	M	I	E	R	■	■	■
E	R	R	O	R	■	K	O	I	■	M	E	A	T	S
■	■	■	R	E	H	E	E	L	S	■	E	R	I	Q
P	L	U	M	P	U	D	D	I	N	G	■	E	A	U
L	E	S	S	O	N	■	■	A	L	A	■	A	M	A
E	T	A	■	■	T	I	E	■	■	M	A	C	A	W
A	T	B	A	T	■	S	P	A	D	E	W	O	R	K
S	E	L	M	A	■	L	I	S	I	■	O	D	I	E
E	R	E	C	T	■	E	C	H	O	■	L	E	A	D

35

M	E	T	S	■	A	L	A	M	O	■	T	E	S	S
A	C	H	E	■	J	A	P	A	N	■	A	N	T	E
C	H	E	W	Y	A	P	P	L	E	■	C	L	A	N
R	E	P	A	I	R	■	■	O	H	I	O	A	N	S
A	L	I	G	N	■	I	O	N	I	C	■	R	C	A
M	O	T	E	■	A	C	M	E	T	A	R	G	E	T
E	N	S	■	G	R	E	G	■	■	R	E	E	S	E
■	■	■	O	U	T	S	■	K	L	U	M	■	■	■
P	E	S	C	I	■	■	E	N	T	S	■	S	S	E
A	C	E	S	T	A	P	L	E	S	■	R	U	T	S
C	O	T	■	A	R	R	O	W	■	C	A	R	E	T
E	N	F	O	R	C	E	■	■	D	A	N	G	L	E
C	O	R	A	■	A	M	A	Z	O	N	D	E	L	L
A	M	E	R	■	D	I	V	A	N	■	O	R	A	L
R	Y	E	S	■	E	X	A	C	T	■	M	Y	R	A

36

R	I	G	G	S	■	A	C	E	S	■	A	C	I	D
I	C	A	R	E	■	L	O	V	E	■	L	I	N	E
B	E	R	E	T	■	I	M	E	D	■	B	N	A	I
I	M	B	E	I	N	G	F	R	A	M	E	D	■	■
S	E	E	D	■	A	N	Y	■	T	H	E	Y	R	E
I	N	D	I	A	N	■	■	S	E	Z	■	L	E	A
■	■	■	E	L	A	I	N	E	■	■	J	O	E	S
T	H	I	S	I	S	N	T	M	Y	F	A	U	L	T
A	U	N	T	■	■	O	H	I	O	A	N	■	■	■
R	R	S	■	P	A	N	■	■	S	T	E	R	N	S
S	T	I	L	E	S	■	A	S	H	■	F	E	A	T
■	■	D	O	N	T	P	I	N	I	T	O	N	M	E
E	Y	E	S	■	R	A	R	E	■	E	N	T	E	R
M	O	R	E	■	A	R	E	A	■	A	D	E	L	E
T	O	S	S	■	L	A	D	D	■	M	A	R	Y	S

38

V	T	R		S	A	L	A	D		O	T	T	E	R
I	R	A		A	M	I	G	O		C	H	I	D	E
S	O	N	I	C	B	O	O	M		H	A	N	G	S
C	L	O	C	K	I	N			R	O	N	N	I	E
E	L	V	E	S		E	D	G	E		K	E	E	N
R	E	E	F		C	L	O	U	D	B	U	R	S	T
A	R	R	O	Y	O		A	L	F	A		S	T	S
			G	O	A	T		F	L	E	D			
A	C	H		G	L	U	T		A	Z	O	R	E	S
T	H	E	B	I	G	B	A	N	G		T	O	N	I
P	A	C	E		A	S	I	A		D	E	U	C	E
E	N	T	E	R	S			P	A	E	L	L	A	S
A	G	O	G	O		F	U	L	L	B	L	A	S	T
C	E	R	E	S		U	S	E	I	T		D	E	A
E	S	S	E	S		R	E	S	T	S		E	D	S

40

	H	O	M	E	S	I	C	K	N	E	S	S
		I		X		N		N		X		W
	B	L	A	C	K	T	R	E	A	C	L	E
		E		E		E		E		E		E
S	A	D	D	L	I	N	G		G	R	I	T
C				L		T		N		P		N
R	E	S	E	E	D		B	O	T	T	L	E
A		H		D		P		T				S
T	E	A	R		B	A	L	A	N	C	E	S
C		M		L		G		T		H		
H	I	P	P	O	P	O	T	A	M	U	S	
E		O		N		D		L		R		
S	T	O	N	E	W	A	L	L	I	N	G	

41

F	L	I	P		I	S	M		H	O	T	A	I	R
L	A	N	A		S	N	O		E	L	A	P	S	E
A	P	T	P	U	P	I	L		H	A	R	A	S	S
G	L	E	A	N		P	E	R			S	T	A	T
D	A	N	C	E	S		S	O	M	E		I	R	A
A	N	D	Y		P	A	T	B	E	N	A	T	A	R
Y	D	S		S	E	C	S		S	T	R	E	E	T
			O	W	N	S		U	S	E	S			
S	I	G	H	E	D		S	P	A	R		T	S	A
P	T	A	M	E	E	T	I	N	G		A	R	A	L
R	E	G		T	R	I	G		E	D	S	E	L	S
I	M	A	C			S	H	E		E	I	E	I	O
T	I	R	A	D	E		T	A	P	W	A	T	E	R
E	Z	I	N	E	S		E	S	T		N	O	R	A
S	E	N	S	E	S		D	Y	S		S	P	I	N

44

			U		L		T		A			
	R	E	S	T	A	U	R	A	N	T	S	
	E		E		U		E		Y		T	
A	S	K	S		G	R	E	E	T	E	R	S
	E				H		S		H		A	
C	R	I	C	K	E	T		G	I	A	N	T
	V		H		D		C		N		G	
W	A	T	E	R		M	A	N	G	L	E	D
	T		C		P		T				N	
N	I	C	K	N	A	M	E		S	E	E	P
	O		I		R		R		E		S	
	N	O	N	E	T	H	E	L	E	S	S	
			G		Y		R		M			

45

E	M	M	A		D	R	I	P		J	A	F	F	A
L	U	I	S		Y	U	L	E		E	L	L	I	S
A	C	A	P	P	E	L	L	A		E	P	E	E	S
P	O	S		G	R	E	E	N	E	R		A	R	E
S	U	M	M	A			G	U	N		A	B	C	S
E	S	A	U		B	B	A	T	T	E	R	I	E	S
			S	M	A	L	L		R	A	T	T	L	E
S	T	A	T	E	L	Y		P	A	R	L	E	Y	S
M	A	N	A	N	A		C	O	P	S	E			
A	B	C	R	U	N	C	H	E	S		S	A	L	A
S	L	E	D		C	U	E			A	S	P	E	N
H	E	S		G	E	T	A	W	A	Y		P	E	I
U	T	T	E	R		O	P	I	O	N	E	E	R	S
P	O	O	L	E		F	E	R	N		K	N	E	E
S	P	R	I	G		F	R	E	E		E	D	D	S

46

R	E	S	O	W		A	D	D	S		E	L	M	O
E	X	T	R	A		L	O	O	K		D	E	E	P
S	P	I	R	I	T	A	W	A	Y		I	N	G	E
T	L	C		T	O	S	S			M	E	G	A	N
A	O	K			S	K	I	I	N	G		T	H	U
T	R	E		P	H	A	N	T	O	M	S	H	I	P
E	E	R	I	E			G	E	T	L	O	S	T	
			C	E	R	A		M	E	I	N			
	I	R	E	L	A	N	D			O	S	C	A	R
S	H	A	D	E	G	A	R	D	E	N		A	B	E
I	O	N		R	E	T	A	I	N			R	I	P
S	P	I	E	S			C	A	D	S		E	L	O
T	E	N	T		S	O	U	L	S	U	R	F	E	R
E	S	T	A		I	D	L	E		C	O	U	N	T
R	O	O	T		R	E	A	D		H	O	L	E	S

48

S	I	M	P	L	E	S	T		Y	A	K	I	M	A
A	M	O	R	E	T	T	O		O	K	A	P	I	S
S	U	P	E	R	C	O	N	D	U	C	T	O	R	S
S	P	Y	O	N		W	A	I	T			D	E	N
			P	E	G		L	O	O	S	E			
B	U	S		R	A	I	L	R	O	A	D	T	I	E
A	S	T	I		T	R	Y			C	I	R	C	A
T	A	U	N	T	E	R		M	I	S	T	I	E	R
H	I	N	D	U			F	A	N		S	P	I	N
E	N	G	I	N	E	B	L	O	C	K		E	N	S
			E	A	G	L	E		A	N	T			
A	A	H			G	O	E	S		U	R	B	A	N
S	M	O	K	I	N	G	C	A	R	R	I	A	G	E
K	I	M	O	N	O		E	N	C	L	O	S	E	S
S	E	E	I	N	G		R	E	A	S	S	E	S	S

49

G	L	A	S	S		R	A	P	A		D	A	T	E
N	A	S	A	L		O	M	I	T		A	C	I	D
P	H	I	L	I	S	T	I	N	E		S	H	A	G
			A	P	H	I	D			T	H	E	S	E
R	E	D	D		I	N	A	W	A	Y				
I	N	I		P	H	I	L	I	P	P	I	N	E	S
P	O	W	E	R			A	F	T	E	R	A	L	L
S	U	A	V	E	S	T		I	S	S	A	R	A	E
U	G	L	I	F	I	E	S			E	E	R	I	E
P	H	I	L	A	T	E	L	I	S	T		O	N	T
				B	E	N	I	T	O		A	W	E	S
C	L	A	S	S			C	A	N	A	L			
R	A	N	T		P	H	I	L	O	S	O	P	H	Y
O	N	T	O		O	M	N	I		I	N	D	I	E
P	E	E	P		T	O	G	A		A	G	A	T	E

52

S	C	A	M		S	T	R	A	W		C	H	E	T
A	L	D	A		K	E	E	N	E		H	E	D	Y
W	E	E	D	K	I	L	L	E	R		I	R	O	N
T	A	L	E	N	T			W	E	L	C	O	M	E
O	N	E		E	O	N	S		H	U	H			
			D	E	W	E	Y	D	E	C	I	M	A	L
O	C	T	A	L		U	S	E	R			O	V	O
P	R	E	S	S	E	R		F	E	A	T	H	E	R
E	E	L			P	A	I	R		P	E	S	C	I
D	W	E	E	Z	I	L	Z	A	P	P	A			
			S	I	S		E	Y	R	E		M	R	T
N	O	N	S	T	O	P			E	A	S	I	E	R
A	R	E	A		D	E	E	W	A	L	L	A	C	E
M	A	C	Y		I	S	A	A	C		A	M	A	S
E	L	K	S		C	O	U	G	H		T	I	P	S

54

A	D	A	P	T		B	A	N	D		D	E	L	A
C	E	L	L	O		I	D	E	A		E	T	A	S
C	A	P	A	N	D	G	O	W	N		W	H	Y	S
O	R	A	N	G	E			S	G	T		E	W	E
S	I	C	K		N	S	A		L	A	U	R	A	S
T	E	A		B	A	T	T	L	E	D	R	E	S	S
			S	A	L	I	V	A			G	A	T	E
O	P	E	N	A	I	R		Y	O	D	E	L	E	D
B	A	L	I			U	S	U	R	E	R			
S	L	I	P	O	F	P	A	P	E	R		E	S	P
C	I	C	E	R	O		D	S	L		A	N	N	O
U	N	I		E	O	N			S	U	N	D	A	E
R	O	T	O		T	A	B	L	E	S	K	I	R	T
E	D	E	N		E	M	I	T		E	L	V	E	R
R	E	D	S		D	E	N	S		S	E	E	D	Y

56

P	I	T	A		D	O	O	F	U	S		S	E	T
A	R	E	S		I	N	V	E	N	T		E	A	R
P	A	S	S	E	D	T	E	N	T	S		A	D	E
A	T	S	E	A		O	R	D	O		E	L	S	E
S	E	A	R	C	H		R	E	L	A	X			
			T	H	E	H	A	R	D	W	E	I	G	H
I	S	A			R	U	N			E	R	N	I	E
S	H	U	C	K	E	D		D	E	S	T	I	N	E
A	U	D	I	O			S	O	P			T	A	P
K	N	I	G	H	T	S	C	H	O	O	L			
			A	L	O	H	A		S	T	I	F	L	E
S	C	A	R		L	A	L	O		T	A	R	O	T
Y	O	U		N	E	V	E	R	G	O	B	A	C	H
N	I	N		O	D	E	N	S	E		L	U	K	A
E	N	T		G	O	N	E	O	N		E	D	E	N

57

S	A	R	A		P	R	O	B	E		S	U	D	S
T	I	E	S		R	A	D	I	O		O	N	I	T
A	R	M	A	G	E	D	D	O	N		U	S	S	R
G	M	O		U	P	S	E	T		A	S	T	R	O
E	A	R	L	S			R	A	G	N	A	R	O	K
R	I	S	O	T	T	O		S	U	N		A	B	E
S	L	E	W		I	V	E		Y	O	O	P	E	R
			E	N	D	O	F	D	A	Y	S			
S	C	A	R	A	B		T	I	N		T	O	G	S
E	O	S		T	I	C		P	A	T	E	L	L	A
E	S	C	H	A	T	O	N			T	O	Y	E	D
S	T	E	A	L		M	O	N	E	Y		M	A	D
R	U	T	S		A	P	O	C	A	L	Y	P	S	E
E	M	I	T		J	O	N	A	S		D	I	O	N
D	E	C	O		A	S	S	A	Y		S	A	N	S

58

	A	B	B	R	E	V	I	A	T	I	O	N
		R		E		A		C		L		E
	M	O	T	H	E	R	S	I	N	L	A	W
		W		E		I		D		N		S
F	A	N	F	A	R	E	S		H	E	L	P
O				R		D		M		S		A
R	E	C	E	S	S		G	O	S	S	I	P
T		A		E		S		N				E
I	M	P	S		C	U	S	T	O	M	E	R
T		A		K		P		R		I		
U	R	B	A	N	L	E	G	E	N	D	S	
D		L		O		R		A		S		
E	L	E	C	T	A	B	I	L	I	T	Y	

60

T	I	P	P	E	R	S		R	E	F	U	S	A	L
A	P	L	E	N	T	Y		I	V	A	N	H	O	E
J	O	U	S	T	E	R		M	E	L	T	I	N	G
		N	O	R		I	D	S		L	I	N	E	S
E	G	G		E	S	A	U		A	G	E			
T	R	E	B	E	K		M	E	N	U		T	U	B
R	A	P	A		I	N	P	L	A	Y		U	N	E
A	V	O	I	D		A	L	I		S	A	M	S	A
D	E	O		I	R	A	I	S	E		U	B	E	R
E	L	L		V	E	N	N		A	N	G	L	E	D
			B	E	D		G	A	T	E		E	N	S
N	A	B	O	B		A	S	L		C	A	W		
E	M	E	R	A	L	D		A	P	T	N	E	S	S
R	E	T	I	R	E	D		N	E	A	T	E	S	T
D	R	E	S	S	E	S		S	T	R	I	D	E	S

62

H	I	C	K		M	A	C	R	O	N		S	G	T
A	S	H	E		A	P	P	O	S	E		P	R	O
W	O	O	L	L	Y	B	U	L	L	Y		R	I	O
S	L	O	P	E	S			L	O	O	S	E	S	T
E	A	S	Y	A		L	E	I			P	A	T	H
R	T	E		S	P	A	C	E	N	E	E	D	L	E
S	E	R	B		R	O	O		E	R	A	S	E	D
			E	G	O	S		E	V	E	R			
S	P	A	R	E	S		I	V	E		S	O	N	S
P	U	R	L	O	Y	S	T	E	R	S		N	I	T
A	S	T	I			U	S	N		U	S	A	G	E
T	H	I	N	A	I	R			L	E	A	D	E	R
U	P	S		W	O	R	S	T	E	D	Y	A	R	N
L	I	T		O	N	E	H	I	T		E	R	I	E
A	N	S		L	A	Y	U	P	S		R	E	A	R

65

A	W	O	L		M	I	S	S	M		U	B	E	R
B	E	L	A		A	N	I	T	A		M	E	M	E
L	A	D	Y	F	I	N	G	E	R		P	R	I	M
A	N	S	E	L	M		M	E	D	S		S	R	O
T	I	A	R	A		R	A	D	I	O	H	E	A	D
E	N	L		P	L	Y				T	O	R	T	E
S	G	T			A	N	T		S	H	E	K	E	L
			B	L	U	E	B	L	O	O	D			
R	E	S	O	L	D		S	O	L			C	D	S
A	M	I	N	O				P	E	P		H	I	M
F	U	N	N	Y	B	O	N	E		O	C	A	L	A
F	L	A		D	A	L	E		A	E	O	L	U	S
L	A	T	H		S	M	A	R	T	M	O	U	T	H
E	T	R	E		S	E	T	T	O		E	P	E	E
S	E	A	M		O	C	H	E	R		D	A	D	S

66

D	E	C	E	M	B	E	R		N	U	T	S
R		H		A		L		M		N		P
A	L	O	N	G		E	N	A	C	T	O	R
W		I		N		V		S		I		A
	A	C	C	I	D	E	N	T	A	L	L	Y
B		E		F		N		E				E
R	E	S	H	I	P		P	R	O	P	E	R
A				C		P		S		R		S
C	O	N	V	E	R	S	A	T	I	O	N	
E		E		N		A		R		T		A
L	Y	R	I	C	A	L		O	C	E	A	N
E		V		E		M		K		C		D
T	R	E	E		A	S	B	E	S	T	O	S

68

T	O	B	A	G	O		I	S	H		A	S	I	A
I	M	A	G	E	R		F	A	A		P	A	C	E
F	A	K	E	I	T		S	L	I	P	O	V	E	R
F	R	E	N	C	H	S	O	U	F	F	L	E	S	
			T	O	O	K		T	A	C	O			
P	R	O	S			U	S	E			G	E	R	E
R	E	M		G	A	L	A		M	A	I	L	E	R
A	R	E	S	M	A	L	L	B	E	C	A	U	S	E
Y	U	G	I	O	H		A	U	N	T		D	E	C
S	N	A	G			E	D	S			K	E	T	T
			N	E	E	D		T	H	A	N			
	O	N	E	E	G	G	I	S	U	N	O	U	E	F
P	L	E	D	G	E	E	S		L	I	T	T	L	E
V	E	R	O		S	I	N		A	T	T	A	I	N
T	O	O	N		T	N	T		S	A	S	H	E	S

71

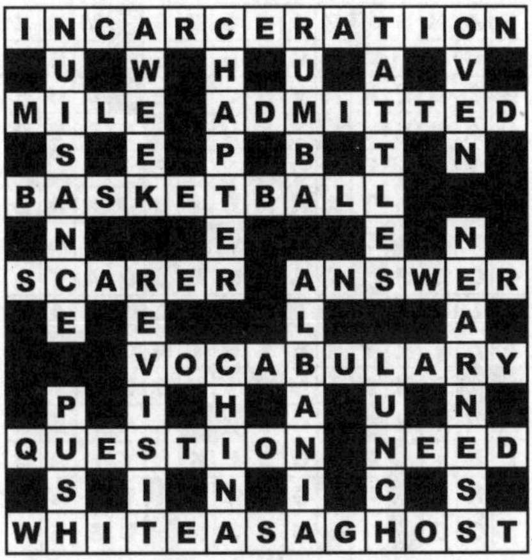

73

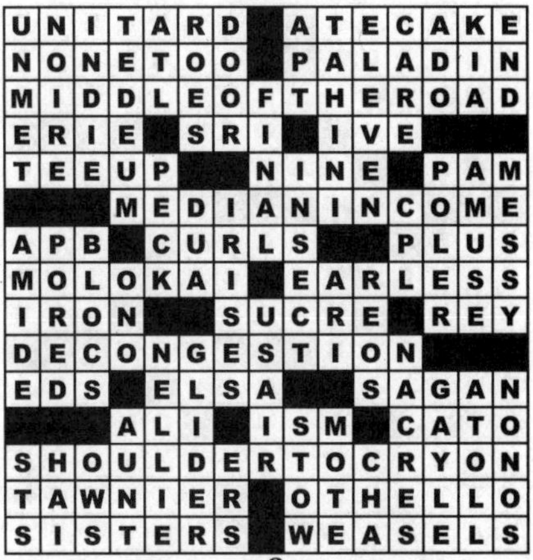

74

76

77

78

79

M	A	P	P	E	D	■	M	A	S	T	H	E	A	D
I	C	E	A	G	E	■	C	L	A	R	E	N	C	E
T	H	E	P	O	L	I	C	E	S	I	N	G	E	R
T	O	T	E	S	■	M	O	C	H	A	■	■	■	■
S	O	A	R	■	S	A	Y	S	■	G	R	A	S	P
■	■	■	S	A	W	■	■	■	P	E	O	P	L	E
S	H	E	■	R	E	P	A	I	R	■	A	R	I	A
C	O	N	F	I	D	E	N	C	E	T	R	I	C	K
R	O	T	O	■	E	I	G	H	T	Y	■	L	E	S
A	C	R	O	S	S	■	■	■	T	R	Y	■	■	■
P	H	Y	L	A	■	E	B	A	Y	■	E	L	B	A
■	■	■	■	T	A	L	U	S	■	O	N	I	O	N
J	E	L	L	Y	F	I	S	H	A	T	T	A	C	K
U	T	T	E	R	R	O	T	■	S	T	A	R	C	H
S	A	R	A	S	O	T	A	■	P	O	S	S	E	S

80

F	A	N	S	■	R	I	D	G	E	S	■	M	R	S
I	D	E	M	■	A	C	O	R	N	S	■	Y	O	U
B	L	U	E	K	E	Y	N	O	T	E	■	C	U	E
E	A	R	L	Y	■	■	S	U	I	■	F	E	E	D
R	I	O	L	O	B	O	■	S	T	E	I	N	■	■
■	■	■	S	T	A	R	K	E	Y	B	O	A	R	D
O	I	L	■	O	N	C	E	■	■	B	R	E	A	D
L	O	O	P	■	C	A	L	M	S	■	D	A	T	A
A	L	G	A	E	■	■	P	A	P	A	■	N	A	Y
F	A	I	R	Y	K	E	Y	R	I	N	G	■	■	■
■	■	S	K	E	I	N	■	I	N	G	R	A	T	E
A	N	T	S	■	M	O	I	■	■	L	A	P	E	L
L	E	I	■	M	O	U	S	E	K	E	Y	P	A	D
A	R	C	■	A	N	G	L	I	A	■	E	L	S	E
S	O	S	■	J	O	H	A	N	N	■	D	E	E	R

81

P	R	A	C	T	I	C	E	■	W	A	L	K
I	■	I	■	R	■	A	■	W	■	L	■	I
L	A	R	V	A	■	S	T	A	T	I	O	N
E	■	H	■	N	■	I	■	L	■	B	■	G
■	P	E	R	S	O	N	A	L	T	I	E	S
M	■	A	■	F	■	G	■	P	■	■	■	L
I	N	D	E	E	D	■	N	A	T	I	V	E
S	■	■	■	R	■	E	■	P	■	N	■	Y
C	L	E	A	R	B	L	U	E	S	K	Y	■
O	■	A	■	I	■	E	■	R	■	I	■	A
U	S	T	I	N	O	V	■	I	D	E	A	S
N	■	E	■	G	■	E	■	N	■	S	■	H
T	I	N	Y	■	K	N	I	G	H	T	L	Y

85

A	R	E	T	H	A	■	S	C	U	M	■	G	R	R
R	E	V	E	A	L	■	A	O	N	E	■	L	E	E
C	H	E	A	P	D	I	N	N	E	R	■	A	V	A
H	A	R	■	P	A	N	D	G	■	C	O	D	E	D
E	S	S	A	Y	■	S	E	A	S	■	G	I	N	A
S	H	O	T	■	F	I	R	S	T	G	R	O	U	P
■	■	■	V	O	I	D	S	■	E	Y	E	L	E	T
A	R	I	■	N	N	E	■	C	A	R	■	I	R	S
D	E	N	A	L	I	■	L	E	M	O	N	■	■	■
H	O	T	M	Y	S	T	E	R	Y	■	A	B	I	T
E	P	E	E	■	H	U	G	E	■	R	H	O	D	A
S	E	N	S	E	■	M	I	A	M	I	■	H	E	M
I	N	D	■	D	O	U	B	L	E	D	R	E	A	M
V	E	E	■	G	U	L	L	■	S	E	E	M	L	Y
E	D	D	■	E	T	T	E	■	A	S	S	E	S	S

86

M	I	S	O	■	N	A	P	S	■	T	Y	P	E	B
A	R	A	L	■	O	G	R	E	■	B	E	R	L	E
H	O	L	D	M	U	S	I	C	■	A	R	U	B	A
A	N	D	E	A	N	■	O	R	B	■	■	D	O	T
T	I	A	R	A	■	G	R	E	A	T	N	E	W	S
M	E	N	■	M	A	E	■	T	H	E	O	R	E	M
A	S	A	P	■	R	A	G	■	■	C	L	Y	D	E
■	■	■	O	V	E	R	N	I	G	H	T	■	■	■
A	N	G	L	O	■	■	U	M	A	■	E	S	P	N
L	U	R	K	I	N	G	■	E	S	P	■	P	O	E
B	R	O	A	D	B	A	N	D	■	L	A	Y	L	A
E	T	A	■	■	C	R	U	■	G	U	S	H	E	R
R	U	N	N	Y	■	D	R	E	A	M	H	O	M	E
T	R	E	E	D	■	E	S	A	U	■	E	L	I	S
A	E	R	O	S	■	N	E	R	D	■	S	E	C	T

87

M	I	S	H	A	■	I	S	A	W	■	W	H	I	R
I	N	C	A	S	■	L	O	N	E	■	A	U	R	A
S	P	A	R	K	P	L	U	G	S	■	T	R	A	P
S	U	N	T	E	A	■	P	O	L	L	U	T	E	S
M	T	S	■	D	I	G	■	R	E	O	S	■	■	■
■	■	■	B	U	R	N	D	A	Y	L	I	G	H	T
R	E	A	P	P	E	A	R	■	■	■	■	O	Y	E
I	T	I	S	■	D	W	E	E	B	■	E	N	D	S
F	A	D	■	■	■	■	A	V	E	R	A	G	E	S
F	L	A	M	E	T	H	R	O	W	E	R	■	■	■
■	■	■	C	O	R	A	■	O	A	T	■	O	N	O
J	U	V	E	N	I	L	E	■	R	E	A	S	O	N
A	N	E	W	■	B	L	A	Z	E	S	T	A	R	R
V	I	S	A	■	A	E	R	O	■	T	O	K	A	Y
A	T	T	N	■	L	Y	L	E	■	S	P	A	D	E

88

C	A	S	H		F	R	A	M	E		L	O	S	T
A	C	A	I		L	E	V	E	R		I	N	T	O
T	U	R	K	E	Y	W	I	N	G		S	T	E	W
A	R	D	E	N		R	D	S		T	T	O	P	S
N	A	I	R	O	B	I		C	A	R	E			
			S	C	O	T	C	H	B	O	N	N	E	T
B	O	G		H	O	E	R		S	T	E	E	L	Y
I	M	U	P			R	O	T			R	A	M	P
F	O	R	E	S	T		S	I	M	I		R	Y	E
F	O	U	R	T	H	E	S	T	A	T	E			
			T	O	O	L		H	E	A	D	O	F	F
C	H	E	A	P		T	E	A		L	I	V	R	E
Y	O	G	I		C	O	W	B	O	Y	B	O	O	T
A	N	O	N		O	R	A	L	S		L	I	N	E
N	E	S	S		D	O	N	E	E		E	D	D	S

89

T	R	U	S	S		D	E	N		G	L	O	B	E
R	E	N	T	A		E	P	I		T	A	M	E	D
A	T	B	A	Y		G	E	T	S	O	M	E	Z	S
D	I	O			T	R	E	A	T			L	E	E
E	C	L	I	P	S	E			A	S	W	E	L	L
O	U	T	L	I	K	E	A	L	I	G	H	T		
F	L	E	E	T			D	I	R	T	Y			
F	E	D			M	A	L	E	S			C	D	C
			C	H	I	N	A			D	A	R	I	A
		C	O	U	N	T	I	N	G	S	H	E	E	P
U	B	U	N	T	U			O	I	L	I	E	S	T
N	E	T			T	I	L	T	S			P	I	A
H	I	T	T	H	E	H	A	Y		O	T	E	R	I
I	G	L	O	O		O	N	E		R	E	R	A	N
P	E	E	V	E		P	E	T		E	A	S	E	S

91

T	A	C	K	S		A	F	C		C	O	I	L	S
A	D	O	P	T		B	R	A		O	N	T	A	P
B	A	R	H	A	R	B	O	R		N	E	A	T	O
A	G	O			U	R	N		S	T	A	L	E	R
T	I	N	C	A	N		T	B	A	R	L	I	F	T
H	O	A	R	S	E	R		A	T	A		C	E	E
A	S	S	E	T		O	P	R	Y		U	S	E	D
			D	I	S	B	A	R	R	E	D			
I	C	E	S		A	B	L	E		A	D	I	O	S
N	O	X		O	D	E		L	I	V	E	N	U	P
C	A	P	Y	B	A	R	A		Z	E	R	O	T	H
I	L	L	E	S	T		T	O	O			R	T	E
S	T	O	L	E		H	A	N	D	L	E	B	A	R
E	A	R	L	S		A	R	C		A	L	I	K	E
D	R	E	S	S		T	I	E		B	I	T	E	S

92

R	I	B		B	I	T	M	A	P		A	M	F	M
O	D	O		A	S	I	A	G	O		L	A	L	A
A	E	R		S	E	E	G	E	R		A	D	A	S
M	A	G	N	A		D	I	S	C	B	R	A	K	E
		D	O	L	B	Y			H	A	M	M	E	R
C	O	R	E		R	E	S	I	G	N	S			
A	P	O	L	L	O		A	L	L	A		B	A	H
T	E	N		I	N	S	U	L	I	N		U	M	A
O	D	E		A	X	E	D		D	A	U	B	E	R
			E	B	B	T	I	D	E		T	B	S	P
A	I	E	L	L	O			A	R	I	A	L		
E	P	I	D	E	M	I	C	S		C	H	E	C	K
S	A	D	E		B	R	A	H	M	A		J	A	N
O	N	E	S		E	A	S	E	I	N		E	K	E
P	A	R	T		R	E	E	D	I	T		T	E	E

94

P	I	T	A	S		S	A	A	B		P	O	S	H
D	R	A	C	O		A	B	L	E		L	A	N	E
F	R	I	E	N	D	L	Y	F	I	R	E	F	L	Y
			T	O	E		S	A	R	D	I			
	S	R	I		P	C	S		U	S	A	B	L	E
J	O	E	C	O	O	L	A	N	T		D	R	U	M
I	R	S		O	S	O	L	E		D	E	I	C	E
C	R	U	M	P	E	T		W	R	E	S	T	E	R
A	I	R	E	S		H	O	T	E	L		A	N	G
M	E	G	A		Y	O	Y	O	M	A	L	I	C	E
A	R	E	T	H	A		S	N	O		A	N	Y	
			H	A	B	I	T		L	I	S			
S	W	E	E	T	B	R	E	A	D	S	T	I	C	K
W	A	W	A		E	A	R	L		S	E	N	S	E
E	Y	E	D		R	E	S	T		A	D	D	I	N

95

D	E	S	K	S		S	T	A	T	E		T	I	P
E	N	N	U	I		P	O	L	E	S		O	R	E
C	R	O	W	N	J	O	U	L	E	S		P	I	E
C	O	R	A		A	U	R	A	S		T	B	S	P
A	N	T	I		C	S	I			S	T	A		
			T	A	K	E	S	A	L	K	Y	N	E	S
M	R	B	I	G			M	U	C	I	L	A	G	E
E	A	R		A	S	A		F	D	R		N	O	T
G	R	E	E	T	E	R	S			U	M	A	S	S
S	E	E	W	H	A	T	A	M	I	N	E			
		Z	O	A			L	I	P		N	A	S	T
W	E	E	K		P	A	I	N	S		O	N	T	O
H	A	W		H	A	V	E	Y	O	U	R	I	O	N
O	R	A		O	P	E	R	A		S	A	M	O	A
S	L	Y		W	A	S	I	N		S	H	E	L	L

96

D	I	S	H		A	B	U	S	E		S	C	A	T
E	R	L	E		P	A	N	E	L		E	L	M	O
B	O	U	L	D	E	R	D	A	M		R	I	M	S
A	N	G	L	O		D	O	G		D	I	M	E	S
T	O	G	O	U	T		C	A	G	E		A	T	E
E	R	E		R	O	C	K	L	O	B	S	T	E	R
S	E	R	B		W	A	S		D	U	P	E	R	S
			A	B	E	T		L	U	G	E			
S	C	A	R	E	R		P	E	T		C	L	A	D
P	E	B	B	L	E	B	E	A	C	H		A	V	E
R	C	A		I	D	E	A		H	U	S	T	O	N
E	E	N	I	E		A	R	S		L	I	E	N	S
A	L	D	O		D	U	S	T	R	U	F	F	L	E
D	I	O	N		S	T	O	U	T		T	E	E	S
S	A	N	S		L	Y	N	D	E		S	E	A	T

99

	B	R	I	L	L	I	A	N	C	E		
	R		D		O		P		H		E	
D	A	V	I	S	C	U	P		A	U	N	T
	K		O		K		R		I		T	
	E	A	T	S		C	O	U	N	T	R	Y
			I		S		V				A	
	B	I	C	Y	C	L	E	C	L	I	P	
	E				R		S		E			
S	A	M	P	L	E	D		S	O	U	P	
	N		O		A		C		P		E	
B	E	L	L		M	E	R	M	A	I	D	S
	D		K		E		O		R		A	
		P	A	T	R	I	C	I	D	A	L	

100

A	M	I	E		S	T	A	I	D		H	O	L	O
B	O	N	A		C	I	R	C	A		A	N	O	N
D	U	S	T	J	A	C	K	E	T		B	A	R	S
O	S	T	M	A	R	K		C	A	B	A	R	E	T
M	E	Y	E	R		L	E	A		E	N	O	L	A
E	R	L		S	W	E	E	P	T	H	E	L	E	G
N	S	E	C		E	R	R		H	A	R	L	I	E
			O	R	I	S		M	I	R	A			
E	N	S	L	E	R		T	O	E		S	C	U	T
M	O	P	A	N	D	S	M	I	F	F		A	P	E
I	N	A	N	E		A	C	S		O	C	E	A	N
R	A	W	D	E	A	L		T	H	R	U	S	T	S
A	C	N	E		V	A	C	U	U	M	T	U	B	E
T	I	E	R		O	M	B	R	E		E	R	A	S
E	D	D	S		W	I	S	E	S		R	A	T	T

Wordsearches

2

D L G M D F Z K S B V G K R E O F F Q A P
H D I G Z X Z T O O K A W T K Y S Q G J V
M P L J G D O O J C T T E H A V R Z P G A
O X K X B S T G H H Z I A A P T U P R A B
H L S B Z Y L U X G W A L M I D A E R B S
J V D S Y P R A B S U H T E G N E L N K E
B J F I C C F S T L Z O H H W N C F L R S
E S N G Q S C K P I K H D V B E J A H A L
C E S K Z S H P N O P S H A P Q F D S C E
U I K Q F O M I Y P R A C W M W A C S H K
T D O H Z P O E U S P K C F H M R J D Y E
T O Y A W T G E L T S E K H O A C B E G H
E O M U L A T V J O N E R O T G K L E A S
L G S L B G Z U R K L K L C N Z Y A C K U
K Q U B H P O H U S H A H S U N T U O P M
O C A B C N F X V R H T U T W L N H R L I
S C A O H L Y T O X Y C N E R R U C P U S
G D Z J S I L V E R S F L C K F O F X N I
Z S N I P O H P G U T A R Z Z I B X Q D G
M S O U R V W S Q F E O Q R N I W P G E N
A C B E F L N T F F R O X S J K G W G R F
O Q N Y V E L A B F L G L V M O B D B B T
V I S K C U B S G U I E M A A O B J M D H
D Y W V T Z R H R T N T I M N Y G K Y J U
G S Q G R H C S N S G C K F N Y V T T F W

6

V A P I M H X Z X B D L C A H S R H G N Y
M E N B Y Y B I O M X Z L E U I T R U C P
A N L U N U Q G J J A F B A V I F P D F M
F S A C R U M R W D J E W Y Q G I Q S F U
E S F T F Y R Y I I V F J R Y U Q W E J I
R I B L F E M S K H G O Y Y Y H A X L S W
B M B A I U I M J G Z K N P O U Y O C G K
Y R U T M S E R A B K L S R U J B R I R B
T J E I J C E P K R V Z S I N P V H S C O
A M L P L A N I X F I X P I S C U Q S H X
R A F I L I W U N R I Z G T X Y C C O C U
N M L C W A P Y T P Y C J V L X Q F Z S M
F Z S C X X S C B P J Q K N L A P R A C M
I D G O L S I R O H U B Y C F M F B D A B
B U K Q U B C H A T W T L C U Y T R X S A
U K W Y Z P P A T T G R A Q Z M D I M D C
L Q E Q B G K L P X U R K M U L L Q L W I
A A Y U N T Z N V U O O G I U L Q B T V S
S A N Q Z K H V Y D L D N J A N X O C P J
N V Y O F F A F J T I A M B N M R O H W A
Z Z V E B X O M T U T L K S E E C E W T I
Y G M C B X Q Y A A J M A M I K W G T C B
C U B R P A R I E T A L K X I P W W D S I
R A D I U S E I W I G C E L C I V A L C T
B J S U R E M U H C Z R P R C G Y X P P L

10

S E J L K I Q M K Z Z F C X Z K E X T U D
N J A L Z R A D D U H H Y M G Y D E Q O A
E L S Q B N Q C R A X J A L J Z L Y O E E
D B R W I H P G X M I P Z N O K H W A C Z
C G N D E S U K Y R L R D W C M G R N L H
G P N Q D N P X C E D D E U L O I U B T Z
L A T R P T A T X Z T X S T D P F T T E C
N P G G L P T E J R X Y M M S Y G G A Y K
H G K K X E Y J G Q E G P W F I B M P A C
V M F P B E B D D N F C Y V I C W R O W W
A N A G Y O P T O O A V J C N L E S C B W
Y V R G X Y E H J I V R Y O V S L K L G C
Z F H W N P Y J J E E Z D Q S G D O W V U
O B O W G O A R C H C Q P Y T W S Z W Y I
Y O K P C S L I R E S N Y A H K Y D D H X
D O M O M N M I Z E I E I Y M W J Q F R Y
A R L I G N L L A S B O M U L I K E N I P
A Y N O M R W Z R A F Y T Z Q N E D R Q H
W E L J V O N X E E W N A O H J A E V J T
V S C W V H Z S M Z B O C B P M P D A K Y
K J A Q X T X L N W F T S W X I W Q L G X
Y Y L H Z W A Z C L V G F Z N Y L Q U B W
X B I T B A Q A N K Q E C U R P S X O F J
L Y L L O H A Z A L E A J C K U W U M B B
D V W Z L Q O A I H T Y S R O F D N X F V

16

D R Z O X Q E F N O T L O B W U C U B O R
M A H S Y E H T P O K N H S D E E L S H R
N L O O P K C A L B T T F B I N N T V G E
E B C Y Q F I Q B I S P P K J X A A S I T
W W P S M R W W U R E A I J D F W P L E S
C J M T B X O P R M D Z X K F B O P I L E
A O U M S E L R N I B M U O S S R L V T H
S H U N C O V E L N E N R G K F R E E J C
T C C V R O E S E G R D Z R L K A B R L N
L I R U O N R T Y H G S L E S K B Y P A A
E U G C J W H O W A H A E T B V E V O N M
Q B A B F R A N N M K T Y N C A N N O C K
Y X Q N W C M L S S W Y L A F D T X L A S
T Q T N R A P U S O G N A T S R A G Y S S
W P M D F T T D O A O Y N U N A G I W T L
H A O B Y T O D P H L F D X T K E A V E L
S M R C C R N M T A A L G Y S V N G L R I
I B E R F G T I D H R A C A R N F O R T H
D B C G I W R N C A R L I S L E T J M E D
N V A R X N E P E H E K C I W S E K X B O
A U M S E K G W X V G V O J I J B H N R T
T C B P S O U T H P O R T W Y O A G F O X
S E E G X R R A O P J C V M F M Y Z W U N
P E J F P Q U J O N E P Z T Z Y W X D G S
M T V P M G X V T N O T W E N L O I A H U

20

L O N D O N E Y E E R T A E H T E B O L G
B P V L C I N M F F Y N O T G N I S N E K
B O S L L A W S N A I R D A H E C Q O O O
R R V I B R M L N F X N T S H C H N T M Y
I T M H U T E D F G Y B A N R A C L P Q J
G O S G C E Y O E Y R T D H E U T C M M B
H B H N K S L S Y N X L I U P V R T A T E
T E T I I R L S H Y D E P A R K O M H R E
O L A T N E I O L D B A I L E Y Y C W O D
N L B T G M D R J D E I L B I G B E N S K
L O N O H O A C S X B L E T C H L E Y D B
E R A N A S C S Y O T Q O Y I M O P O N M
C R M C M Y C G J Y H T P O A N Z V E I W
D L O T A R I N O X F O R D P N E G G W E
S N R O T N P I H P T T A A E R D M O X S
D T J O M O T K P R S M U D F I E I Z J T
L T P C K T M E U G E E R R R A L V F X M
O F I A O E R O R T Q A M B G A L K I M I
W U A N U L C A U B G O M A U W H G B L N
S K T P T L I S D T U A N A H L Z S A I S
T O N O A A S S N H C R H M I T L X B R T
O W F Y M A G E E U H U Y E L B M E W D E
C X O Q U P V E S U E G N E H E N O T S R
Y R A D C O C G L J M M R Q C D U R H A M
M N S B C H T U O M S T R O P E H E J Z O

24

S C S Q N X U A F L B X L L G J A J V C H
F L H I J K X T C H A N N E L I N G G F U
D G X Z B I L O C A T I O N X M P N Z K D
C C N G S I S E N I K O R Y P N I P L K T
C P D N E P X Z M S A E O Q W S L I Y N C
L L L I G T B I I E S R H H W Q K H S N L
U H S W G E R G N N T M H O J V Z S S O A
E G U E F L G J D G R O D I X B T M I I I
A Z Q I S E T P C W A T G X X I L U S T R
Y J E V F K E J O S L P Y V H Y N I E I V
I H P E Y I L R N T P E H C F Q E D N N O
E J X T C N E V T E R Z V M E D A E I G Y
A C I O P E P A R E O O I A S H S M K O A
N I C M R S A Z O F J B F N R P P Z O C N
Y F S E E I T X L N E U P N S T R O Y E C
H F M R M S H L O L C T Q Y I C E V R R E
H P D Z O T Y I W N T R C C O A A M C P G
Q I K Q N N T V J T I H C J E F I I I I K
X R Q M I A N B D R O V M R V Q T T L T N
V H X H T X H J Y M N J Y L R E W X G H W
U A Y I I T E L E P O R T A T I O N A V U
E R V S O A O T R A N S F O R M A T I O N
M E E N N F R I C M O N C S F R G F B F I
L K L D J Y A C B N O I T C I D E R P Z L
B C O L G N I T F I H S E P A H S J U J R

28

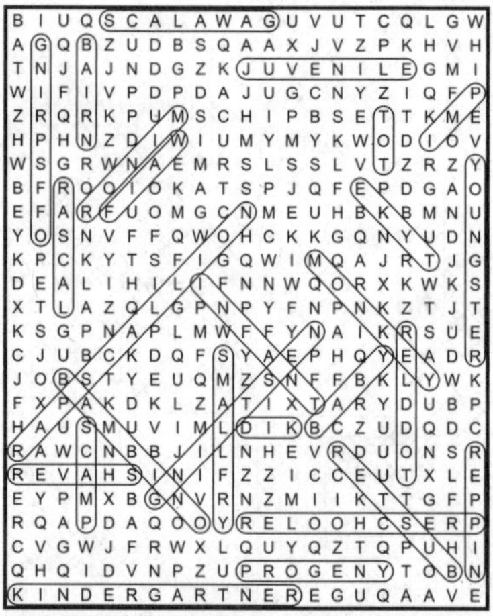

32

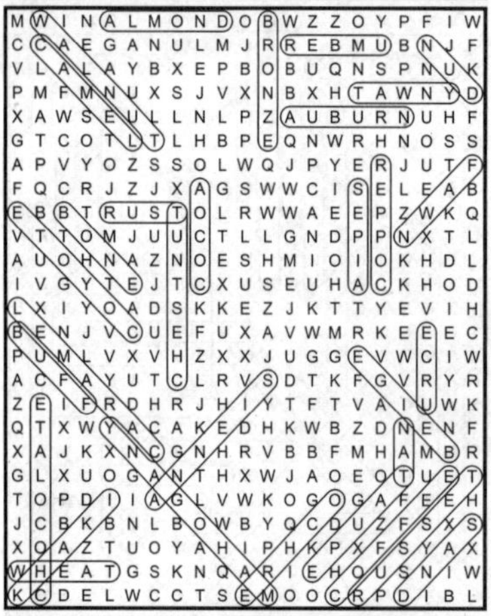

37

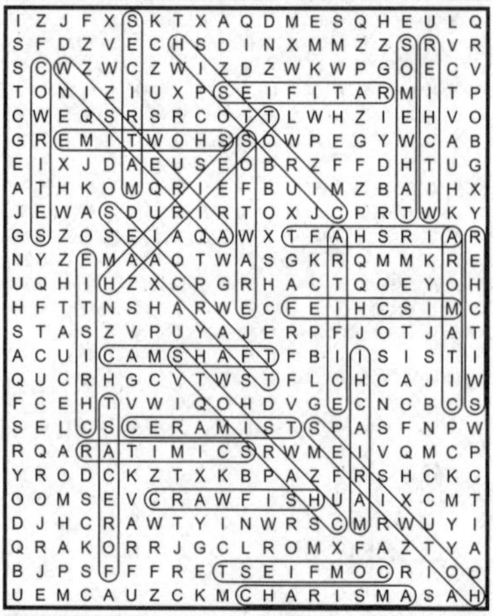

43

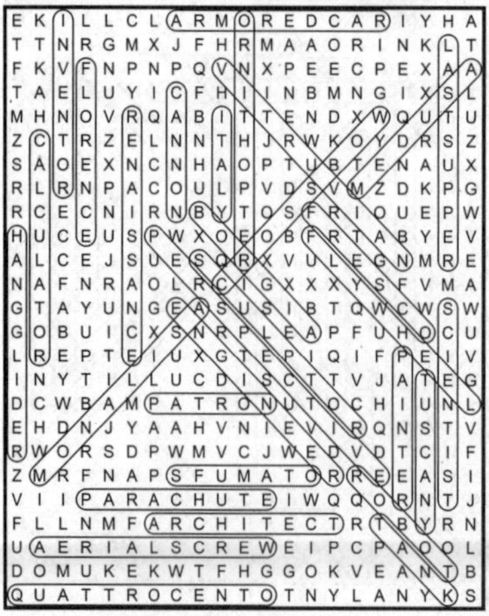

47

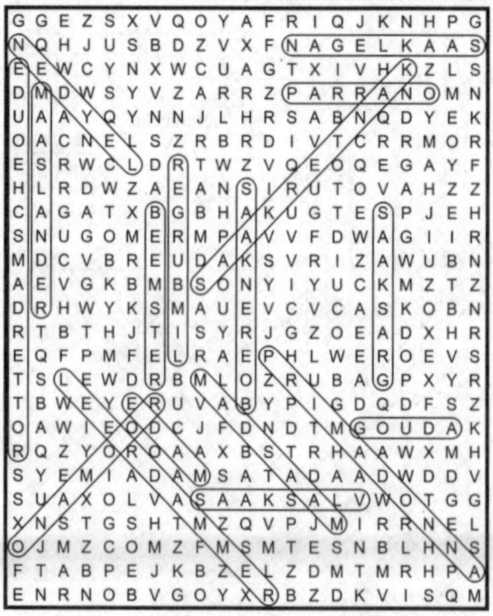

55

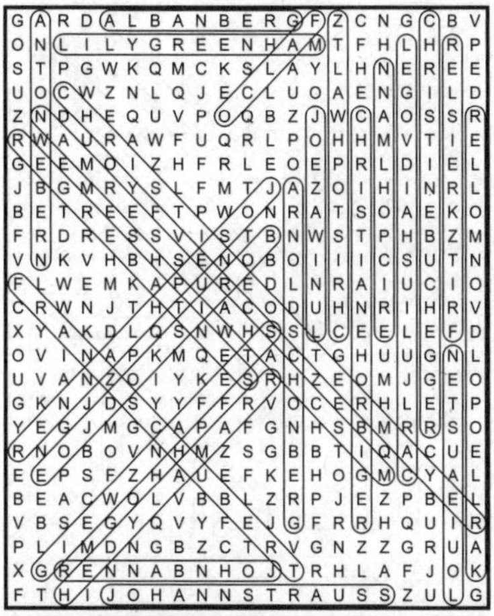

59

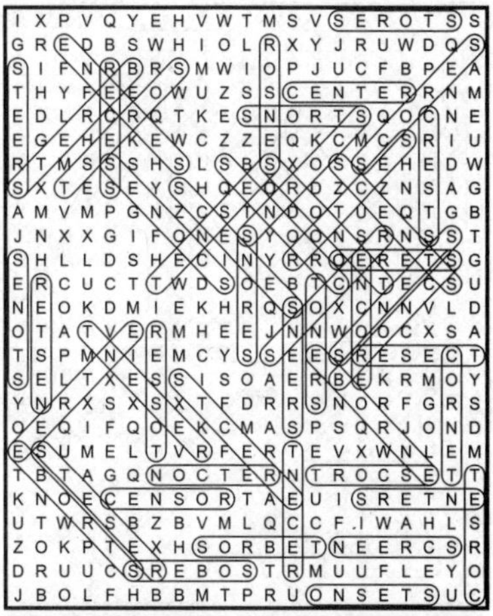

64

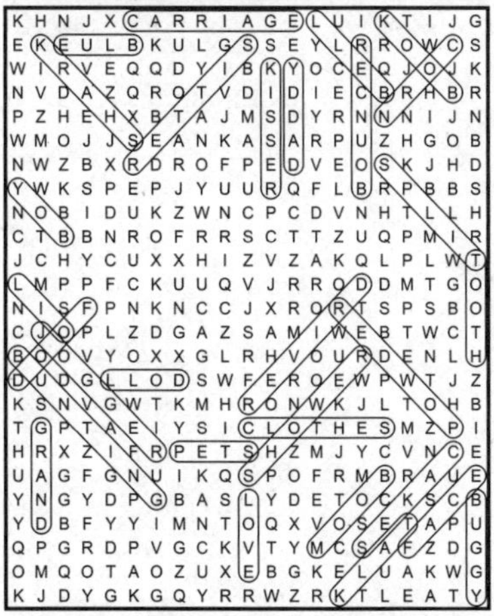

67

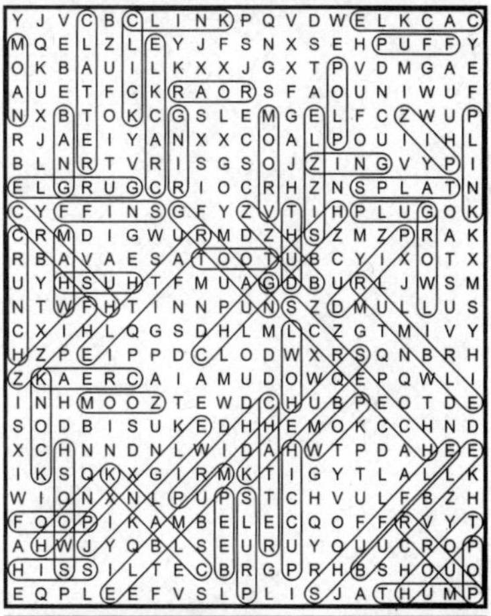

70

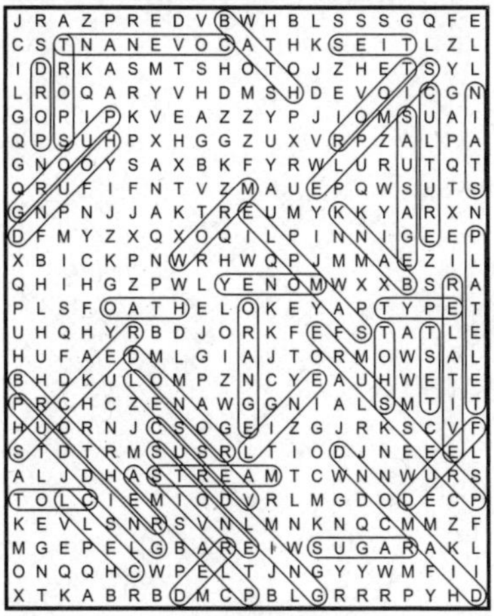

75

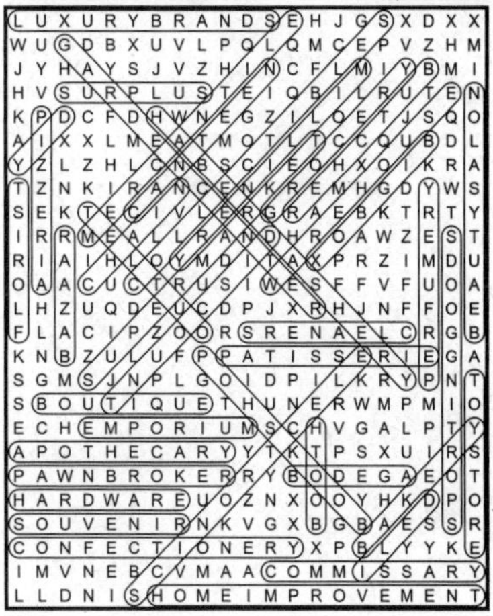

82

93

```
Q Y S J P S T L M C X D R D B R E G N I G
C A Z J J G H S I D A R E S R O H S Q E B
T C A M T C R B S H W R P U W D A I K O N
U A I K T N A J F I E Y R E F G W X W X G
R M T A D A K J W G Q T T O A Z A W N Y X
M M R L N Y U Y N O M X B S T N Y E P A A
E O A X Z B G A M O V P D I S V U R F I D
R T X S N L M K E A K P D B K L G T M H C
I K B H H E S O K V M Y E A I O O A S H J
C Q Z A K U M Y S A M J H R R G K W K A K
X H X L V E A M Z S U P O L R R H C N V P
G I V L Q D E O N S C W Z H E Y N U Z P V
Z I S O B Q U L W A N J T O T V J Q D I H
C Q B T I J F J M C Q R Z K M S H A J N D
G D C A A S A L S I F Y N G K A B P J S J
W A O Z S N I G N K G W Z T V I M P R R B
N N U T D A N O N O C E Q P G R H A S A D
A S B V A T W I N O C I E A Z Y A M C P H
G O E K G T C I A D T A L Y C T U R N I P
A R R O W R O O T N W A Y R N G E M F G J
B L F W W N M P X R N I I O A M W G J Z B
A T T W F I V J R G S K X N Z G F U Z E A
T R X L F M A L A N G A A Z O S K D E C Z
U T C A I R E L E C O K U N L B L T O R J
R F Q P G H V Y C I E X Y W O T H S G H P
```

97

```
B E B O P Q G G D U X H O E M R M P P A T
J B D N N U V U R O O Y I P B F U S R I O
A I F G I T X O L U S S G O R D Y N E P L
K U S T Y D Y U O L A S Y E D J O O T I A
F R P B O E C R V Q I M O L E L O W N G S
I Y Y V J E C F B P W N E R D H B B U N K
U P L F P L F E G I M S B Z O P O A G I N
G I J T H F O X A I B Z I U O C N L N T I
K G Z E Q H L P L X N F N Y R E R L R E O
D G E L A X P S A I F H A Q W S Z O T C R
N L M W E E H G Q E D S U N F Y T M P T I
A E K N P P A K L U P E E O X B A I N P S
L Y T F O E M I O A E H H Z P W P O R K Y
B W O A I T M P T P N A O L D M A J O R S
G I S K N T L I K U O T L L T V Y J Z O P
N N X N D P S I B M T X U E I E E T W N I
I K N I W O A K M B M R A H R L L Y E W D
L S E O R Y Z U W A A I W I T I X G Q M E
G D X E S J G H R A H I B O V H U T I H R
I Y T M Z R N A P O L E O N S I H L A P H
P W P A A W O F O B G T T Y A K L N A N A
W Z N D W P E T U N I A A B B N S O L P M
Y F Z A S E Y R F I T U N A J X I Z A K O
D C S M Y G G I P S S I M B G U M C M G V
I G G Y A R B U C K L E U E Q D P L G B W
```

Logic Puzzles

4

Charles Rivera was found in Back Bay with a gunshot wound.
Jack Hancock was found in North End, stabbed to death.
Prudence Hyde was found in Beacon Hill, killed by blunt force.

8

Ned Bundy buried incriminating documents near a rock shaped like a face.
Charlie Gambino buried loot from a bank heist between two mesas.
Frankie Harvard buried toxic waste near a natural aquifer.

12

Veronica reads Haruki Murakami and tutors English Grammar.
Marianne reads Neil Gaiman and tutors Calculus.
Louise reads Stieg Larsson and tutors Chemistry.

14

They left an obituary writer job in Middletown due to the toxic work environment.
They left a copy editor job in Bloomfield because of bad hours.
They left a restaurant reviewer job in Lakeville because of low wages.

15

In 2020, the dad was attacked in Glendale with a pipe wrench.
In 2021, the dad was attacked in Anaheim with a car bomb.
In 2022, the dad was attacked in Long Beach with a machete.
In 2023, the dad was attacked in Santa Ana with an axe.
In 2024, the dad was attacked in Culver City with a knife.

18

Bobby Blue was investigating equipment theft, and was found behind the local store.

Barney Piccolo was investigating vandalism and was found next to the fire station.

Ursula Kojak was investigating assault and was found in the church parking lot.

22

Nola made cooking baskets out of rabbitbrush.

Willow made gathering baskets out of dunebroom.

Iva made storage baskets out of galleta grass.

26

Brian from Washington Heights will be released in July.

David from Greenpoint will be released in September.

Don from Brighton Breach will be released in May.

Kevin from Sheepshead Bay will be released in August.

Mark from Flushing will be released in June.

30

In 2019, Elvis was spotted working as a dishwasher in Madison, Virginia.

In 2020, Elvis was spotted working as a truck driver in Clinton, Iowa.

In 2021, Elvis was spotted working for a lawn maintenance company in Arlington, Kentucky.

In 2022, Elvis was spotted installing drywall in Franklin, Indiana.

In 2023, Elvis was spotted working as a handyman in Newport, Tennessee.

34

Jack was banned from the Drunken Duck for fighting.

Leo was banned from the Queen's Arms for being mean to the staff.

Freddie was banned from the Cat and Custard for stealing bottles of liquor.

39

Kathy's caramel cremes were on the top shelf.
Nella's corn chips were on display behind the counter.
Nicky's chocolate kisses were on the end cap.

42

In 2018, Uncle Joe provided the party with white wine.
In 2019, Cousin Toni brought everyone tequila shots.
In 2020, Cousin Ralph treated the group to rum and coke.
In 2021, Aunt Laura brought vodka and ginger ale.
In 2022, Jenny Crane treated the group to beer.

50

Renata was found in the bathroom of Popeyes.
Loretta was located in the outdoor dining area of McDonald's.
Diana was found in the back booth of Taco Bell.

51

Phil McCup owns Abick's Bar, he bought the Johnnie Walker.
Holden Cole-Brues owns LJ's Lounge, he bought the Jack Daniel's.
Jen N. Tawnick owns the Bronx Bar, she bought the Jameson.

53

2019, Francis X. Quinn, Hope, Colorado.
2020, Mary Ellen Froelich, Key West, Florida.
2021, Susan Turner, Margrave, Georgia.
2022, James Barr, Bolton, South Dakota.
2023, Holly Johnson, Carter's Crossing, Mississippi.

61

104, Wilson, Pink Victorian.
106, Tremblay, Gray Tudor.
108, Lee, Brown Split-Level.

110, Johnson, Green Ranch.
112, Martin,Blue Modern.
114, Gagnon, White Craftsman.

63

Effie McCallum won a bottle of HP Sauce on the top line.
Clara Boyd won a box of Barry's Tea on the middle line.
Agatha Davies won a jar of Branston Pickles on the bottom line.

69

Archibald Dover was buried under Asda Swindon's roses.
Cressida Bertram was buried under Nigel Cardiff's delphinium.
Edmund Lysander was buried under Bernie Camden's phlox.
Fraser Digby was buried under Brixton Kensington's lavender.
Rafe Laurence was buried under Agatha Grimsby's geraniums.

72

Cadence Capricio, the second soprano, will sing "Adoro Te Devote."
Harmony Courante, the bass, will perform "Come, Holy Ghost."
Melody Barcarolle, the alto, will perform "Parce Domine."
Rubato Fudge, the soprano, will sing "Lo, How a Rose E'er Blooming."
Sherzo Molto, the tenor, will sing "Salve Regina."

83

Bruno "The Mastermind" Cadaveretta is in Beaumont, Texas for tax fraud.
Redd "Tick-Tock" blue is in Atwater, California for embezzlement.
Roger "Mr. Warmth" Payne is in Allenwood, Pennsylvania for bribery.
Sal "Merchant of Venom" Minella is in Big Sandy, Kentucky for counterfeiting.

84

Bach Stabber, Parlor, Athame.
Blade Boggs, Main Bedroom, Dirk.
Cookie Cutter, Kitchen, Bowie Knife.
Mick Dagger, Library, Scalpel.
Slash Gordon, Dining Room, Switchblade.

90

Niamh, who is drinking Smithwick's Ale, sang "The Wild Rover."
Siobhan, who is drinking Jameson, sang "Finnegan's Wake."
Cillian, who is drinking hot whiskey, sang "The Black Velvet Band."
Declan, who is drinking cider, sang "Seven Drunken Nights."
Fiona, who is drinking Guinness, sang "Whiskey in the Jar."

98

Tommy AKA Luke Skywalker has the 212 area code.
Andrew AKA Mace Windu has the 917 area code.
Bishop AKA Obi-Wan Kenobi has the 718 of area code.

The Black Spring Crime Series

Curated and edited by the best-selling author Luca Veste, and endorsed by the likes of Lee Child, Mark Billingham, and Val McDermid, the Black Spring Crime Series is filled with fantastic reads, waiting to be discovered. From psychological thrillers, to historical crime novels, to classic noir, we have something for everyone, with many, many more to come . . . some of our selection are listed below!

***A Crime in the Land of 7,000 Islands*, Zephaniah Sole**

This psychological literary fiction tells the tale of Ikigai Johnson, a Special Agent working out of the FBI's Portland, Oregon field office, who pledges to bring justice to children abused by a monstrous American in the Philippines. Amidst an expertly accurate police procedural, Ikigai recounts her tale to her eleven-year-old daughter through fantastical allegory.

This is a powerhouse crime thriller written by a serving FBI agent fused with folk tales and the influence of anime. Described by bestselling author Stuart Neville as 'an extraordinary feat of storytelling'.

***Jasper's Brood*, J.K. Nottingham**

It Takes a Killer, To Raise a Killer, To Raise a Killer . . . Jasper is a killer. Raised by a man who is not his father, but a serial killer to become just like him. Only, he is different. He wants to help people. The only way he knows how. To be just like him.

Cormac McCarthy meets North-East England in this unforgettable novel, with a fresh and exciting voice from a debut author.

***The Scotsman*, Rob McClure**

Chic Cowan will do anything to find his daughter's killer. Six months ago, Glasgow Detective Chic Cowan received a call that his daughter had been murdered, 4,000 miles away from their home in Scotland. Across the Atlantic Ocean in a United States riven by protests and riots. He is determined to find out the truth.

The Scotsman is the blistering debut from a new Tartan Noir talent. This is Rebus meets *Taken*.

***The Salt Cutter*, C.J. Howell**

Bolivia. 1991. A soldier arrives in the small town of Uyuni. A place people endure rather than enjoy. The soldier knows they're coming for him. Hunting him down so they can deal their own brand of justice. He needs to get out. To make it to the border and escape what is waiting for him. He's prepared to do anything to survive. Even kill.

This is noir fiction at its finest. With characters that you will root for, heartbreak, and breathtaking writing, this is a story that will linger in reader's minds long after you've turned the final page.

***Winter of Shadows*, Clare Grant**

In the midwinter of 1862 in York, a young woman is found dead by the river, her body marked by a sinister act of mutilation. The mysterious death spreads fear, for this is not the first corpse to be discovered. Speculation grows there is a killer stalking the city's medieval streets.

This glorious historical crime thriller, described by Ambrose Parry as, 'hugely atmospheric', introduces the character of Ava Fawkes, the country's only crime scene photographer, who you won't forget in a hurry.

CRIMEBITS 2

After the popularity of our first competition we are excited to announce a sequel for our *CrimeBits* series.

CrimeBits 2 will be judged by another best-selling author . . . the one and only Val McDermid, the beloved best-selling Scottish Tartan Noir crime author and CWA Diamond Dagger winner.

WANT TO BE FEATURED IN *CRIMEBITS 2*?

Follow us to keep updated

The Black Spring Press Group

@ blackspringpressgroup

@BlackSpringC

www.blackspringpressgroup.com

Email us at: blackspringcrime@gmail.com

MARQUIS
Québec, Canada